# JAYDIUM

## DEBORAH WHEELER

DAW BOOKS, INC.
DONALD A. WOLLHEIM, FOUNDER
375 Hudson Street, New York, NY 10014
ELIZABETH R. WOLLHEIM
SHEILA E. GILBERT
PUBLISHERS

Cover art by Vincent Di Fate.

DAW Book Collectors No. 913.



First Printing, May 1993

1 2 3 4 5 6 7 8 9

DAW TRADEMARK REGISTERED
U.S. PAT. OFF. AND FOREIGN COUNTRIES
—MARCA REGISTRADA
HECHO EN U.S.A.

PRINTED IN THE U.S.A.

To the memory of my parents

Allan Ross (Alter Rosenberg) 1907-1974

Jane Ross (Marie-Jeanne-Léonie Jean) 1916-1986

## ACKNOWLEDGMENTS

No novel is ever written in a vacuum, but short of including everyone who's ever been a part of my life, I want to single out a few people for special thanks:

The West L.A. writers group—Anne Pautler, Kathleen Tyler, Cynthia Applewhite, Lynne Hamilton, Tim Weedlun, Chris Kamens and especially Jim Brunet—who minced no words telling me just how atrocious the first draft was and spared no praise when I finally got it right;

Cynthia Felice, who critiqued my very first effort at a novel with such diplomacy and honesty; Marion Zimmer Bradley, who kept telling me I was a writer and buying my short stories to prove it;

And most of all, my family—Richard, Phyllis, Sarah, and Rose—who believed in me every long step of the way.

# Chapter 1

*Dust,* Kithri thought as she shoved her shoulder against the door of The Thirsty Miner Tavern. The pitted duraplast jerked open, sending a drift of gray-brown powder over her boots. *My whole life is turning to dust.*

Dust was everywhere on the single inhabited continent of the planet Stayman. It clung to the folds of Kithri's dun-colored overalls and sprinkled her ragged brown curls. Sifting past the shutters or tracked in at the door, it invaded even the corners where shadows lay thick and stale.

The Thirsty Miner gathered its fair share of dust. Other bars catered to insystem traders, the few Federation agents who cared to rub shoulders with locals or the farmers who, when they came into town at all, kept stubbornly to themselves. But this bar, small and far from the center of Port Ludlow, attracted only its regular customers, jaydium miners all.

*Look at them,* Kithri thought, pausing as the door swung shut behind her. *They're already drinking up every credit they've made on this run.*

Old Dowdell and his two tavern buddies, identical in their rumpled miners' overalls and grizzled faces, looked up from their usual places at the centermost table. Kithri turned her back on them and leaned her elbows on the bar. The barkeep set a mug of brew in front of her.

*A few more years, and I'll be just like them.*

This was not strictly true. Although Kithri had come to Stayman as a homesick adolescent, she would never be anything but an outsider. One day her clear gray eyes might dull under the faint film which never seemed to leave the other miners' eyes and her youthful skin might dry up into a mass of crevices like theirs, but she could never change who she was—the daughter of a Federation scientist.

Kithri might not belong to Stayman, but Stayman had left its mark on her. The heavy fabric of her overalls could not hide the long curves of her thighs, or shoulders grown muscular from years of chipping jaydium. She rubbed her nose where it had once been broken and sipped the tepid brew, wishing for the hundredth time that morning there was somewhere else to go, something else to do. She could drag out her outdated astrophysics texts and pretend to study, but what would be the use?

*I'm never going to get off this miserable planet! Not to University, not to anywhere!*

"Hey, Bloodyluck!"

"Dowdell," she muttered without turning around, "there's nothing you have to say that I want to hear, so stuff it."

"I hear Nash's looking for a whore on his insystem route. Fix you up good, you might do."

Kithri took her mug and stalked over to the farthest, darkest corner. Dowdell's raucous laugh followed her, ". . . 'course we'd all expect free samples . . ."

At the rate she was going, flying *singlo,* it would

take years to save the rest of her passage offplanet. The Federation freighters came too infrequently and too much of her earnings dribbled away just to survive on this desolate hunk of rock. But if she could find someone else trained in *duo*—someone besides that dustbug Dowdell—all it would take would be one, maybe two good runs. She could even make another haul before the freighter took off tonight.

Kithri leaned against the grimy ash-brick wall and closed her eyes, trying to remember Albion's rivers and flowered fields, the clear blue sky, the billowing golden clouds. The images were fragmentary, a child's memories, luminous and blurred. Albion itself was now a radioactive cinder.

Lost in her daydreams, Kithri didn't look up as the door swung open again and a man stood there, silhouetted against the glaring daylight. His offworlder clothing—closefit pants, shirt and vest, laced boots—did little to mask the hard, lean contours of his body. Close behind him came a stunningly beautiful woman in a tailored medic's uniform and a taller man, brassy-haired and smiling. Dowdell let out a long whistle and glanced toward the corner where Kithri sat, her eyes still closed.

The barkeep set three mugs of brew in front of the newcomers. "Hank," he nodded to the tall man. "Been a while."

In her corner, Kithri opened her eyes, slowly focusing on the three newcomers. Her expression hidden by the dense shadows, she got noiselessly to her feet.

The woman looked down at her mug and wrinkled her nose at the dingy, froth-covered liquid. "Is *this* all there is?"

"Avery, my love, you wouldn't want to try the alternatives," said Hank. "The water's laced with metal salts and the rotgut's only good for a three-day drunk."

The second man lifted his mug to his lips. His vest fell open and revealed a leather shoulder holster carrying a force whip, an exotic weapon for a planet where simple stunguns were the norm. "It's better than aardwolf piss," he commented.

"Such language, Eril!" said the woman. He leaned toward her, laughing, a male version of her beauty—dark hair, faint epicanthic folds of the eyelids, golden skin. But while she was all silky curves, there was nothing effeminate about him. Instead, he was sleek and taut like a sand-leopard, the kind of predator that relishes trouble.

Hank turned away from the bar, unaware of Kithri's silent approach. "Yes, my love, this lowly tavern was the scene of many a youthful adventure of mine. I remember the time this trader took the notion one of the miners'd hyped his stash. Now, I knew Grizz'd done no such thing—all the man knows is jaydium and getting drunk, in the reverse order. And besides, the trader's so stoned on bloodroot he can't even remember where he put his own head. He pulls out a knife as long as your forearm—" Hank gestured dramatically, "—screams like bloody hell and goes ramming for Grizz. Well, what was I to do, let an honest miner get his kidneys chopped? I vault over those three tables there and foot-sweep him. Bam! Down he goes! Then I break a chair over his head, wrestle the knife out of his hands and—"

"You're nothing but a dustbug liar, Hank Austin!" Kithri slammed her mug down next to his. "In case you've forgotten, it wasn't a *chair* I smashed over the trader's head, it was a *bench.* All *you* did was stick your foot out and pick up the pieces afterward."

"Kithri! By all the powers of luck and space, what are you still doing here?"

She winced. "It's great to see you, too. C'mon, if we scramble we can make one more *duo* haul on this run. There's five, almost six hours until lift-off."

"Who *is* this . . . person?" asked the petite beauty, slipping her hand through Hank's arm and narrowing her eyes.

Hank straightened up. "Avery, my love, meet my old flying partner, Kithri Bloodyluck. Ask me sometime how she got that name. It makes the other story sound like an old ladies' tea party. Kithri, this is my wife."

"Your . . . wife." In her soaring excitement, Kithri had barely noticed the two strangers. She swallowed hard, her tanned face flushing to an ugly shade of copper. The dim light of the tavern masked it and her voice was steady enough. That was lucky because she could feel the eyes of the other miners on her, searching her for any hint of weakness. They'd given up any pretense of lack of interest and were staring frankly. After Hank had signed on as a Federation pilot, she'd had her fill of speculation about their having been lovers—and who would take his place. The thought of another round of Dowdell's jokes was enough to turn her stomach.

"I wanted to show Avery where I used to hang out before I enlisted," Hank said. "Now that the war's over—" He paused, his handsome brow furrowing. "You didn't think I came back here—just to run jaydium, did you? I'm not that crazy, and besides, there's my bonus money."

Kithri picked up her mug. The brew tasted flat and bitter. "It's nice *one* of us doesn't have to work for a living."

"What about you? You're not still running jaydium, are you?"

"What else should I do on this dustball planet? Open a beauty parlor," she jerked her chin toward Dowdell and his cronies, "for the likes of them?"

Hank spread his hands apologetically. "Hey, it's nothing personal."

"The whole thing's too damned personal, if you ask me." Kithri strode out of the bar, leaving the rest of her drink. Dowdell let out another long whistle as the second newcomer slapped his own mug down and hurried after her.

Too angry to think straight, Kithri hurried down the broad unpaved street that lead to the jetport. Why, why, *why* had she allowed herself to hope—even for the briefest moment—that Hank might have come back to help her, as he'd promised when he left? After flying *duo* together, she knew what he was—a self-centered, vainglorious bastard who happened to fly like a dust-devil. And who kept his promises only when it was convenient and profitable. There was no hope for her, and what's more, there never had been. What a fool she was!

Against her will, tears spilled down her cheeks. She broke into a headlong run. Here at the edge of Port Ludlow there were only a few straggler buildings, ash-brick like The Thirsty Miner. Nobody would see her weakness. The locals were all in their favorite drinking places, getting sensibly plastered.

"Kithri!" came a shout behind her, a man's voice. "Kithri Bloodyluck!"

She slowed, turning her head, ready to keep going if it were Dowdell or one of his pals, unable to resist the temptation. It was the second man from the bar. Relieved and curious, she slowed to a walk. The next moment he caught up with her.

"Who the hell are you?" she asked.

"Eril, Eril Trionan. I'm Avery's brother."

Kithri scrubbed at her tears with the back of one dusty sleeve. Her eyes smarted in protest. "That scrub-pilot-turned-war-hero married your *sister*?"

"Hank's not so bad, as long as he thinks there's something in it for him. And he's one hell of a good pilot—"

"Don't apologize for him. He only came back to show off and laugh at the local brushies. He thinks he's so tough—well, I could fly circles around him in my sleep. Lucky, that's all he is. What d'*you* want?"

"I can fly *duo*."

For a long moment Kithri could do no more than stare at him. Her eyes rested on the tiny jagged scar on one cheek which saved his face from outright prettiness. His dark eyes measured her in return, and she wondered what he thought of her broad shoulders and slightly crooked nose, so different from his sister's daintiness. Finally her brain got itself back into gear. What did it matter what he thought of her? He was probably no different than Hank. She'd had enough of pretty fly-boys and their promises.

She forced her lips to move. "Ratshit."

"In space. Hank was my copilot," he answered, grinning. "Try me."

"You want to go on a jaydium run . . . with me?" Her eyes narrowed. "Why?"

"What else is there to do here? Get drunk? Listen to Hank tell barroom lies I could make up better myself? The one thing Stayman has to offer is jaydium, and that's halfway across the continent." His words, although spoken firmly enough, didn't have the right ring to them. A bored tourist he wasn't, but that was his business.

*What does that matter?* whispered through her mind. *It's one more run, the best chance you'll get. You wouldn't have to promise him anything, just let him fly with you. . . .*

"I'd be crazy to do it," she said, but not as forcefully as before.

"You'd be crazy *not* to," Eril answered good-naturedly. He gestured back toward the tavern. "Hank's not running jaydium any more. Not now, not ever again. He said the only other miner here who was trained in *duo* was some old sourbug named Dowdell and that you'd kicked him halfway to Hyades when he got so horny he wouldn't take no for an answer."

"Hank said that, did he?"

The mental backlash of emerging from *duo* affected people differently, the most common reaction being a brief but intense erotic rush. Kithri had never experienced it herself, but she'd had her fill of its consequences. For all his faults, Hank had enough sense to back off and look for easier pickings elsewhere.

"What else did Hank tell you about me?" she asked.

"That you were damned good."

Kithri bit her lip, considering. The angry flush had drained from her face, leaving her cheeks a light, even tan against the rich brown of her curls. She studied Eril speculatively. "You ever chipped jaydium before?"

"I'm willing to learn."

"It's no picnic, I can tell you. The work's rough and dirty and the flight across the Cerrano can kill you. Why would you want to risk it?"

"You want the truth?" Eril stopped grinning. "All right—it's the money. Hank told me what you made on a *duo* run, with the jaydium still intact. If he's too love-addled to take it, I will."

Kithri nodded, relaxing. Greed was something she could understand. "You might change your mind once you see *Brushwacker*. But it won't hurt to take a look."

The Port Ludlow jetport was definitely third-class. The only landing space worth anything was currently dominated by a single, heavily-guarded Federation shuttle, used for ferrying hauls of jaydium ore to the orbiting freighter, where it was sealed in hard vacuum to prevent further deterioration. A few battered insystem traders sat behind it, looking like poor country cousins. Miners' scrubjets lined the paved runways at the edge of the field. Farther south and west, patches of muted green marked the beginning of Stayman's insular agricultural community. The patches centered on prewar tapwells, for Stayman's water resources lay deep within the bedrock aquifers.

Kithri ran one hand over *Brushwacker*'s blunt nose

and sent the thin layer of dust up in little billows. Like her, it was different, set apart. Its metalloceramic skin wore only a dull patina from years of abrasion by the ever-present dust. The other miners painted and repainted theirs with bright, outlandish designs—flames and snakes with gaping mouths, jagged lightning, women with wings. Each one tried to outshine the others.

The stubby, wide wings which gave *Brushwacker* its unusual maneuverability were set in specialized mountings that permitted minute changes in angle. The engines, too, were capable of rotating to vary the direction of thrust. The narrow body of the scrubjet acted as a secondary airfoil and within its curved contours, space was at a premium. Since the death of Kithri's father, no one but she had sat in the pilot's seat. Hank—and Dowdell for that one ill-fated flight—had always taken second place.

She slid the door open and stepped back for Eril to take a look. He poked his head in and said, "Looks like there's enough room to take a deep breath, but skies help you if you get the urge to scratch your *pitouchee*."

Kithri raised one eyebrow, not quite ingenuous enough to ask what a *pitouchee* was. "Still game?"

"Compared to the new needle scouts, this is positively spacious."

"In you go, then. You run the copilot's check, and if you get it right, you're on."

Eril climbed into the second pilot's seat and pulled the harness straps around him. He took a few moments to study the panels, then began his inspection. Kithri watched him, liking the way he moved in the cramped space, sensing where the 'jet's walls were without having to bang his elbows into them, liking the meticulousness with which he double-checked everything. But he'd had an unforgiving teacher—in space, carelessness was invariably fatal.

He looked up as she folded herself into the seat before him, her shoulders between his knees. She didn't touch him as she checked his work again. "All right, you pass," she said, closed the door, and thumbed the engines into life.

"What's the drill?"

"Manual in the 'port and out past the hills. That'll take us to the Cerrano Plain, a good three thousand miles across. Then into the Manitous themselves."

"How deep into them?"

"Depends on where the jaydium is. Could be as much as ten miles. You ever flown a tunnel?"

Kithri nudged *Brushwacker* from its berth and along the runway leading east toward the hills. The tiny ship moved smoothly under her hands, as if it were a living thing that knew her touch.

"No, but I've heard they're as predictable as a trader's promise. A system of natural tunnels that run all through the mountain range."

Kithri laughed. "That's not the half of it. There's no jaydium worth having on the surface, so you have to follow the tunnels deep into the mountain. They twist worse than a dish of noodles—one wrong turn and you'll end up plastered against the wall."

"You're not the noodle type," he said. "And neither am I."

# Chapter 2

"Assist?" came Eril's voice.

The long muscles in his thighs flexed alongside Kithri's arms as he settled the auxiliary foot controls. With an effort, she ignored the sensation. "Take us due east to the hills, then through them along the lowest route."

"Speed?" There was no hint of excitement in his voice.

"Don't get us smashed."

Kithri rested her hands lightly on the controls, sensing the subtle changes as Eril eased into command and increased their speed. He flew with almost arrogant confidence, but he wasn't greedy—he'd left a good twenty percent to her discretion.

They reached the first wrinkle of hills at moderate subsonic speed. Eril guided the scrubjet along the narrow gullies where vegetation covered the jagged rock like splotches of green-black ink. At first his handling felt rough-edged, his reactions to the winding canyon jerky. Kithri nudged the stabilizers and tried to keep her muscles loose. He was doing a hell of a lot better than she had on her first try.

She'd been eleven, less than a year on Stayman and still homesick for Albion's flowers. That was before the war, when the Federation still manned the colony and provided services to the jaydium miners and their families. That was when they still had families. Her father sat before her in the pilot's seat, his body a bulwark against this unfamiliar, desolate world.

"All right, Kithryne Sunnai," he said. He was given to using her full name when he wanted her to pay particular attention. Sometimes when a topic was really important to him, he sounded like one of his own geology lectures. Even now, she could remember the rhythm of his words, his voice, his hands covering hers on the scrubjet controls.

"Stayman's your world now, and you've got to learn her like the inside of your own room, learn her mountains, her Cerrano Plain, learn how to chip and run her jaydium. Learn the dangers of her coriolis storms and alkali pits. So you can take care of yourself when—if anything happens to me. This scrubjet will be your friend when there's nobody else you can trust. . . ."

Had he known, even then, of the neurodyscrasia already setting its fatal enzymatic markers in the deepest recesses of his brainstem? Had he known how little time they had left together? Had he guessed what her life would become, between Hank's broken promises and dustbug miners like Dowdell? Was he trying to warn her, to prepare her, to give her what she'd need to survive?

The little ship had flinched under her childish touch like a wild creature shying away from human control. "No, don't fight her, don't think of *Brushwacker* as an enemy you've got to conquer," her father said. "Think of her as an extension of yourself, just as your arms and legs are. Know exactly where and how you want to go, and then put her right . . . there. . . ."

A swerve of the scrubjet jerked Kithri's attention back to the present. Eril had been flying in graceful, even swoops along the canyon floor. The walls narrowed and he'd oversteered in bringing them back to a straight line. Quickly, he compensated and evened out. Then they began to climb, snaking through the twisted passes, always clinging to the ground. The ink-blotchy vegetation grew sparser, ragged-looking, and finally gave way to yellowish lichen.

They reached the crest and looked down from the last hill. The vast Cerrano Plain lay before them, flat from scrubjet nose to horizon. Alkali-tolerant scrub grew in patches, blending in the distance into a swath of silver-gray. The pale soil underneath was so fine it was almost powdery. Wherever the first human explorers had driven their heavy land-moving equipment, they'd torn away the thin protective crust. Over the years, wind had eroded the trails into wildly sculpted gullies like scars on the Plain's fragile skin. Plumes of dust rose from the old trails, blown aloft by the constant winds.

Kithri reached for the headsets which would join her mind to Eril's and to the computerized shipbrain. As she leaned forward, her arm brushed against the inner surface of Eril's thigh. She wondered what it would be like to touch him deliberately, to run her fingers over the warm, sleek flesh beneath the layers of clothing. Her heartbeat soared.

What was happening to her? She'd never reacted to a man like that before, certainly not to the tavern dustbugs or Hank with his hyperinflated ego. Yet ever since Eril had come racing after her, this awareness of him had been growing.

*Get yourself under control, Kithri! The jaydium's the important thing, not a few jerk-you-around hormones.*

Kithri pulled on her headset and slid the padded neuroprobes into place. The gel contacts felt familiar and cool on her skin. She blinked, her brain refusing at first, as it always did, to integrate the vibrating double images, the overlay of her own organic vision on top of the computerized analysis. The equipment which made *duo*flight possible by linking two human minds to shipbrain was a highly sophisticated adaptation of the apparatus used to link an ordinary computer to its human operator. Several additional safety devices had been added, notably the unspoken emergency abort command which would disengage the entire system. Kithri could have chosen her own phrase, but she'd kept the one her father had programmed. *Terminal Escape Velocity.* She'd never had to use it, but sometimes it sifted like a ghostly echo through her dreams.

The visual images blended together as shipbrain fed data into Kithri's mind and her temporal lobes sent back fine-tuning signals. The effect was very like the addition of another sensory dimension. A moment later, Eril completed the *duo* configuration.

Whenever Kithri linked with Hank, she always felt a flash of searing pain before he settled into synch. She'd studied enough physiology to know it was due to the differences in their synaptic patterns, but that didn't make it any easier. Old Dowdell's mind had been repulsive rather than painful, and she could no longer remember what it had been like when her father taught her. She held her breath and Eril joined with her.

There was no sudden agony, but a silken touch, a whisper of delight, and then Eril was *inside* her mind. For a dazzling instant their awareness merged, they thought as one organic unity. Shipbrain receded to a background monotone.

She was Eril, he was Kithri and, miraculously, there was no difference between them. She saw through his eyes. She felt the warmth of her own shoulders between his thighs. Her skin tingled, her heart beat wildly, and tantalizing shivers rippled through her nerves.

The moment of merging faded like honey melting on the tongue, and Kithri was once more a separate entity floating in the web of Kithri/Eril/shipbrain.

*Ready?* Kithri put *'Wacker* in a straight path across the Plain as she and Eril sorted the housekeeping. The division of tasks which she and Hank had worked out was irrelevant now and she wanted to put it all behind her.

*Bio-homeostasis?* Eighty percent to Eril, without a question. Kithri's heart rate and blood pressure were almost back to normal under his sure touch. She shifted the remaining twenty percent as emergency backup to the ship. Navigation was hers, eighty-five with fifteen percent to ship memory, and power train and life-support split a ragged three ways.

*Down to business.* Kithri took hold of the helm, using shipbrain's external sensors for orientation. With a sure touch, she steadied the 'jet and sent it supersonic across the Plain.

After a few minutes, she felt Eril relax, lulled by the flat, featureless expanse below them and the empty indigo sky above. His calmness sent ripples of relaxation through her own body. Yet years of running jaydium had taught her better than to trust the Cerrano for even a moment. She kept watch with *'Wacker*'s senses as well as her own.

Within minutes, shipbrain alerted her to a massive circular air disturbance ahead, three hundred miles in diameter. Instantly she recognized it as a coriolis storm. Driven by the immense heat gradients built up over the reflective plain and amplified by the rotation of the planet, coriolis winds whipped to hundreds of miles per hour. The eye was usually still, but severe local turbulences along the periphery could prove deadly to even the most skillful pilot.

Kithri tightened her grip on the controls. *Trouble coming.*

*I don't see a thing,* Eril said.

*Clear-air coriolis, a big one. Check the infrared, not visual. We'll try to stay out of the worst of it. Hold on!*

*'Wacker* accelerated smoothly to match the wind speed. Then the tiny ship touched the invisible edge of the storm. It shuddered and bucked, spinning out of control.

An imaginary hand crushed Kithri's chest, forcing the air from her lungs. Struggling for breath, she tried to brace herself against it. The harness straps bit deep into her flesh as they held her firmly in her seat. She gasped and shut her eyes. Ordinary vision was useless here—she couldn't respond quickly enough. No single unaided human could, only two minds linked in *duo.*

Kithri drew on shipbrain, using her years of experience in dealing with minute shifts in wind direction and velocity. The connection to the computer was solid, the ship responsive. She reached for Eril to take up the data sorting and sensor management she couldn't handle.

Instead of the silken unity of their first moments of fusion, Kithri collided with a mental blank like a solid wall. She recoiled, stunned.

*What the hell?*

One moment Eril had been part of her, the next he simply wasn't there. Kithri's first thought was that he was dead, but no—his mind had gone suddenly opaque. More than that, in her moment of confusion he'd somehow managed to grab a huge percentage of helm control.

What did Eril think he was doing? Was he trying to get them both killed? Did he think he could pilot *Brushwacker* better than she could?

*My ship! Give me back my ship!*

Furious and terrified, Kithri signaled for manual control. She'd been caught in worse and survived, flying *singlo,* just her and shipbrain. But she'd never had to fight for command of her own ship before. After an agonizing delay, the scrubjet responded. It felt as agile as a wallowing barge in the raging air currents.

Half of Kithri's mind was deep in the meld with shipbrain, while the other half struggled to hold the ship steady. Her sweating hands clenched the manual helm. She leaned forward, using her muscular shoulders to force the ship toward what looked like a clear path ahead. Ever treacherous, the winds shifted, lifting and twisting the tiny craft. Suddenly *Brushwacker* slipped sideways, plunging toward the heart of the storm.

Her life on Stayman might not be much, but she wasn't ready to die. Not yet, not like this.

*Damn it, Eril! Stop playing hero and let me fly this thing!*

Kithri's words, or the desperation behind them somehow got through. Eril's resistance passed as quickly as it had arisen. His mind linked smoothly with hers again, a pulse of solid support. He kept her adrenaline levels steady as he channeled more and more data to shipbrain.

Kithri felt as if she'd just been pulled out from beneath a Manitou avalanche. Quickly she switched back from the manual. The scrubjet moved light and nimble under her control. A moment later, it leveled out, flying with the storm. Power, there was so much power streaming into her from Eril's mind. He took up so much of the data selection that all she had to do was imagine the ship balanced and steady.

Now to edge back toward the periphery of the storm. . . .

But the coriolis wasn't done with them. Before they'd gone a hundred feet, *'Wacker* struck a local turbulence. Clear winds churned and swirled like a miniature tornado. Gusts slammed into the 'jet and its metal frame wailed with strain. Data, fluctuating wildly from one moment to the next, flooded the ship's sensors.

It took all of Kithri's will and years of experience not to panic. She'd never been caught like this, nor known anyone who had and lived to tell about it. Now she rode the winds with all her skill and intuition, sweating and trembling, searching for a way back into the main current of the storm.

Then Eril's mind surged up and blended with

hers, holding the 'jet steady with unerring control. She nudged the helm, flying with the winds and using their raw power instead of uselessly fighting them. Under Eril's sure touch, the engines rotated, compensating exactly for the turbulences. They worked together as smoothly as if they were part of a single mind. *'Wacker* leveled out and slipped easily through the air streams, once more speeding east.

# Chapter 3

Relieved she was still alive, Kithri signaled shipbrain to begin the disengagement from *duo*flight. She resolved not to say anything about Eril's brief mutiny. They were still alive, she'd never see him again after today, and perhaps the storm itself had taught him better than to try it again. This wasn't space, where he knew all the dangers and how to deal with them. Yet she couldn't help thinking that in the end, when it mattered, he'd come through better than she expected. With him as a partner, she could *duo* her way through a black hole.

She knew she was rationalizing, making excuses. If she had any sense, she'd turn around and fly back to Port Ludlow right now. But if she did, she'd be throwing away her last real chance to get off Stayman. . . .

*It's just one run. I can survive anything for just one run.*

With the end of *duo*linkage, Kithri's vision returned to normal. She slowed the scrubjet to subsonic. To the north, just inside the boundary of the Plain, lay a pile of partially completed permacrete structures, the abandoned first colony site. Fine white dust rose from the disturbed soil where the slow-growing scrub had not yet, after centuries, reestablished its dominion. The merest breeze blew it aloft, an eloquent reminder of the fragility of Stayman's ecology and the dismal failure of the first spaceport. The Federation had long since moved its base to the current location, where water was more readily available. It had never tried to revive the first site, a costly and difficult project. There was no reason to, as long as the miners were willing to haul the jaydium across the Plain.

Kithri lifted her eyes to the vast, whitened Manitou range, rising high above a line of brownish dust haze. Peak after purple peak surged skyward, hard-edged against the dark blue horizon. The drifted snow on the summits glimmered in the sunlight.

Behind her, Eril drew a quick, hissing breath. She was still in such rapport with him that she experienced his awe as if it were her own. The pleasure she felt at his mental touch built into a preorgasmic thrill. She caught her breath, her heart pounding in her chest.

Kithri drew the scrubjet to a halt at the rocky edge of the Plain. Her fingers flew across the buckles of the restraining straps. She yanked the door open and scrambled, breathless, to the ground. Eril tumbled out after her and caught her in his arms.

She held him tightly, fiercely, as if she could press her flesh through the layers of clothing and into his. His mouth on hers felt like velvet and then like steel. He cupped her head with his hands, his fingers stroking the smooth skin behind her ears. She slid her lips over his cheek, down the line of his jaw to the soft hollow of his throat, tasting him, inhaling his scent like perfume.

*It's like making love to myself,* she thought in amazement. *The male self that is my perfect complement.*

Kithri drew away, eyes closed as she drew his hands over her breasts. She swayed, almost overcome with the intensity of her feelings, and sank to her knees.

She put one hand to the barren ground for balance. A sharp-edged stone cut deep into her palm, drawing blood. The pain shocked her halfway back to rationality. The pounding in her ears faltered as she stared at the red droplets staining the grit on her hand.

*That's my life draining away into the dust.* Her stomach twisted into a knot of ice.

She drew herself upright, her sensual rapport with Eril shattered. "That's quite . . . something. . . . I'd wondered what it was like—the backlash," she murmured, glancing away. "Hank always got randy after a *duo* flight, but I didn't feel anything."

"The women I trained *duo* with—we never connected like this." Eril's voice sounded husky and his pupils were so huge, his eyes looked totally black. "If you didn't feel anything for each other to begin with—there was nothing. Sometimes Hank and I would make bad jokes about it when we weren't in a scramble." His fingers sank into her shoulders and he pulled her closer, caressing her mouth and cheek. "Who cares what it was like *then*?"

Kithri pushed him away, wiped her eyes with the back of one hand and clambered to her feet. "This isn't getting us any jaydium."

Eril lunged upright, his breath coming in huge gulps. "That's all there is to it, then? We go on as if nothing had happened— "

"What do you expect?" she snapped. "Instant affinity? Eril, we don't even *know* each other. Yes, I wanted you—I wanted *us*. A moment ago—if there'd been room in *'Wacker* or grass instead of this cursed rock—well, there wasn't. Life's like that. It's over now. It's time to get back to work."

He caught her arm as she started back to the 'jet. "Have it your own way. But the next time we *duo* it'll happen again. Maybe worse. Do you think you'll be able to walk away from me then?"

Kithri turned from him, unable to reply, and jumped back into *Brushwacker*.

They flew slowly along the rapidly climbing slopes, past the altitude boundary of the meager vegetation. The familiar rhythm of the scrubjet soothed Kithri's jangled nerves. Her awareness of Eril's touch on the controls lingered as if they were still joined in *duo*, and that disturbed her. His parting challenge would not dissipate as simply as a few ephemeral hormones. She would have to find a rebuttal for him, for her own peace as well.

*I always seem to want what I can't have. Why can't I take what little comfort life has to offer?*

She had no answers. Not for him, not for herself.

As they climbed, the automatic pressurization came on, compensating for the thinner air. Kithri spotted the first few tunnels, some half-blocked with fallen rock. She pointed them out to Eril. The early settlers had thought them volcanic because of their superficial resemblance to lava tubes, but more detailed studies revealed that they ran through, rather than along, the crustal plates. The conventional opinion was they couldn't be natural and they couldn't be anything else.

Kithri's father had been particularly intrigued by the traces of odd organic acids in the slag. He hoped they might lead to understanding why jaydium was not found anywhere else in settled space. Pearls, amber, coral—each planet had its own distinctive varieties. Jaydium was unique, found only on Stayman.

Although it had not been his primary assignment, jaydium and everything associated with it had been Raddison Sunnai's abiding passion. He was a chemical geologist, one of the last scientists the Federation sent to Stayman as dwindling resources and escalating internal chaos forced a reordering of priorities. Then there was the war and no more Federation ships, only demands for more jaydium.

Kithri helped him with what research he could continue, chipping jaydium to pay the bills and buy enough books to pass her University admissions equivalency. After the war began, however, there were no more scholarships. Jaydium mining itself could not pay for interstellar transport and off-planet tuition, not after supplies of the space-crystallized drug, lithicycline, had wiped out their small savings. Lithicycline was the only treatment known for neurodyscrasia, and it was a palliative at best.

It had taken Raddison Sunnai three years to die. The lithicycline shipments had stopped after one.

Left with nothing but memories, Kithri flew frantically, going without sleep and often without meals during the brief visits of the Federation freighters, only to find that half or more of each haul had deteriorated past recovery in the slow *singlo* flight back. Then Hank came along and she made more on the first two *duo* flights than she had in the whole year before. Almost the entire haul had been good, and for the first time she began to think that she might stand a chance of buying her way off Stayman. Then Hank enlisted in the Federation forces, and her savings slowly trickled away, along with her hope for the future.

If her father hadn't taught her to fly *duo* she wouldn't have had even that. For a brief, heart-wringing moment she remembered the shock as her mind first blended with his. And then . . .

The memory hit her smack in the solar plexus—the tumult of her awakening adolescent sexuality and her father's ashen face, his trembling hands carefully avoiding even the most casual touch. She remembered thinking, *This isn't happening, oh, please let this not be happening! I will just close my eyes and still my heart and all will be well. . . .*

In desperation she'd made that one run with Dowdell. The *duo*touch of his mind had been like a creeping itch, and the light in his eyes as he reached for her had given her nightmares for a solid month. She could still taste the metallic tang of adrenaline and blood. She'd thrown him against the dusty rock hard enough to break his collarbone. After that she refused to share *Brushwacker* with anyone except Hank, who had never reached past her barriers . . . as Eril had.

*I just have to get through one trip,* she told herself. *Eril will never come back to this chip of rock, and that'll be the end of it. One thing's for sure, I won't be following him into space, so it's better—for both of us—that we leave it this way.*

For a moment, she almost believed it.

# Chapter 4

Slaty gray stones lay tumbled around the tunnel entrance, partly blocking it. About fifty feet inside, the passageway widened and curved, then straightened for another twenty or thirty feet and turned again. In the diffuse illumination of the scrubjet's running lights, the walls alternated between matte and highly reflective gloss. Sometimes the rock surfaces looked as smooth as melted glass, sometimes so rough and jagged that slivers of it could double as knives.

The tunnel twisted into the heart of the mountain for a half mile. Then it divided, one branch leading up and back toward the surface and the other downward at a steep angle.

Eril, watching Kithri maneuver the scrubjet through the tangle of intersections, considered how easily *singlo* flight could lead to disaster unless the 'jet was kept at little better than a crawl. The craft itself was maneuverable enough to fly at two or three times their present rate. It was the slowness of their unaided human reflexes which would send them crashing into a curving tunnel wall.

Thinking analytically about the difficulties of tunnel flight was pure evasion, and Eril knew it. *Duo*-flight required teamwork, although he'd rarely flown secondary. When they'd sorted housekeeping, he'd agreed to let Kithri handle the controls. So why had he fought her like some rookie, too green not to panic the moment they hit the storm? Had this mission robbed him of all common sense?

*Instinct. Blind instinct,* he told himself. *Whenever there's trouble, you never let anyone else make decisions for you. You live—or die—by your own mistakes.*

But was that any way to inspire Kithri's trust, by trying to take her ship away from her?

Weiram, his squadron chief, had berated him more than once for being a loner.

"You're a fine pilot, none better," the old man had said. They've been sitting in the disordered cavern that passed for his office, aboard the flagship which was his last command. His silver-white hair looked sallow in the ancient jaydium light.

"But once the laser fire starts, you forget everything you've learned about teamwork. You go on as if you're a one-man squadron and can take all the risks yourself. That's not a disaster when all you're responsible for is a stinger, but you can't run a battleship that way."

Later, much later, speaking from his coldly efficient administrative suit in the Federation Control Complex, First Councillor Eades had echoed that judgment.

"The new Corps needs people with initiative and self-control, not glory-hungry troublemakers."

Eril kept his face blank and his eyes on the uniform of unadorned black which was Eades's trademark. He didn't know what it was that drove him into one scrape after another, but it wasn't hunger for glory.

"Even with your war record, that last stunt you pulled in New Paris can't be ignored," Eades said. "Five civilians injured and a star-class navigator out of commission for months. What are you, some kind of thrill addict? I should shunt you straight into Exploration, as far away from civilized space as I can put you."

Eril held his tongue. The New Paris riot had started innocently enough, a few friendly drag-sprints down the back alleys. By the time the crowd mushroomed into a frustrated, war-sickened mob, he'd been long gone. But people recognized his face from all the news tri-vids. They remembered him as the instigator—Colonel Eril Trionan, the war hero.

"Your father was in Exploration, wasn't he?" said Eades, as if that explained all of Eril's transgressions.

"My father," Eril said through clenched teeth, "disappeared when I was five. And, yes, he was in Exploration. But I'd rather stay where the action is. Sir."

"Weiram put some rather glowing words about you in his last report," Eades said, "so I'm willing to forgo my better judgment. For the record, I do so reluctantly. Still, I suppose some allowance might be made for the fact that until three years ago, you were a source of pride rather than embarrassment to the Service."

Eril tried to look trustworthy as he waited for Eades's decision.

"If you want a shot at the Courier Corps so much, Colonel Trionan, you go find your own *duo* partner. If you can convince anyone to fly with you—someone who qualifies for the Corps in his own right—*then* I'll believe you really mean it."

*Easy,* Eril had thought. But the other veterans, even his squadron mates, shuffled around as they found one polite excuse after another to say *no.* They respected him, true, but none would trust him that far. He'd been too much the hothead, the hero, the loner.

Luck finally turned his way again when Hank, who wanted nothing móre to do with the Federation, suggested his old jaydium running partner. "Flies like a space devil," he'd said, "and hungry, real hungry to get off Stayman. Assuming she's still there, you two might suit. That is, if you don't kill each other first."

Now, for all he knew, Eril had already managed to alienate her. Fighting her for control of her own ship was not an auspicious beginning. Maybe Eades was right and he'd be better off with the Explorers, going years between touchdowns on settled worlds. At least the only hell to pay there would be his own.

But maybe he still had a chance. Eril remembered the silken heat of Kithri's mind in his. That hadn't been an illusion on his part, had it? He'd made a bad start, but she hadn't dumped him at the earliest opportunity or headed right back to the 'port. She must feel something of the same attraction, no matter what she said. It was too soon to give up. Somehow he'd find a way to win her over.

Kithri slowed the scrubjet, leveling off in a still narrower branch, and Eril turned his attention back to the tunnel walls. They were passing through a particularly reflective section, but the passage seemed more closed-in, not less so.

"It feels like the tunnel's swallowed us up," he said aloud.

"Hank had the same reaction," Kithri said. "It drove him to jitters sometimes. He kept looking over his shoulder to see what was watching."

Eril had trouble imagining Hank Austin subject to "jitters" of any sort. Despite his looks, he'd been an able copilot, or neither he nor Eril would have made it out of the war alive. Eril didn't want to waste his breath defending him to Kithri. He changed the subject. "Where's the jaydium?"

"Hold on, we still have to get past the old workings—see, there." Kithri pointed to a section of wall which looked to Eril exactly like the rock around it, except that it was perfectly smooth from floor to ceiling.

"Tell me something about the stuff," he said conversationally. "Something I wouldn't learn from the technical tapes."

"Hank's probably told you more miners' tales than you ever wanted to hear." After a pause, she added hesitantly, "Did you know that when jaydium was first discovered, they thought it might be an organic residue?"

"I thought it was quasi-crystalline."

"There's no identifiable cellular structure, I didn't mean that. But it doesn't *behave* like an ordinary mineral."

Eril remembered his Academy physics instructor insisting that if jaydium existed anywhere else besides remote Stayman, it would have been discovered hundreds of years earlier and drastically altered the course of human spaceflight. Even now, its nature was still poorly understood. Get any three experts from the Jaydium Institute together, and you'd have five different theories as to why it acted the way it did.

Jaydium gave off light indefinitely in the absence of oxygen, but more than that, its light was *tunable*, generating a faster-than-light field around anything it enclosed. Before its discovery, Terran scientists had already developed a fabulously expensive fusion-powered drive. Jaydium's light-field effect slashed the cost of spaceflight and sent humankind to the stars in hordes instead of trickles.

Jaydium's primary drawback was its perishability when exposed to air. Properly sealed, it would last longer than the vessel itself, so the replacement demand was small, except when ships were regularly getting smashed to powder. Eril had piloted some antiquated fighters late in the war, but their jaydium panels still shone bright and clear. Sometimes the jaydium was the only thing on those ships that still worked right.

They brought *'Wacker* to a halt where three convoluted branches joined in a miniature cavern, far more spacious than the tunnels they'd been traveling. Eril drew in a tentative lungful as Kithri unsealed the door. The air felt thick, as if it had sat undisturbed for centuries. He detected a peculiar, almost metallic odor. "Are you sure this stuff's safe to breathe?"

"Jaydium does have a distinctive smell, doesn't it?" Kithri answered. "Hank always said I was imagining it."

"He also swore his nose was fine-tuned only to Centurion brandy."

"Well, you're not Hank, are you?"

"I'm glad you noticed the difference," he said, and caught her startled reaction.

Their boots rang as they stepped out on the rock floor. *'Wacker* stood on a patch of roughened surface, and the traction was good. Kithri opened an external storage drawer and took out canisters of sealant and pouches of storage containers. Upon contact with oxygen, these would foam up into solid, insulated boxes, capable of accommodating a range of cargo shapes and virtually impervious to mechanical assault.

"As soon as we chip a piece, we seal it in slickoil and spray epoxy, then the insulation," she told Eril. "That'll give us about six hours before degeneration starts. We should have plenty of time to *duo* it back to Port Ludlow."

"That'd hold *me* until the next glacial age."

She picked up the laser cutting tool and handed it to him. "You chip first and I'll pack. When you've had enough, we'll switch. You can cut for only so long before your shoulders get the jangles."

Eril glanced from the precision light generator to the cleft Kithri indicated as their chipping site. "*Jangles?* From what? These cutters can go through titanium steel without a shiver."

"Jaydium's different. Jaydium's *always* different."

Kithri showed Eril how to make shallow vertical cuts in the tunnel wall. "Don't burrow, no matter how tempting it seems," she advised. "The bedrock's stable. It won't collapse on you. But once you start chipping into a cavity, you get weird vibrational resonances. We wouldn't be fit to fly again for hours, and that's if we're lucky."

Eril swept the focused light along the exposed tunnel surface. A layer of dark stone fell away, shattering as it hit the floor. The laser felt familiar enough, although its size was better suited to Kithri's smaller hands. He'd used a similar tool for emergency repairs.

Kithri stood at his shoulder as he worked. "Don't *push* the cutter through, *stroke* it through," she murmured. "Follow the way the stuff *wants* to be cut. Give it a chance to open up in front of the laser, and ease up when you finish the stroke."

He tried his best to follow her instructions. After a few passes, an insidious vibration began to creep up his forearms. His wrists and elbows felt as if tiny mallet-wielding devils had taken up residence there. Any sudden maneuver intensified the sensation. Only the smoothest movement kept the tickling under control.

"Okay," she said, still watching, "you're almost there. Just keep on like you've been, nice and easy. . . ."

Eril managed not to break his rhythm when, a few minutes later, the light of raw jaydium burst through the slivers of dark rock. Sealed jaydium tended to be yellowish or orange, green when it deteriorated, but this was rose tinted, so subtle it was only a hint of color. Fist-sized slabs of it glimmered from the surrounding stone, illuminating the entire tunnel.

Kithri took a fragment from his hands and began swabbing it with slickoil. She looked very young in the pink light, almost pretty with her huge dark-lashed eyes and ruddy cheeks. The dent in her nose was barely noticeable.

"Keep going and don't wait for me," she said without looking up. "I can seal just as fast as you can chip."

As Eril went back to work, his confidence returned. He knew he was doing a creditable job, even for a rank beginner. There was nothing like hard labor for taking your mind off past indiscretions. Kithri was clearly willing to work with him, for the time being anyway. Sooner or later they'd stop and he'd find another opening.

They worked on, cut and seal, until the passage of time muted in the monotony of repetitive action. Eril's hands and arms began trembling. Prickles shot through his upper body with each sweep across the jaydium face. He switched off the laser tool and arched his back. His muscles shrieked in protest. He stepped away from the rock face.

"Is it—all right—to leave that?" He gestured toward the facet of glowing, exposed jaydium.

Kithri nodded as she placed the last sealed chip in the insulated storage container. "After a few hours, a layer of ash will reseal the face."

She took the laser tool from him. "Your turn to pack. First the oil—remember, be generous—and then the spray epoxy. Keep the stuff off your fingers if you can, because I don't have much solvent. Stop me if I get ahead of you."

The sealants proved tricky to handle and the oil had an unpleasantly bitter odor which masked the tang of the jaydium. Kithri cut for roughly twice as long as Eril had, but she looked tired when she finally put down the laser tool.

"Let's stow what we've cut," she said. "We've got enough time for a bite to eat and another round apiece."

They hunkered down beside the far side tunnel wall with slabs of hardbread smeared with canned cheese from Kithri's supplies. "Why are you here?" she asked. "And don't give me that line about the money again. Anyone who can fly like you can doesn't need to run jaydium, not unless he's made himself downright unwelcome everywhere else."

Eril took a gulp of stale water from the flask. "Why are *you* still here on Stayman?" he countered. "You're young, obviously educated, and you've got your whole life ahead of you. Is *this* all you've ever wanted?"

Kithri snorted in derision. "Before the war I'd have killed for a chance to get off this rock. To University . . . to anywhere. My father—he was a chemical geologist—he tutored me for the entrance exams when he wasn't studying everything he could get his hands on about jaydium. But then . . . we had some expenses. Now with the Federation hanging on by its toenails, even running jaydium won't buy me a passage to someplace better. Not flying *singlo,* anyway."

"That's exactly what I'm doing here."

"Talk sense."

"It's true that Hank married my sister," Eril said slowly, not wanting to rush things. "But he was also one of the best *duo*pilots in my squadron—"

"*Your* squadron?" Her gray eyes widened.

"The war's officially over," he went on, "but we're still scrambling to keep order in the settled worlds. You've been lucky here on Stayman—not like Pandora or Albion or half a dozen other worlds that somebody considered easy pickings. The Fed protected you better than most because of the jaydium."

Eril paused. Stayman could barely feed herself as it was, and it had been nothing short of criminal to abandon the scientists and their families here. He didn't want to appear to be defending the Fed. "I'm not on a pleasure trip, I'm recruiting."

*"Recruiting?"* Her eyes got even bigger.

He smiled. "Hank told me about this brushie he'd run jaydium with. He said she could fly circles around him in her sleep. I had to see for myself."

"Hank said that? About me?"

"You got any other candidates? I didn't come five parsecs across space to fly *duo* with that old sourbug in the tavern."

Kithri choked down the last of her bread, lowering her eyes so he could no longer read her reactions in them. "Entrance," she repeated. "To what, exactly?"

"Courier Corps."

She shook her head. "Never heard of it."

"It never existed before, it's the brainchild of First Councillor Eades. The Council's too isolated and settled space too spread out. They need agents who can be their eyes and arms out there, so their resources get put where they do the most good. There are lots of situations when speed and inspiration are needed more than brute force. At least that's the theory."

"And you're recruiting for this thing?"

He nodded.

She took a deep breath and looked away. "I can fly surface, yes, but space—that's something else. I don't have any formal training, my astrophysics is ten years out of date—"

"Never mind the rest," he said, trying to keep his voice smooth. "You've got what it takes, all right.

Compared to a coriolis, space is a vacuum, remember? You kept your head in that storm, so I know you can think straight." It was a risky thing to say, but if she was going to hold what happened against him, he might as well know now.

Kithri scowled, her face flushing. "Why me? There must be more than enough out-of-work veterans begging for the job."

"Can you picture Hank on a diplomatic mission?"

"Skies, no!" The scowl vanished into a fleeting grin.

"Actually, that's not the real problem," he said. "The training sessions will teach you whatever you need to know. The problem is finding the right people, and it's even harder when you're looking for pairs who can fly *duo.* Yes, we can recruit from within the Service, but too many of those pilots are like Hank, and those that are left are spread even thinner than before, with all our losses and the number of trouble spots to watch. Eades wants new, fresh blood."

He studied her face and saw mostly confusion. But there was something darker behind her eyes. Something he could not put a name to. He decided to take a chance and push harder.

"What do you say? Or are you so afraid of trying something new that you'd choose a jaydium tunnel over the stars?"

"No! I— I—" Kithri stammered. "I'm not afraid. It's just that I don't like to be pushed into things." She was talking too fast, her words tumbling over one another. "Of course I'd jump at the chance to get off this dust-chip. Your offer sounds good—*too* good. There's got to be a hitch somewhere. Like—

like, why should I give a damn about your Federation?" Her voice turned harsh. "They were the ones who left us here to rot, cut off the lithicycline, stuck Port Ludlow *there* when the jaydium was *here* because they didn't give a *shit* about what the miners had to go through to scratch out a living. I just want *off* this rock, not into someone's Do-Good Club!"

Eril brushed the rest of the bread crumbs from his fingers to give himself time to think. He'd expected her to object to him personally or else to vent some vague resentment against the Fed. He hadn't expected this raw hostility.

No, not hostility, he realized with an echo of their brief *duo* rapport.

Pain.

"If that's the way you feel about it," he said quietly, "we'd better get this jaydium back to Port Ludlow." The muscles behind his shoulders felt tight, as if the only way to release them was to hit something. He forced gentleness into his voice. "Think about it, would you."

She looked away. "Maybe I will, maybe . . . when I've got a choice."

# Chapter 5

For a moment Eril considered telling her the truth, that he had as much chance of getting into the Corps without her as she had of getting off Stayman without him. In the mood she was in, she'd probably tell him to stuff a comet up his *pitouchee.* The only thing to do was to keep his mouth shut and wait for another opening. He hoped he'd get one.

Kithri picked up the water bottle, took a long swallow, and then dropped it, sputtering. She pointed down the tunnel.

As he followed her gesture, Eril's mouth went dry. The last time he'd looked, the tunnel had been empty except for the two of them and the scrubjet. Now a man-shaped mist hovered there, one moment diaphanous, then condensing into near solidity. In stark contrast to the rosy glow of the partly-sealed jaydium, it was a clear, untinted gray. Eril made out a bulbous head, two arms, and two splayed-out legs. He thought he saw markings on the head section, but they faded so quickly he could not be sure.

"What the hell is *that*?" Kithri whispered. "I've been running these tunnels for years, and I've never seen *anything* like it."

"Space ghost," he said, dredging his memory. "They're sighted along the old interstellar routes. There are only about six or seven documented cases known, never this close to a planet. By our best guess, they're relics of early attempts to exceed the speed of light. Residues of energy that just happen to be shaped like humans. They probably don't actually exist in three-space."

As he spoke, the figure descended until its feet seemed to touch the tunnel floor. For a moment it stood there, motionless. Then it began to move. First one leg and then the other stretched out and swung back as it drifted along in a mechanical parody of walking.

"Whatever you are," Kithri called out, "you stay away from my ship!"

"There's no danger. The ghost can't interact with ordinary matter," Eril said with a confidence he did not feel. It was one thing to listen to a lecture on "quasi-dimensional oddities" when you were sitting safely in an Academy classroom, and quite another to confront one in the middle of a jaydium tunnel.

"There's nothing to worry about," he repeated. "It'll dematerialize again in a moment." *I hope.*

Moving one awkward step at a time, the shape continued to advance, not toward the two humans, but toward the scrubjet and its precious cargo. Kithri jumped to her feet, as tense as a coiled dust-viper.

"I don't care what that thing is, if it messes with my 'jet— "

Eril grabbed her hand. "You stay here. I'm going in for a better look before it disappears."

He shoved her bodily behind him and took a couple of steps toward the diaphanous figure. For a moment he wondered if her instincts might be right about the thing's nature. A familiar thrill shot down his spine, reminiscent of the moments before his first battle in space. He'd been just as terrified as all the other rookies, but he'd never before felt so intensely, exhilaratingly alive.

Maybe Eades was right. Maybe he was some kind of thrill junkie, a real glory-boy.

The ghost was close enough to the scrubjet to touch it, still floating stiff-legged, as if all its joints were frozen. It stretched out one thick-fingered hand, now clearly visible as it took on greater and greater solidity. Eril saw the arm reach for the curved side of *Brushwacker*—

*"No!"* Kithri screamed. She shoved him aside with surprising force and lunged for the scrubjet.

Eril grabbed her shoulders and jerked her to a halt. She pushed against him, hard. He wrestled her around to face him, holding her close to his chest. She wasn't trying to hurt him, just struggling ineffectively to get free.

"Calm down!" he said. "There's nothing to be—"

Kithri twisted away and dropped her weight, breaking his hold. Too late, Eril realized that in their struggle she'd slipped his force whip out of its shoulder holster and was now pointing it at the shape leaning toward her ship.

*Ineffective, indeed!* He'd never underestimate her like that again.

Aiming mostly by instinct, Kithri pushed the force whip trigger, a broad, flat lever set in a protective groove. Eril grabbed for the weapon, but the beam of the whip was already arcing through space. It touched the phantom shape and exploded in a tiny noval flare.

Eril gasped as a shock wave rattled his teeth. Tears blurred his vision but not enough to obscure the figure still looming near the scrubjet.

Kithri raised the whip again, this time holding it in both hands and carefully sighting down the barrel. Eril caught her hand, pulling it backward before she could press the firing stud again.

"You idiot, it'll go away on its own!"

"Skies damn you, Eril! If you don't want do something about it, I will! I won't let that thing mess with my ship!"

Kithri yanked the force whip around again. It lashed out, this time in a wide, unfocused sweep. She clung to the firing button despite Eril's attempt to pry her fingers free. The whip beam spiraled downward to touch the point of the specter's shoulder.

A blast of air and searing brightness, many times more powerful than the first, stunned Eril. In an instant, the breath was stolen from his lungs, the strength from his muscles. He staggered under the sudden impact of Kithri's weight and they both went down.

The light gave way to enveloping darkness. For an agonizing moment, Eril was afraid he'd been blinded. He struggled to sit upright, blinking furiously.

"Of all the comet-brained things to happen . . ." moaned Kithri.

"I warned you," Eril grumbled. "We had no idea how the whip's energy would interact with that thing. I'll bet your damned heroics haven't even touched it. The ghost will disappear in its own sweet time when the dimensional gap shifts. Meanwhile, there's no way we can *duo* that jaydium back now. We're half blind—hardly fit to fly—or at least I am. Can you see anything yet?"

"No . . . yes, I think that blob is *'Wacker.*" Her voice took on a new, urgent tone. "Eril! There's something on the ground next to it."

Eril forced himself to concentrate on the gray soup before his eyes, with very little success. "Don't trust your vision, not so soon after a blast like that. Our eyes were pretty well dark-adapted—"

"Stuff it!" She pulled herself free and clambered to her feet. "There *is* something. Something which *wasn't* there before."

Eril's vision cleared as he stumbled after her toward the nebulous shape of the scrubjet. Tone-on-tone gray replaced velvet black, slowly resolving into the outlines of objects. No rosy glow came from the cut jaydium face. It must have become sealed under a layer of protective ash, quicker than he'd thought possible.

They were almost on top of the sprawled figure before he was able to make it out. The thing was flat gray instead of its previous luminous transparency. The bulbous head absorbed light without any hint of gloss.

Eril touched it cautiously with the tip of one boot. The surface yielded like stiffened cloth. His vision cleared a little more and he saw—not a ghost, nor any inhuman figure—but a Terran spacesuit of ancient design.

"There's someone inside!"

"He's not a space *ghost,* that's for sure," came Kithri's voice from beside him. "But what—who *is* he?"

Without waiting for his answer, she knelt down. Eril crouched beside her and began searching for the seals of the globe helmet. In a few moments, he found the primitive lock-clasp. As they wrestled the helmet free of its moorings, he wondered what they would find inside—a human spaceman, in all likelihood long dead—or something else, some horrendous relic from the depths of space? A thrill raced along his nerves.

The opaque globe came free with a snap and a burst of humid but not stale air. Inside was no desiccated corpse, but the fully fleshed head of a living man, lolling in unconsciousness. Eril shoved the helmet into Kithri's hands and ran his fingers along the man's neck. The flesh felt warm and resilient under his touch. "I've found a pulse. Slow, but he's alive."

Kithri sat back on her heels. "Where did he come from? How did he get from deep space to the middle of this tunnel? And, more to the point, what are we going to do with him?"

"Take him back to Port Ludlow," Eril said. "He seems stable enough to move. He's breathing regularly and his pulse is steady. Do we have room for him in the hold?"

Kithri considered for a moment. "We've more than half a load of jaydium, but if we leave the sealing equipment here, we can make it. It'll be a tight fit."

"Don't worry. Our friend here is in no position to object."

Kithri insisted on reorganizing *Brushwacker*'s hold by herself. She managed to create a space large enough for the spaceman. Together they lifted him in and strapped him in place.

As they flew back through the tunnel maze at *duo* speed, Eril marveled again at the sensitivity of Kithri's handling of the tiny ship. By all the powers of luck and space, he wasn't wrong in thinking what a great team they'd make! Look at the way they'd gone into action together to detach the spaceman's helmet. She might be impulsive, but that was no crime. So was he. And to fly *duo* with her, not down some cramped jaydium tunnel in a patched-up scrubjet, but through the starfields in a proper ship. . . .

They burst from the tunnel into solar brightness. Kithri cried aloud and dropped them jarringly out of *duo*.

The pain of Eril's watering eyes blanketed a fleeting moment of erotic backlash. He squinted reflexively. The quality of the light was too vivid, as if somehow cleansed of the omnipresent dust. He leaned forward and looked down over Kithri's shoulder.

No barren plain lay at the foot of the Manitous, no endless expanse of rock and drought-tortured scrub. No curling plumes of dust where trails had carved through the fragile crust.

*Forest.*

Lush, exuberant green stretched as far as his eyes could follow. Shade upon shade of it filled the bowl of the Plain and spilled on to the sheer sides of the mountains. Trees massed so close and dense they seemed to be a single growth.

"Eril . . ."

"I see it," he said in the same hushed tone. "I see it. But I don't believe it."

# Chapter 6

"What's happened?" Kithri gasped. "Where the bloody hell *are* we?"

Eril didn't answer. For the moment, he had no ready answers. Adrenaline thrilled through his veins, bringing his vision into sharp focus—every instrument on the scrubjet's panel, every tone of green filling the endless Plain, every brilliant mote of sunlight.

Silently they circled back and brought *Brushwacker* to a halt on the wide, wind-scoured ledge. In contrast to the debris-strewn entrance they'd flown into, here they found ample room to land. Otherwise, the treeless purple-gray mountainside looked just like the one they'd left, but that was the only familiar feature of the landscape.

Kithri yanked the door open and jumped out, Eril at her heels. "The Plain, the dust—it's gone, all gone!" she cried. "Where—Oh, god, where did all those trees come from? Even the sky looks different, it's . . ." Her voice trailed off into a whisper. "It's so beautiful. . . ."

Eril had to agree with her. Standing there open-mouthed and momentarily speechless, he could see for hundreds of miles, clear to where the dazzling azure sky melded with the forest in a thin, hazy line. From this height, the expanse of green resembled a felt-topped gaming board. He'd seen forests before, on Terillium, where he was born, and on the two worlds where he saw ground action, but compared to this one they were nothing but pale, manicured gardens. He imagined tigers prowling the depths, hunted by spear-wielding woodsmen who guarded the ruins of once fabulous cities, the last remains of a race of galaxy-spanning telepathic tyrants. . . .

*Argh! I must have seen too many bad tri-vids as a kid.* But his nerves hummed with a familiar tingle and his confidence soared. If it wasn't woodsmen out there, it was something else . . . something wild and wonderful . . . just waiting for him. . . .

"Wh–where are we?" Kithri grabbed his sleeve. "We can't still be on Stayman, can we? Then how did we— What the *hell* is going on?"

Eril put one arm around her shoulders and grinned. "One *colossal* adventure."

She jerked away from him, scowling. "Be serious."

"I *am* serious!"

"Then where are we?"

"Looking at it logically, we must still be on Stayman," Eril said. "No insult intended, but your little 'jet isn't exactly spaceworthy. For another thing, look out there and imagine this place without all the trees. You've got the mountains here," he pointed, "the Plain out there, just the way it was before. Come nightfall, I'll bet we even see the same constellations. So what d'you think, have we fallen down a colossal time-travel hole, or what?"

"It's— That's just not possible. All we did was fly down a tunnel and back out again, the same as always." She still sounded confused, but less panic-stricken than a moment ago. "That spacer's suit is so old. You think we've somehow gone back to *his* time?" She hugged her arms to her body and shivered. "No! Things like this just don't happen!"

He grabbed her elbow and pulled her toward the scrubjet. "C'mon, let's take a closer look."

Kithri's voice suddenly regained its usual edge. "Not a chance, fly-boy. I've got a half load of jaydium that's decaying by the minute. Not to mention what we're going to do with our friend in the suit."

Eril clambered into the scrubjet and folded himself into the copilot's seat. Kithri might have a point about getting back, but he refused to worry. In five years of dogfights and sabotage missions, he'd always found a way out of the tightest corners. Now he figured his luck hadn't deserted him, it had presented him with a plum.

He looked back at her and said, as reassuringly as he could, "Trust me, I'll think of something. But later, after we've had a chance to look around. We can't just turn around and go back, not with a whole new world waiting for us out there." He added, seeing the stubborn set of her chin, "You can have my half of the haul, if that's what's bothering you."

The corners of Kithri's mouth twitched in something that might have been a smile. It was more than Eril expected. She climbed into the pilot's seat. "You owe me."

"I got you off Stayman, didn't I?"

She laughed, a little nervously. Activating shipbrain's automatic radio frequency search, she began their descent from the ledge. Eril, thinking of his woodsmen, added infrared and motion scans. Neither of them were much surprised when the first sweep turned up nothing more than small birds and insects.

As they passed below the tree line, the first hardy conifers multiplied into a dense, exuberant mass, their needles almost blue-black. Down a little farther, bright green deciduous species infiltrated the evergreens. Eril could almost smell the profusion of scents through *'Wacker*'s air seals. He marveled at how many shades of green there were, more than he'd ever imagined possible.

The forest canopy no longer presented an unbroken appearance. Here and there the flinty, leafless trunks stood vigil over blackened patches, encircled by vigorous younger growth. Sometimes the forest thinned around patches of brush and grass.

"Eril, look! Three o'clock! See it?"

Eril caught a glimpse of something blue and orange, shaped like a giant butterfly, darting from one leafy shelter to the next. Kithri swung the 'jet to follow, but it vanished as quickly as it had appeared.

Later they saw reflections of water running like silver veins along the forest floor, and once the infrared scanners picked up the distant, smoldering remains of a fire. Suddenly a huge meadow, frosted with yellow, crimson, and lavender, opened out below them.

"Flowers!" Kithri cried out. "Fields of flowers! Look at them!"

She sent *Brushwacker* in a ragged dive. Eril's teeth rattled as she dropped the scrubjet on the field. She scrambled out in a time that would have earned her an Academy record and bolted through the waving knee-high meadow. She fell to her knees and stretched her arms wide, gathering sweeps of flowers to her breast.

The field sizzled with midday heat and the insistent whine of insects. Eril took a few steps and was quickly inundated by color and head-spinning scent. He stopped to snap off one long-stemmed lavender blossom and run his fingertips over the wedge-shaped petals. They were surprisingly rigid and gave off a faint vanilla scent. The pollen grains which clung to his hand were deep blue. Scattering whirring creatures, he waded through the tall stalks to where Kithri knelt.

She lifted her face to him as she accepted the flower. Her cheeks were flushed and wet. "I thought I'd never see fields like this again," she said in a husky voice. "It's just like when I was a kid."

"Oh. Where was that?"

"Albion," she murmured, dropping her eyes.

Eril had heard of Albion's flower fields and how the planet was so beautiful that no one emigrated. He wondered why Kithri had. "I'm sorry."

She glanced up again, and this time he had to look away. There was something behind her eyes, some shadow that threatened to rise up and engulf him. He hurried back to the scrubjet and lounged against the opened door.

*Albion. By all the powers of space, no wonder she's so wary of anything remotely military.*

Eril had seen Albion only once, from space, a cloud-laced blue-and-green pearl, but he'd had no chance to appreciate it. He and Hank were in the team Weiram had dispatched behind the far moon, holding them in reserve against the impending stalemate. It was a sensible tactical move that took everything into account, everything except the desperation of the Alliance raiders. Eril had seethed with frustration at being ordered away from the center of the action.

Battle-fever scoring his nerves, he'd watched on the scanners as the fight turned in favor of the Federation. Behind him, in the copilot's seat, Hank wondered aloud how soon the surrender would come. Then, without a shred of warning, a blanket of electromagnetic noise paralyzed the stinger's scanners. The static deafened his ears for a terrifying moment.

As soon as he could move his hands on the controls, Eril sent his ship darting out from the moon's protective shadow. The struggle was all but over, so what had happened? Where was the battle? Where were the Federation ships, poised for the kill?

A snowstorm of tiny fragments glittered momentarily in the holocaust which had once been a planet. Eril slowed, unable to believe his eyes. Numbly he thought, *That mote of fire was once the flagship, that one a stinger, that one a medic unit, that one a living human. . . .*

Then he could see nothing at all.

When Eril's light-seared vision cleared, the sparkling cloud was gone. The fireball had already begun to dim. As he and Hank drifted and waited, their communications equipment damaged past repair, he heard someone weeping—dry, heart-shredding sobs.

Now, three years later, leaning against a tenth-rate scrubjet on an unknown planet, Eril shied away from the memory.

It must have been Hank sobbing in the darkness. It must have been. *He* was fine, just fine. The medics had cleared him of any radiation damage. He'd made it out of the war alive and with a bucket of medals, hadn't he?

In the middle of the field, Kithri jerked upright, and the movement caught his eye. The flowers in her arms had darkened, wilting. She brushed them from her, letting them drop as she got to her feet. The broken flowers lay in a little heap.

As she came toward him, Eril saw she still held the one he'd given her. Its inky petals drooped like the tentacles of an octopus. When she reached the scrubjet, he could smell its rankness. She paused, her eyes flickering to the mangled blossom, and dropped it.

Eril took a deep breath and wished he hadn't. The whole field reeked with decay. Even his saliva tasted bitter. Silently he climbed into the copilot's seat and slid his hands over the controls. They felt familiar and solid.

Kithri scrubbed her face with the back of her hand, slipped in front of him, and pulled the door shut. "So much for flower fields," she said in a voice tight with secrets. "Let's see what else this place has to offer."

Neither of them said anything about going back.

# Chapter 7

As they continued across the massive forest, shipbrain sketched details of a variety of animals—insects, amphibians in the rivers and ponds, and reptiles, some of them the size of wolves. There seemed to be no recognizable primates or felines. Shipbrain continued to report nothing on the radio frequencies except natural background noise.

*So much for my woodsmen.*

Without checking the scrubjet's chronometer, Eril couldn't be sure how long they'd been flying, watching, and scanning. It felt like forever, suspended between forest below and equally endless sky above. Kithri said nothing about the flower field and very little about anything else.

The novelty of the planet quickly wore thin on Eril. He found himself itching for something—*anything*—to happen. This couldn't be all there was—a few tantalizing mysteries and then nothing but hours on end of unremitting pastoral peacefulness.

He signaled shipbrain to pipe the radio scans to his headset. Maybe there was something out there after all and the dumb machine was too limited to recognize it. He listened, hearing nothing but uncommunicative noise.

Eril's thoughts turned to the unconscious man in the hold. Maybe they should find some place to set down and try to rouse him, find out who he was and where he'd come from. The stranger might even be from this world, might have been peacefully exploring the tunnel when he and Kithri jolted out of nowhere. Eril instantly discarded the notion. For one thing, they'd been in their own Stayman—a normal jaydium tunnel of it anyway—when the spacer appeared. For another, the suit was clearly designed for work in space. Who in their right mind would go exploring a *tunnel* in extravehicular gear? Boredom must be corroding his brain, to even think of it.

*Squawk! —BURST—bzzz—BURST— Squawk!* came shrieking over the headset. Eril nearly leapt out of his seat.

"What the hell was that?" Kithri demanded.

"I don't know," he said, quickly scanning the location functions. "It's gone now. Damn!"

"I'll check shipbrain's analysis." After a brief pause, she said, "Inconclusive. Could have been some natural source—lightning, something like that."

"No lightning made that sound."

"You know something shipbrain doesn't?"

"I gotta hunch. I gotta hunch of a hunch. Where's the source?"

"Shipbrain pins it near Port Ludlow—or where it used to be. We could fly there in an hour, if you want to check it out."

"You bet I do!"

*Brushwacker* cleared the last ridge. Eril and Kithri looked down into the depression where Port Ludlow had lain baking in the sun. No low, flat-walled buildings of ash-brick greeted them, no spaceport with its battered insystem traders and field of garishly painted scrubjets. No distant fields of sallow, struggling green, no tendril roads spewing forth plumes of powdery dust. After the forest, Eril hadn't expected any of that. But neither did he expect what he did see.

Once, when he was a boy of four, the year before his father had disappeared on that Exploration mission, Eril's mother had taken him and his sister to an antique crafts exhibition. There he watched a glassblower fashion a fairy castle, looping and twisting the liquid glass into filigree designs. It was his earliest childhood memory. Six-year-old Avery chose a winged horse for herself, but Eril had eyes only for the tower. It stood on his dresser, a touchstone for his imagination, until . . . he could not remember what happened to it. Now the memory of that childhood treasure rose up in front of his eyes, magnified a thousandfold and tinted like a watercolor rainbow, a crystal city set in a cup of living green.

"Lo-o-ok at that," Kithri said.

Eril leaned forward across her shoulders, straining for more, hardly daring to breathe lest the city shimmer and evaporate like a fever-born mirage. Even at this distance, he could distinguish individual structures. A ruby spindle shone in the late afternoon sun, dwarfing a flat rectangular block of pearlescent lace and a chain of smaller towers linked at every level by bridges of the same translucent material. A series of causeways, sapphire blue and turquoise, wound through the forest of towers.

As they drew nearer, Eril realized that the city was

not nearly as large as it had first seemed. He was accustomed to the scale of artificial satellites or ancient mega-cities like New Paris or Terillium City, where ten thousand might live and work within the same self-contained scraper. These shining buildings before him could not be more than three or four stories high. It was their slenderness and composition which made them seem so elegantly tall. Judging by Fifth Fed standards, he put the city's entire population at fifty thousand people, no more.

*Or perhaps they aren't human. Perhaps we've discovered a new race of intelligent aliens!* That had only happened twice before in humankind's exploration of space and in neither case were the aliens this sophisticated. He'd met a few during the early years of the war, semitelepathic anthropoids who quickly withdrew to their own planets at the first sign of interstellar warfare. The pseudofelines were even more reclusive and limited their own colonies to less than a dozen individuals.

When he first went into space, Eril thought he wanted adventure, the biggest there was. Before him lay the wildest discovery he could ever hope to make, even in the far-flung Exploration Corps.

A long-remembered quiver shot through him like an ember leaping into flame. At any moment, the city people would spot the scrubjet and send out an envoy.

*Wait until the Council gets my report—first the spaceman and now a whole new civilization! If only Weiram could see it. . . .*

"Whatever made the radio signal, it wasn't that city," Kithri said in a puzzled voice. "There's nothing alive down there."

Eril's mind still rolled with images of a brilliant new interspecies alliance. "What are you talking about? It's *got* to come from there. It couldn't have been anything else. I'm betting we've just made First Contact with a new civilization!"

"I'm betting you've got rocks in your skull," she retorted. "I've been monitoring the infrared and motion scans, and there's not a trace. And no radio, either. The burst must have been a natural fluke, just like shipbrain said. If anyone was there, their radar would have picked us up by now and they'd have sent someone to check us out."

Eril's skin prickled. Logically she was correct, but it wasn't logic that had kept him alive through one dogfight after another at the end of the war. Maybe he was fooling himself, maybe he *wanted* the city to have inhabitants. Maybe he wanted an excuse not to go back—not yet, not empty-handed. Whatever his rationalizations, he couldn't shake the bone-deep certainty that the noise burst had been from some advanced, power-using intelligence.

But would such an intelligence necessarily be friendly? The two alien races known to the Federation were timid and anything but warlike, but he had no way of knowing if they were a fluke or the rule.

*Their radar would have picked us up,* Kithri had reminded him. Were they even now being tracked by hidden weapons? Was the city's silence an absence—or a lure?

Kithri brought *'Wacker* down into the shallow bowl of parkland that surrounded the city. With a sinking heart, Eril recognized the signs of deterioration—

the splintered towers, the shredded supports beneath the causeways, the bridges whose lacy structures had crumbled in patches. The cores of the buildings still stood upright, lonely and proud as they slowly lost their battle with the elements. His fairytale city was nothing but a decaying ruin.

"Eril, wait!" Kithri said suddenly. "On the infrared—I'm picking up something moving on the far perimeter, something small, or maybe there's only one of them. I—you could be right. . . ."

*An alien survivor,* Eril wondered, *or only a large animal, something we missed in the forest?* Hope soared in him again.

They came around to the far side of the city, following the location of the reading, to hover over a belt of velvety tree-dotted lawns. Eril had seen similar gardens on long-civilized worlds, intricate orchestrations of botanical species chosen for their nonproliferating nature. They required little maintenance to preserve the original landscaping.

On the far side of the park lay a huge, flat field. Where it was not pockmarked by faded blast sites, the surface was smooth, the color of cream instead of the charcoal ceramic asphalt used by the Federation in its spaceports. A chain of crumbling buildings, most likely control towers, ran down the center like the shattered fragments of a spinal column. Nothing else, not even the rusting framework of an abandoned ship, rose above the level surface.

"You could berth twenty—no, thirty starcruisers out there without being crowded," Eril said.

Kithri's voice sounded tinny in the cramped cockpit. "Even during the war, we always had *something,* if only some old insystem junker."

"Jaydium kept us coming back. Even with the Fed falling apart, that was too valuable to forget."

"But they didn't come back *here.* Eril, could that mean—no Federation at all, no space travel, maybe the whole place left to rot like some sort of graveyard planet?"

"If you'd built a spaceport that size, and a city like that, would you just leave?"

"Not if I had any choice," she answered bleakly. "But if they weren't human, why should they even think like us?"

"There's got to be something left," he said stubbornly. "*Something.* Where was that heat source?"

"It's gone out of range. Or maybe the detector malfunctioned and it never was there at all."

"No matter, we'll be waiting for it when it sticks its *pitouchee* out again."

"Uhn!" came from behind them, a voice barely recognizable as human. The spaceman, as if following a carefully orchestrated script, had woken up.

# Chapter 8

They dragged the spaceman from *Brushwacker*'s hold and laid him under a massive tree whose branches spread out like an umbrella from its knotted trunk. Although the spaceman was still unconscious, his breath came in hoarse grunts as he jerked his head from side to side. Eril knelt beside him. The shade felt cool and damp after the sun's brassy heat and the crushed grass gave off a sweet, earthy smell.

Kithri touched the side of the man's neck. "His pulse is faster. Skin temperature feels okay. Shouldn't we do something for him, like get him out of his suit?"

"I don't think so," Eril said. If this suit was anything like the extravehicular gear he knew, it had its own life-support function. It might be safer not to tamper with it.

Kithri gave him an exasperated look. "We can't just sit here like a pair of brainless sand-hens! We've got to *do* something! Look, I've got some more water in stores. How about if we bathe his face? That can't hurt, can it?"

The spaceman quieted as she wiped a damp cloth across his cheeks and brow. Slowly his breathing deepened, and the color of his skin changed from waxen to pink. His eyes moved behind his closed lids and suddenly jerked open.

Before, the face had been one of an ordinary, fairly young man, neither handsome nor ugly. When his eyes opened, so red-brown they looked auburn, they transformed his face into one of startling intensity. His pupils dilated and constricted as he shifted his gaze from Eril to Kithri.

Eril put his hand on the spacer's shoulder. "You're all right now," he said, with his friendliest smile. "We're friends."

"Uh . . . Huh?"

"Friends," Eril repeated slowly. "Can you understand me?"

The spaceman wet his lips. "Whuh hept? Whirrmy? Whirrs the shih?"

Eril exchanged puzzled glances with Kithri, then tried again. The spacer seemed confused, although not frightened, as he answered. "Wirron—explorshon miss—Nited Therrin Spay Cummin—AlfaCentaw to Peers sunstar—we mit liestor—I win offboar—then I wek up here. Hoor yoo?"

"I'm sorry, we can't understand you," said Eril.

"No, wait," Kithri said. "It's like an archaic form of Pan-Anglish. *Therrin,* that's like *Terran,* Old Terran! That almost-last bit was, 'Then I woke up here.' Can't you hear it?"

Now that she'd pointed it out, he could. Eril dredged his memory for the history lectures he'd sat through only because the Academy required them. He never thought there might be anything useful in them. "There was something about a Terran Space Cum-something—Command? United Terran Space Command?"

After a fraction of a second, the spaceman nodded vigorously and gestured toward himself. The movement was hampered by the bulky suit. He repeated in a louder voice, even more heavily accented. "Nited Therrin Spay Cummin—Cummind Pascal, Lennart Pascal."

*Commander Lennart Pascal.*

"Eril Trionan, Kithri Bloodyluck," Eril said, pointing at himself and Kithri.

"Whirrmy?"

*Where am I?* Not a bad question to begin with. Before Eril could explain that they didn't know where they were, either, Lennart Pascal tugged at the catches across his chest with his heavily gloved hands. "I'm bow too suffcay. Yoofol could hell me owtta this thin?"

Even though Eril didn't understand all the words, their meaning was clear. "Just lie back and we'll get you out of it."

With Kithri's help, Eril unfastened the complicated series of clasps and locks. Underneath, Lennart wore a jumpsuit with embroidered patches on the chest and upper arm—stylized rockets and lightning bolts ringed with unrecognizable script. He grinned at them as he sat up and gestured around him.

"Won thin shoor, thiz play naw AlfaCentaw. Beezmee whuh hept, maybe Einstein rie bow tie trav. Yoofol see fren enuh. Shors a pritt plan yoo gaw."

"Look, I don't know how much of this you can follow," Eril said, "but when you popped out of—wherever you were—it seems *we* popped into this place. Do you understand?"

While Lennart clambered to his feet, Eril repeated

himself, pointing toward the city, the deserted spaceport, and the scrubjet. Lennart nodded before answering, "Alnoo, yoofol, too, heyh? Hot damn. Maybe niz we could bett unnerstan chothre, sin we stuh kere for why. Weefol splore lessgo citee, heyh?"

"Explore the city?" Eril guessed. "My thought exactly. No point in waiting for a formal invitation."

"Before we go anywhere," said Kithri. "I'm stashing what's left of this haul."

With visible reluctance, Kithri allowed the two men to help her unload the packaged jaydium and set it in a pile well away from the tree. She opened a safepocket in the scrubjet's inner wall and drew out a small device. Eril recognized it as a guardsafe-field generator. She set it on top of the pile and stepped back. After a short delay, the field ignited over the pile, shimmering poisonous ocher for an instant before it flickered into invisibility. No sign remained of the jaydium stash or its safekeeping system. Lennart watched the whole proceeding intently.

Eril slipped the force whip into its holster and slung his small pack over his other shoulder. "Who do you think's going to steal your jaydium out here?"

She paused, considering. "I don't know—it's just habit, I guess. It's probably only a matter of time now until the stuff goes to junk."

"Kithri, do you have some kind of weapon?" As he'd unloaded the insulated jaydium, Eril had considered the problem of self-defense. He'd even thought of the laser cutter, but rejected it as too heavy and cumbersome to be of much use. He found the idea of Kithri wandering unarmed through an alien city unaccountably disturbing.

She studied him for a moment before nodding,

then brought out a battered stungun from beneath her pilot's seat. Eril recognized the palm-sized gun, a combination short-range nonlethal weapon, heat beam—for cutting thin sections of metal and starting fires—and emergency beacon. He carried a survival unit very much like hers, only his had a hollow handle containing a back-sharpened knife blade, a length of permawire and three large-eyed needles.

"I've got the whip and my emergency kit," he said. "You take your little stun-popper there, and the water container." He turned to the spacer and said slowly, emphasizing his words with gestures, "Lennart, I don't have a weapon for you, so I want you to stay close to us. In fact, I want us all to stay together. No exploring on your own, and if I say 'Jump,' I don't want you to stop and ask 'How high?' I just want you to *do* it. Understood?"

"You're taking a lot for granted, throwing around orders like that," Kithri said, lifting her chin. "We're not a pair of recruits—or babies."

"And I'm no nursemaid," he said. "But we don't know what nasty surprises the city builders left for us. You haven't had training in how to deal with such things, and I have. I may not have any fancy infiltration equipment, but I'll do my best to keep us alive."

A stormy expression flickered across Kithri's gray eyes. "Okay," she said after a moment, "you've made your point. You don't have to rub it in. I'll go along with you. For now, anyway. You, too, Lennart?"

"Dun luh to me lie arm fortreh, buh I'm ease. Tever yoosay, baw."

The parkland ended abruptly in a narrow apron of quartzlike stone. The grass grew right up to it, and on the other side lay pale satiny pavement that marked the beginning of the city. Eril kept to the cover of overgrown bushes and umbrella trees as long as he could, searching for any traces of automatic weaponry. There was no response when he hailed the city or rolled a clod of earth over the threshold. He took a deep breath, drew his force whip and stepped cautiously into the open.

He wasn't sure what he expected to find or what he'd do when he found it. Neither his Academy training nor his wartime experience had prepared him for First Contact. If the city builders—assuming there still were any—were anything like the gentle, timid aliens known to the Federation, then the last thing he'd want to do was blast them away with the force whip. He slipped it back into its holster and adjusted the straps so he could draw it again quickly.

Eril started down a broad avenue flanked on one side by a lacy, pearlescent rectangle. On the other side sat a delicate spindle, two stories high and faceted like rubies. His boots crunched shards of multicolored crystals which littered the street. There was no other sound except for the rasping of his breath in his throat and the muted pounding of his heart.

He cupped his hands around his mouth. "Hallo! Anybody out there? Hallo!"

"H-a-a-l-o-o-o . . ." His voice echoed down the spacious avenue. It sounded eerie, barely human.

He stopped in front of the spindle and studied it for a moment. It was about fifteen feet on each side of its square base, and deep crimson in color. The nearby buildings, shades of pastel, looked anemic by comparison.

"Eril!" Kithri yelled from the bushes. "What's going on out there?"

"Nothing so far," he called back. "Stay where you are! I want to check—"

"The hell you are!" Kithri strode across the stone border, Lennart at her heels. She halted in front of Eril and set her fists on her hips. "We're not going to wait back there while you go off by yourself!"

Eril, realizing the futility of arguing with her, turned his attention back to the spindle. Kithri followed his gaze, throwing her head back to stare.

"Wow," she said in a hushed voice.

Lennart grinned, poked Eril with one elbow, and repeated, "Wow."

Eril placed his flattened hand on the side of the spindle. The faceted wall felt hard and smooth, like gemstone. It was slightly cool, but warmed almost instantly. He jerked his hand away.

"What is it?" Kithri asked.

Eril shook his head. "Damned if I know. It's not like any substance I've ever seen before." His right hand went automatically to the hilt of the force whip as he began searching for a door. There was none he could identify.

After a few minutes, they gave up looking and went on. Several blocks southward, they spotted a squat lavender pyramid with a curious fuzzy surface which contrasted sharply with the smooth exteriors of the other buildings.

A few buildings later they came to a single-storied cylinder of light, clear blue, like blue topaz. A doorway gaped before them, wide enough for all three to pass through abreast. They went in, cautiously picking their through the piles of splinters which had fallen from the causeway overhead. The doorway was slightly elevated from street level but there were no steps, only a smooth ramp.

Inside they found a single central room, about twenty feet in diameter and ringed with delicate fluted columns of the same pale blue. With the exception of some multicolored dust piled up along the curved wall, it was completely empty.

Eril took a few steps on the unexpectedly spongy floor. When he prodded it with one heel, it didn't give perceptibly although it effectively muffled his footsteps. He glanced up and saw the blurred outlines of nearby buildings through the translucent roof. Kithri and Lennart spread out, examining the walls.

"What would you *do* in a place like this?" Kithri murmured. She wiped her hands on her dun-colored overalls, which looked even dingier than before.

"Space only knows," he answered. "Hold a tea party?"

"Nobodd home," said Lennart. "Nafor lon tie. Whoover bill thiss playz grayon dezih buh litt shor onth upkee." He held up his hand, his fingers coated with rainbow-colored sparkles.

Eril nodded, getting the general idea that Lennart didn't approve of the current standard of housekeeping. *I hope we understand each other better before some crisis lands on us. Most of the time I'm only getting one word out of three, and it's probably the same for him.*

Beyond the blue cylinder, they found a series of spacious, interconnected courtyards, lined with opal-tinted benches and abstract sculptures. The street slanted down into a broad trough lined by knee-high curbs. At regular intervals, round openings appeared in the lower part of the walls. They looked to Eril like water pipes rather than drains. He knelt to inspect them, but could discover no trace of liquid or other contents. Nor were there any discernible seams in the paving material.

Here, near the center of the city, the buildings stood closer together, their shapes and vibrant colors clashing. Eril thought them the visual equivalent of the Academy banquets he'd been forced to sit through, getting more glazed in the eye and queasy in the stomach with each passing course. The red of rubies, the purple of amethysts, the blues of sapphire and turquoise formed a riotous mixture of color, with only narrow corridors separating the towers.

Kithri pointed to the tiny tracks skirting a pile of grit-fine dust. "Something lives here."

"Something the size of a lizard," Eril commented.

"You'd think there'd be something more," she said. "Weeds poking through cracks, the local version of cockroaches." She grimaced. "Believe me, you never get rid of *them*."

Eril ran his hands over the seamless paving material. He glimpsed something moving at the far end of the dust pile and bent to examine it further. He saw what it was and chuckled. Not one of Kithri's cockroaches, but an ant. Every planet he'd ever been on had them. This one had eight legs and bright red antennae. It seemed to be a lone scout, quite uninterested in the dust granules.

They went on for a while, deeper into the crowded heart of the city. Some of the courtyards were sunken, accessible only by ramps. After a while they no longer exclaimed at each new building, as if their capacity for awe had gone numb with overload.

Eril knelt and picked up a fist-sized piece of flame-colored glass shaped like an elongated teardrop. Was it a sculpture, a thing of deliberate beauty, or only a fragment that happened to have a pleasing form?

Straightening up, he saw that the sun had begun to dip behind the horizon. A chilly, moisture-laden breeze sprang up, whistling eerily between the towers. The crystal buildings seemed even colder and less human as daylight left the sky.

# Chapter 9

Eril unfolded Kithri's micropore emergency blanket and spread out their meager supplies while she went in search of dead wood for a fire. He added the contents of his own pack to the pile and sat back to contemplate the situation. The food supply was meager, just the lunch leftovers and emergency rations, his and Kithri's. They could find water in the forest, but they had no purification unit or anything to hunt with, except the force whip and stungun. Prudently, they should return to their own Stayman tomorrow. Given that he didn't know exactly how to get there, they ought to be trying right now instead of preparing for a camp-out.

*Just one night won't hurt anything,* Eril told himself, knowing full well that he was rationalizing. The truth was that he wanted the city to himself for a little longer, before it swarmed with Federation scientists.

Lennart hunkered down beside him, looked over the assembled gear and said something incomprehensible. Eril pointed to the variable-insulation fabric. "Blanket."

"Bee-ann." Lennart nodded and grinned.

"No, no, you're saying it all wrong. The word has an *L* and a *K*. Blan-ket. Say it, Blan-ket."

Kithri dropped a double armful of fallen wood next to them. It rattled like dry bones as it hit a patch of bare earth. She scowled. "Don't patronize him."

"I was just—"

"He's not an idiot. He knows what you mean." She brushed off her hands and set them on her hips.

"We've got to understand each other better," Eril said. "Since there're two of us and one of him, it makes more sense for him to learn our dialect."

"Sokay, pal," said Lennart. "Doanfi vermee. Telps f'yoo tak slow, buh nawso bad. I gih the gennel driff."

Kithri turned her back on both of them and began making the campfire.

Eril pointed to the force whip. "Do you know what this is?"

Lennart shook his head. He looked troubled when Eril explained that it was a weapon. "Yoofol kep, yoòfol yooz," he said, shaking his head. "No thin, no tall, no damm guh! Nessep—whar! Unnerstan?"

After a moment's uncomfortable silence, Eril went through the assembled items, naming each one and watching the spaceman's response, either recognition or puzzlement. As he did so, he sorted them into items better stored away for safekeeping and those needed at hand. The water in particular would have to be rationed until they could find a safe source.

Lennart pointed toward the place where Kithri had set the guardsafe-field. "Is wazz?"

"A device," Eril answered, "for hiding something valuable, keeping it from being stolen. You understand?"

"Hies reel weh, yoono. I can see a thin. Whuzzo valla? Hoo'd stee sumthin tauheer?"

"Sorry, I don't understand."

Lennart took a deep breath. "Whuh—arr—yoo-fol—hie?"

"Nothing much, only a half-load of jaydium."

"Eril!" Kithri whirled around from the newly lit fire. She'd used her stungun to ignite the tinder and now she waved it in his direction. "That's *my* jaydium!"

"What is he going to do, walk off with it? Out here in the middle of nowhere? When he doesn't even know what a 'safe-field is? A moment ago you were charring *me* for treating him like an idiot!"

Kithri pressed her lips together. "It's not your haul, not even half. So it's not your decision to make. Where I come from, letting strangers know you're carrying jaydium is damned dangerous."

Lennart took advantage of the pause in their argument to ask, "Waz this jhaydiuh?"

"Jaydium. How can you not know about jaydium?" Kithri asked. "You're a spacer, aren't you?"

He stared back at her with a bewildered expression and started speaking rapidly and incomprehensibly.

"Jaydium—a mineral used in spaceflight," Eril managed to interject. "Faster-than-light, do you understand?"

"Fazzer thah lie? Snaw possuh. You can seed Einstein's limm forwhy mass sponenshul incree as the Niverss Nuhcertent Prinz varz wih thinver of—"

"Hold it! Slow down, I can't follow you. Kithri, did you get any of that?"

She shook her head. "Just that he seems to have

all sorts of reasons why faster-than-light travel isn't possible."

"I'd already gathered that. I wonder how long ago . . . Lennart, what was the year? The date? *When* do you come from?"

"Day? Yoofol doano day? I coobe owtaheer few mozz maybe, shibee arawn fie-fhay."

By scrawling numbers on a patch of dirt next to the fire, they were able to establish the length of the year and fix Lennart's time somewhere around 3508 Common Era. Common Era, that unimaginably ancient time from the Lost Eras before the First Federation. Almost nothing was known of that time, beyond its mere existence.

"You're from our far, far past," Eril said. "So long ago we don't use that dating system, not even in history texts."

Lennart looked bleak and nodded. "I thaw nivver see the few. Spay the close I get, buzz kine lone, heyh? Can exa befrenn theyfol can unnerstan the say lang." He combed back his hair with one hand. "So whenz weefol now?"

"It's 107-Five," Eril answered, "counting from the founding of the current Federation."

"That's assuming," Kithri added, "that he's come *forward* into our time instead of us going back into his."

"We'll have to check the stars tonight to be sure."

Eril gazed at the parkland, where the weirdly elongated shadows of the umbrella trees striped the lawn and shivered inwardly. Kithri could well be right, much as he hated to admit it. But what kind of disaster could turn such a dense, exuberant forest into the desolate Cerrano Plain? *And the city . . . Surely some trace of that should remain. . . .*

"Yoofol fly awtie fazzer than lie?" Lennart asked suddenly.

"We've always had superlight speed, that's what's made the Federations possible. During the First Fed, roboships brought back the first samples of jaydium." Eril had only the vaguest impression of the bulky sublight barges of pre-First Federation spaceflight. It was jaydium which reduced the prohibitive cost of the fusion-driven faster-than-light drive and made possible the exodus of humanity into space that marked that golden era.

"Yoofly fazzer than lie in *thah* shih?" Lennart asked, pointing at *Brushwacker.* There was only a faint lemony light remaining in the western sky, and twilight softened the tiny ship's scars. "Doan luh lie muzz, buh can telmuh fruh th'ex. Yoofol gaw allsore noo gadges, whomy t'say whuh theyshuh loo lie? Eril, yoogaw one pritt spiff shiheer, heyh?"

"It's *mine,* not his," Kithri said, biting off the words.

Lennart looked from one to the other, his expression unreadable in the gloom. "Hot damn."

*Exactly my sentiments,* thought Eril.

"Yoofol show me insie?"

Kithri hesitated so long that Eril was sure she'd refuse, but in the end she didn't. Lennart was so eager to see all the new aircraft developments over the years, his enthusiasm was irresistible. Finally, exasperated with the limitations of language, Kithri shoved him bodily into the copilot's seat. Eril stood at the opened cockpit door and watched, trying to keep a straight face as she ran through the equipment and explained everything again in words of one syllable. From the look on Lennart's face, composed of equal parts of delight, concentration, and bewilderment, Eril couldn't tell how much he really understood. But one thing was sure, the ancient spaceman was crazy over anything that flew.

The second run-through exhausted Kithri's patience. She ordered Lennart out, turned off the ship's lights, and closed the door firmly behind them.

The fire had died to a heap of embers and the damp breeze felt even colder. Kithri put the last of the wood on the fire and rolled up in one of the emergency blankets, her back to Eril. Lennart crawled back into his spacesuit and wished them both the equivalent of a good night.

As he lay looking up at the stars and waiting for sleep, Eril's thoughts drifted to the burst of radio noise and the infrared trace which had vanished so mysteriously. They couldn't have been natural. Somewhere in that seemingly deserted city there was something alive, something which used machinery. . . .

Eril knew that Kithri was gone even before he came fully awake, as if some part of his mind, even sleeping, was aware of her. He raised his head and looked around. A few feet away, Lennart lay stretched on his back in his space suit, snoring gently. From the overhanging branches came the occasional twitter of night creatures.

Silently Eril got to his feet and stepped out from the shelter of the umbrella tree. Above his head, stars swam in a profusion of milky light, dense and luminous. One small moon wore a faint blue halo as it rose on the far side of the city, flanked by two steady points of planetary brilliance.

*Anybody out there?* He waited there for several minutes, just beyond the perimeter of the tiny camp, head thrown back, staring at the celestial display. Then he spotted a dark figure against the paleness of the spacefield.

Kithri stood hugging her arms to her body as he walked up to her. After a pause, she said, "We've got the answer to one question, at least. That's our night sky up there. Ours today, not thousands of years either way. I've looked up at those stars a million times, dreaming of the day I'd be out there, too. See that one?" She pointed. "The miners call it The Dewdrop. When we first came, I used to wish on it."

Eril shifted his weight from one foot to the other. He cleared his throat. "What do you think of our spacer?"

"I know exactly how he feels."

"Me, too."

"Don't talk scut!" Kithri snapped. "All *you* had to do was get back on your ship and take off! You could jet over to Terillium or Nouvelle-France whenever you wanted to! You have no *idea* what it's like to be buried alive down here—no cities, no trees, n–no flowers. Nothing but dust." Her words came out in a flood, hot and wild like tears. "Oh, sure, there are choices, even for someone like me—whoring insystem or marrying some farmer who might say two words in a year. Or chipping jaydium. All those years of running and hoping. . . . What a fool I was to think I'd ever make it!"

Eril's tongue wouldn't move. A wave of unexpected empathy surged through him—what would it have been like for him, stranded on such a desolate world, looking up at the sky night after night? Knowing that the jaydium he sweated for would see the stars before he would? He'd end up even more bitter than she was.

They stood in silence, looking up at the stars. After a while, he said, "So we're on Stayman, but it's not our Stayman. If this can happen to us, anything can. Out of all that glory up there, what do you want, really want?"

She shuddered and whispered something he couldn't hear. He tried to put his arm around her and she shied away like a frightened deer. "I made you an offer in the mountains," he said, "and I meant it. But until we get back—I don't want things to stay this way between us—all prickly, as if we had nothing—"

"One trip down a wormhole is hardly enough to make us lifemates."

"Kithri, let's not throw away what happened to us in *duo*. It's still there, I know you can feel it, too. We need time to know each other better, to learn to trust one another. . . ." There was much more he wanted to tell her, far beyond these stumbling words. He let them trail off.

After a pause, she said, "Do you think we *can* get back . . . to our own Stayman?" Her voice sounded low and tired, as if all the fight had gone out of her.

"I think it's too early to give up."

He reached out again, fully expecting her to jerk away. "You're wound up tighter than a drum. How about I rub your back for you? No—" to her quick flinch, "I meant a back rub, nothing more."

Kithri followed him back to camp and stretched

out on her stomach on one of the micropore blankets, her head pillowed on her arms. Eril lay down beside her and pulled the second blanket over both of them. Using his free hand, he began rubbing her back with the gentle, insistent pressure he'd learned years ago.

Her muscles were stronger and better defined than those of the women he'd trained and flown with. Slowly the tautness seeped away, leaving a supple resilience he found pleasurable to touch.

"Mmm, that's nice," she murmured. "Hank and I sometimes swapped shoulder rubs after a haul, when he was still hoping it would lead somewhere."

"Sounds like Hank. Did he ever give up?"

"Let's say we reached an agreement. If I wouldn't whore for my passage, it didn't make sense to do it for my *duo* partner and then pay twice to get offplanet."

"Hank wouldn't have seen it as payment. More like a privilege. According to Avery, he was quite a catch, and she's got high standards."

"I tried that—before Hank—for the sake of a warm body the next morning. It didn't help. It only made things worse, like he was in bed with my body and not even me."

"What about—us in *duo*?"

She sighed so gently he felt the passage of her breath through the air, rather than hearing it.

Eril laid his head down, still stroking her back. His hand brushed her curls. An image leapt to his mind, amplified by the residue of their *duo* unity—Kithri as a young girl, her hair long and loose, streaming down her back. Kithri dancing through fields of flowers, her bare feet kicking up little sprays of pollen. Then he saw her, curls hacked short and skin choked with dust, clutching a mug of stale brew, sitting alone rather than endure the old lechers in the tavern. He wished he hadn't tried to defend Hank.

Kithri rolled on her side facing him, the blanket draped like a tent between their bodies. Eril let his hand slip from her shoulder. They were so close he could feel the heat of her body on his face. He remembered her mouth on his and the softness of her breasts against his body.

She said, "What was all that recruitment stuff really about? I don't doubt there is such a thing as the Courier Corps and that you have something to do with it, but I don't know what. If they picked you as a spokesman, they're a pack of idiots. You sounded worse than a tri-vid advertisement. And if that's all you are, why is it so damned important that I join? Do you get a bonus for signing me up, or what?"

Eril hesitated, thinking how he'd handle one of Avery's friends. He could tell her how much he wanted her, how beautiful she was in the light of the two moons. He could promise that this time she would really see the stars, that *he* was her ticket, not the jaydium. She'd fall into his hand like a ripe peach.

"Or did you mean it about learning to trust each other?" Kithri said, and all his schemes fell apart.

"The Corps is real, but I'm no spokesman for it," he said slowly, a little astonished at what popped out of his mouth. "In fact, unless I show up with a qualified *duo* partner in hand, I'm not in it at all." *That is, if we ever get back. . . .*

"You, or every applicant?"

"Me."

"Why you?"

"Because I messed up once too often."

There was a moment of silence, during which something seemed to be wrong with Eril's heartbeat—too loud, too fast, rattling the bones behind his eyes.

"I thought you were some kind of war hero, like Hank."

"Oh!" His laugh came out a sharp, bitter bark. "That part's true. I have a drawerful of medals to prove it—Four Sectors, Albion—"

"Albion! You were there?"

Eril nodded, even though she couldn't see him. She said, "And you—you must have been the team that survived. . . ."

"I went where my squadron commander said to. It was ratshit luck. You got away, too."

"That was years ago, before the war," she said. "I was still a kid, I had nothing to say about it. In fact, I was damned pissed when I found out we didn't *have* to leave."

"I thought people didn't."

"My father volunteered for the Stayman mission. *Volunteered!* I suppose it was a good thing in the end, or neither of us would've made it."

"I take it he didn't."

Another sigh in the darkness. "He died . . . after a long illness."

*Back in the tunnel she mentioned cutting off the supply of lithicycline—that's the treatment for neurodyscrasia.* Eril shuddered. No one deserved to die like that. She must have nursed him through it.

"It never made sense why he'd leave Albion for

someplace like Stayman," she continued. "It was years before the Alliance Declaration. Sure, some people must have seen the war coming, but who'd've thought Albion wouldn't be safe? Anyway, the Feds snapped him up. They needed a chemical geologist, so they didn't ask any questions. So we went, and stayed alive." She turned back on her stomach, facing away from him.

As Eril began rubbing Kithri's back again, he was struck by the bland, dispassionate tone in her voice. With *duo*enhanced awareness, he could feel her desperate homesickness, her anger and confusion at her father's actions, shadows of the things she couldn't tell him. Well, he hadn't been forthcoming with all the unflattering details of his own fall from official grace, his own shadows.

*Time,* he had said, they needed time to learn to trust each other. *Time . . .*

Still, it was surprisingly pleasant, lying beside her on a star-strewn night, feeling her warmth and the gentle rise and fall of her breathing.

# Chapter 10

Night-faring insects chirped and whirred from the foliage of the umbrella trees, a descant counterpoint to Lennart's rhythmic snores. Eril wasn't sure of the exact moment Kithri fell asleep and her muscles went from tense to buttery under his fingertips. Her breathing became soft and regular. Soon he, too, drifted off, one hand flung across her back. His body grew warm and heavy, so heavy. . . .

So heavy, gravity sucking him down into the denseness of the earth. . . .

*Heavy.* . . .

Suddenly Eril was no longer lulled three-quarters into sleep. He didn't know exactly what was wrong, but something. . . .

Lennart snored on, oblivious, but the insects had fallen silent. The instincts which had warned Eril of impending disaster so many times during the war now shrilled in alarm. He tensed to scramble to his feet, force whip in hand and ready for action.

The world froze around him.

He couldn't move, not even his eyelids. He could barely breathe as an iron band held his ribs like a vise. Something warm and steely clamped tightly over his mouth. Prickles of ice flared up all over his body.

*Air!* screamed his burning lungs.

Calm—he had to stay calm. Just one breath, he swore to himself—one breath, nice and slow. *Air in . . . air out. . . .*

Panic receded to a muted roar.

*Air in . . . air out. . . .* He could feel a faint, shallow movement in his chest. His heart raced loud and strong in his ears. Cold sweat covered his face.

The next thing Eril felt was a slight stinging on his temples as something was torn loose.

"Ccan yyou unndersstand mme?"

The words reverberated in his ears with a curious, distorted echo. Somehow he managed to open his eyes. His vision whirled, doubled, and finally came to an uneasy fusion. A moment later he made out a slender silhouette, backlit by artificial yellow-green light, bending over him. The clamp over his mouth was suddenly released. He felt a gentle touch behind one ear.

"There, the translator should be working better now." The voice was light, flowery, and unmistakably feminine. "The sound-duplication effect will fade as your auditory associational cortex filters out the redundant signals. You can understand me, yes?"

"Nn-unh!" Eril tried to sit up, but his body was still inert as frozen clay. His mouth flooded with metallic-tasting saliva. He swallowed hard.

"The tangle will wear off in a few moments. Don't worry, it's a harmless dose. As soon as you've recovered sufficiently, I'll release your companions. I'm sorry to have to restrain you, but under the circumstances the precaution was unavoidable."

*What circumstances?*

The female humanoid—Eril immediately thought

of her as a woman—disappeared from his field of view. He took another breath, deeper than before, and found he could move a little if he didn't do it too fast. Tingles shot down his arms and legs. The sensation of being half-frozen eased. Moving slowly and deliberately, he managed to haul himself upright.

The woman adjusted her portable light source to illuminate the camp circle. Eril's vision cleared enough so he could make out Lennart, unbound and apparently unharmed, several yards away.

Kithri sat at a point equidistant from both of them. Her huge gray eyes were pools of darkness above her sallow cheeks. She rubbed them with the back of one hand.

"Kithri? Lennart—are you all right?" Eril's voice came out in a croak.

"What happened to us?" said Kithri, equally hoarse.

"Holy shit," Lennart groaned, shaking his head as if his ears were plugged. "Is this what you folks call a welcoming committee?"

Eril's mouth jerked open, despite a wave of protest from his still-numb muscles. Surely he'd misheard the spacer—he must be more befuddled than he realized.

"I apologize if the tangle disoriented you," their captor said. "I didn't know who you were and the only people who could be here without my prior knowledge would be either pirates or illegal amateurs. I had to discover which you were before you damaged the site."

She moved into the circle of light, still talking. Eril got his first good look at her. Unbound shoulder-length hair floated like a golden cloud around her oval face. Full, crimson lips and dark eyebrows contrasted vividly with her flawlessly pale skin. Her chin was softly rounded, her neck long and graceful, her eyes as green as almond-shaped emeralds. She wore a one-piece garment like a tightly belted jumpsuit, which accentuated her narrow waist and curving hips.

"I had to use the tangle to keep you safe until I could be sure," she continued. "As soon as I saw your craft, I realized you were neither of these, were something unknown, and then I needed to install the translators in your cerebral speech centers. It was just as well you were unconscious. I didn't have to anesthetize you."

"Tr–translator?" Yes, she said something about a translator. Something *surgically* implanted?

"So that's why you started coming in loud and clear all of a sudden," Lennart commented. "I thought my brains were still on strike."

Kithri scowled at the alien woman. "Who the hell are you?"

"My name is Brianna Jheridian." She turned slowly toward Kithri and answered calmly. "As a licensed xenoarchaeologist, I am legally authorized to be on this planet. Now you tell me who *you* are, and where you came from."

"Give us one reason why we should trust you!" Kithri said. "You sneak into our camp, knock us senseless with that tangle thing, plant your translator devices in our brains, and now you expect us to just *tell* you—"

"No, you misunderstand my intention," Brianna interrupted. She sat down beside Kithri, positioning herself so that the light fell full on her face. Kithri stared back, drab and rumpled beside her.

Watching the two women, Eril felt his hackles rise.

"Listen to me, No-body out of No-where," Brianna said to Kithri. "I am a *scientist,* first and foremost. I neither deal in nor condone political manipulations. My goal is the preservation and appreciation of intelligent species' diversity. Yes, I had to safeguard this site. But I treated your bodies with the same cautions I would have used on my own colleagues."

Brianna's tone impressed Eril as much as her words. He realized he'd been unconsciously swayed by her beauty, which was enough to turn the average man to putty. But *unfavorably* swayed, because he'd grown up scrapping with an older sister who was every bit as gorgeous. Avery wouldn't have hesitated to use all her allure to get what she wanted, even if it meant playing to the two men, polarizing the group and making Kithri look unattractive—even ugly—by comparison, in order to discredit her. For a dangerous half-second, Eril had been tempted to judge Brianna by Avery's behavior.

Not fair, he realized. Also not wise, when she was offering a reasonable explanation for her actions. He couldn't think of any graceful way of saying, *So sorry I knocked you out and treated you like criminals, but it was all a misunderstanding. I was just doing my job.*

She wasn't their enemy, and wouldn't become one if he could help it. But he had to take that risk and trust her first.

"I'm Colonel Eril Trionan," he said, "of the Fifth Federation Star Service. And that's Kithri Bloodyluck of Stayman and Commander Lennart Pascal of the United Terran Something-or-other."

"Space Command," said Lennart.

Kithri glared at Eril, but said nothing. He thought she looked more miserable than angry.

"I don't know any Federations, fifth or otherwise," Brianna moved closer to Eril, shaking her head. He saw, for the first time, the lines of tension around her mouth, the faint trembling of her hands with their shadowy markings. She was every bit as scared as he'd been—and in a much more vulnerable position, one against three. It must have taken courage—or desperation—to let them wake up instead of finishing them off while they lay helpless.

"Unless you're from outside the Dominion Sphere . . ." Brianna said, curiosity wrestling with caution on her features. "You clearly aren't Tribesmen. You'd need a galaxy-class starship to cross those distances, and only a zipper could have landed without my alarms sounding. So how did you get here?"

"We don't really know," Eril said. "But one thing is sure, we didn't travel through space. Kithri and I started out on Stayman, a world of great arid plains with only a few marginal settlements, nothing even remotely like the crystal city. We were mining in the Manitous, that mountain range on the eastern side of the forest, and Lennart there fell out of an interdimensional time gap."

"Oh, is *that* what happened to me?" Lennart said, rubbing the back of his neck.

"An *interdimensional time gap*?" Brianna raised one eyebrow, although her expression remained perfectly serious.

Praying he wouldn't sound totally unbelievable, Eril related how Lennart had been caught up in a time-space disturbance and had appeared suddenly in the tunnel.

"Actually," said Lennart. "I was outside the ship, repairing the medial ramscoop struts. We were traveling at a significant fraction of light-speed and if a lightstorm had caught us crooked like that . . . I've seen what was left of the *Verne,* half the tail blasted into nothing and no sign of the crew. Anyway, one moment everything was going fine, the next I looked up and there was the storm. I was sure I was dead but the *next* moment these two were welcoming me to the future."

"The . . . future?" Brianna repeated.

"By all the geological and astronomical evidence, we're still on the same planet, in the same time," Eril said. "Lennart's been frozen—suspended you might say—for millennia."

Brianna folded her arms over her chest and pursed her lips. "I see what you're suggesting. It's never been proven, of course, but it's not impossible by the current theory of temporal mechanics. *If* Lennart were 'suspended' in a mass-space-time anomaly, then whatever factor released him would experience an equivalent vectorial displacement."

"Huh?" said Lennart and Eril together.

"When Lennart fell out of the thing, we got knocked sideways," Kithri said. When they all stared at her, she added, "I think."

"Theoretically—and I must stress the hypothetical nature of this line of reasoning," Brianna gestured with her hands as she talked, "time isn't linear but divergent. At each intersection point, each crucial event, two or more subsidiary time lines are produced."

"Like the world where the dinosaurs didn't become extinct and went on to explore space?" said Lennart.

"It's all speculation at this point," Brianna said. "And if you tried it again with Lennart, since he's the focal point of the displacement, you might just as easily travel linearly instead of horizontally. Back to his own time, I'd guess. But if you *did* come from an alternate probability world . . . and we could find some way to *reverse* the process . . . and open a door between our two worlds . . ."

She raised her shoulders in a little shiver of excitement. "The Institute scientists will be crawling over each other to help you get back, not to mention creating a two-way portal."

"It's my guess all we have to do to return to our own world is to retrace our steps," Eril said, ignoring Kithri's snort of derision. "But if that doesn't work, we'd be grateful for your help."

Brianna's green eyes narrowed speculatively. "What were you mining here? There were no commercial options when the Institute issued the excavation permits."

For a moment, Eril considered keeping the jaydium a secret. It might make a powerful bargaining tool, yet Kithri had been so damned sensitive about his even mentioning it to Lennart.

*That was just conversation, but this is important! To hell with her paranoia.*

"We were chipping jaydium, deep in the tunnels," he said.

"I'm sorry, I must have misunderstood you," Brianna blinked. "Did you say . . . *jaydium*?"

"Maybe you call it something else and your translator garbled the meaning," Eril suggested.

"I've never heard of the stuff before," said Lennart.

"I *know* what jaydium is." Brianna got to her feet

and began to pace. "Everyone knows that faster-than-light spaceflight requires jaydium. The Dominion wouldn't exist without it. Slow-light generation makes the relativity warp impossible. But how could it be *here*?"

"Where else?" Eril said, startled. "This is the *only* place it's found. That's why the Federation kept the spacelanes open through the war."

"*Only* place?" Brianna paused, her eyes widening. "Oh no, our surveys would never have missed it or released this planet for scientific study if there were even the remotest possibility. Don't you realize how rare—and how essential, how irreplaceable—jaydium is?"

"Where does *yours* come from?" Lennart asked mildly.

Brianna lowered her eyes.

"And you asked *us* to trust *you*," Kithri said.

Brianna looked up, stung. "Not *here*. It's restricted to two planets, the most heavily guarded in the Dominion Sphere."

"Oh!" Kithri laughed humorlessly. "That's not so bad. In our world, it's found on only *one* planet. But I bet you don't pay your miners any better."

Brianna looked puzzled for a moment before saying, "If there's a new source of jaydium here, we can't leave it undefended. Come on, I'll take you back to my camp and call the Institute authorities."

# Chapter 11

Kithri followed Eril and Brianna through the shadowed parkland, Lennart at her side. The short grass cushioned her step and gave off a tangy smell. She glanced up at the stars, but they were blotted out across half the sky. In the other direction, one moon burned stark and white through a rift in the clouds. The first cool drops of rain spattered her face.

*Rain!* Memories flooded up in her of that last evening on Albion, walking in the pastel twilight through a field of tall, waving skyflowers. She'd stayed out until the rain had washed away her tears and she was soaked to the skin. Her father hadn't said a word.

"Hurry!" called Brianna. She'd been heading toward the city, but now she veered off into a clump of low trees. Dense foliage blocked all but a gentle mist and the faintest dappling of moonlight. Low branches pressed in on both sides, forcing them to go single file.

Kithri walked slowly, feeling her way through the near darkness. Her moment of astonished joy at the rainfall had vanished. It was difficult to hurry and think at the same time, especially when a chorus of contradictory voices took up residence in her skull.

*How do I know this Dominion isn't just as bad as the*

*Fifth Fed?* one part of her said. *I'll probably end up stranded on some backdust world that's even worse than Stayman.*

*I should've insisted on staying behind with* 'Wacker, another part grumbled. *Who knows what might happen to it out there?*

And yet, to see the Dominion woman's camp, to ride in her ships, maybe to reach those stars which were so like the ones she'd dreamed of. . . .

Kithri tripped on a knotted tree root, caught herself, and swore under her breath. Lennart, who was walking behind her, hooked one hand under her elbow to steady her.

"Th–thank you."

"My pleasure."

*Your . . . pleasure?*

She wasn't sure what to say to Lennart, caught between a flood of questions about his world and an irrational fear of revealing to Brianna how little they knew each other, as if that were a fatal weakness. Miserably, she turned back to her deliberations.

*Everyone else is so pleased by what's happening, and all I think about is the things that can go wrong.*

She *ought* to be excited or at least pleased. This was what she dreamed about, wasn't it—a whole new world to explore? And, as Eril had pointed out, she was off Stayman. So what the hell was wrong with her?

Brianna's voice floated back to her. "I can't handle the security for a jaydium find by myself," she was saying to Eril. Her speech sounded as natural as if she were speaking their own language without any mechanical intermediary. The echo effect had completely disappeared. "If it's really there, we can't risk someone else discovering it before we get to it and either mining the stuff for themselves or holding it for ransom."

"We'll cooperate in any way we can," Eril said.

Kithri scowled again, her saliva turning acid. "Why should you trust us, anyway?" she asked Brianna. "How do you know we aren't pirates ourselves? We could've lied about the jaydium."

"My scientific training enables me to understand cultures from their physical remains," Brianna replied over her shoulder. "You couldn't fool me even if you tried. I instructed the translator to analyze your language for aggressive concepts, and it would have picked up a mercenary's specialized jargon. Your naïveté is one of the most convincing arguments for the truth of your story."

Kithri shut her mouth and vowed not to put her feet anywhere near it again.

At the center of Brianna's camp stood a wide-based dome tent ringed with smaller storage bubbles. The mottled green and ivory structure blended with the grove as if an artist had designed the ideal marriage of tree and human dwelling. Brianna swung open the translucent door and led them inside.

Lights flashed on automatically at their entrance. Kithri glanced around, trying not to look impressed. Inside the spacious central laboratory, instruments and specimen containers covered the rows of free-standing shelving and tables. She recognized spectrophotometers, miniaturized nucleomagnetic resonators, qualitative analysis gear, and a computer for analysis and data storage. She knew enough about scientific apparatus to realize the sophistication—and cost—of Brianna's equipment.

Yet the laboratory seemed subtly wrong—too big, too spread out, as if it had been designed for more than a single researcher. Kithri had only her memories of her father's tiny laboratory to compare it to. It had been compact for efficiency, not out of necessity. On Stayman, space had hardly been at a premium, but it made no sense to walk halfway across the room to take a sample from one instrument to another. Here, the areas that looked well-used were scattered, interspersed with others that seemed to be mere storage.

Brianna seated herself at a desk and removed the protective cover of a small instrument that seemed to be mostly mirrors and a square keypad. "You're familiar with the principle of the neo-ansible?"

"Something like that," Eril answered.

Brianna settled the threadwork headset over her ears and activated the device. She tapped a complex pattern on the keypad. After a few moments, the triangular screen flashed yellow.

Kithri noticed the lines of Brianna's profile and how the folds of her jumpsuit hugged her full breasts and hips. She rubbed her nose where it had been broken and remembered Avery's pristine beauty. Then she saw the half-healed scars, pink and raised, covering Brianna's hands. The nails were short and misshapen, some of them blackened as if they'd grown out after being smashed.

Kithri turned on one heel and strode to the far side of the laboratory. Lennart followed her at a more leisurely pace.

"Do you recognize any of this stuff?"

"Not the specifics, no," she said. "But it all looks familiar." She ran one finger along a small lensed instrument, noticing the film of dust. "This looks like a holographic camera, but I've only seen them in textbooks. Nobody on Stayman could afford one."

"Then what was all that business with the force-field? I thought from the way you protected it that your jaydium was valuable."

"Yes, but we miners weren't the ones making the fortunes. I don't know who did, maybe the processors. Then there was the cost of shipping anything—anything at all—to Stayman once the war started."

"War . . ." Lennart took a deep breath and his cheeks paled. "I thought I'd never hear that word refer to something outside the history books. We thought we'd ended armed conflict once and forever, back in the 2500s. All those slogans about war being a contagion and we'd found the final vaccine. Guess we were wrong on that score, hey? F-T-L travel coexisting with warfare—civilization sure went forward and backward at the same time."

Lennart jerked his chin in Eril's direction. "He's carrying around more than a few scars from it."

"How would you know that?"

"The way he throws around orders, the way he snuck us into the city. Suddenly all that paranoia makes sense. What a world I've fallen into."

Brianna disconnected the neo-ansible. "I've made my report," she said, "but they want me to check out your find before they investigate. The regular Institute ship isn't due to make its rounds here for months. It would take a verified discovery to merit a special probe."

"We've got a half-load of jaydium back at our

camp," he said. "It was all we cut before Lennart made his appearance. Would that be proof enough?"

Something inside Kithri exploded. "In case you forgot, the jaydium is *mine*!" She rushed toward them, barely avoiding slamming one hip into a table laden with equipment. "It won't do you a damned bit of good to look at it. The stuff's completely sealed with ash by now."

"I have the equipment to expose a slice for examination," Brianna said calmly. "I'd have to rely on spectrographic analysis for a positive identification anyway. Even then, I couldn't be sure the source was local and not an imported sample. It would be better if I could inspect the site itself to prove your specimen isn't a plant. There would be details you couldn't fake."

"Fine, we can—" Eril began.

"Just how do you propose to get her out there?" Kithri broke in. She halted in front of Eril and put both hands on her hips. "Walk?"

"In the scrubjet, of course."

"*Brushwacker* seats two, no passengers, and besides—"

"We carried Lennart back in the hold."

Kithri jabbed one thumb in Brianna's direction. "*She'd* end up like a corkscrew after five hours!"

"I wasn't planning on flying her there *singlo*," Eril retorted.

"Are you crazy? Fly *duo* with her in the hold? With *her*? Have you forgotten what happened the first time?"

Eril set his lips together. For the first time, his voice took on an edge to match hers. "Have you forgotten what *didn't* happen?"

"What's *duo*?" Brianna asked in a puzzled voice.

"Eril, don't even think about telling her!" Kithri snarled.

"Kithri, what is wrong with you?" he said. "Why are you acting like this?"

"What's the matter with *me*? How about what's the matter with *you*?" Kithri knew she was making a fool of herself, but she couldn't stop. The words kept pouring from her mouth, faster and hotter than ever. Her hands moved of their own accord, gesturing wildly.

"This Brianna seems harmless enough, but what about her Dominion or those space pirates she keeps talking about? We're the outsiders here. Who knows what *'nasty surprises'* are waiting for us? And you're greeting them all with open arms, giving away everything I've got! Our lives won't be worth a thing! We'll have nothing left to bargain with—*nothing*!"

Brianna leapt to her feet, knocking over the low padded stool she'd been sitting on. Her white face stood out in stark contrast to the glowing red of her lips. Even angry, she was lovely. "Bargaining—for lives, for knowledge? What kind of monsters do you think we are? The Dominion is a union of civilized worlds and I am a *scientist*—"

"Kithri, you've gone too far," Eril said. "What do you think is going on here? Some hole-in-the-rock bazaar? We're talking about an *alliance* with Brianna and her people. It could be the greatest thing that's happened to us since . . . since spaceflight itself! And I won't let you ruin it with these petty, provincial hysterics. If the Dominion needs more information about the jaydium site, it's a small price for what we'll get back. I'm taking Brianna out there if I have to fly her *singlo*."

Kithri set her lips together, her face burning as if suddenly scalded. Her eyes went from his honey-gold skin to Brianna's delicately flushed cheeks. Whatever was waiting for them on this new world, she wouldn't be a part of it. She might have been trapped on Stayman, the stars beyond her reach, but at least she had *Brushwacker.* At least she had what little hope she could wrest from running jaydium. Now all she wanted was to run as far and as fast as possible.

Lennart touched her arm gently. She flinched as if he had struck her. "Come outside with me for a moment, would you?"

Outside, the dome's artificial lights clashed with the brilliant apricot dawn now drenching the eastern sky, and the night squawkers had grown quiet. The rain had stopped, but the moist, chilly air made Kithri shiver. Lennart put his hands on her shoulders and turned her around to face him. She didn't protest.

"You got to calm down, lady, or you and the boss there are gonna start World War Four."

"What the hell do you—" Kithri stopped herself. Lennart, after all, hardly qualified as an enemy. She couldn't think straight, not with her heart making such a racket between her ears. "But those two, they're going to . . ."

"You're feeling pissed and left out, but that's not the end of things," Lennart said. "You're not alone, you know."

She took a deep breath, searching for words. Eril's enthusiasm for the crystal city, with its mysterious, desolate beauty, was one thing. The city wasn't stealing her scrubjet as well as her jaydium. But ever since they'd woken up in the clutches of that Brianna woman. . . .

"Now that we know this world is part of a space-faring Dominion, Eril won't listen to sense," she stumbled. "It's never occurred to him to ask what I—what either of *us* wants."

"Eril and that Brianna, I've seen their type before," Lennart nodded. "They're always so excited about what they're doing, they never look to see who's bringing up the rear."

"And that's us?"

"In a manner of speaking. I don't know what your story is, but I always figured that being a loner was the price of spaceflight. It never seemed like too much to pay before. Most other people couldn't understand what I wanted, anyway. But maybe it was the opposite, that *I* never got close to *them* because I knew I'd only have to leave."

"So you pushed them away. Are you telling me *I* do the same thing?"

Lennart shrugged. "I'm not saying it's *bad* to do that. You make your choice and you live by it."

"But I *didn't* choose this!" Kithri's nerves sizzled. "I had nothing to say about any of it! First I get dragged off Albion, then the goddamn war strands us in the dustpit of the universe, and now this crazy place—"

"And you're pissed at Eril because he sees it as a chance instead of a dead end?"

Something hot and red welled up inside Kithri until she could hardly see. "Why should you care what I feel?"

"Because you could use a friend."

For a moment Kithri saw herself reflected in his

eyes, saw beauty in the taut, muscled grace of her body, the ragged curls. He stood before her, his big hands at his sides. The sky was light enough to reveal the startling red-brown of his eyes.

"A . . . friend," she repeated.

He smiled, one corner of his mouth turned down. "And so could I. Whether we stay here or make it back to your Fifth Fed, nobody's going to run me through a weekend refresher course and zap me back into space. I'll be lucky to get a job pushing a broom."

Kithri didn't understand the exact reference, but she caught his meaning clearly enough. "Not you. With your luck, you'll end up someone's prized museum specimen. *I'm* the one who'll end up . . . 'pushing the broom.' "

*But not if I have anything to say about it! Not while* 'Wacker *is mine!*

"I don't believe in luck," he said. "Only, like they say, the luck we make for ourselves."

Kithri glanced back toward the makeshift camp, then forced herself to stand still. Lennart was a sharp one. The moment she moved, he'd know what she meant to do. But would he try to stop her? How much of a friend was he?

"You could use a little time alone . . . to think things over." Without another word, Lennart disappeared back inside the dome.

For a moment Kithri hesitated. Maybe she should go after Lennart, ask him to come with her. He wasn't any more use here than she was, and he'd said he was her friend. But Eril would think—

*Damn Eril! Damn him or anyone else who tries to tell*

*me what to do with my 'jet—or my life! Damn Brianna! Damn Lennart! Damn the whole dustbug lot of them!*

*'Wacker* stood waiting in the makeshift camp, cold and familiar. Kithri threw one of the micropore blankets into the hold, along with what was left of her own food and water, and scrambled through a criminally rapid preflight check. She hardly saw the instruments under her flying fingers. A dense, black urgency rose up in her, consuming her until only a paper-thin shell remained.

She guided the scrubjet through the low hills bordering the Cerrano Plain, but took none of her usual joy in the intricate twists and valleys. The last time she'd flown this route, the hills had been scrub instead of green. She'd ridden between Eril's thighs, his hands light and sensitive upon the controls, his mind like silk against hers. . . .

She thought belatedly of the jaydium under the 'safe-field. She'd been so crazy desperate to leave, she'd actually forgotten it. But it would have taken too long to reload it and besides, it was probably no good by now. She could always cut more.

The emptiness behind her eyes yammered at her, demanding more speed.

She looked down to find her fingers entangled in the *duo*apparatus. She shoved the headsets back into their storage slots and wiped her hands on her overalls as if a suggestive film still clung to her fingers. The 'jet shot over the final pass, skimming the forest that now covered the Plain.

Mile after empty mile passed with nothing but unbroken green below and hazy sky above. Ten miles became a hundred, an hour became three, then five.

Her body settled into the endurance mode she'd learned running jaydium *singlo* and her thoughts melted into the rhythm of the tiny ship. The unbroken sky broke into billowy clouds and at last the Manitous came into view.

Kithri signaled shipbrain to run a memory trace on the tunnel they'd left. There it was, high above the tree line where the wind-scoured rock stood out in a sharp contrast to the forest. She slowed *'Wacker* and dove into the entrance.

Once she left daylight behind, she almost convinced herself the whole adventure was a wild hallucination. Here she was, as usual, running jaydium all by herself, crazy from so many years of stress and loneliness. She went a little way in and flew back out, fully expecting to see the arid Cerrano Plain stretching beyond the mountains.

Forest. *So much for Eril's idea about retracing our steps to get back home!*

Dry-eyed, she stared at the impossibly lush green and remembered the feel of rain on her face.

Kithri flew back down the tunnels until shipbrain indicated she'd returned to the same jaydium site. She brought the 'jet to a halt and climbed out. Her packing equipment lay in a pile, just as she'd left it when she'd made room for Lennart. There was something wrong about the tunnel, the stale moist air, the hollow way her boots rang with each step. But that could just be her shredded nerves.

She pulled out the laser cutter and chipped through a thick slice. Instead of the sweet, rosy light of raw jaydium, she found only rock.

Dead, dark rock.

*It's just the thickness of the ash layer,* she told herself.

She cut again and again, digging savagely into the tunnel wall. But no matter how deep she sliced, she found only rock. She tried one place after another, some on the same side, some opposite, some farther down the tunnel, all with the same result. Her hands shook so badly she could barely hold the laser. And not, she knew from the *jangles.* She might have missed a narrow vein of jaydium, but she'd felt no hint of the disturbing resonances which should accompany undercutting.

Kithri sat back and studied the hollowed tunnel wall, forcing herself to think.

*There's no jaydium here, not even a whiff of it. Not in this tunnel. Maybe not in this whole world.*

The tunnel closed in on her, black and dank like a tomb. She could feel the mass of the mountain above her, the unfeeling weight and cold. Heart skittering, she scrambled back into the 'jet and sped away. Only when she'd reached the surface did she draw an easy breath.

Numbly Kithri flew back down the mountainside and found a place to set down under the trees. She disengaged *'Wacker*'s engines and let it sit cooling in the greenish shade, while the dense alien quiet seeped into the tiny cabin.

# Chapter 12

Three days after she'd left Brianna's camp, Kithri sat alone on a hillside at the western border of the forest, watching color slowly saturate the sky. Without dust to burnish it to eye-searing gold, the dawn glowed with a gentle, lingering light. Below her, the bushes covering the scrubjet looked soft, like brushed velvet.

She could not stay hidden long, she knew. Brianna would have metal detection scanners and any search would pick up the scrubjet. But first they'd have to know what area to fly over and she was a long way from the Manitous. She had time before they came after her . . . if they did. Time to think, time to decide. Time, but not much food or water.

Kithri jerked her hand away from her mouth before she could chew off another fingernail. *It's time to make up your mind. Do you want to be on your own again, maybe forever alone, or are you going back to deal with Eril?*

No, the problem wasn't Eril, although thinking about him sometimes left her feeling she'd gotten caught in a coriolis storm. *He* hadn't dumped her on Stayman to rot. In fact, he'd offered her a decent way out and she'd been too ratshit scared to take it.

What did she expect, that he *wouldn't* be thrilled by the discoveries they'd made?

*The problem isn't Eril,* Kithri repeated to herself. *It's me. Here I am with the same wonders in front of me, but all I can see is dust.*

She brushed away a tear with the back of one hand, remembering the first joyous shock of the flower field and how quickly its sweetness had gone rancid. It had been easy to cry these last few days, without anyone to judge her weakness. Her eyelids burned as if they'd been scoured raw.

*Albion is dead. I can never go back and I've let that poison everything I touch.*

She set the scrubjet down near the site of their original camp beneath a clump of umbrella trees that crowded between the crystalline city and the spaceport. The city looked exactly as she'd left it, but the vast cream-colored field was no longer vacant.

A bullet-shaped ship sat on the pavement, flat black where it wasn't pocked by space damage. Kithri guessed it could hold a crew of six and it looked spaceworthy if unglamorous. It must be from Brianna's superiors, come to investigate the jaydium story.

*They got here fast enough.*

Something about the brooding, bloated shape set her skin crawling. *If this is what the Dominion is like, I don't want anything to do with it. Nobody nice designed that ship.*

Kithri sighed at herself. If she was going to try to fit in, she ought to do it in earnest, with goodwill, and not create more excuses to turn back. She'd have enough problems explaining why she'd run away that night.

She touched the stungun tucked securely under her belt. The tiny weapon didn't give her much comfort.

She caught a glimpse of Brianna's camp through the surrounding bushes and then, moving as quietly as she could, circled around for a closer look. The door to the central dome hung wide open, but there was no sign of anybody present at the campsite. Something rust colored was smeared on the outside control panel.

It could be blood. At this distance she couldn't tell. As she slipped the stungun from her belt, she thought that either Eril was the biggest sham she'd ever run into or else there wasn't much he couldn't handle.

Maybe everything was fine, maybe they'd just had a minor accident and gone back to their ship for bandages.

*Maybe not.*

Seeing no further sign of life, Kithri left her cover and went in for a closer look. Inside the main dome, Brianna's instruments lay scattered on the floor, most broken past repair. The communications device had been thoroughly smashed.

Kithri bent her head to the rusty stain on the door frame and sniffed. The tang of blood filled her nostrils. Then she remembered why the Dominion agents would have come, what they'd be looking for.

*The jaydium.*

She bolted for the hidden cache. After so long, with only the temporary sealing designed for short transit times, it must have deteriorated past any hope of salvage. But would the others know that?

The tiny guardsafe-field generator lay in splinters on the turf, and only a few bent blades of grass indicated where the insulated storage containers had lain.

Had Eril led them to the cache and shown them how to open the 'safe-field? That was difficult but not impossible, and he knew the underlying principles. A glory-boy like him would think nothing of a little casual theft for his own good cause. But was he a prisoner or an ally of Brianna's Dominion? And Lennart—had the blood been *his*?

One thing was clear—she wasn't going to get any more answers either here or in Brianna's deserted camp. She'd have to look for them in that lump of metal out on the landing field. She drew a deep breath, tightened her hold on the stungun and started across the deserted spaceport.

The landing gear was familiar in concept if not in specifics, six flat pods on hydraulic extension wedges, capable of being drawn flat into the sides of the ship during flight. The exhaust of the ship's descent left no marks on the cream-colored field. It could have come and gone without a trace, and Kithri would never have known it had been there at all. Luck had been with her this time.

The portal lay on the far side, angled toward the rear. Kithri kept close to the bulk of the ship as she circled it, expecting to be challenged at any moment. The stairwalk looked flimsy with neglect, its pleated railing splintered completely away on one side. She bent over to look up through the opening, one hand resting gingerly on the rough skin. She heard no sound, neither voices nor the thrum of engines. The metal beneath her fingertips carried no hint of vibration. Cautiously she set one foot on the stairwalk, then another.

By the time she got to the portal itself, she was sure that sophisticated sensors had already detected the beating of her heart and that Dominion forces were even now waiting for the order to attack. Any moment now neurotoxin-bearing slivers would pierce her skin or the pain of sonic-disrupted organs bring her to her knees. Her imagination roiled with alternatives, each more horrible than the last. Her breath came in a papery slither, the tread of her boots scarcely louder. But there was no response, no alarm, no sign of outraged Dominion agents.

Kithri stepped through the arch of the portal and swung herself along the catbars, past the gaping air locks and along a capillary ledge toward the bridge. She eased open the partly-telescoped iris leading to the control center of the ship and slipped through it. The room, placed just behind the blunted nose, was tiny and round, its floor and control banks mounted on gimbals to adapt to varying gravitational vectors. In a corner lay the crumpled remains of her jaydium storage containers.

She held her breath, again waiting for the alarm. Again, none came. She crouched down and ran one hand over the fragmented container. The tough material was scored from rough handling and the jaydium was missing.

*Jaydium . . .*

Her eyes flew to the control banks. In addition to whatever jaydium-dependent stardrive they'd developed, these people used it lavishly. Every crucial system she could identify was laced with the stuff.

This ship's jaydium was in a sorry state. Under Federation conditions, instrumentation panel jaydium was nearly as immortal as the ship itself. Kithri had seen meticulously maintained Federation jaydium installations, still glowing white-gold even after a generation of pilots had come and gone. The light from these banks were harsh and tinny, greenish where it wasn't flecked with areas of gray.

*Reading them in a hurry must be maddening. No wonder this Dominion is desperate for fresh jaydium.*

She left the bridge and began a systematic search of the rest of the ship. Life-support and power units appeared to be completely self-contained except for coded repair accesses. There was a tiny multifunction chamber which included a galley, records, and what she guessed was personal storage, each compartment individually sealed.

At last she found the entrance to what must be living quarters of off-duty crew, a narrow room in the insulated heart of the ship, gimbal-mounted as the bridge had been. The door was secured from the outside, but not locked. The wheel-screw turned freely under her hands.

Kithri pulled the door slightly ajar and peered inside. The tiny room was dimly illuminated by a few strips of jaydium, flanked by others obviously deteriorated past the point of usefulness. Strap-down bunks lined the walls. An inert body lay facing away from her on the lowest, farthest bed.

For a moment, she hesitated, her fingers tightening around her stungun. Could one of the crew be here, asleep? How had she been able to penetrate the ship this deeply without arousing him?

*Him?*

As her eyes adapted to the dark, she realized from the generously curved outlines that the body must be female. Cuffs bound the slender wrists and a heavy chain anchored to the metal cabin wall. Frothy golden hair dropped forward across the face.

*Brianna? That doesn't make sense. Why would she be a prisoner of her own Dominion?*

Brianna's ribs moved slowly and evenly. She gave no sign she'd heard the door open. *Drugged or stunned?* Kithri wondered.

She stepped into the room, moving silently toward the bunk. Just as she cleared the partly-opened door, she caught a flash of movement from the side. She couldn't see it clearly, only an instant of looming shadow before the man-shaped figure burst from the corner and lunged at her. Without thinking, she whirled and brought her stungun up. A booted foot lashed out and collided with her forearm. It was a glancing blow, jerked up short, hard enough to break her aim but not loosen her grip entirely. Her arm muscles went numb; she grabbed the stungun with the other hand—

Before she could fire, her assailant fell heavily to the floor beside a bunk which had been concealed by the door. If she'd opened it all the way, she would have seen him plainly. "Kithri?" The voice was slurred but recognizable.

*Lennart!*

He grinned crookedly up at her and said in a harsh whisper, "You are a welcome sight!"

The next instant, she slipped the stungun through

her belt and was kneeling at Lennart's side. A trickle of dried blood ran from his hairline down one cheek. Like Brianna, he was chained to the wall, so that another inch would have taken Kithri entirely out of his range. A quick glance around the room revealed no other hidden prisoners.

"What the hell is going on?" Kithri asked in a low voice. "Where's Eril?"

"Damned pirates took him back to the city."

"Pirates . . ." Kithri inspected his wrist cuffs. She didn't recognize the mechanism, nor could she identify any mechanical hinge closure. "They found my jaydium—I saw."

"They must have been monitoring Brianna's transmission," Lennart said. "They knew we had a cache, and that there's a source somewhere in this planet."

Kithri yanked at the chain which bound Lennart's cuffs to the ship wall. "Get back, and I'll do what I can do about this." She adjusted the stungun's simple controls and aimed the heat beam at the loop. Sparks shot outward and ozone stung the air, but the thick dark links were almost severed. Another pass, more sparks, and then Lennart pulled his joined hands free. He leaned against the wall, breathing hard.

Kithri glanced at Brianna, still lying unconscious across the room. "What's the matter with her?"

"Once they decided Eril knew more about the jaydium source than either of us, they put us out with some kind of shock device. I'm still a little muzzy-headed, but it hit her pretty hard."

Kithri crossed to Brianna's side and softly called her name. There was no response. She took Brianna by both shoulders and shook her with such vigor that Brianna's limp body slithered to the floor and reached the end of the heavy chain with an emphatic *clump*!

"Damn you, Brianna, wake up!" she hissed, trying to keep her voice down. "I swear, if you don't open your eyes this instant, I'll leave you here and serve you right!"

Still muttering, she hauled Brianna to a sitting position. She did not have the chance to find out if she could really have carried out her threat, for after an instant of head-lolling limpness, Brianna whimpered, "N–no, don't. . . ."

"Brianna! It's me, Kithri!"

"You—what are you doing here?" Brianna stared at her, emerald eyes wide and unfocused. "You stole the surface craft—you selfish bitch! Eril was so angry—"

"Save it!" Lennart broke in. "We've got to get out of here!"

Brianna gulped and held still as Kithri burned through her chains. A few moments later, she was free.

"I can't do anything about the cuffs," Kithri said.

"They're sonic locks," Brianna said in a shaky voice. "I've got a tuner back at the camp, if it's still functioning."

Lennart led the way back, swinging agilely along the catwalks and capillary ledges despite his bound hands. Even Brianna was able to manage surprisingly well. Once moving, her body was much steadier than her words. Kithri had to help her around only one difficult corner. They clambered down the battered stairwalk and on to the smooth pavement of the spaceport.

Kithri paused to scan the field and surrounding parkland from the shelter of the ship's bulk. "It's probably as safe now as it will ever be." In the daylight, both Brianna and Lennart looked ashen.

"Why'd they take Eril back to the city?" she asked Lennart as they hurried toward the relative cover of the parkland.

"To make him show them where you got the jaydium," he said. "I guess they figured if any of us knew, he did."

"They think we got the jaydium from a ruined city? Don't they know jaydium's got to be mined?"

"Where—some imaginary site in the mountain range?" Brianna panted, one hand pressed to her side as if to ease a cramp. "The pirates didn't believe it, either. The city was the only place it *could* have come from. That's where it's found, in ruins."

"*Ruins*! That's the most ridiculous—"

"Why do you think my superiors wanted me to see the site for myself?" Brianna cried. "They'd never heard such an outlandish thing, either! It was the one part of your story that made absolutely no sense."

Kithri brought them to a halt under the first thick clump of bushes. Her heart slammed against her chest. Blind panic wouldn't get Eril free. She had to think, to plan. "Your superiors—can we call them for help?"

Brianna shook her head. "The first thing those *untranslatables* did was to disable all my communication devices. When they don't hear from me, the Institute will send a probe to check." She ran one hand over her reddened, sweating face. "That might take weeks. Without a positive find, they might just wait for the regular supply ship."

"Your Dominion isn't any better than the Fed," Kithri said acidly. "They both dump people in the middle of nowhere and then forget them. Let's get those cuffs off. We've got a rescue to plan!"

# Chapter 13

Kithri stood at the entrance to the dome and scanned the surrounding brush for any signs of discovery. Behind her, Brianna alternated between cursing under her breath and choking back sobs as she and Lennart sorted through the wreckage. Kithri kept her eyes away from the interior of the laboratory. The waste—the vicious, wanton waste—was more than she could bear. The central room, once filled with marvels of technology, was little better than a junkyard. The pirates had carried off some equipment and systematically rendered the rest useless. Splintered glass and twisted metal housings lay everywhere, mingled with record books in sodden reagent-soaked lumps. Acids still smoked from the rubble that had been the main computer.

Kithri could understand disabling the communications gear, but to deliberately destroy scientific instruments. . . . She remembered when her father would have given all he had for such treasure, now smashed past any hope of salvage.

The pirates hadn't overlooked much of value, although Brianna's sonic tuner was still functional and Lennart had found some short lengths of monofilament rope. The emergency medical kit was gone, along with the water purification supplies and the best of the survival clothing. They'd also taken the tangle, Brianna's only effective weapon, and disabled her surface transport. There was no way Brianna could have gone searching for Kithri across the forest-covered Cerrano Plain.

Kithri's fingers ached from gripping the handle of her stungun. The camp and the surrounding bushes still looked peaceful, but it was only a matter of time before the escape was discovered, and every passing moment increased the chances of their being tracked here. She took a deep breath, hoping she wouldn't jump out of her skin at the first sign of trouble.

Lennart emerged from the laboratory and finished packing the rope lengths, along with some clothes and empty water containers. Brianna rummaged through a disorderly heap of papers on a desk top.

"What are you bothering with those for?" Kithri scowled. "I said to take only what we need."

"Ah!" Brianna slid a thin sheaf into her pack along with the other gear. "My field maps!"

Kithri held her breath practically the whole distance to the city. As they darted from one clump of brush to the next, she felt entirely too exposed. She wanted solid walls around her while they planned their strategy.

*Too damned much time spent down jaydium tunnels. It's better to see the enemy coming.*

The city, Brianna insisted, was the last place the pirates would think to search for them if their escape was discovered. The three of them took cover in the squat lavender pyramid near the western outskirts.

Its walls, although opaque from the outside, admitted a diffuse pastel light. Shards of tinted glass cilia, once as thick as fur over the building's exterior, littered the street beyond. The inside walls were smooth and there was no trace of internal furnishing. The arched doorway faced southward, hidden from both the parkland and the center of the city.

In response to questions from Kithri and Lennart, Brianna produced a wealth of detail about each building's exact dimensions and wall thicknesses, as well as the chemical composition of the various materials.

"The construction techniques are like nothing we've ever seen," Brianna said. "They're neither assembled, like brick or adobe structures, nor layered like concrete over reinforced steel. The material is homogenous, both by penetration analysis and cross section. It's as if the stuff had been molded, although I don't understand how you could smelt something that size."

"Smelt?" Lennart asked, looking astonished.

"The material has some of the characteristics of silica-based materials. It resembles organically adulterated glass. Sometimes it will shatter and leave a sharp edge, like those capillary needles outside, but other structures which look equally delicate are virtually unbreakable. Yet my instruments can't detect any chemical difference between them. The material exhibits much of the diversity of living tissue. Of course, despite the odd organic contaminants, it's quite definitely mineral."

Kithri thought of the mysteries of her own Stayman that she'd had to pass over for more immediate concerns—the tunnels, the desert ecology in the presence of plentiful bedrock water, the jaydium which had been the focus of her father's researches . . . all the questions which she would never have the chance to answer now.

"Tell me again about the pirates," she said.

"There are six of them," Brianna said. "From the Tribes, though that won't mean anything to you. They're nomadic, with whole families spending their lives on their mother ships. Most live on the fringes of trade and engage in low-grade charter. They're a closed society and won't allow our anthropologists to study them, not even for the usual living-cultures stipend. When times are hard, it's common for them to slip across the line of what's strictly lawful. When they turn raider, they can't afford to take prisoners—air and food cost too much. I don't think anything is known of their private customs or languages."

"We can understand them, though," Lennart said.

Brianna nodded. "Yes, the translator I implanted in you handles the basics well enough."

Kithri glanced from Lennart's face, set and tight-lipped, to Brianna's. The other woman no longer looked sweetly pretty, but taut and pale in the lavender light. She'd tied her flyaway golden hair into a knot at the nape of her neck. A purpling bruise had developed on one cheekbone, with several more on her chest and throat.

"This bunch is spaceborn," Brianna went on, "so they're big, but they're not as strong as they look because of all that time spent off-planet. Their bones are thin and their postural muscles fatigue easily in normal gravity."

"They were strong enough to take the three of you," Kithri pointed out.

"Hell," Lennart said, "they could have *sat* on us and we'd have been out. Bri wasn't kidding when she said *big*."

Brianna shivered, her green eyes hard and flat. "They have blasters and heavyweight rods with an illegal convulsant setting."

A vision arose unbidden in Kithri's mind—Eril, his back arched, jaws clenched, muscles locked in spasm, eyes white with pain. . . .

Her throat constricted painfully. She forced herself to ask, "Is there any . . . any permanent damage from the rod?"

"There shouldn't be." Brianna lowered her gaze and cleared her throat. "Not physical, anyway."

"What else?" Kithri asked.

"The leader's Teeg," Brianna said. "Bald, albino eyes, lots of hidden weapons. And not stupid. His second's called Quick. He knows he'll never have the top spot and gets whatever he can from backing Teeg. I've seen the same character type at the Institute. I didn't catch any other names, but I'd mark the red one as a pathological sadist."

"All male?" Kithri asked.

"Is that an issue?"

Ignoring Lennart's startled glance, Kithri studied the other woman, sensing the steel beneath the flower-petal exterior. She didn't like Brianna, but she was beginning to trust her, just as she was beginning to not trust Lennart. But she needed help from both of them. "You tell me."

"They didn't try raping me," Brianna said slowly. "Not yet, anyway, and Teeg at least should know he'd have to inactivate my infraprotection."

"Your what?"

"Infraprotection. Aren't you bio-equipped against sexual assault?"

Kithri shook her head. People on Stayman came together for all sorts of reasons besides love—loneliness, egotism, the easier path after seasons of harassment—which made her think of Hank. Actual rape was uncommon, even in Port Ludlow, which was why Dowdell's attack had shocked her into such a violent reaction. Yet Brianna casually referred to the possibility and was surgically prepared to resist it. What did this say about her precious Dominion? Kithri was not at all sure that this world, no matter how green and inviting, offered any real advantages over her own.

Brianna finished enumerating the weapons she had seen and those probably hidden. "And all we've got is your little survival-gun."

"We can't meet those goons force to force," Kithri said, "not even if we each had a gun."

"And I'm not about to go firing a gun at anybody," Lennart added in a ragged voice.

Kithri ran one hand through her unkempt curls, thinking hard. "We'll have to separate them. That shouldn't be too hard, here in the city. We know our way around, or rather, Brianna does, and with her maps, I can manage."

"Separate them?" Brianna arched her eyebrows expressively. "How do you propose to do that? Invite them individually to a festive dance?"

"We use you as bait."

*"What!"* Brianna's face turned three shades whiter. Spots of color stood out on her cheeks like dabs of fresh-spilled blood.

"Listen, as far as they know, they left you both

stunned and tied up," Kithri explained. "All we have to do is let them catch a glimpse of you—free and following them. They'll send someone after you—one of the underlings most likely—and I'll stun him. Then we repeat the process."

"What if something goes wrong and they capture her again?" Lennart shook his head. "If it's got to be anyone, I'll go."

"They'll send more men after you than they will after her," Kithri pointed out. "You're bigger and—that's what I'd do in their place. Besides, I'll need you for backup."

Brianna wet her lips nervously. "I don't know if I can."

"What's to stop them from sending more than one after her?" Lennart said.

"Why should they? If they're not used to gravity, they won't want to do any more running around than they have to. They'll have to leave someone behind to guard Eril. Besides, I don't hear you making any better suggestions."

"First we have to find them," Lennart said grudgingly.

"All right, so let's find them."

The pirates left a trail of broken crystals that anyone could follow. Kithri grimaced at the imprint of a boot across a fallen, sapphire-tinted cylinder.

"Don't they care what they destroy?" Lennart asked.

"About these artifacts, no," Brianna said in a tightly controlled voice. "You can't eat or breathe them, so they're of no value in space. All the pirates want now is the jaydium." She brushed a pile of glittering splinters with her boot. "It wasn't this bad when I first came."

They heard the pirates before they saw them, masculine voices booming through the ruins. Kithri caught a glimpse of them along a colonnade of opalescent spires as they moved through the overlapping multihued shadows. Before the three of them scuttled back under cover, she counted five big men dressed in skintight jackets and pants of black and midnight blue. Beneath their barrel-chested torsos, their legs looked unnaturally thin. One bald head gleamed in the sunlight.

Eril stood on the far side of the group, flanked by two guards. His hands were bound behind him. The leather holster which had once carried his force whip hung empty, and his sleeveless jacket was missing. Kithri thought he looked like a sand-leopard in a pen of black bulls.

Kithri pulled Brianna and Lennart back into an alcove of garnet and lapis, praying they had not been seen. Long heartbeats later, there was still no outcry, and she breathed easier. Brianna reached into her pack and drew out the map, silently pointing out their location. Kithri traced out their route with her finger as Lennart looked over her shoulder. Brianna nodded in agreement. One more careful scan of the map, and then Kithri gestured for her to put it away and leave the pack.

Kithri tried not to imagine what Brianna must be feeling as she headed toward the pirates' voices. She hadn't even asked whether Brianna was willing to risk herself to rescue Eril. She didn't owe him any loyalty. Yet Kithri had been furious when Eril presumed to make the same sort of decision for her.

Now it was too late to say anything to either one of them.

Kithri tightened the pack on her shoulders and waited. Before too much time had passed, she heard male voices shouting and then a high, thin shriek, not of shock or pain but surprise. It was Brianna playing her part, she hoped, and not some unpleasant new development.

Kithri gestured to Lennart and took off at a run, following the planned route. Their pounding feet threw up puffs of sparkling powder. The particles smelled acrid, like jaydium gone bad.

Breathing harder and clenching her stungun, Kithri sprinted down the narrow corridor which connected two main avenues. Brianna raced into view, her arms pumping frantically. A black-clad pirate was almost upon her. They burst into a little circular courtyard, darting past the amethyst obelisk which stood at its heart. The grit on the ground lay thicker here, like drifted sand.

Suddenly Brianna skidded and slipped on the dust. She screamed, landing obliquely on one hip. But she had no time to regain her footing before the pirate backhanded her across the side of her face. Kithri heard the sickening *whap!* as Brianna's body flew into the air.

Before Kithri could take aim, a second pirate lumbered into the courtyard, breathing hoarsely as he rolled along at a heavy-footed lope. Lennart, who was right behind Kithri shoved her. He hurled himself into the air and tackled the second pirate around his hips. They went down in a flurry of pulverized crystal. Lennart yelled something she couldn't understand.

The dust made for unexpectedly slippery footing. Her aim broken, Kithri scrambled to keep her balance. In that moment, the first pirate whirled, spotted her, and reached for something at his belt. She didn't recognize it, only his intent. She steadied the stungun with both hands and fired.

The pirate arched backward, suspended in space, and for a moment Kithri feared the stungun's charge was too weak to numb his bulky body. He turned slowly toward her and she took a step backward. Then she saw the whites of his eyeballs, rolled up in his head. He landed with a *thump!* across Brianna's legs.

Lennart and the second pirate still wrestled on the ground, although Lennart was on top and seemed to have the larger man's arms pinned. Kithri took careful aim at the pirate's head and fired. He went limp instantly.

Face flushed, Lennart nodded and got to his feet. He pulled the first pirate's body off Brianna while Kithri shoved her stungun through her belt and fumbled for the monofilament rope in the pack.

*"Untranslatable,"* Brianna moaned as her eyes fluttered open. "Not again. . . ."

"Are you all right?" Lennart asked, helping Brianna to sit up. "Did he hit you hard?"

Brianna ran her fingertips over her jaw, wincing. "Obviously, he hit me *hard*." She nudged the fallen pirate with one foot. "My head feels like he's still sitting on it. I c–c–can't . . ." Her face turned gray and her eyes didn't seem to track properly. She propped her head in her hands, elbows supported on her bent knees, and for a moment she seemed to be steadier. Then she fell over sideways in a dead faint.

Cursing, Kithri scrambled to Brianna's side.

"Fellows!" barked a masculine voice from behind her. "Both fellows! Stand away from her!"

# Chapter 14

"Stand away from her, both!" The voice repeated in the same staccato bark. "With respect to the blaster I hold, unless you desire to become imitation of city dust!"

Kithri raised her hands and slowly got to her feet, her back to the voice. From the corner of her vision, she saw Lennart do the same. What a dustbug idiot she'd been, so sure of herself. Now the three of them were in the pirates' clutches, with no one left free to plan a real rescue, and it was her own damned fault.

She wondered fleetingly if she could snatch the stungun from her belt, whirl around, and aim it before the pirate could fire his blaster.

*Talk about idiotic ideas!*

"Fellow! Turn slowly around."

Kithri obeyed. It was the bald head, Teeg, a glistening black egg on stilts. In one fist he held a wide-muzzled pistol of dull orange metal. A squirrelly looking pirate in blue knelt over the first one she'd stunned. Behind them moved a shadow of a man of their height but thinner and red-haired. He carried Eril's force whip, tucked through his wide leather belt. Kithri saw his eyes and swallowed hard, struggling to keep her face impassive.

"No fellow, this. Female!" The squirrelly one grinned in Kithri's direction. She decided he must be Quick, Teeg's second.

Red-hair slipped forward and proceeded to search both prisoners with ruthless efficiency. When her turn came, Kithri tried not to flinch from the soft, intrusive patting of his hands. He tugged the stungun free of her belt and tossed it to his leader. Quick bent once more over the inert pirates. Kithri heard the click of a metallic instrument and then groans as the two stunned men regained consciousness.

Without speaking, Quick and Red-hair hauled the other pirates to their feet. Kithri found the silence between them almost as unnerving as Red-hair's lingering touch as he tied her wrists behind her back and pushed her forward. Quick slung Brianna's body across his shoulders and followed.

Eril lay crumpled in the center of a small courtyard ringed by low benches of emerald and aquamarine. Rather than leave additional men to guard him, Teeg had simply eliminated any threat he might pose. Another massive pirate, clad in black like their leader, looked both grim and bored where he sat on the fragments of a fallen column. He held a second orange pistol. Kithri wondered where the other one was . . . still hunting for jaydium in the city?

Red-hair smiled unpleasantly as he forced Kithri down on a slab of blue fire opal and secured her wrists to a metal loop recently drilled into the stone. She suppressed her instinctive revulsion at his touch.

Teeg stood in front of her, his stork-thin legs braced in an aggressive stance. Red-hair grabbed her jaw and wrenched her head around so she was forced to look directly into the sun.

"Jaydium, say where is source." The pirate leader's face was shadowed and unreadable.

Caught in Red-hair's iron grip, Kithri could hardly breathe, let alone talk. She managed to blurt out, "I don't know—what you're—talking about."

Teeg backhanded her full force across her cheek and she reeled with the blow. Had it been only her imagination or had Red-hair thrust her against it, anticipating his captain's attack?

With a sudden shiver, Kithri realized she could not save herself by giving Teeg what he wanted. The physical condition of the prisoners didn't matter. The pirates were going to kill them anyway. Teeg would indulge Red-hair in his pleasure for as long as it served his own aims. The very best she could do was pray they made a crucial mistake while she could still take advantage of it.

There was a movement at the far end of the courtyard. Kithri's doubling sight showed her a bland-faced giant entering the courtyard. He grunted, "Got lost," and took a place in guard position. Teeg did not take his eyes off Kithri or give any sign he'd heard.

Before Kithri's vision cleared completely, Teeg rumbled again, "Jaydium, where."

She shook her head, *No.*

Again came another blow, and again the jerk on her head. Pain reverberated through her skull and her stomach knotted.

"Jaydium, where."

Kithri squeezed her eyes shut. On the opposite side of the courtyard Eril had come awake and was watching her. She could not see him, but she could sense the tension of his muscles in the pit of her belly.

She felt him sit up, alert and clearheaded. His face glimmered like a beacon behind her closed lids—expressionless as a carved statue, honey-smooth skin, tiny scar high on one cheek, a few strands of hair fallen across his forehead. Black eyes shone with fiery intensity.

Now Kithri sensed something more than his eyes on her, as if there were an invisible rope stretching between them. For an instant the pain in her head felt distant, barely noticeable.

*Eril, don't you break because of me! Let them do whatever they want, but don't give them anything for it. You hold on just as long as I do!*

Slowly, deliberately, with the same timing as before so that it came exactly when she expected it, Teeg and Red-hair coordinated another blow. The force used was identical, only this time the agony which lanced through her head was magnified tenfold. And then, before the pain died down, another blow—*Eril, hold on! Don't leave me now!*—a sharp uppercut that caught her in the solar plexus and sent her reeling.

And then another. She clung to the image of Eril's impassive face, measuring the shallowness of her courage against his silence, until she could no longer see anything at all.

Water splashed against her face and up her nostrils. Kithri sputtered awake and struggled to open her eyes. Red-hair released her head with a savage jerk and her weight fell forward on her bound wrists, twisting her shoulders.

"Jaydium. Where." Again the implacable, inflectionless voice.

Kithri ran her tongue over her dripping lips, tasting salt mixed with stale water. One lip had split open, though she hadn't felt it at the time. Her voice came as a meaningless syllable. "Uhh . . ."

"Hit again."

Somehow she summoned the strength to gasp, "You wouldn't—believe me—if I told you."

Teeg drew closer again, hovering over her. His bulk blotted out the searing sun, but Kithri felt no relief in his shade, only intensified menace. He would beat her senseless again, no matter what she told him. Already she felt too concussed to think coherently.

*Eril, don't give them anything! Hold on for me, hold on. . . .*

The words echoed through her skull like a monastic chant. Kithri closed her eyes again, numbly awaiting the next blow.

She opened them some time later, aware that she had been drifting in and out of consciousness. Her temples reverberated at every pulse beat and her swollen lids opened with great reluctance. She moved her mouth experimentally. The cut lip stung in protest and her bruised torso ached all over. A needle of pain shot across her lower ribs with each breath. Her shoulder joints burned from being twisted behind her and she guessed she'd been hanging there for some time. She tried to focus on the shadows moving around the pastel-lit courtyard, but her vision doubled rebelliously.

"Jaydium, where."

She knew that voice, although it seemed curiously distant, like something at the end of a long, twisted tunnel. It was a voice that brought pain, that demanded something she had no power to give.

Kithri winced involuntarily, anticipating the next blow. But it never came, although she heard the *slap!* of flesh against flesh.

"Not going to tell us," said someone else.

Kithri's vision steadied enough to show her Quick, Teeg and Red-hair clustered around Eril. The front of his shirt glistened red, but she couldn't tell how badly hurt he really was. She knew from her own broken nose how freely even trivial face and scalp wounds could bleed. She'd kept right on punching that damned claim-jumper, bloody nose and all. The smells and sounds of the Port Ludlow bar rose in her memory, the jeers of the miners dying into grudging respect as she alone heaved herself to her feet. "Just her bloody luck," they'd said, and it had stuck for all these years, her brush name, so much her identity that Eril had apparently not known she had any other.

*Okay, namesake, where are you now? We're going to need a little bloody luck to get out of this one alive.*

Kithri's head hurt past hurting. She felt nauseous and disoriented as she struggled to assess the situation. Brianna huddled whimpering on an aquamarine bench in the shadow of a fourth pirate. Lennart stood nearby, his hands bound behind him. The sixth pirate covered him with one of the orange blasters. Lennart seemed uninjured, although dazed, maybe in shock. His eyes stretched wide and white, like those of a man on the verge of an abyss.

Eril bent over between his captors, his ribs heaving. If he could breathe that well, Kithri told herself, he couldn't be in all that bad shape.

"Not break for self, that fellow," said Quick, gesturing at Eril. "Maybe for this one." He turned and stared at Brianna with deliberate intent.

Red-hair strode over to her and caressed the misty gold of her hair with a lover's touch. Suddenly he sank his fingers into her hair and twisted hard. Brianna gasped. He smiled and forced her face up and back. His look of anticipation shook Kithri far deeper than Eril's beating had.

Brianna's face paled as Red-hair bent closer, his lips puckered in an obscene parody of a kiss. Kithri could hear her labored breathing.

"You—you c–c–can't do this to m–m–me," Brianna said, but there was only desperation, not strength, behind her words. "I'm a *s–s–scient–t–tist. . . .*"

"Hostage worth nothing," said Teeg, his face bland. "Jaydium."

"It wasn't m–m–mine, it was theirs!"

Teeg gave her a look of utter disgust. "Fellow!" He lashed out at Eril with one heavy black boot. The toe caught Eril in mid-chest and threw him backward. A pirate caught his shoulders and dragged him upright.

"You tough fellow," Teeg said to Eril. He nodded toward Kithri, "That one also. But *this?*"

Red-hair ran his fingers along Brianna's cheek and down her neck. He paused one finger at the hollow between her collarbones, forcing her head back so that she opened her throat to him as if in surrender. He made a quick movement, a jab so short and swift as to be barely noticeable except for the shriek which rang through the courtyard. Smiling tenderly, his hand still twisted in her hair so that he controlled every movement of her head, he changed to another target, approaching slowly, languorously, then striking like a sand-viper.

Brianna convulsed upward. Her breath came in ragged cries. She twisted frantically, bucking and heaving when he flung her down across the slab. Her skull made a sodden sound as she slammed against the unyielding stone. She kept struggling when Red-hair threw his body across hers.

It couldn't go on for long, Kithri realized. Even adrenaline-fueled, Brianna would tire. She couldn't breathe with that monster across her ribs. Kithri jerked against her own bonds, only to have a massive hand clench her throat and drag her back.

Red-hair moved his body on Brianna's, and Kithri recoiled at the triumphant, almost orgasmic expression on his face. He moved his hands down along the sides of Brianna's body. This time her screams came as raw, unfocused sound, no longer human.

"Stop it! For god's sake, stop it!" shouted Lennart. His words spilled out, broken. "Can't you see she doesn't know anything?"

Kithri forced herself to remain still. It wasn't Lennart's words that shook her to her core, but the desperation behind them. In the brush, she reminded herself savagely, you never *ever* gave a claim-jumper something to hold over you. Eril, with his sand-leopard reflexes, he understood that. If Lennart did not, it was too bad.

Teeg grunted. "More."

"No, please!" begged Lennart. "No more! I'll do

anything—I'll give you whatever you want, just so you stop!"

"*You* know nothing," Teeg said contemptuously.

Tears mingled with the dried blood on Lennart's face. It had been years since Kithri had seen a man's unhidden weeping, not since her father died. Those final months he'd been like a child, laughing, crying, whimpering in pain. His skin had grown more and more translucent until it seemed his heart had turned to glass and every naked emotion shone out from it. Now Lennart had somehow stolen past the barriers she'd built in all her years on Stayman. She felt the unmoving ice in her own heart and was ashamed.

Lennart's eyes locked on hers, pleading. *It's only a goddamned chunk of rock,* his voice rang through her mind. *Not a living person.*

*That's easy for you to say,* another part of her raged. *You had the stars and all I had was one beat-up scrubjet!*

And besides, she had no choice. There was no jaydium site in the mountains to trade for Brianna's life.

Red-hair towered over Brianna, anchoring her shoulders to the stone. He released her hair, and her head fell back, her mouth opened in wordless anguish. Looking down at her with a lover's gratitude, he moved one hand into the periphery of her vision and her whole body shuddered soundlessly.

Kithri could not look away. Her determination felt brittle as glass, ready to shatter into a thousand pieces. *If not the jaydium, then what? Would anything I do save her?*

*You can't know that. You can only know what you'll live with if you don't try. . . .*

Any moment now she would explode like an Albionese fairybird egg and then there would be no hope for any of them.

*Oh Eril, hold on for me. . . .*

"Enough."

It took Kithri a long moment to realize she had heard rather than thought it. The word, barely more than a whisper, came from Eril.

"Enough," he repeated. "I'll tell you."

Teeg, with the first sign of genuine interest yet, lurched stiff-legged to Eril.

"The jaydium . . . ore . . ." Eril paused and ran his tongue over his ragged lips. "Is from a site . . . in the mountains . . . across . . . forest plain."

Teeg's expression of satisfaction evaporated. "Fellow, fool us not. This be rough-sealed jaydium, not long dead. Flight across forest takes too long."

"Special . . . equipment . . . faster than . . . manual pilot."

Teeg nodded to Red-hair. "More."

Brianna began gently sobbing. The sound shook Kithri even more than her screams had. It curled around her heart like a dust-viper and sank its poisoned fangs deep.

"You bastards," she hissed. "You're so dense—you don't believe—the truth—when you—hear it."

"Knows nothing, either," Teeg said.

"By the bloody balls of hell, who do you think runs this operation?" she screamed. "Some nincompoop of a glory-boy? Of course he thinks I got the jaydium in the mountains! I told him so. If you had him for a partner, would *you* tell him where you found the jaydium?"

The corners of Teeg's mouth twitched. Kithri stormed on, barely pausing for breath.

"If you want the jaydium so much, you give me a good reason to tell you."

"Do the same. To you."

Kithri prayed her swollen face hid her instant panic at the suggestion. She summoned up the image of every lewd-mouthed, sodden-drunk claim-jumper she'd ever known. She saw herself putting a fist through Teeg's bloated face and then spitting on the bloody splinters. Fury raced like quicksilver through her veins.

"You already tried that with me and it didn't work," she sneered. "Do better."

"Share jaydium. You take part."

The pain of her body lessened with her soaring adrenaline. *He's making a fool's offer. Maybe I've bought us a little time.*

Teeg folded his arms across his barrel chest, waiting. Brianna stopped sobbing, and no one else made a sound. Lennart's face had gone flat white. Kithri dared not meet his eyes.

*You've done enough damage, Lennart, making me go all soft like this.*

"Let's not play trader games. You let my friends go, give them a fair start, then I'll take you there. You'll still have *me* for insurance." Kithri lifted her chin. "It's that or nothing."

For the next few moments Teeg stood like a statue, completely unresponsive. Maybe he found her proposal so absurd that he refused to even consider it. Then his face showed a fleeting shadow of a smile and he uncrossed his arms. He nodded to Red-hair.

"Loose."

*He thinks he's pulling one over on me. He'll send his men after them the moment my back's turned, and he thinks they can't get far on foot.*

Brianna lay across the stone, breathing hoarsely. Released, Lennart went to her. He touched her face. "She's out cold."

Teeg lifted one eyebrow. "Deal."

"Get her out of here, any way you can!" Kithri said. *If you don't make it, then my devil's bargain is for nothing.*

"I never want to see your dustbug faces again!" she continued. "Eril, after what happened to us when we *first landed,* I hope you'll take proper care of *brushwackers.*"

Eril stood up, rubbing his wrists with swollen fingers. Under the bruises and swelling, his expression was unreadable. Lennart hoisted Brianna's inert body across his shoulders, grunting with the effort.

Kithri watched them disappear past the opalescent columns. Eril must have understood her, he *must.* With any luck, they'd get far enough in the scrubjet to stay hidden, either in the forest or the Manitou tunnels, until either the pirates gave up or Brianna's Dominion sent that probe to investigate.

Kithri waited until she thought a chase would not catch them before they reached the scrubjet.

"All right," she said, praying that her memory of Brianna's maps was accurate. "Now I'll take you to the jaydium."

# Chapter 15

Red-hair gripped Kithri's elbow as she led them past archways of splintered topaz and amber. Sunlight fractured against the ruined lacework and spilled ribbons of color over the pirates' pale skins. They made no comment as they marched along, grinding the shards under their heavy space boots.

She guided them around another corner, three turns and then back down the long avenue where freestanding walls made a maze of light and shadow. The tension in Red-hair's hands increased as they went along, the group bunching closer together. Spacebred, they relied heavily on their navigational instruments, while Kithri's years in the brush had developed both her directional sense and a keen memory for landmarks. Now she prayed to all the powers of luck and space they were truly as disoriented as they seemed.

*I must pretend I've been here before.*

Kithri kept her features impassive as she identified her goal, a truncated green pyramid located diagonally across a plaza bordered by hedges of intricate braided crystals. She squelched any temptation to pause and stare at its perfect balance and grace.

She stepped through the doorway and into the

spacious central chamber. The opaque, mint-colored threshold muffled the tread of the men's boots.

The interior was surprisingly bright, considering the thickness of the deep-hued emerald walls and the absence of windows. A shallow, unrailed balcony ringed the central chamber. Kithri's gaze raced across the shadowed doorways as she searched for the entrance Brianna had described.

*I've been here before, I know where I'm going.*

As she drew closer to the far wall, Kithri noticed the intricate patterns which alternated with narrow openings. She wished she had the time to examine them more closely. The entrance could be any one of them, but which? She couldn't afford to show any hesitation, not with Red-hair's hands on her. He'd catch the smallest lapse in her concentration. There was a limit to what she could improvise, and so far she'd already used up more than her share of bloody luck.

The first slit was narrower than the others, barely wide enough for her shoulders, let alone the men's bulk. Brianna would have been able to slip though it without too much trouble, but would she have described it as a passageway? Kithri felt a gust of cool air on her face. It was nothing more than an air vent. She went on to the next one.

She had narrowed her choices to three possibilities when Red-hair pulled her around to face Teeg.

"Jaydium."

She hesitated, not understanding.

"Building empty. Where jaydium?"

Kithri seized the small pulse of anger that flared up at his demand. "Not *here*, you dustbug. You don't find *jaydium* in *buildings*." She pointed vaguely in the direction of the remaining three openings. "Below."

"Under building?"

"That's the story. Now are you going to let me get on with it, or are we going to stand here all day jabbering?" She jerked her elbow away from Redhair and put both hands on her hips in an aggressive stance.

"You go first," growled Teeg.

Kithri sniffed with as much arrogance as she could muster and headed for the farthest doorway, the one closest to the corner. To her surprise, the indirect lighting in the corridor beyond was as good as in the central chamber. The faint green cast did little to improve the pirates' space-bleached complexions.

At the end of the short corridor was a broad ramp, spiraling downward. There were no handrails, but Kithri plunged down it with determination. Past the first spacious landing with its tributary corridors, she kept to the central ramp and picked up the pace, flexing her knees to shorten her stride. One of the pirates stumbled as he misjudged the ramp angle. Kithri hoped that, with their bulkier bodies and weaker thigh muscles, they'd tire sooner than she would. She should have an even greater advantage climbing back up—if she was still alive to try it.

Past the third landing, the light grew noticeably dimmer, turning yellow and then reddish. Kithri silently blessed Brianna for her precise, detailed maps of the subterranean system. She'd have to steer clear of the large area Brianna had blocked off with crosshatching. Brianna had offered no explanation but only replied, tight-faced, that those particular tunnels were impassable.

At the fourth landing, Kithri headed along the westerly corridor instead of continuing down. The passage ran straight, then curved unexpectedly into a downward ramp. Now came the really difficult part, a series of branches and spirals as complex as any she'd ever flown. It must have taken Brianna a solid year to map them all in the subdued light, and she'd only done the arterials.

The pirates said nothing, but Kithri felt their tension level rise again. The underground must be unnerving after so much time in the freedom of space. She hoped they were thoroughly and miserably confused by the constant switchbacks. As the walls narrowed into low-ceiling, branching tunnels, the mazework felt surprisingly comfortable to her, as familiar as Manitou tunnels. Her confidence began to rise.

They emerged into a small circular chamber, crimson-lit as if from badly sealed jaydium. This was the first of a series of rooms, strung out like interconnected beads. Brianna had not discovered their purpose, nor could Kithri imagine one. South, southwest, and then due east again. . . .

Teeg grabbed Kithri's shoulder with one massive hand and jerked her to a halt. His features, shadowy in the dim red light, twisted with some unnamable emotion. Was it fear, she wondered, or just plain greed?

"Jaydium!"

"We're close now, can't you smell it?" Kithri's voice sounded tinny and unsure to her own ears.

The pirate leader shoved her backward.

"You going to stop—*now*—when we're almost there?" she asked.

He pointed one blunt finger toward the last chamber. "Same." Toward the one before them, "Same." And toward the one that lay beyond the slender passageway, "Same, everywhere same. No more stalling. Say where is jaydium."

Teeg knotted his hand into a fist and tapped his knuckles against Kithri's chest, deliberately gouging the bruises Red-hair had given her in the courtyard. "Where?"

Kithri staggered under the sudden pain. "Don't—rush me!"

He hit her again, harder. She jerked away from him and fell against Red-hair. His hands closed around her left wrist and forearm like silken gloves. In one fluid movement he twisted her arm behind her. The instant agony in her shoulder took her breath away.

"We had deal. Friends for jaydium." Teeg pressed his knuckles on the bruises again until his weight crushed her under waves of charring pain. Red-hair stood behind her, an implacable wall of flesh. The butt of the force whip tucked in his belt dug into the muscles of her back.

"Deal! Now jaydium!"

"I—"

"No more words! Jaydium!"

For a frantic instant Kithri thought, *What does he want me to do? He won't listen to me!* Then she realized that cutting her off was only one more intimidation tactic. She let her head hang forward, her curls shadowing her face.

The grinding agony eased. Red-hair loosened the

twist on her shoulder, but Kithri did not straighten up. She must give them every reason to think she was beaten into submission.

"Jaydium now." Teeg's words were flat, with no hint of a question.

*Please, please let him think he's won.*

Kithri nodded, keeping her face hidden. Red-hair released her so quickly that she flailed about for balance. She fell heavily to her knees. Although it went against her every instinct, she grasped his hand to pull herself up, grasped it and pulled down hard and fast. His body yielded slightly, and puzzlement replaced his expression of gloating certainty.

Kithri's free hand shot upward, her fingers curling around the force whip handle, finding the controls even before she had it fully free. Without pausing for aim, she thumbed the whip into a broad sweeping beam. Someone screamed, and at least one body toppled to the stone floor.

Red-hair grabbed for her, but she was already sprinting past him for the nearest passageway. He lunged and she jumped free and whirled to face him. For an awful moment her nerves froze. Then she brought the force whip up again, snapping the energy beam like a barrier between them. The harsh light of the weapon shone on his face, contorted into a mask of fury. He bellowed at her like a maddened beast and reeled backward, hands fisting over his eyes.

Kithri wheeled and darted down the nearest exit. A short tunnel brought her to a larger chamber. She counted four entrances, plus the way she had come. Westward would bring her back to the room where the pirates waited, perhaps recovering even now. She plunged into the southwest tunnel.

From the next circular room she had only two choices, due west or north. If memory served her, the same would be true for the next chamber—yes, it looked identical, only this one allowed her to circle around where she'd left Teeg and his gang.

She raced northward and then northeast. Even with adrenaline fueling her aching muscles, she had to take the ramp slowly. Flight after uneven flight quickly took their toll. Before long, her breath rasped in her ears and the pounding of her heart filled her head. Her body radiated heat like an oven. Sweat drenched her hair and clothing. She strained her ears for any sound of pursuit, found nothing she could recognize, and forced herself upward again.

Kithri held on to the doorway to the pyramid's central chamber for a moment, struggling to catch her breath and force her burning muscles to move. Her legs trembled so badly she could hardly stand. Her head throbbed and she lost all sense of time. She had no idea how long she stood there—a few seconds, a few minutes. Then she thought of what Teeg might let Red-hair do if they caught her, and somehow found the strength to stumble onward.

Outside, she paused again in the blindingly bright light and rubbed her watering eyes, for a moment unable to believe what she saw. In the exact center of the open space, its landing path a swath of shattered rainbow glass, sat *Brushwacker*.

Eril jumped from the cockpit and sprinted toward her. "Kithri! Brianna said you'd be here!"

"I told you to get the hell out of here!" She meant

to scream, but her voice came out as a reedy whisper.

Eril gave her one swift, unreadable look. The bruises on his face and chest glowered like a patchwork of livid purple. He set one shoulder against her waist and threw her across his back.

"Put me down! What do you think you're doing?"

"Rescuing you—you ungrateful dustbug! What did you think?" He heaved her through the opened door and threw her in.

Kithri's surge of anger evaporated. Her whole body was a solid mass of pain, but what hurt most was the sudden lump in her throat.

"You didn't think I'd leave you in the hands of those monsters, did you?" Eril said.

For an instant she couldn't answer. Then she said, "Where's Brianna—and Lennart?"

"In the hold. Now to *duo* it out of here—"

Kithri blinked as his words sank in. At *duo*flight speeds, they'd be thousands of miles away before the pirates realized they'd gone. The pirates would have to tear the planet apart before they'd find them.

Suddenly the lacework of pink opal to her right shattered into dust grains. "Move not!" bellowed a sickeningly familiar voice. "Or same to ship!"

*Teeg! How could he get up the ramp so fast?*

Eril was still kneeling beside the scrubjet, his shoulders blocking Kithri's view of the emerald pyramid. She couldn't see exactly where the pirates were, but judging by the sound of Teeg's voice, they were some distance away. Maybe she still had a chance.

Kithri glanced down at the force whip tucked inside her belt. Praying that Teeg wouldn't see the movement, she reached for the handle. Her fingers settled on the controls. Eril's black eyes flickered in agreement. She took a deep breath.

"You comet-brained burned-out crop of dustbugs! You want us so bad, you come and get us!"

"Too gentle blaster—little sniveling pieces of you will be telling us where is jaydium!" Teeg shouted back, and Kithri got a fix on his location.

In one fluid movement, Eril ducked and Kithri thumbed the force whip into life. The pirates were more than halfway from the pyramid to the scrubjet—Teeg, Quick and another she did not know. But not Red-hair.

The leading edge of the whip caught Teeg glancingly across the chest. He screamed and jumped back. She glimpsed the raw burns across his cheeks.

Kithri could not hold the whip handle steady in her trembling fingers. She grabbed it with her free hand, but it was no use. The tip of the beam splayed backward and touched the scrubjet for an instant. There was a horrendous clap of sound and then light seared her eyes into blindness.

Suddenly Kithri no longer sprawled across the scrubjet pilot's seat, she floated in a frigid, spinning void. She opened her mouth to scream, but no sound came out. Whatever the force whip was doing to them this time, it was very different from the jump which had brought them to Brianna's world.

Unknown forces plucked at her, drawing her out like taffy, stretching her body thinner and thinner until she thought if it went on for another moment she'd snap like an elasticized band. Instantly the pull vanished, along with all sense of direction, and she went hurtling through the darkness.

* * *

Her next awareness was of the warmth of Eril's arms around her legs and the coiled tension in the muscles of his back. His head lay in her lap and her upper body had fallen forward on top of him. She didn't remember dropping the force whip, but her hands were empty. Her vision was all one gray blur.

"Eril," she whispered, "Eril, can you—see anything?"

*Where are the pirates? Why don't they attack again, now while we're helpless?*

"No, only shadows. Wait, it's clearing a little."

Kithri strained to make sense out of the roiling gray shapes. They bore no resemblance to the brilliant crystal garden, but that was all she could tell. Even as she stared, squinting her watering eyes, she caught the ripple of something moving toward them, something like an elongated silvery pearl.

"Are you thinking they are intelligent, clan-superior Raerquel?" The voice was deep, hovering at the lower end of what human vocal apparatus could produce.

"Behold! Indwelling artifact is indicating complex technology!"

Kithri's vision cleared a little more. The pearl now tapered upward into a headless neck. It slithered rapidly toward her. She thought of giant amoebas, of fat, slimy worms and the boneless jelly things she'd seen in tri-vids. Tentacles began to unfold from the neck section and reach out for her.

Then she felt herself slipping sideways and the entire world went black. The *basso* tones rang in her fading consciousness.

"Rest they need, rest and healing."

# Chapter 16

No light, no taste. Silence. Anesthetic numbness filmed her skin. Her mouth—surely she should have a mouth below her sightless eyes. Her mouth—open or closed, she could not tell. Teeth and tongue, lips—were they wet or dry or coated with a thick gel?

Kithri struggled to pull herself upright, but there was no sensation of muscles contracting or joints flexing, no tug of gravity to orient herself in space. No change to prove she had actually moved.

*I must be dead, then,* she thought, and fled back into unconsciousness.

Some time later, she woke again. Her skin was slick and icy, her first reaction one of relief to be feeling something again, even if it was unpleasant. After a few moments, she noticed the feathery swish of air through her lungs. Her chest rose and fell rhythmically. Something flat pressed against her back, firm but not hard.

If she could feel her body, then she was still alive. And if she was not dead at the hands of the pirates, then what she had seen before she blacked out must be real and not an hallucination born of dying brain cells.

An image flashed unbidden across Kithri's mind. Man-high and twice as long, the rounded body had tapered upward, like a mound of silver jelly drawn erect at one end. Four platelike disks covered the highest tip. Below them, boneless appendages uncurled and lengthened, reaching for her—

*No, don't think about that!*

—and there had been a voice, she remembered, two voices, deep and resonant.

"Ah! Your recovery is proceeding well."

Kithri sat bolt upright. She was no longer in the crystalline courtyard or the scrubjet. She was sitting, stark naked, on a low table in an otherwise unfurnished room of neutral gray.

She shivered and hugged her arms to her body. A thin film covered her skin and peeled away at the lightest touch. Slowly her eyes locked on the rounded silvery shape. She'd remembered the creature's size and color right, but the head disks were tinged with shades of copper and blued steel, resembling four oblong coins. They were set in the place of eyes but showed no hint of pupil or other marking. Coiled tentacles covered the upright section of the body, varying in thickness and arranged in no discernible order.

A webwork of centrally located neck slits vibrated as the deep-toned voice spoke again. "Please do not be alarmed. No aggression toward you is being intended."

Now there was no possible doubt she was awake. Not only awake, but facing something which looked like a giant silver slug.

"Please do not be attempting to communicate verbally," the thing said. "Your universal-meaning unit has not yet been installed, although the artifact previously implanted in your cerebral cortex is permitting you to comprehend my words."

*Artifact? Brianna's translator.*

One of the creature's neck coils uncurled into a slender appendage, which it extended in her direction as it moved closer. Kithri leapt off the table, putting its bulk between her and the creature. It withdrew, folding its tentacle into a series of graceful coils.

"Your companions have previously indicated the desirability of synthetic integument. To obtain this, I must be manipulating this building-appendage," it said. "Then I can be fitting you with a device permitting mutual conversation."

Without waiting for her response, the alien glided to the table. Its neck section shrank back into the mass of the body as it uncurled several slender upper tentacles and began stroking the base of the translucent gray pedestal.

Kithri jumped back a few steps. She pressed the knuckles of one hand against her teeth, forcing herself to breathe slowly and evenly. It was ridiculous, to be so afraid. The thing hadn't harmed her or even threatened to do so. In fact, unlike the pirates, it seemed to be making every effort to reassure her. *Your companions,* it had said. *Eril, the others—alive, too? Then where are they? What's happened to them?*

*Slow down and think!* she told herself sternly. *If they've been asking for clothes, how bad off can they be?*

The slug creature finished whatever it was doing and undulated back across the room, revealing a cubbyhole in the table's pedestal base. Kithri cautiously approached the table, knelt, and reached in.

Her fingers closed around a bundle of silky cloth. This proved to be a loose, sleeveless shirt, long enough to come halfway down her thighs, a length of fabric to tie around her waist as a belt, an undergarment somewhere between a loincloth and a bikini—she wondered whose idea *that* was—and tubelike socks.

Trying not to take her eyes off the creature, she pulled the shirt over her head. The thin gray fabric felt unexpectedly warm against her skin. Instantly it shrank in some places and stretched in others so that it fit her body perfectly.

When she straightened up, the silvery alien was holding a small rectangle of grayish glass between two of its feathery upper tentacles. "It is now necessary that I approach you more closely for the installation of universal-meaning device. The process is brief and without risk. The panel will adhere to your synthetic covering, not your integument. I assure you, I mean you no harm."

Kithri pressed her back against the hard, rounded edge of the table. She forced herself to stand still as the thing slithered closer. A cold sweat drenched her hands. Her breath came in punctuated gasps, so shallow she felt dizzy. She wet her lips with a tongue gone curiously numb.

*It isn't going to hurt me—I think—and besides, where could I run to? There's not a door or window in the place. It's* stupid *to be this scared.*

The giant slug was almost upon her now. Kithri expected to smell its foul, decay-laden stench, but there was only a slightly acidic odor, not at all unpleasant. The panel was inches from her heaving chest now. She caught a glimpse of it, a thin tile of the same watery-gray stuff as the table and walls. She held her breath.

The slug-voice said, "I am of the clan Hath, rank Djan, and my personal name is Raerquel."

After a long moment Kithri began breathing again. The alien had retreated to about ten feet away, and she hadn't felt a thing. It had just formally introduced itself.

She cleared her throat. "I'm—I'm Kithri—Kithryne Sunnai. Human. Woman. Are you male or female—what *are* you?"

No sounds came from the "translator" panel on her chest, but with each word a ripple of white light danced across the surface. She took a deep breath and watched the panel flex with the movement. It did not change brightness, so it must be sound and not movement that was the activating energy.

"My species is the pinnacle of molluscan evolution, and calling ourselves—" the translator in her skull hesitated, "—*Gastropoideus sapiens sapiens*. The question of gender is of concern only to lesser orders which have a constant preoccupation with genetic recombinant reproduction. We have no such drainage on our mental energies."

The gastropoid came closer in a gliding movement. This time, instead of recoiling in horror, Kithri watched it curiously. It did not ooze along on a carpet of slime like the slug it superficially resembled, but propelled itself on a rippling ridge of muscle. The movement of the flesh suggested some sort of internal pumping mechanism or hydraulic system. That would make sense, since there would be no bony skeleton to support so much mass. She couldn't be sure. Her training in xenozoology was sketchy at best, most of it centered around the two alien races which were known to the Fifth Fed. Her textbooks hadn't even considered the possibility of invertebrate sapience.

"I am a scientist studying vertebrate life forms, my particular interest being mammalians," the gastropoid said. "Your species is most unusual, if you will forgive any inadvertent discourtesy in my saying so. I have never had the opportunity to converse with an intelligent vertebrate before. All the mammalians we have studied have been tiny and nonsentient."

Kithri thought wryly that they'd certainly gotten things backward here. She'd seen slugs before. Stayman had several varieties of shell-less snail, tiny, slime-coated creatures which ravaged the farm plots and dug deep beneath the soil to conserve moisture. A person could survive on them in an emergency if he could bring himself to eat them. Kithri had never needed to.

She shifted away from the table and said, "So you're a scientist. Is that what you want, to study us? Is that why you separated us?"

"Yes, I am desiring you to answer questions. Preliminary noninvasive evaluations of your structure and physiology have been completed during your period of unconsciousness."

"Questions . . ." Kithri folded her arms protectively across her body and suppressed the impulse to pace. The gastropoid seemed perfectly comfortable sitting—or lying—there.

"To begin with, what are you and where did you come from?"

Kithri was tempted to laugh, *Is that all?* "I told you, I'm human. As to how I got here, your guess is as good as mine. I'm not even sure where *here* is. It's not the Stayman I started out on, that's sure."

"You consider yourself a *person?*"

She paused, a little puzzled. Brianna's translator seemed to have confused the meaning of the word "human." "That's my species, yes. But doesn't every race define itself as 'people'?"

Instead of replying, the slug asked her again where she'd come from, and how, and for what purpose. What planet was she from? Did her species have interplanetary flight? How had she gotten to this world? Who sent her and why?

"I don't know," she said, as often as she was asked. Her own mind was spinning with questions. What *had* happened to them this time? Had they traveled again through alternate probabilities? Or some inexplicable, instantaneous shift through space? Or through time itself and if so, forward or backward?

"I've already told you!" she said. "If you don't like my answers, go ask someone else."

"Are you wishing a reunion with your companions?" the slug said unexpectedly, as if this explained her lack of cooperation.

"Of course I want to see them!"

To her surprise, the gastropoid asked no more questions. It crawled over to a blank stretch of wall and touched it with a thick lower appendage. A door appeared on the smooth surface and slid noiselessly open. Beyond lay a hallway of the same featureless gray.

*These gastropoids must be damned good engineers to camouflage the door that well. I wonder what else I missed.*

As she followed the alien along the narrow, curved passageway, Kithri realized that, for all her uneasiness in her new surroundings, she was no longer in physical pain. It took her a few moments to remember the last time she'd been awake. Her face had been beaten into bruises, her lip cut and swollen, skies only knew how many ribs cracked, her shoulder wrenched half out of its socket, other damage which blended together into one enormous pain.

*Gone, all of it.*

She ran one hand over her chest, feeling only the curve of breast and muscle under the silky cloth. She might have lain for weeks under some sort of suspended animation while she healed, unless the gel itself possessed unusually potent regenerative properties.

They came to the end of the corridor, turned left, and crossed under a wide archway. Raerquel halted at the threshold of a spacious courtyard.

Light drenched the open space, reflected and magnified by the mirror-bright towers. Some looked slender and delicate like glass filigree. Others rose in solid blocks of gray or white like highly polished alabaster.

Kithri squinted and shaded her eyes with one hand, feeling as if she were standing in the center of a brilliant-cut diamond. Then her vision adapted and she realized the effect was partly due to the water, clear and sparkling, which filled the courtyard.

Several aliens went by, half-crawling, half-swimming, weaving among sculptures which looked like petrified waterfalls. Others rested like beached seals on the flat, rectangular islands.

Raerquel started across the pond, its undulating movement smoothing into a glide. Kithri hesitated, her gaze once more drawn aloft to the glittering towers. They reached no more than a story or two, but the graceful spires and causeways made them appear taller. She spotted other, lower buildings interspersed with the towers. Her eyes lit on a wide pyramid a few blocks away and she shuddered. The last time she'd seen a structure like that, it had been emerald green.

Kithri's heart did a curious little flip. Take away the slugs and the water, and color the city in gemstone hues—and she'd be right back in Brianna's world. Here she saw only shades of gray and silver, heard only the lapping of the water and the muted *basso* rumbling of the giant slugs.

And yet . . . the resemblance was so uncanny, she *recognized* some of the towers.

Raerquel halted and turned back toward her. She took a hesitant step into the sun-warmed water. It seeped through her tube socks and between her toes, stirring childhood memories of flower-banked streams.

At the far side of the pond, Kithri spotted round pipe openings, and felt the faint tug of circulating water.

*Just like in the other city, only we didn't realize what they were for. And those islands, we thought they were benches.*

Kithri stumbled. *It is the same city, it's got to be! And this one's inhabited, so it must have come first. We must have traveled back in time . . . To Lennart's time?*

She waded slowly, shuffling her feet and looking around her. When she'd first woken up, her impression had been of an austere, sterile world. Now, splashing through the knee-high water, she imagined herself treading a sea of shining light. Brianna's city seemed like a tawdry imitation of this city's subtle-toned brilliance. She felt as if the dust of Stayman were at last being washed from her pores.

Raerquel led her up a ramp and along a dry avenue. Kithri followed, her socks dripping for a few steps before they shed their wetness. The gastropoid crawled through the open doorway of a wide, squat cylinder. Inside was a circular wall, forming a corridor along the building's circumference. Although Kithri could see no markings indicating its location, the gastropoid opened a second door in the inner wall. A ramp spiraled down to a blank-walled corridor filled with indirect light. Kithri followed Raerquel downward. The gastropoid created another door, this time at the end of the lower corridor, and stood back for her to enter.

# Chapter 17

Even before Kithri stepped through the doorway, she recognized Brianna's voice.

"—positive evidence it's the same. I've spent a whole year studying this site and—"

Lennart spotted Kithri and jumped to his feet. He and Brianna had been sitting on a low bench in a large, light-filled room. Kithri caught a glimpse of his unbruised face before he enveloped her in a hug.

"They swore that magic ointment would fix you. . . ." Lennart ran one hand over Kithri's face, touching the lip that had been cut.

*If it had been me with Red-hair instead of Brianna,* Kithri thought, *he would have tried just as hard to stop him.* She flinched and took a step back.

Brianna stood up. She, too, wore a belted one-piece tunic with a translator panel across her chest, but on her figure it looked alluringly feminine. There were no traces of the hollows around her eyes or the patchy texture to her skin that had appeared with her first capture by the pirates.

Kithri looked away. She didn't want to be reminded of how willing she'd been to let Brianna suffer. "You're all right, too."

"As you can see," Brianna said stiffly.

Kithri's eyes darted around the room, the low broad bench, the two blank walls and third wall of shallow built-in shelving covered with mysterious-looking glass objects. Raerquel had disappeared, along with any trace of the door. "Where's Eril?"

"Still recuperating, is my best guess," said Lennart.

Kithri caught the undertones of worry in his voice. Acid filled her mouth and a throb of pain shot through her temples. Even though her physical injuries were healed, some part of her was still back with the pirates, still holding on. . . .

"Did you recognize the city when you were outside?" Brianna asked suddenly.

"It looks just like yours, except for the color," Kithri said.

"Come here, look at this." Brianna grabbed Kithri's hand and pulled her to the far wall, where rows of clear glass artifacts lined the shallow shelves. She picked up a crystal tube, colorless and unmarked, and handed it to Kithri. It felt warm and very slightly supple, not like ordinary glass.

Kithri wondered if it would shatter if she hurled it against the opposite wall.

"You see?" asked Brianna. Her eyes gleamed with undisguised enthusiasm.

"I have no idea what it is," Kithri said. "Do *you?*"

Brianna ignored the barbed question. "Watch what happens when you put it back."

Kithri replaced the tube on the self. It rolled a little and then halted abruptly, as if held by a magnet. She tried sliding it along with her fingers, but it would not budge until she gave it a sharp upward tug.

"And there's the malleable quality of the building

material," Brianna went on quickly, before Kithri could say anything more. "You've seen the gastropoids sculpt the stuff with their appendages? We've tried it, but without result. Maybe our body temperature's wrong, or else it might require a special catalyst. In the Dominion, we have plastics that can be reshaped and set using liquefying agents and fixatives, but nothing this durable."

Kithri ran one fingertip along a chain of fist-sized crystal bubbles on the next shelf. Brianna's words swept by her like a dust zephyr. Her nerves felt as if they'd been scoured raw.

Lennart stroked a slender frosty-white rod and said, "Bri was just telling me—when you walked in—she thinks we got zapped into another dimensional whatcha-call-it. Only this time we've gone back in time and this is an earlier version of the same city."

"I warned you that might happen if we were transported with you along," Brianna told him, as if it were somehow his fault. "I don't know what created the astonishing colors in my city—or what *will* happen, rather. They've always reminded me of the artificially brilliant hues produced when mediocre gemstones are exposed to ionizing radiation. But that's clearly not the case here. Ah! There's so much to learn—such an unparalleled glimpse into the past!"

"If this is the past and I somehow dragged us back here," Lennart said thoughtfully, glancing upward, "then somewhere out there my people—the United Terran Space Command—are just beginning to settle space. And from here history goes two ways—your Dominion and the rainbow city or the Federation and Kithri's desert planet."

A shadow flickered across his russet eyes. "My god . . . what's going to happen to this city—to this whole world?"

"We don't know that anything *does,*" Brianna said briskly. "We can't assume this is the cataclysm point—we can't assume *anything* on this time line. That's why it's so important to study this civilization, to learn everything we can."

Kithri folded her arms across her chest and turned away from the shelves. This wasn't some fantastical tri-vid drama they'd stumbled into, despite Brianna's speeches. And yet, time-travel—or dimension-travel—wasn't any more improbable than anything *else* that had happened to her since she'd been fool enough to take Eril Trionan on a jaydium run.

*Eril . . .*

Her thoughts jumped around like sand-fleas. "What about the—slugs? It's hard to imagine them building this place."

*"Gastropoids,"* Brianna said, as if explaining basic facts to a slightly retarded delinquent. "Intelligent, civilized *gastropoids*. And yes, capable of creating this city. From what I've already observed of their ability to manipulate the building material, I'm certain of it."

"In my time we'd never met an alien race, intelligent or otherwise," said Lennart, still sounding shaken. "We sent out probes, searched the night sky, and analyzed every blip on the radio waves, but we never found anything. For centuries, our writers imagined what they might be like, everything from bug-eyed monsters to telepathic crystals."

"In all my people know of present-day space, we, too, are alone," Brianna said. She walked over to the bench and sat down again, clasping her hands around her knees as if to forcefully keep them still. "Maybe there are alien races out there among the stars, waiting for us to discover them, but I—" she hugged her knees hard to her body. Her voice was low and vibrant. "I could only *dream* of them as I sifted through their ruins. All my life I'd been trying to make dead cultures come alive . . . and here one is, just waiting for me."

"That's assuming they'll let you." Kithri couldn't bear to stand still any longer. She began to pace up and down. "What do they want us for, anyway?"

"Given how different we are," Lennart said, "you can't blame them for wanting to know something about us." He seemed to be regaining his usual equanimity.

"So we're more like scientific specimens than prisoners," Kithri said.

"It doesn't *matter!*" Brianna exclaimed. "None of this matters except they're *real* and I'm *here*. And every moment I learn something new."

Kithri kept on pacing. There was no place to run. *Let her study the slugs all she likes, and I wish her joy of them.* "So what are the rest of us supposed to do while you find out all this stuff?" she said under her breath, not expecting an answer.

And Eril—what would Eril be doing now if he were awake? Playing wonder-boy diplomat, scheming to pioneer gastropoid-human relations? Mankind's first ambassador to the slugs?

Kithri smiled humorlessly at the thought of Eril in a tux-suit, sipping cocktails and making small talk with a giant snail. Unlike him, she had not dreamt of discovering alien races or exploring strange new worlds. She had only dreamed of escaping Stayman's everlasting dust. What she would find to replace it had never been more than a nebulous memory of flowery fields and cloud-dotted skies.

She stood still. *Lennart, how right you were about us both being outsiders. Exiles is more like it.*

Eril's words came back to her, *"Out of all that glory up there, what do you really want?"* And again she had no answer.

"What about the door?" she asked, turning her thoughts in a more practical direction.

Brianna shook her head. "We spent a long time trying to find it, but we can't determine its position. The seam melts right back into the wall." She shrugged. "It's beyond any technology the Dominion has."

"Where was it, about here?" Kithri asked, running her hands over a section of uniformly smooth wall. She rapped on it, listening for the hollowness that might mark the slot for a sliding door. Her knuckles jarred against the unyielding surface.

"What exactly do you think you're doing?" Brianna asked, scowling.

"I don't like the idea of being anyone's prisoner," Kithri said. "I've had enough of that, thank you."

"But we aren't—" said Brianna.

"Let Kithri try if she wants to," Lennart said in his gentle, easy voice. "Who knows what she might find? She's got the best survival instincts of any of us."

*Survival?* Kithri wanted to laugh in his face. Jaydium running could be hazardous, but being beaten up by space pirates or marooned on a world of talking slugs wasn't her idea of an improvement. Her bloody luck had saved her skin, but that was about all. She might need a good deal more than luck for whatever came next.

The door slid open suddenly, almost in front of Kithri's nose. She jumped back as a giant gastropoid slithered into the room. In its lower tentacles, it carried packages wrapped in the same silky fabric as their garments. At the sight of it, a rush of adrenaline surged through her, setting her heart pounding and her muscles aching to run.

"Greetings to you, our guest-humans," the gastropoid intoned.

Lennart walked over to the silvery alien, close enough to reach out and put an arm around it. "Hello, yourself. Pardon my asking, but which one are you?"

"Personal name being Duvach, assistant to clan-superior Raerquel. You are being reassured as to the well-being of your companions?"

"All except the last one," Lennart said. "How's he doing?"

The gastropoid said, "Now let you be partaking of food. Since the sustaining effects of the rejuvenation matrix are time-limited, nourishment is required to continue your healing process."

"What about Eril?" said Kithri, surprised to hear how strong her voice sounded. "Why didn't you answer us?"

"You are already in possession of most recent information regarding the status of your fourth companion," the silvery alien said. Its voice sounded flat and bland, almost mechanical. "There is nothing I can be telling you which you do not already know."

Kithri exchanged an astonished glance with Lennart, but neither of them said anything. The hard things in life, she reflected, weren't tangling with pirates or *duo*ing through a coriolis storm—they were things like waiting. Waiting and guessing.

The gastropoid Duvach laid down its packages and, using its sturdy lower appendages, stroked the material of the floor in front of the low bench. The translucent glass grew up and outward under the alien's touch, at first resembling an amorphous lump, then expanding to a huge flat mushroom, and, finally, a low but serviceable table.

Kithri watched the procedure, her uneasiness melting temporarily into fascination. Where did the material for the table come from? There was no trace of a depression in the floor, nor could she detect any mechanism by which more mass could have been carried to the surface. Superficially, it looked like the slug was stretching the floor up and outward, the way Albionese children pulled stretchy-candy. Kithri glimpsed a flash of light, like a reflection on a liquid surface, where the tentacles touched the metamorphosing table—an illusion, a coupling agent, or—or was the slug *secreting* the stuff out of its own body?

The alien proceeded to create a second bench adjacent to the first. It placed the packages in the center of the table and settled itself in the opposite corner.

"Appropriate environment for human partaking of nourishment, as described to us, this is correct?"

After a pause and another exchange of glances, the three humans took their places at the table and began opening the packages. The first two intricately folded fabric packages contained thick-stalked leaves.

Kithri took a tentative nibble of purple-hued stuff. She didn't recognize it, but she'd eaten stranger-looking things in the brush. It was salty and slightly rubbery, with a surprisingly pleasant tang. As she swallowed, she realized how long it had been since she'd eaten anything solid. Her stomach growled appreciatively, and she took another mouthful.

Brianna licked her fingers delicately. "This is seaweed, isn't it?"

"Is this not adequate mammalian human food?" Duvach asked. "Our biochemical studies verified digestibility and suitableness of nutrients."

"It's not what we usually call *lunch,*" Lennart said good-naturedly. "But I guess it's the best you could do. I don't suppose you could come up with something like a steak?"

"We're fine as vegetarians," Brianna interjected. She added as she scooped up a fingerful of pale green strands, "Many molluscan genera are strict herbivores. We don't know what cultural taboos we might violate by even asking for animal flesh."

"That's all right by me," Lennart said. "I'm happy eating just about anything that doesn't bite back. I just hope there's a pile more of this seaweed stuff around, or we're all going to end up a lot hungrier."

Kithri opened the next package, which proved to contain cubes of something pale and lemon-scented, and offered them around. She bit into one, surprised at the smooth texture and pleasantly tart taste. Whatever it was, it was a more concentrated food source than the greens. With food in her stomach, she found herself thinking more clearly. The slugs—*gastropoids,* she reminded herself—had shown them nothing but goodwill so far. They'd escaped

Brianna's pirates. Eril would be all right. And wherever this place was—*whenever* this place was, it sure wasn't Stayman. Her spirits began to recover.

Brianna meanwhile had finished the last of her pale-green strands. "Is this the sort of food your people eat, too?" she asked the gastropoid.

Duvach sat motionless for a moment before answering, "Your pardoning, friend-human, but I have been instructed by clan-superior Raerquel not to be answering any questions. The intention is not to be impolite, but to avoid the appearance of cultural contamination."

Kithri didn't know exactly what the gastropoid was referring to, but she had a feeling that it wasn't good.

"*We,* contaminating your culture?" Brianna asked. "I don't understand." She did not, in Kithri's opinion, look in the least puzzled. *Avid* would be a better word. "You've given us the freedom of this laboratory—it *is* a laboratory, isn't it?" Brianna turned and gestured toward the shelves. "Surely you meant for us to study these artifacts?"

But Duvach was already undulating rapidly toward the door. It ignored her as it sealed the opening behind itself.

"I have the feeling we've gone and done it," Lennart said somberly, "but what *it* is is anyone's guess."

Kithri found she had to agree with him.

# Chapter 18

In another part of the laboratory complex, Eril wrestled with an entirely different set of problems. Opposite him, just beyond arm's reach, sat the gastropoid Bhevon, Raerquel's assistant and clan-inferior, patiently going over its questions one more time. As he formed his answers, Eril tried to analyze each one critically and to keep his own curiosity under control.

Yet his eyes sometimes strayed to the glass instruments lining the walls and he couldn't shake the feeling of relaxed well-being, as if there had been some euphoric drug in the healing gel. All traces of the pirates' handling, even the pain from his fractured ribs, had vanished completely.

To make matters worse, his chair, which had been sculpted to his individual dimensions, was so comfortable, it presented a constant temptation to relax. That was a luxury he could scarcely afford, now of all times. How he handled these questions was crucial, even if the gastropoids seemed friendly enough to begin with. It wasn't just his own impression that was at stake but that of the whole human race.

*What was his species?* Terran human, technically *Homo sapiens*. He hoped the translator panel would make something coherent of the archaic terminology.

*His individual name?* Eril Jermaine Trionan. Colonel, Fifth Federation Space Service.

*His phylogenic ancestry?* Primates, and before that, mammals, and before that, some kind of reptile, he supposed, and before *that.* . . . Well, certainly, they were all vertebrates, clear back to whenever animals developed internal skeletons.

*By what means had he appeared in World-of-Home?* That was a hard one. Some sort of time-space disequilibrium must have transported them. No, not across space, they were still on the same planet, except it was different. Either they'd gone back in time, or history had taken a different direction, or both. If the gastropoid thought this a preposterous explanation, it gave no indication.

*How did his species differ from other animals? Why did they consider themselves human?* At least, that was the word Brianna's translator came up with.

*What were they doing here? Who sent them?*

Eril ran one finger along the edge of the translator panel on his chest, feeling the slick, slightly warm surface. He couldn't judge his answers, since he had no idea what Bhevon really wanted or what its values were. He might be a hot-shot pilot, but he was definitely not a diplomat with a gift for saying nothing in the smoothest way possible. He felt overwhelmed by his own ignorance, a child, alone as he'd been for so many years with only himself to rely on.

"You will be rejoining your comrades soon," the gastropoid said, its neck slits vibrating with each syllable, "waiting only for the resuscitation of the one most severely injured, yet there is a caution to be given."

*Injured? Kithri?* A vision rose unbidden in Eril's

memory—Kithri glaring at him across the shattered crystal garden—Kithri screaming defiance at the baldie leader, spinning a web of lies and courage—Kithri outraged that he'd risk her third-class, down-at-the-fins scrubjet for her very life.

"All four human specimens are given positive prognoses," Bhevon said. "Caution is with regard to your status as persons, not your physical well-being."

The memory of the pirates had wiped away much of Eril's euphoria and reminded him that he was in the midst of an alien culture, cut off from his friends. The gastropoids could probably do anything they pleased with him. He certainly had nothing he could use in self-defense except his fists—for all the good they'd do against a creature that size, with no obvious vulnerable points—and his still-addled wits.

"Clan-superior Raerquel is asserting that, despite manifest differences, you possess other characteristics which qualify you for consideration as persons. It believes, in defiance of all tradition, that personness is not limited to those of proven—" the translator hesitated, "identicalness."

*Personness? Identicalness?* Had Brianna's translator gotten the words right?

"Raerquel wishes you to understand that its enlightened opinion is not endorsed by other clans."

Eril hazarded a guess. "You mean Raerquel's willing to talk to us, but others might not be?" That might make for an awkward beginning but didn't seem to be insurmountable. With time and communication, humans and gastropoids would learn how to relate to each other, respecting each other's abilities and diversity.

"*Talking to* is but a minor example of considering

personness," Bhevon answered. "Many beasts are capable of primitive, sound-mediated signaling. The mere production of noise patterns is not causally related to self-awareness or social conscience."

The gastropoid's booming voice was as devoid of emotional nuances as ever, and Eril found himself wishing for some hint of its own personal opinions. For all he could tell, it was only cooperating with Raerquel's orders because of clan loyalty. There was no warmth, no excitement, not even curiosity coming from its impassive silver bulk.

"Have you not in your own ecological system living entities which possess some degree of intelligence but do not qualify as social or moral equals?" Bhevon asked.

"Are you warning me that we're apt to get treated as some sort of *animals?*"

"Yes, undesirable lower creatures. Vermin."

Eril closed his mouth.

The alien stirred, a faint ripple flowing from its blunted head section down the tapering neck. "You must understand that clan-superior Raerquel thinks far beyond tradition-honored wisdom. Identicalness has always been considered the most fundamental prerequisite for personness, since we share conscious identity only through our unity in Flesh-Before-Naming. It is inconceivable to consider personness coexisting with differences."

Eril found his voice again. "But surely you can recognize that we're *intelligent.* We may come from different phyla, but we can use language to communicate with one another. We can think, reason, solve complex problems. And our technology—you saw the 'jet we came in. It didn't build itself. The definition of intelligence is the ability to make and use tools, isn't it?"

"*Using* tools is not the same as *making* tools," Bhevon replied. "Any moronically-minded, uncivilized offspring-of-degenerate-monotreme can *use* the tools it does not understand."

"We make the tools we use!" Eril protested. "From toothbrushes to starcruisers. In fact, on our planets, we're the only species capable of it."

For a long moment, the gastropoid sat motionless. The clear light of the room glinted off its head disks. "A convincing argument this would be, if you can create the means to modify your environment. We had assumed that your mammalian origin would preclude this ability. Please to be demonstrating it."

Eril glanced around the room, seeing only the banks of unfamiliar instruments lining the walls. There was no furniture other than the seat he occupied, and that had been sculpted for him by Bhevon. He dredged his memory for the survival tools he'd been taught about in the Academy. They didn't assume much, just wood, cleavable stone like flint, and plant fibers. In theory he could kill and cook his own dinner or sabotage an Alliance installation, using only materials found on any habitable planet.

Now he spread out his hands and asked, "With what?"

"What could you possibly be needing to make tools? Are external substrates necessary for generating the mammalian equivalent of *therine?*"

Eril very nearly snapped, "What the hell is *therine?*" Instead he said slowly and calmly, "I can't make tools out of empty air. I have to have raw materials and something to work them with."

Another ripple went down Bhevon's body. Eril had the feeling that, given its wish, it would have gone humping away from him in disgust. After a long pause, it said, in a monotone that he found infuriatingly pedantic, "Raerquel's scientific explorations are advancing the theory that personness should be redefined as the capacity for both altruism and individual initiative, which require intelligence as well as self-awareness. It believes you humans fulfill these theoretical requirements. However, many scientific colleagues will be challenging this premise and rejecting our evidences. Why, they will surely ask, should they extend serious consideration to specimens which fail to share the most basic skills with us?"

Eril squashed his immediate impulse to get up and do something drastic. Adrenaline crept along his nerves, but no familiar thrill. His belly twisted as if he'd swallowed a bucketful of ice. *What would we do with an unknown animal? Probably put it in a zoo, if we didn't slaughter and dissect it first. Is that what's in store for us?*

Bhevon took Eril down the ramp to the big underground laboratory. When he stepped through the doorway, Brianna greeted him enthusiastically, followed by Lennart, who hugged him and slapped his shoulders as if they were long-lost cousins.

Only Kithri hung back. Her eyes jumped around, never still, although otherwise she looked fit enough. Her skin was clear and unbruised. As she walked toward him, the silky gray tunic outlined the muscles of her shoulders and thighs. By contrast, Brianna's opulent curves seemed flabby.

Kithri reached out and touched him hesitantly, as if needing to reassure herself that he was solid flesh. She wouldn't meet his eyes, and yet in that brief contact, he felt an unexpected intimacy with her. His skin tingled where her fingertips brushed against his arm. Feelings rushed over him, things he wanted to say to her, things he had no words for.

Then the moment was gone and the four of them gathered around the table, comparing experiences. They argued a bit as to whether they had any privacy. Eril thought they did, because the gastropoids seemed to require direct visual contact with the light translator panels. There had been several instances during his questioning when he'd turned away and Bhevon hadn't been able to see the panel. It had to ask him to repeat what he'd said.

Brianna pointed out that the light panels were still operative, ripples of brightness covering them with each sentence. The gastropoids could easily watch the conversation.

"If they're going to spy on us, there's not a lot we can do about it," Lennart said, making swirling patterns with his fingers on the smooth table surface. "What are we going to do, stop talking to each other—or invent a common sign language? We still don't know if we're guests or prisoners or what."

"I don't think they've decided that yet, themselves," Eril said. "The next move's theirs."

"Running us through their tests to see if we're worthy of, how did you put it, *personness*?" said Lennart.

"And if they decide we're not?" Kithri said, half-bitter, half-anxious. "What happens then? Do we get stuck in a cage for the rest of our lives?"

Eril remembered the *therine* incident with Bhevon. Being able to exchange abstract ideas, use recorded language to bind time, manipulate tools—all the measures of intelligence he was familiar with—none of these might count if the aliens' standards for "personness" were truly that different. But he couldn't bring himself to say it aloud, to feed Kithri's mood. She had good cause to be uneasy. They all did. They'd been separated, questioned and kept in suspense about each other. After their ordeal with the pirates, that was more than enough to erode even the most optimistic spirits.

"You can sit around feeling incompetent if you want to," Brianna told Kithri, "but I'm not going to join you. It takes time to understand any new culture, and time is what we've got. Besides, Raerquel, the chief investigating scientist, is already our advocate.

"Which reminds me," she paused, gesturing with her hands, "I need some sort of recording medium. There're only so many details I can memorize before they all start to run together—"

Lennart laughed and told her she was incorrigible.

"What's the point of keeping notes, when we might be trapped here for the rest of our lives?" Kithri said. "We could die here, alone, prisoners. Don't you even care?"

"What would you do if you could break out?" Brianna said waspishly. "Go running off to the hills like you did before?"

Kithri drew in a quick breath and clamped her lips together. Her hands curled into fists, the muscles of her shoulders bunching.

"It's too early to be making plans," Eril said. "Not

until we know what our situation is. The slugs could turn out hostile, or they could just as easily become our allies. Maybe we'll find a way back to Brianna's world, or Lennart's, or our own. Or a way of traveling among all three. Who knows?"

Kithri swiveled on the bench to look him full in the face, her eyes like pools of still water. The dent in her nose stood out sharply. For a moment, Eril saw her as a wild young thing, bewildered and alone. Brianna was in her element here, and Eril couldn't deny his own hopes for dealing with the aliens. Lennart seemed as relaxed and good-natured as usual, but where was there a role for Kithri? Here there was no jaydium to run, no scrubjets to pilot. . . .

Was *that* what she was thinking?

"We're all in this together." It was a stupid platitude, but the best he could come up with at the moment. The expression on her face had left him awkward and unsure.

She looked away and said in a voice that tore at his heart, "If you say so."

# Chapter 19

The living quarters were the most boring Eril had ever laid eyes on. *If this was a hotel, I'd turn around and check out now. How can these creatures make buildings that are so beautiful on the outside and so dull inside?*

The four windowless rooms opened to a spacious central area furnished with a table, benches, and a large shallow pool of water, constantly circulating through pipes at either end. The table was more birdbath than eating surface, its water replenished like that of the pool. The sleeping cubicles were empty except for an unadorned couch and a shallow ceramic fixture set in the floor, with perforated openings at one end and a large drainage hole at the other, like an awkward cross between a urinal and a bidet. Everything from the walls to the benches was the same neutral, indirectly-lit gray.

Kithri threw herself down on one of the beds, her back to the others. Brianna darted about, examining everything from the pool to the table to the cubicles with great enthusiasm. Lennart slouched on a bench, encouraging her until Eril wanted to scream at both of them to shut up. When Bhevon returned and indicated that Eril was to return to the laboratory, he went cheerfully.

What followed was the strangest examination Eril had ever undergone, and he'd passed some sadistically inventive Qualifiers at the Academy. The chair, again sculpted to his own dimensions, was superlatively comfortable, yet now he felt penned-in, cornered. Another of Raerquel's many assistants, Possiv, had drawn six-foot high panels out of the bare walls and surrounded him with them. The panels were close enough for Eril to touch. They completely cut off his view of the laboratory.

Apparently all he was expected to do in this test was watch the patterns of light which flashed across the screens. Ripples of the subtlest shades of gray, barely distinguishable from one another, alternated with loops and squiggles of brilliant white and black. Occasionally they broke into stark geometrical patterns like aerial views of a psychopathically conceived labyrinth.

Eril couldn't decide if it was the brightness that made his eyes water and ache, or it was the rapidly changing patterns. His leg muscles twitched and his hands curled unconsciously into fists. Something grated on his nerves, as if he were about to fly smack into an ambush. He couldn't put his finger on what made him feel so jumpy. Whatever it was, it was getting worse by the moment. His vision blurred and the blood vessels behind his eyeballs began to throb.

He briefly considered jumping up from his chair and cutting the whole thing short, but he managed to restrain himself. There was too much at stake here. He'd find some way to put up with it.

"How much more is there of this tri-vid show?" he said. "The visuals are great—I think—but the plot's a little thin and the characters could use some juicing up."

The panel in front of him shifted from a grid of hair-fine lines to a display of eccentrically spiraling bull's-eyes. A moment later, it slid to one side and Raerquel's head emerged through the gap, coppery-steel disks reflecting the lurching zigzags.

"Eril-human, please repeat your communication. Are you in distress?"

Eril tried to stand up, but his muscles wouldn't obey him. His stomach rolled over three times. He sat back down and buried his face in his palms, his mouth filling with acrid saliva. The spasm of nausea eased, but the pain in his head hammered on like a molten pulse.

He tried to breathe. "Uhhh . . ."

"Assistant Possiv! Immediate cessation of experiment!"

"I'm all right," Eril protested, sitting straight again and swallowing rapidly. He winced as light blasted once more on his eyes, but kept his hands away from them. "It's just a headache, that's all. We can—"

"You are in *pain*, Eril-human. I cannot permit this to continue," Raerquel said as it flicked its stout lower appendages over the screens. One by one they went blank, melting to the gray tones of the divider panels. Possiv slid the subdivider panels back into the walls.

"I didn't do too well on that one, did I?" Eril muttered.

"Do not berate yourself." Raerquel placed itself alongside Eril's chair. "It is a deception that because we possess efficient translating devices, we are therefore capable of instantaneously understanding one another. Your absence of reaction merely indicates the depth of our differences."

*Absence of reaction? It calls this headache an* absence *of reaction?*

Eril shook his head, hoping to ease the pain which had caught his skull in a bone-crushing vise. His vision steadied, but the agony continued unabated. He rubbed his temples, feeling the underlying muscles as tight as strings of steel.

"I *did* react," he said, trying to sound more coherent than he felt. "Like I said, it's just a headache. I'm not the type that uses them as an excuse. Let's go on."

"Be covering your eyes," Raerquel commanded. *"NOW!"*

Eril complied. Whatever came next couldn't be worse than the light displays. He was unprepared, and therefore startled, when he felt a moist band encircle his head. He reached up and touched something smooth, almost snakelike, and under it a sticky wetness—

His eyes flew open as Raerquel withdrew its tentacle and recoiled it neatly on its neck.

"You—you *tricked* me."

"Would you have permitted me to be touching you otherwise, Eril-human?"

Eril rubbed his fingers together, feeling the liquid harden quickly to a gel. He blinked. The throbbing headache had vanished. "I didn't have my eyes closed more than a second before you smeared me with that stuff. There was no time to dig out a container. Where did you get it?"

Raerquel swung its head away, as if preparing to join Possiv in dismantling the screen panels. Eril lurched forward in his chair, reaching out with one hand. If Raerquel had been human, or even some type of animal, something with fur or feathers or even *bones,* he would have pulled it around to face him. But, he thought as he hesitated, fingers still outstretched, he had *already* touched the thing, and it hadn't been horrible. Smooth and cool, more like marblestone than worm slime. . . .

"Did you secrete that stuff from your own body? Was—was it *therine?*"

"No."

"No, what? You didn't squirt it out on me, or it isn't *therine?*"

Raerquel's head tilted back toward him. "It is not good for you to know the answers to these questions. Clan-inferior Bhevon has already explained to you the dangers of any suspicion of cultural contamination. The day following this, the preliminary scientific inspection team will be reviewing my researches. If I am able to convince them of your potential for personness, then we can begin meeting each other as civilized equals. If not—"

"Then we go back to being pet cockroaches?"

"Then we must gather more proof until we cannot be controverted. And for this we will need the establishment of ignorance, are you understanding? For some on the committee will not be believing even if your only interaction with us was through automatic computing devices."

Eril sat down, shutting up with a considerable effort of will. Finally, when he could trust himself not to come out with something totally idiotic, he said, "Whatever it was, your stuff cured my headache. I'm ready to go on now."

"I am appreciating your cooperativeness, Eril-human. Come here."

One of the coiled appendages high on Raerquel's neck uncurled into life. Smooth and slender, it ended in a blunt, featureless tip. It gestured toward one of the instrument banks which lined the laboratory walls. "Please to be observing."

Eril got up and followed the creature to the side. The various devices were difficult to distinguish because they were all made of the same highly reflective, glasslike substance. A large rectangular screen had been set in the wall at the height of the gastropoid head disks.

Raerquel uncoiled several of its lower, thicker tentacles and stroked a row of small knoblike projections. Under its touch, they lengthened into thick levers. Something white and brilliant fluttered in the center of the screen, spreading quickly into a discernible image. Eril recognized the characteristic silhouette of a gastropoid. Shades of gray, from almost-white to dark charcoal, created scintillating patterns along the bottom and two sides of the screen. Raerquel waited, apparently watching Eril, and Eril waited for something else to happen.

"It isn't going to do any good for me to look at this if I can't understand what it's saying," he said after a few minutes.

"Is translator device being inoperative? You are unable to understand me now?"

"Yes, I can understand you. But I can't read *that.*" Eril pointed to the rippling lights.

"You cannot read?"

Eril forced himself to take a slow, deep breath. It helped keep his temper under control. "I can read my own language. But I've never learned to read *yours*."

"Your species has to be taught interpretation of vision?"

Interpretation—of vision? Eril thought of the educational programs developed for the born-blind, fitted as children with computer implants. It was certainly true that they had to learn to interpret the electronically enhanced signals. But what did that have to do with reading, an acquired skill?

"Look," he said, "I don't think we're talking about the same thing. That stuff—" indicating the bands of patterned light, "looks like a *visual* record to me. Your people may learn it awfully young, but you weren't *born* knowing it. It's not inherently obvious, at least not to this space-bum."

"You are in error, Eril-human," Raerquel said after a brief pause, during which Eril wondered what new diplomatic outrage he'd unwittingly committed. "Comprehension of what you call a secondary recording is indeed inherent in my species. What we now spew into the air, these patterns of sound vibrations, *these* are the learned analogs, useful for redundancy in storage, but fraught with potential for error. Light, in its infinite meanings and shadows, light is the true language. Everything else is compromise."

# Chapter 20

Having determined for the hundredth time the door to the living quarters was undetectable when sealed and being unable to think of anything more constructive to do, Eril wandered restlessly through the common room. He knelt by the pool of running water and dipped his fingers into it, noticing for the first time the four shallow depressions on the bottom. They were long and narrow, as if designed to cradle four prone bodies. Was the pool meant as a bath? The water, while not exactly cold, was far from a comfortable temperature. And, he discovered as he put his fingers to his lips, it was slightly salty.

*Damned if I know what the thing is for.* He got to his feet and tried the table water. It was fresh and cool.

There was no one to discuss the water and its significance with, and for some reason that bothered Eril. The entire suite of rooms felt echoingly empty. Kithri was still sleeping, or whatever she was doing in her cubicle. First Lennart and then Brianna had been taken away for testing.

Eril tried to ignore how much their absence affected him. What did he think existed among the four of them? Some kind of solidarity because they were all human? He didn't even *know* these people.

There was no reason one brief adventure should make a difference. For the past five years, neither constant danger nor Weiram's powers of persuasion had ever made him feel like part of a team.

A door appeared in one wall, whispered open, disgorged Lennart and just as quickly sealed itself behind him. Lennart went to his empty bed and sat down. A trace of healing gel gleamed on his forehead and his eyes held a tight, strained look.

Eril leaned against the doorway, watching him. Memories stirred uncomfortably. "You don't look too well."

"Yeah?" Lennart stretched out his legs on the bed, one by one, and leaned back against the wall. He closed his eyes and rubbed his temples. "You were no prize, either, when you came back."

"How did it go?"

"Slugs two, humans zero, the best I can tell. I don't know what they were after with that light show, but they sure didn't get it from me."

"It makes you wonder, doesn't it, what they're *really* up to," Eril said, thinking aloud. His eyes wandered back to the empty common room and pool of salt water. "Raerquel admits we're intelligent, but it talks about proving our 'personness'—the local passport to first-class treatment—as if that were something quite different." He shook his head. "We didn't make such a distinction in the Fifth Fed."

"That's hard to believe. Every government on my Earth defined citizenship in a way that kept *somebody* out, whether it was women or foreigners or AIs." Lennart's voice was rough with fatigue. He sounded more pessimistic than Eril had ever heard him.

Eril sat down on the edge of the bed, next to Lennart's feet. "But we both agree that intelligence isn't limited to the human race, don't we? These gastropoids don't seem to think anyone else even qualifies for consideration."

"Except for Raerquel, who's our local version of a freethinker. And it's only dancing the dance for the sake of its grant committee. It doesn't give a hoot about this 'cultural contamination' stuff, or it would never have let us peek at that lab, let alone turn us loose there. It would have just stuffed us into a Korzinowski box."

"A what?"

"They wouldn't have shown themselves to us."

"Unless they've never dealt with an intelligent alien species and it hasn't occurred to them that this half-assed isolation isn't very effective," Eril said. "We may not have a free spin of the place, but Brianna's studying them as hard as *they're* studying *us*. She's not being particularly secretive about it. They're pretty sloppy if they're really worried about 'cultural contamination.' "

" 'Cultural contamination,' my ass," Lennart said. His mouth twisted downward. "There's more than a few tourist traps they're hiding from us."

"Such as?"

"Such as there's a goddamned power struggle going on and we're smack in the middle of it. Everything Raerquel and its friends have told us reeks of it. If it were just up to Raerquel, we'd probably be guests of honor, right? Instead of being put through one idiot-minded test after another. So what does that suggest to you?"

"The Admiral's inspection tour," Eril couldn't resist saying. "Seriously, it suggests Raerquel has an agenda of its own, and that agenda is *not* popular with the higher-ups."

Lennart shifted uneasily on his bed. "We'd better keep our eyes open tomorrow. We don't want to bonker Raerquel's game, but we sure don't want to get labeled the sweetest pets in town just to save its professional hide."

"For a guy who comes from an age when warfare was a dirty word, you have a surprisingly suspicious mind," Eril said.

"Suspicious, devious, and downright sneaky," said Lennart with a very unhumorous smile. "That's me all over. I didn't get into space by trusting in universal sweetness and goodwill. Think on this, captain—there were a thousand applicants for every place, all of them just as qualified as I was. What got me in?"

Eril flinched, as if Lennart had just shoved a plasteel rod up his spine. "What did you call me—*captain*? What kind of joke is that?"

Lennart buried his nose in the crook of one uplifted elbow and slid down on the bed until he was completely horizontal. "No joke. And nothing wrong with your hearing, either. Who else do you think is holding this circus together?"

Eril stared at him long and hard. "Thanks," he said in an unexpectedly rusty voice, "but I think you've got the wrong candidate." He headed back to his own cubicle with what poise he could summon.

Eril paused at the entrance to Kithri's room. She lay on her side, her back toward him and knees drawn slightly up, her brown curls spilling over one shoulder. The supple fabric of her tunic clung to the curve of her waist, outlining her back and hips.

As if sensing his presence in her sleep, she rolled partway toward him. One small breast formed a rounded silhouette against the pale gray wall. Eril caught his breath, remembering the surprising softness of her body against his. Like melting honey—no, it was *he* who'd melted. When she'd pushed him away, the separation was only partial.

He held on to the door frame so hard his knuckles cracked. The sound brought him back to the present. The Cerrano Plain receded, worlds away. Maybe millennia away. He shouldn't be standing here, watching her sleep, even if it weren't for Lennart next door and Brianna sweating under the lights.

He cursed softly as he walked away.

Duvach appeared shortly before the morning meal to tell the four humans they wouldn't be needed in the laboratory. The inspection committee was going to spend most of the next day with Raerquel, going over the results of its research.

*If it had been Bhevon,* Eril thought, *it wouldn't have even told us that much.*

So they waited in their quarters. And waited. They moved restlessly around the room, tension building until even the most casual comment seemed intolerably irritating. Eril decided they'd been cooped up too long. Thinking it would bring them together and give them something to do, he began telling his favorite war stories. He had plenty to tell, even without the battle at Albion and the last escapade on New Paris, the one that led him to try recruiting Kithri as a *duo*partner. He wasn't ashamed of these two incidents, but he somehow wanted to tell a better story than he'd lived.

Kithri and Brianna listened, Kithri relaxing enough to laugh at the right times and Brianna looking as if she'd rather be taking notes. Lennart, his face set, got up and strode over to the other side of the room.

Brianna's narrative, a string of anecdotes of research expeditions on one meaningless planet after another, also sounded suspiciously edited. If she'd gathered that much professional prestige, Eril wondered, why wasn't she a hot-shot professor somewhere? What was she doing all by herself on Stayman? Where were the shadows in *her* past?

As Brianna came to the high point of her story, Lennart walked slowly back to the table. He held his arms crossed tightly over his chest, his hands in fists. When he sat down, Eril saw a new, stormy light in his eyes, a tension around his mouth that hadn't been there since the pirates.

"I've had about all I can stand of this let's-tell-each-other-how-wonderful-we-are," he said. "I can't judge your academic credentials, Bri, but I know hypocrisy when I hear it."

Brianna recoiled as if he'd struck her in the face.

"I don't mean it personally," he continued before she could protest. "I know you think what you've done is wonderful and you're so proud of how *civilized* your Dominion is. But all this talk of 'universal cultural understanding' is just a scab covering over a festering sore. Like they say, violence is contagious. It doesn't exist in a vacuum. Those space pirates—and everything they stand for—" he jabbed one forefinger at her "—that's how your people *really* treat each other—that's the true soul of your Dominion."

Brianna set her whitened lips together, but she didn't flinch again. She gathered herself for a reply, but Lennart gave her no opening. By look and gesture, he shifted his focus to Eril.

"And you—to think that all this time I've been envying you! I thought I'd woken up in the future of my dreams. It was all I could do not to sound off like a damned propaganda chit—'O glorious new horizon!' and all that. I didn't want to see the truth."

"And what is the truth?" Kithri asked in a tight, quiet voice. "If Brianna's people are no better than her pirates, then what are *we?*"

Eril could hear her thoughts, *We who blow up whole planets and turn children into scrub-rats?*

"You don't know what we had to give up for space," Lennart said. "It's *so damned easy* for you. You don't have to give up a thing! You have it all. You've got ships that can take you halfway across the galaxy as if the speed of light was nothing. And what do you do with them?"

"You don't understand," Eril jumped into the pause. "Everything's different now. It isn't that war is bad and peace is good. *Nothing's* that simple, not any more. Settled space is too big, political problems too complex. You can't judge us by what happened thousands of years ago."

Lennart's eyes shone like polished cinnabar. "Can't I?"

"Your people weren't so great with your vaunted age of peace," Eril shot back. "It didn't last, did it? It ended so long ago, we've even forgotten it existed. But we haven't given up! In fact, we're still fighting for the same thing."

Watching Lennart's face, Eril remembered his expression as Red-hair had reached for Brianna that last time. He also remembered thinking a man who looked like that was capable of anything. Eril could have throttled him then, before he infected Kithri with the same deadly recklessness. She, too, would have thrown away all their lives for a moment of hopeless compassion if he hadn't stepped in. He saw that same desperation in Lennart's eyes now, but then the light shifted and it was gone.

*"Fighting?"* Lennart repeated, his voice laced with sarcasm. "For *peace?*" Something like a bark shot from his mouth. "Maybe I'm too dense to see it. Maybe things have changed so much I *can't* see it. But I do know this—we didn't have to be afraid of each other. And you do."

*I'm only one man,* Eril thought desperately. *The civil war was no more my doing than the pirates were Brianna's. I'm on the other side, building something better, or trying to, for god's sake.*

It wasn't fair to blame him for something he had no control over. Even less fair to blame Kithri, who hadn't had the chance to fight back. But every answer that came to his mind sounded defensive, an adolescent whine.

"We don't know why it ended. It was a special, isolated time," Kithri's voice broke in on his thoughts. She was talking to Lennart in slow, careful tones, whatever hurt she'd taken from him well hidden. "Maybe it lasted until the First Fed. We can only guess. But once we discovered jaydium, we exploded through space. Everywhere. Distance didn't mean anything any more. People could just take their problems somewhere else. We didn't *have* to live together on one planet."

*And if we* hadn't *discovered jaydium . . . The stuff's like a cancer, devouring all our lives, not just Kithri's.*

*Without it, there wouldn't have been a Fifth Fed or Brianna's Dominion. Or the pirates, either. We'd still be back in Lennart's time, cooped up on a handful of planets, taking decades to travel between them.*

"You're saying war's inevitable, given human nature," Lennart said bleakly. "In our genes, like some hereditary disease. I can't accept that. It wasn't true then and it's not true now."

"Things change!" Eril insisted. "People change."

"No. Some things don't change, captain. War isn't bad one time and good the next. We built you a world of peace and you threw it away."

*Of all the narrow-minded, comet-brained, opinionated—*

"Hold on, you two," Brianna cut in. She'd been listening to their debate, her face grave with concentration. "*All* civilizations go through natural cycles of conflict and resolution, if they last long enough. Mine did, but with each round of tensions, we got farther away from wide-scale fighting. It's only in the early trigger-happy stages—by accident—that interplanetary destruction is a possibility."

*Albion was an accident?*

The conversation came to an abrupt halt as the door became visible and whispered open. Two gastropoids stood outside in the hallway. Eril identified them by the pattern of their neck slits. Duvach and Possiv.

Duvach extruded its head section into the room. "It is time for personal inspections by the Council committee. Kithri-human, please to be accompanying us."

Kithri straightened her shoulders. A few stray curls had fallen forward on her brow, and she brushed them back.

"Why her?" Eril said. "She missed the tests the rest of us took."

"Obviously, the Council committee members are wishing to witness firsthand the duplication of previously reported results, using a naive subject," Duvach answered in the same expressionless voice all the gastropoids used.

Eril shut up, wishing he didn't feel so damned protective. Kithri gave him a small smile on her way out.

"I'll be all right," she said. "After all, *you* made it through the other day."

# Chapter 21

*What are they doing to her? She's been in there longer than all the rest of us put together. It can't be more than a bunch of stupid light tests. . . . Raerquel might be willing to stop with a headache, but what about this Council committee?*

Eril found himself pacing again. It had been several hours—three or four at least, it was hard to tell—since Kithri had been taken away. One moment he was sitting at the table with Lennart and Brianna, sipping table water from the cups they'd convinced Possiv to sculpt for them. Pretending to listen to their few attempts at conversation, going over the same speculations and words of encouragement. Trying not to feel how slowly time passed, as unbroken as the blank gray walls. The next thing Eril knew, he was on his feet, his body moving of its own accord through the common room.

He skirted the shallow pond, resisting the urge to jump in and kick up some waves, the way he had as a boy at the summer lake on Terillium, waves that left only a temporary mark on the surface of the water. It would do no good and space only knew how the gastropoids would react. The water was important, he could feel it even if he didn't understand why.

*Damn! What was taking them so long?*

Was that any reason for him to fall apart? Whatever happened next, he'd need all his wits where they belonged, not scattered halfway to Hyades, which was where they were heading at the moment.

He stopped right where he was and took a deep breath. Where was that cool, level head that had gotten him through so many squeaks? How could he expect to handle the gastropoids—or anything else—if he couldn't even sit still?

Slowly the room came back into focus. Lennart was watching him, eyes shadowed and brows in a single straight knot, and Brianna was tracing patterns in water on the table top. Eril walked back to the table, every step smooth and controlled.

He never made it. A door formed in the wall, first a hair-wide outline, then a narrow opening. Kithri stumbled through, gasping and ashen-faced.

Eril was beside her before she'd taken two steps into the room. He caught her in his arms. For a moment, she sagged against him as if her legs could no longer hold her. She trembled and her skin felt clammy against his.

Then she pushed him away and sprinted for the back of her cubicle, one hand over her mouth. She threw herself on the floor beside the sanitary facility, retching. It took Eril a moment to realize that she was neither badly injured nor in shock, and by that time Lennart was kneeling at her side, one arm across her shoulders.

"Go away," she snapped at him. "I don't need any help to puke."

Lennart returned to the table where Brianna still

sat. He glanced at Eril with a wry expression. "She insists on doing everything herself, heyh?"

Kithri emerged a few minutes later, still pale but steadier on her feet. She'd used one of her socks for a washcloth, and her face and hair were sopping wet. She sat down on one of the two empty benches and Eril took the other. Lennart solemnly dipped some water into a cup and handed it to her.

"Well," she said after she'd downed the water, "that's over with."

She glanced at their expectant faces and cleared her throat. "I guess you want to hear about it, huh? Mmmm . . . There were four or five tests with different kinds of lights, just like you told me, a couple of drills with small objects, and then a thousand questions, most of which Raerquel had already asked."

As she talked, her color returned and her voice began to sound normal again. "I don't know how much good any of it did. They must have asked me twenty times how we got here, and even then they didn't believe me."

"You did the best you could," said Lennart.

Kithri didn't respond, not even a flicker of her gaze in his direction. Eril understood. Maybe things were different where Lennart came from, but here you didn't get any credit for trying. What you got was dead.

"Any idea how long before they make up their minds about us?" he said.

Kithri shook her head.

"If the gastropoids work anything like Dominion funding committees, it could be months," Brianna sighed. "They delight in keeping grant applicants as anxiety-ridden as possible."

Kithri managed a brief smile. "My father always said it was a foregone conclusion. The grant people only took their time when the answer was *no* and they were obliged to go through the formalities anyway. But he said you already knew it. Of course, none of this may apply to the sl—gastropoids. Who knows what they're looking for? I sure didn't."

The door slid open with the faintest of whispers and Raerquel undulated into the room.

Eril got to his feet. News, this must be some kind of news. He held his breath, wishing that the gastropoid's metallic-tinted head disks were either more like eyes or less. He kept expecting to be able to read some expression in them and feeling frustrated when he couldn't.

Raerquel paused beside the shallow pool. It lowered its head section and uncurled several feathery upper tentacles until they touched the rippling water. For several moments, it held them extended and dripping.

"Your ways are not ours, your . . . water is not ours," it said. "Yet I honor the light within your water. I invite you, if you are so . . . moved, to be reciprocating."

Without thinking clearly what that meant, Eril dipped his fingers into the pond and held them out, watching the drops fall into the water. *One body,* he thought, *and then separate, and then one again.* A profound gesture, he realized in retrospect. His impulse to act for all of them had been sound.

Raerquel slithered up to the table and halted, unfurling more appendages. "My mammalian friends, without yet knowing how much we have achieved together, still I thank you for your cooperativeness.

Especially you, Kithri-human. I am aware of the pain you suffered for the advancement of scientific truth. To my thinking, your ability to transcend the discomforts of the body for a higher goal is itself proof of your personness."

Kithri reddened and ducked her head.

"Any of us would have done the same," Eril said. "It's important to establish a relationship between our species and yours. If we've got to satisfy your superiors as to our intelligence, or whatever they're looking for in us, then we'll do whatever we can."

"We would have much to learn from your kind," Raerquel began. "We—"

Whatever the gastropoid scientist was going to say was cut off as a rumble like faint thunder filled the air. It started low, barely more than a vibration. It felt to Eril like a starship taking off from a nearby field. Kithri and the others scrambled to their feet. The shaking escalated sharply. The room shivered, slid sideways with a stomach-twisting jerk, and shivered again.

*Earthquake!*

"Let's get out of here!" Eril shouted. "Fast!" He yelled at Raerquel to open the door.

But the gastropoid scientist sat as if glued to the floor. Its thick head section wavered back and forth as it spoke. "Be calming yourselves until this activity has subsided and further information is forthcoming."

Eril did not feel in the least calm as the room rocked again, rolling and swaying. Legs braced and apart, he rode the next wave. His skin felt cold and prickly. He tasted a familiar tang like the thrill before a battle broke loose.

"Our dwelling constructions are possessing considerable elastic properties." Raerquel continued in its expressionless voice. "Only detachable external ornamentations present any immediate danger. Whatever the cause of this disturbance, the greatest protection lies within these walls."

*"Elastic properties."* That was so much comet dust! Eril knew glass when he saw it and he'd been through the Academy's survival drills. Even the doorways—if they could find them—wouldn't provide decent protection in an earthquake. Any moment now, the walls would crack and shatter under the strain. They'd be buried under tons of splintered crystal. And, despite its infuriating calm, Raerquel would be buried along with them. The slug wasn't going to do a damned thing to save them!

At times like this, Eril knew he couldn't count on anyone but himself. If there was any way out, he'd have to find it himself. But what? Where? Knowing he had to act now, he took a step toward where the door had been.

A muffled cry broke through the low rumble. He spun around to see Brianna hunched over the bench she'd been sitting on, her head buried between her knees. Her ribs, visible through the supple alien cloth, heaved in shuddering, soundless sobs, one after the other. Lennart wrapped her in his arms and rocked her back and forth, murmuring syllables of comfort.

Kithri stood behind Brianna, knees flexed, looking frightened but alert, ready for anything. She glanced down at the other woman and a puzzled expression flickered across her face.

Eril stared at them, momentarily baffled by Brianna's reaction. What the hell was going on with her? She'd been through a bad time with the pirates and then the lights, but he couldn't see her panicking like this, going half catatonic. Not from something like an earthquake. She had her limits—so did they all—but she was tough and self-reliant, too. She'd have to be to work alone on a site like Stayman. Now she curled into a helpless ball, trembling violently.

Eril took a step toward her, not quite sure what he was going to do—drag her to her feet, slap her to break the shock? Throw her across his shoulders and carry her? Carry her *where?*

Suddenly Possiv burst through the doorway, propelling itself across the smooth floor in a flurry of leaps. "Clan-superior Raerquel! We are receiving information from City-of-Light headquarters. NewHome has carried through with the threatened detonation in the Northern Arctic Desert. The emergency negotiation committees are disbanding—"

Raerquel slithered to the doorway with unexpected speed. It paused, head disks gleaming kaleidoscopically, and turned back to the astonished humans.

"Urgent matters require my presence elsewhere," it said. "Wait here, where you will be safe!"

# Chapter 22

The room shook as if Raerquel had slammed the door behind itself. Then came more rumbling, wave after wave, eventually dying into silence.

Kithri stared at the blank wall and the water which had splashed around the lip of the shallow pool where only a few minutes ago, Raerquel and Eril had performed that strangely moving ritual. Now her heart pounded and her hands clenched unconsciously into fists. Her mouth tasted metallic as if she'd bitten her lip. Brianna might have turned inward on herself, shutting out the world, but what Kithri wanted to do—*needed* to do—was to run, strike out, hit something. Adrenaline, shock, conditioning—that's all it was. Not enough to save any of them now.

Brianna and Lennart had not moved. Neither had Eril. He'd been standing with his back to Kithri, taut and poised for action. He turned and his eyes locked with hers, burning as they had in the shattered crystal garden. She felt him reach out an imaginary hand to her and felt herself grasp it. Fire and hope surged through her.

She took one slow breath and then another. Her heartbeat quieted and she realized the quaking had stopped. The room was silent except for Brianna's sobbing.

"It's all right," Lennart murmured, stroking Brianna's hair. "It's all over now."

Kithri and Eril sat down at the table again. Kithri felt even more useless than she had at the camp. There was nothing she could do for Brianna that Lennart wasn't already doing. He kept talking to her, gentle soothing nonsense about how they'd be fine now and everything was going to be all right.

It worked better than the truth would have. Brianna stopped crying. By gradual degrees she unlocked her arms, straightened her back and lifted her head. Her hair hung around her face in damp curls and her cheeks were flushed, dark lashes beaded with tears. She dipped her hands in the table fountain and rinsed her face.

"You all right now?" Kithri asked.

Brianna turned reddened eyes toward her. "As much as any of *you* are."

"I meant—about the way you reacted—"

"I *know* what you meant!"

"I know when something's none of my business," Kithri said.

Brianna pulled away from the circle of Lennart's arms. "I'm sorry. You're right. I owe you—all of you—an explanation."

"You don't owe us anything," said Lennart.

Brianna looked up at the ceiling, blinking back fresh tears. "We're locked in here," she said, each word a visible struggle. "There's nothing we can do. But if it had been some other circumstance . . . if some action on our part had been required and I had *'reacted'* like that. . . ." Her gaze was steady and level now, her voice surer. "I could have cost us all our lives. I owe you that."

"All right," Eril said quietly. "What happened to you?"

*And,* Kithri thought, *will you do it again, the next time something deadly dumps on us?*

Brianna took a gulp of air and pushed her hair back from her face. "You have to understand, nothing bad ever happens—*happened*—to me. The security routines, even the infraprotection, they were just an exciting game. I even did my doctoral field work on Ytervi, with all those active volcanoes. But they went dormant the whole year I was there. I almost thought—no, I *did* think—I had a magic touch.

"Anyway, we'd been here about a half-year when it happened. We were mapping the underground chambers, working late because it was such a long climb back up and—"

"Wait a second," Kithri broke in. "Who's this 'we'?"

"The others. There were four of us—Fabrice, the senior scientist who got us the grant to study the city, myself, and two graduate students."

"So where are they? I thought you were alone."

"Please!" Brianna held up her hands, eyes wide and white-rimmed. "I'll get to that! Just let me . . . tell the story."

Kithri heard the grief and terror ringing through Brianna's words. She held her tongue and waited.

A few heartbeats later, Brianna took up the story again. "I'll never know if we got careless and didn't check the seismic predictors or if it was freak chance. We were below, as I told you. There was a quake—a big one—and a slide. Crystalline wall material, rock, dust. Everything. We were trapped. It might have been better if we'd all died then. But we didn't. It took three days. And the last day I was alone."

She placed her hands, palms down, on the narrow strip of table surface. The scar tissue stood out, livid and shiny. Her fingers, with their blackened, broken nails, curled into claws. "The last day . . . I dug. And dug. . . .

"I suppose . . . I've been a little crazy since then. I don't even remember how I got back up. I remember climbing out of the resuscitation unit. . . ."

The sobs had left Brianna's voice, replaced by a dispassionate calm. Only her phrasing, clusters of words parenthesized by almost inaudible breaths, betrayed her.

"The computer's psychiatry module kept me on medication therapy for weeks. I could even go below for short times. To map the slide area. There wasn't much burial I could . . . needed to do. The Institute said I was well enough to continue on alone until they sent the regular resupply ship."

"You mean they'd send a special ship for the jaydium but not for you," Kithri said bleakly. She thought of the weeks and months, waiting for the lithicycline shipments that never came, watching her father grow weaker and weaker, of the terrible moment when she realized there would be no more.

"None of it matters now," Brianna said. Her hands moved like drunken moths, taking in the room, the shallow pool and the city outside, "Here is a whole new civilization—a *living alien* civilization—all mine to study! It makes everything that's come before it insignificant—the quake, the recovery—yes, even the pirates! Can you understand that?"

"Yes," said Lennart, "I think we've all felt that way about something. I did about getting into space."

Eril's eyes were grim, his expression cryptic. "We may have stumbled into more than any of us imagined."

Brianna smiled, taking his words for agreement, but Kithri suppressed an instinctive shudder, hearing the warning in them.

An unfamiliar gastropoid brought them food, which they ate more for something to do than out of any real appetite. They were sitting around the table, picking at the last bits of seaweed and going over Possiv's message, when Raerquel came back. It paused again beside the shallow pool and repeated the ritual dipping into the water. Eril got up and did the same.

"I honor the light of your water."

"And we honor the light of yours."

Something in Raerquel's eerie silence as it settled itself on the floor nearby prevented them from deluging it with questions. They waited.

Raerquel's upper appendages curled and uncurled repeatedly. It reminded Kithri unexpectedly of an old jaydium miner coerced into giving a public speech. Dowdell had once looked like that, when his drinking buddies at the Thirsty Miner found out it was his birthday, and made him stand up and tell a joke or else buy a drink for every man there. She could see him, face flushed, shoulders hunched, pulling at his overall pockets and looking around for some place to spit. She almost smiled at the memory, but then the old feelings—the pain and the desperate loneliness—rose up in her to wipe away any hint of nostalgia. Did she really want to go back to *that?*

Raerquel began speaking. "Everything I have learned of you is convincing me that you are an intelligent and conscience-gifted species. You are my honored guests, not research animals to be kept ignorant for the sake of experimental protocol."

"Ignorant? Of what, exactly?" Eril asked as he sat down again. As he spoke, Kithri watched his face. A few minutes ago, going through the water ritual, he'd looked so calm, like a tri-vid hero. Now he seemed more human.

"The quaking we experienced was not a natural phenomenon," said Raerquel.

"But if it was artificial," Kithri said, puzzled, "it must have been *enormous*."

"The detonation of interplanetary missile at uninhabited northern polar region was indeed enormous," replied Raerquel. "Fortunately, the NewHome leaders were not intending the destruction of life, only a warning."

"Oh, my god," Lennart said, running his hands over his flushed face. "Not here, too."

"What kind of warning?" Eril asked.

"It is as I feared," Raerquel said after a brief hesitation. "Offspring planets NewHome and Tomorrow reacted to our arrogance with even greater belligerence, which must breed only more hostility. A trade embargo they could abide, but not the seizure of assets and expulsion of their diplomatic staffs. As long as we continued discussions, there was hope that irrevocable action could be avoided. Now the first blow has been struck—a warning only, as I told you, but enough to frighten our own leaders into more desperate measures."

Kithri's chin jutted upward as if it had a will of its

own. "I've heard this kind of talk before," she said. " 'Desperate measures.' 'Irrevocable actions.' Nothing but excuses to do what they damned well pleased—and we were already in the midst of an interplanetary war."

She narrowed her eyes. "How do we know this story isn't just another of your *tests* to see how we'll react?"

"Excellent questioning," said Raerquel, continuing the graceful, rhythmic motion of its tentacles, "but you must inform me what proof you will accept. News broadcasts, which could be prerecorded in a dramatic manner? Verification from other clan superiors, who could be likewise deceitful? Personal observation of the blast site, which could be falsified?"

"How about the simple truth?" Lennart looked up, eyes shadowed. "Like they say, that's the best place to begin."

"Is there such a thing, my human friend, as a *simple* truth? Not in this world, I am assuring you. Perhaps they are correct who believe that, by our own ambition in colonizing the stars, we have split our race into irreconcilable opponents. If so, does not each faction offer its own *simple* truth?

"Once," the gastropoid continued, "in our dimmest past, we were only one clan. We all shared the same Flesh-Before-Naming. Such dissension as we now face would have been unimaginable. Then many clans arose, still sharing the same birthing place. Ocean-of-Home grew more and more crowded, until finally we were forced to emigrate, first to the land and then the heavens. We found and settled two ocean worlds, NewHome and Tomorrow."

Brianna leaned forward, her voice steadier. "Since

an aquatic environment is necessary for reproduction of your species, you chose compatible ecosystems. You must still share common experiences . . . a sense of shared origin. . . ."

"They are our offspring worlds. Why should we mistrust them because their waters are different from ours? One clanmate does not take another hostage."

"So what are you fighting about?" Lennart asked.

"*I* am not fighting, I am committed to *preventing* that most terrible disaster. Council-of-Ocean and other governing bodies fight because they fear their own blindness. They have given surrender to the illusion that light is divisible, that the light of NewHome—or Tomorrow—or even the strange world which saw your hatching—is in some fundamental way separate from the true light."

The alien paused, then continued in its expressionless voice, "Hope for reconciliation has been advanced by only a few, such as myself, but even that small chance is now fading quickly. Last *untranslatable*-four, the leader of our peace faction was arrested for treason, and is now facing execution. Yet better the death of one individual than that of three living planets."

"I *still* don't understand what you're fighting about," Lennart said. His voice sounded harsher than Kithri had ever heard it. She'd always thought of him as gentle.

"Does it matter?" Eril said. "As you pointed out, *we* found plenty to fight about. And a lot of good people died trying to keep the Fifth Fed from falling apart."

Listening to them, Kithri shivered involuntarily

and hugged her arms tight to her body. *This can't be happening, Not like Stayman. And Albion. . . . Skies, I don't want to think about it! I just want to get out of here!*

"As to destructive capability," Raerquel said with an incongruently airy wave of one tentacle, "it is a small matter of utilizing the atomic constituents of water, slightly modified."

"You mean you're using hydrogen-fusion bombs?" Lennart asked. His face paled visibly.

"What's that?" Eril turned to him.

A flicker of something dark and unreadable passed across the ancient spaceman's eyes. "So your historians lost that particular achievement, heyh? Forgot your worst mistakes so you could make them all over again."

"How could my people not know water and its deadly secrets?" Raerquel said. "It is our beginning, our ending. Our nourishment and our life."

Raerquel swung its head section in Lennart's direction. "You have come from a world without armed conflict. Therefore, it must be possible to achieve. You can tell us how it was accomplished, guide us, lend us the wisdom of your success. You will do this for us?"

Lennart lowered his eyes. "I . . . I don't know how much help I can be. We didn't *make* the peace, we only *inherited* it. It all happened hundreds of years ago! What good would it do now to hand you a bunch of slogans? Like they say, *this* and like they say, *that*? Oh, we studied all the historical speeches, the treaties, the Great Preamble. We had aggression-release and compromise training drilled into us from the time we could talk. Those that didn't—or wouldn't—pass the screener got mindwiped or sent to the asteroid mining camps where their so-called *violent tendencies* would at least be functional."

"You exiled all the wolves and turned yourselves into a nation of . . . sheep," Eril said. "The price of peace?"

"The price of war is a whole lot higher, captain," Lennart said grimly.

"How dare you say *no* now, when these people ask you for help!" Kithri flared. "After all you've said about Brianna's Dominion and the pirates, about the Fed, about how we threw away your age of peace. It was all ratshit, wasn't it, all empty words."

"Words, yes!" Lennart cried. "That's how we made peace—empty words, repeated over and over in every conceivable combination until one day they weren't empty any more!"

He turned back to Raerquel. "I could tell you everything I remember—where the negotiations were held, which nations signed which accords, which leader gave which famous speech. But would any of it make sense to you? Would our human solution work here?"

"It *must* work," said Raerquel. "Something must."

After a long moment of silence, Brianna spoke up. "I don't understand your references to the aquatic origin of your species. Isn't this city—"

"Only an adaptation. I will be sharing with you the waters which are the true source of our life, not these houses of dust. Soon, when Council-of-Ocean questions you. And once again you will tell us of your world, Eril-human-leader, and how you came here."

Kithri's stomach gave a sudden lurch. "Does he have to go through that again? Your committee's already heard everything we have to say. One more time isn't going to make them believe us."

Raerquel swung its tapered head section around so that all four disks gleamed in the laboratory's indirect lighting. The thing was *studying* her again.

She swallowed hard and went on, "And what do *we* have to do with your war? We sure as hell didn't start it, and Lennart's right, there's not a thing we can do to stop it."

"If I can be providing proof of your personness," Raerquel answered slowly, "then I can be showing that beings not of oneness with Flesh-Before-Naming are deserving of personness. Surely if consideration can be extended to something so alien as a *mammal,* then the inhabitants of our offspring planets, who are otherwise so like us, also merit it. Are you not receiving the translation of my words? Do you not understand why you humans are so important to me, aside from mere scientific curiosity? *You* are my key to ending this war."

# Chapter 23

Progress to the periphery of the city was slow, but they had time to get a good look at it. Kithri recognized one structure after another. She wondered what had happened to the vibrant colors of Brianna's city, and then corrected her thinking. *This* was the original and the other only a ghost transformed by some unimaginable process. If they were now in the far past, Lennart's past, this planet might well be the point of divergence, the origin of both her world and Brianna's. A disturbing thought snaked through her mind. Had the gastropoids blown themselves up and was her Stayman with its alkali pits and dust-filled Cerrano Plain the result?

She shivered in the warm air and wondered what would happen to Raerquel's peace movement if it accepted its own annihilation as its *inevitable* future.

*Will Eril tell them what their war will do to this planet, in the hope of getting them to keep talking instead of bombing?* She was grateful the decision wasn't hers.

At the edge of the city lay parkland, very much like the green stretch where she'd first set *'Wacker* down. In the distance, a few gastropoids, their silvery hides gleaming in the sunshine, herded a flock of long-bodied, rattailed creatures who lifted their heads curiously and then returned to grazing. Kithri thought they might be furred, but couldn't be sure.

At the very edge of the pavement, a row of flat, sideless vehicles hovered only a few inches above the milky-quartz threshold. Several gastropoids were in the process of disembarking.

"Hai, Raerquel Hath'djan, so those are your alien mammals!" boomed one of them. "You have scientific proof they are truly sentient?"

"I am seeing you, Suppbril Ad'herim. Any news from NewHome station?"

The other alien rippled enigmatically. Kithri watched Raerquel in sympathy. *How would I feel if I had a bunch of intelligent aliens in my custody on the eve of Albion being blown into bits? Would I care—would I show them the consideration Raerquel's shown us?*

The other gastropoids undulated away toward the city. Raerquel slithered onto the platform, occupying most of the front portion. The four humans followed and seated themselves in the center and rear.

Kithri smoothed her hands over the platform, wondering where the control mechanisms were. The surface felt slightly yielding, not brittle like true glass. "This can't be the same stuff the city's made out of, even if it looks like it."

"Looks?" Raerquel asked. "Ah, to your eyes all water is appearing the same."

Raerquel telescoped down the erect portion of its body until it reached the platform with its lower appendages. Then it stroked the clear surface like the Port Ludlow guitar player Kithri had once seen coaxing a harmony from his battered instrument. In response, a series of bulbous-tipped knobs rose above the surface. As Raerquel manipulated them, the vehicle lifted slowly to a height of several feet and then began to glide westward.

"You mean this material *looks* different to you than the city buildings?" Eril asked.

"Functional optical molecular qualities are quite distinctive," the alien replied, finishing its stroking. "Underwater, these differences are enhanced. Here, in this dry place, there is little true light."

"You were able to construct buildings—like those—*underwater?*" asked Brianna.

Raerquel gestured with a delicate upper tendril. "Once all this was part of the sea of life, before the land changed. The mountains pushed upward and Ocean-of-Home shrank. Much was lost as we adapted to dry living. We built new cities here, on the banks of the old seas, cities like the one we are now leaving, cities of working, dreaming, waiting. . . ."

"To return to the water?" Kithri asked.

"Even now, we must. For eggs to hatch and water-breathing trochophore younglings to grow. The Flesh-Before-Naming. For the dying oldsters, for the sick in spirit. We adults are able to utilize gaseous oxygen, and our integument is tolerant to the dryness of land with the aid of the healing gel. Terrestrial adaptation, although unpleasant, is possible."

"Just because a thing is possible, doesn't mean it's good," said Lennart. Again, some bleak undertone in his voice stung Kithri.

"Wise you are, my human friend. These cities here," Raerquel gestured from the way they had come, "cities of light, and cities of darkness in the mountains, they are not enough for us. Who can say if our present desolation is beginning then, with the loss of our water home, and not with our estranged offspring planets?"

The transport platform floated above the parkland and began to circle the city. As they came around, Kithri caught her first glimpse of the spaceport in its living state, not deserted as it was in Brianna's time. Row after row of teardrop-shaped ships filled the field. Some were slim and tight like the needle-jets Eril flew late in the war. They seated one, maybe two—she couldn't be sure about the gastropoids. Other ships were clearly meant to carry more, including one massive vessel which must surely be a freighter. The trading ships she'd known on Stayman were squat, space-scarred buckets, not smoothly rounded crystal. She had a sudden vision of the ships lying broken on the cream-colored field like bits of shattered glass.

Beside her, the two men sat silently staring. The naked hunger in Lennart's eyes made Kithri flinch and look down. She felt something hot and wet on her face, and scrubbed it away before the others could notice.

They angled along the vee-shaped pass and cut through the last green-cloaked hills. Something flashed before them, blinding in the sunlight. Kithri sat straighter, straining for a better view. She blinked, expecting at first to see the vivid green forest of Brianna's world. Instead, as they started down the final slope, a vast shallow sea stretched before them and into the blurred horizon.

Brianna murmured something unintelligible and Lennart made a comment about this place being different, but Kithri ignored them. How could you make jokes when there was so much *water* out there? So big, and glassy calm beyond the narrow line of surf. The reflected light filled the sky and caught in her throat.

The coast curved inward to a little bay, with a cluster of sparkling buildings and a broad, low pier spun of moonlight-frosted glass like something from a fairy tale. Gastropoids jammed the strip of beach, spilling into the shallow water. A few swam out past the surf line, dipping through the waves like elongated pearls. On the beach itself, the bodies thronged together.

Raerquel lowered the platform until waves splashed against the sides. It cantilevered its upper body over the water until its delicate upper appendages skimmed the surface. Then it extended its dripping tentacles, rigid and unmoving.

She had never seen Raerquel so still before. The scientist's extremities were usually in constant motion. A faint light glimmered over its skin as it slowly recurled its tentacles.

Kithri looked away, out across the sea, and took a deep breath. The air here tasted different from anything she'd known. She felt the moisture on her skin and inside her nose and throat.

Above them, a slender-winged flier hovered and dove, emitting an abrasive whine. Kithri wondered what it was. The shape seemed wrong for a bird, judging by Stayman's desert-adapted scavengers.

"What was that?" Lennart asked. "A giant dragonfly?"

"Dragonflies don't make noises like that," Eril said.

*"Pseudo-avian,"* Raerquel commented. Kithri thought

that wasn't what it actually said, but only the best interpretation of Brianna's translator.

The platform sped on, leaving only a shadow for a wake. Below them, the water was clear enough to reveal a sandy bottom. The ocean floor slanted gradually deeper and deeper, darkening to blue.

Kithri squinted in the brightness of the reflected glare. There was a mist ahead, low and close to the water. Its sharp boundaries struck her as peculiar, but what did she know about water vapor? She was a stranger to Stayman's single hypersaline sea and Albion had been a world of lakes and rivers, not oceans.

When they were about a mile offshore, the mist resolved into detailed structures. Kithri stared open-mouthed at the outskirts of a gigantic crystalline city which dominated the center of the ocean. Much of it lay underwater, visible only as masses of glittering peaks interspersed with darker areas of red-brown and muted green. Causeways and platforms jutted skyward, spires and towers spaced by avenues, broad enough for the free circulation of water. Gastropoids dove through the waves, sleek and round, their heads emerging here and there to dot the surface like a constellation of pearly beads.

"Tell me I'm not seeing this," Lennart murmured.

"It's so *big*," said Brianna in a high, breathy voice. "How do they deal with tidal currents?"

Kithri's heart seemed to have crawled into her throat. She could barely breathe, let alone speak. Her longing for Albion's beauty seemed no more than a mistaken hunger, when before her lay a feast. It was not her world, not her city, or even one that her kind might build. Yet something stirred deep within her, a longing which had been buried all those years beneath Stayman's dust. She'd wept at the vision of the crystalline ships smashed into dust. Now she could not bear to think what might happen to this city.

They arrived at an elaborate complex built above the water, a pavilion of soaring buttresses and wide horizontal panels of transparent lace. Here Raerquel brought their transport to a halt. They climbed the ramp to the wide central stage, where a small group of gastropoids waited. Others moved into position around the perimeter of the platform, encircling them, while below the water teemed with silver bodies.

Sunlight filtered through the crisscrossed filigree of the high arched dome and dappled the glassy floor beneath Kithri's feet. A breeze whispered through the open walls, bringing her the tang of seawater.

Five massive gastropoids sat in a semicircle. Kithri recognized one from the laboratory examining committee, the one on the far left with the iron-gray sheen to its head disks and the neck slits in an inverted chevron pattern.

After cautioning the humans to remain together and to speak only when requested, Raerquel pointed to each gastropoid and named it. "There is Fillo-'hip, leader-elect of the Council . . . Shuwash from the mountain cities, Nadilith . . . Ru-elliven of the scientific committee . . . and Eatonne."

As Raerquel spoke, ripples of brightness flowed over the latticework of the platform's walls. Kithri craned her neck to watch the patterns of light flare up and then dim as Raerquel finished. The panels should be visible for miles on a day as fair as this one.

Its introductions finished, Raerquel undulated forward. "Esteemed Council-of-Ocean and others," it gestured with one constantly moving tentacle toward the gastropoids floating in the waters outside. "I present to you a scientific marvel—intelligent mammalians."

"Whether these creatures are a *marvel* is remaining to be demonstrated," said the gastropoid Raerquel had named as Fillo-'hip, overriding the murmured reaction from the crowd below. It was a massive creature, easily the largest Kithri had yet seen. She found herself distrusting it intensely. The arrangement of its neck slits resembled sand-hen scratchings, and the motion of its lower appendages, so different from the flowing gestures of Raerquel, made her think of writhing worms.

"We have studied your reports and the evaluation of the scientific review committee," Fillo-'hip continued. "In these, we find more questions than answers. We are here to find those answers, not to stare like witless hatchlings at your prize exhibits. What secrets have you been witholding from us, Raerquel? There must be an extraterrestrial origin for these creatures, yet your findings indicate the craft in which they were found is inadequate to the depths of space. Where is the explanation for this matter?"

"The discovery of another habitable world, one adaptable to our colonization, would be greatly altering the balance of interplanetary power," added another gastropoid.

"Perhaps Scientist Raerquel has failed in rigorous pursuing of this information for reasons having to do with the *political* consequences."

Kithri wasn't sure which gastropoid had uttered this last statement. Some quality of the open space played havoc with her sense of sound direction. She scanned the neck sections of the Council before her, searching for any hint of motion.

"No conclusive proof of the origins of these humans is yet available," Raerquel answered temperately. "The artifacts accompanying their sudden appearance are currently undergoing analysis. Ghembaya and others have speculated that, had invertebrates not dominated the evolution of life here on Planet-of-Home, some other group—perhaps vertebrate—*perhaps mammalian*—might have developed intelligence. This is what makes these creatures so miraculous! Listen to them and judge for yourselves if such an evolutionary development has not already occurred, on a world which is separated from ours not by space but by probability. A world in which the unfolding of life has taken this fascinating divergence!"

Raerquel pointed one graceful tentacle at Eril, who stepped forward. The Council came to a sudden halt, upper tentacles extended like frozen feathers. Kithri, standing behind Eril, saw him square his shoulders. A few of the Council members rumbled ominously. For a moment, she feared he wouldn't be allowed to speak. Then they quieted, a semicircle of fleshy gray monoliths, their expressions utterly unreadable.

One of them said, "This is irrelevant to the central point under discussion—the true motivations behind Scientist Raerquel's treasonous opinions."

"Let us at least hear this argument," replied another. "We would not have it said we gave Raerquel no opportunity to present its . . . evidence."

# Chapter 24

Eril stood quietly, hands at his sides, facing the semicircle of giant silvery bodies. He took a deep breath, his shoulders rising and falling. Then he began to speak. "We greet you in peace and friendship," he said. At his words, brightness shot through the platform wall panels, leaping with energy. "We represent two starfaring empires, the Fifth Federation and the—er, Dominion. We welcome you with open—er, with eagerness. In all our settled worlds, we have never encountered intelligent life like yours. You are unique, and we would like to have you as friends and . . . allies."

*It could be worse,* Kithri thought, even if he did sound like a pompous diplomatic ass. He was doing a whole lot better than she would have in his position. And it couldn't be easy for him, knowing how much rode on his words. Sweat plastered his black hair to his neck and tension roughened his voice. Despite this, he held himself erect and graceful. The wall lattices danced with light in response to his words.

As Eril spoke, the giant molluscans of the Council began slowly shifting their positions. At first, they swayed from side to side as if they were restless or bored with his speech. Then Kithri realized that they were actually creeping across the platform, back and forth in a complicated weaving pattern. No matter how she tried to concentrate on Eril, her eyes were drawn to them. As they moved, the rhythm of their rocking became more apparent and more disturbing. She caught a faint, hypnotic pulsation of light in their bodies.

*I'm seeing things. That must be it.*

"Raerquel told the truth," Eril went on. "We did *not* travel here across space. You already know our 'jet is capable of surface transportation only. We came here across a time-space discontinuity, but the planet we left is a desert, no more than a minor outpost of the Federation. There's no indigenous intelligent life, no cities—just a few settlements around the spaceport. Brianna's world, where the—where history diverged from ours, is green and fertile like this one, but there's forest here instead of ocean, and our city—" he pointed back toward the shore, "—is a single, brightly-colored ruin."

*Don't posture, Eril, they'll think it's a made up speech you learned from Raerquel.* Kithri fought against the dawning certainty that the hearing was merely a formality, like the grant applications her father said would never be seriously considered. The damned slugs kept moving around, as if they were engaged in a ritual dance. For god's sake, weren't they even *listening?*

"We are convinced these two worlds represent divergent possibilities, of which yours is the precursor," Eril struggled on. "My world may well be the future in which your civilization destroys itself. In

Brianna's, some other catastrophe might occur, one which turns this ocean into a forest floor."

He took another deep breath, as if gathering himself. "Scientist Raerquel told us you're on the brink of an interstellar war. If this actually happens—and either of our worlds are the consequence—"

"Dangerous it is to be listening to this primitive vertebrate performance!" Ru-elliven interrupted. "As dangerous as giving credence to the heresies of NewHome and Tomorrow. I warn you, once we allow it, then our own thoughts will become polluted beyond repair!"

During Eril's speech, the gastropoids had intensified their bodily pulsations. The reflections glinting off their silvery skins now made Kithri disoriented and nauseated, much as the light displays in the laboratory had. During the moment of silence that followed Ru-elliven's outburst, she glanced up at the glittering towers. Something flooded up behind her eyes, the same something which had roused at the sight of the crystalline ships. She saw the sky darken to the emptiness of space. The spires and towers fractured into a million bits, scintillating in the light of a massive fireball. Wild, anguished wailing lanced through her mind—a name she did not recognize—and then she was staring at the intact lacework panels as another gastropoid voice boomed out.

"—Scientist Raerquel's sympathy with the NewHome degenerates is clearly stemming from its perverted fascination with subsentient animals—"

Brianna pushed forward, jerking away from Lennart's restraining hand. Crimson had risen to her cheeks, leaving the rest of her face waxen pale by comparison.

"You cannot dismiss us like this!" she said. "I am not some degenerate animal, I am a trained scientist! I don't give an *untranslatable* about your adolescent politics. My sole loyalty is to the truth. If you only let us, we can—we *will*—demonstrate all the attributes of a civilized species. Language. Abstract symbology. Time-binding. Complex social interactions. The ability to modify our natural environment."

She calmed down as she went on, sounding less irate and more rational. Her face regained its natural color. "Even if you reject our oral arguments, you must still consider the evidence of our vehicle. My people have colonized fifty planetary systems to your three, and studied a hundred more. How can you possibly deny our technological achievements?"

"If this is true, the creatures are deserving a deeper investigation," said one gastropoid. Nadilith, maybe.

*It actually paid attention to what she said,* Kithri realized. *Maybe there's some hope here after all.*

"Association is not proving origination!" Ru-elliven insisted, barely pausing in its undulating movement. Its resonant voice filled the platform space.

"Then where did they come from?" Nadilith said. "Not from Planet-of-Home, or they would have been discovered centuries ago."

"It does not matter where they are coming from! What matters is Raerquel's attempt to brainwash this Council using pseudo-scientific trickery!" Ru-elliven said. "You have all received my committee's report."

"Your committee," Raerquel interrupted, "is having its collective cerebral ganglia embedded in fixative before consideration of actual data. If I were to train mammalians to mimic the characteristics of personness, surely I would choose some less preposterous history for them."

Raerquel shuffled forward into the open space between the Council members. "Set aside what you think of my political affiliations. They are not the issue. Look at these creatures! They are mammalians, true, but highly evolved, gifted with conscience and awarenesses that rival our own. Forget their outlandish skeletal shapes and trichotiferous integuments. Listen to the *meaning* of their words, the universality of—"

"This Council is already sufficiently acquainted with your delusions!" bellowed out another voice. "Too long have we tolerated Raerquel's dissident political views and unnatural dabblings with lower life forms, for the sake of its honorable Clan." This was Eatonne, Kithri was sure, standing just to the right of the giant Fillo-'hip. "Many warnings we have given you of the dangers of deviant social thought."

"Thought of choice is the right of all persons, regardless of Clan or rank!" Raerquel rumbled, withdrawing from the eye of the circle. "It is unethical to conduct scientific investigation to the bigotry of molluscan superior-morality!"

Fillo-'hip undulated forward, still keeping well within the group's subtly circling pattern. "This is not a simple matter of thought freedom, but the derangement of a once brilliant scientist."

Another gastropoid spoke. "Unusual researches can be tolerated only so long as the behavior of the investigating scientist remains within proper ethical boundaries. Now, with regret, this Council has discovered positive proof of the criminal actions of Raerquel Hath'djan."

"Neither this Council nor anyone else can be discovering what is not existing!" thundered Raerquel.

"Evidence will be presented at your trial," said Ruelliven.

"*Trial!* On what charge?"

"Mental contamination," answered Fillo-'hip. "I am sorry of this necessity, my old colleague, but the second and more serious charge is *treason*."

Raerquel humped forward, then drew itself up to a tower of silver flesh. "Injustice! This opposition to my mammalian experiments is merely a ruse to silence my attempts to achieve peace with our offspring planets!"

The gastropoids had extended the range of their movements so they almost surrounded Raerquel and the humans. The pulsation of their bodies grew brighter, echoed and intensified by reflections from the wall panels. The rhythms built like a sea-storm. Kithri felt herself drowning in it, dissolving, breaking into a thousand helpless pieces. The individual patterns of light blended, merging into a single, battering wave and there was no way she could stand against it. The air in her lungs became thick and impenetrable, the dappled sunlight on her shoulders ice-edged.

Raerquel stood in front of her, erect and immobile, a pillar of defiance. Kithri kept her eyes locked on Eril's steel-straight back and tried to keep breathing.

The Council halted abruptly in its circling movements. Every second or third gastropoid from the perimeter of the platform slithered forward. The four humans and their scientist ally were completely encircled.

Kithri drew in her breath, mentally cursing herself

for not having seen this development earlier. No matter what Brianna said, the Council clearly considered them as Raerquel's *specimens*—or, worse yet, evidence of its treachery. And evidence would be disposable once a verdict was rendered.

"You will now be surrendering yourself and your specimens pending your trial," said Fillo-'hip.

The gastropoids began closing in, and the mindless revulsion Kithri had first felt at Raerquel's first approach returned in full force. Whatever happened, she did *not* want those things touching her.

"Do not be provoking retaliation by assaultive behavior," Raerquel said.

"Tell that to *them,*" Eril muttered.

The circle of gastropoids grew tighter. "Control your research animals, Raerquel Hath'djan!" Shuwash called out.

"Scientist Raerquel," said a calmer voice, the gastropoid to the far right. "If you cooperate with us, we are prepared to suspend the usual procedure of euthanasia for dangerous specimens, pending your trial. If not, you will be endangering their lives as well as your own legal defense. They themselves will confirm the charges that they led you into violent anti-civilized actions."

Kithri felt something snap inside her, like a rupturing balloon. It was the pirates all over again, only this time she had no promises of jaydium to throw at them. Here they were, in the middle of the ocean, surrounded by hostile slugs. But she couldn't just sit there and let herself be taken prisoner. Every second she delayed, she lost more options.

She darted forward, hoping that a quick shove would be enough to unbalance the nearest gastropoid. Then to hustle Raerquel down to the transport platform and run for it—

A faint hissing sound was all the warning she got. The two closest gastropoids uncoiled their appendages so quickly that all she saw was a blur between the feathered tips. Jets of clear liquid shot out from those delicate strands with such force they crisscrossed over her head. A moment later, the stuff thickened, falling across her like a net. Its first touch was icy cold before the heat of her body warmed it. Then she was held fast, like an insect in an arachnid's web.

The net hardened instantly. Kithri thrust against it with the full power of her shoulders and thighs, toughened by her years in the jaydium tunnels. There was no give in the net and no way to gain leverage against any individual threads. Only the gentle draping around her torso gave her enough space to breathe.

"You are not helping by generating antagonism," pleaded Raerquel. "The best chance for all is convincing the Council of your capacity for personness, even as I was convinced."

With a sense of blissful relief, Kithri felt the strands around her soften. They did not fall away entirely, but relaxed enough to permit her slow movement. When she pushed against them with more than the lightest force, they instantly became rigid again. She turned around to see the others. They, too, were caught in webs of gleaming crystal, no more able to move than she was. Eril met her eyes, but she read no censure in them. As for Raerquel, it had disappeared in the crowd of rounded silvery bodies.

# Chapter 25

After their capture, the four humans were half-pushed, half-carried to a small satellite platform. This was no more than a cell surrounded by featureless translucent walls, unbroken by door or window. Above, far beyond their reach, a filigree canopy admitted splotches of brilliant sunlight. Here the restraining webs were removed, melting at a touch from their captors' tentacles, and they were left alone.

"We have a proverb to describe situations like this," Brianna said, wringing her hands and moving restlessly back and forth. "We say, 'From the cookpot down the gullet.' An inelegant expression, true, but at this moment I feel much like the food animals it refers to."

Kithri leaned against one wall, watching the other woman. Her body tingled with the aftereffects of adrenaline, her arms and thighs smarted where the restraining webs had cut deep into her skin, and she wished Brianna would settle down and stop fussing. Sometimes Brianna made her itch all over.

"We're not the issue here," Lennart said tightly. He sat with his back against the opposite wall, elbows resting on his bent knees. "The Council had it in for

Raerquel, and not just because of its *scientific* interests. They're out to get it discredited any way they can. We just gave them a convenient excuse."

"You're right," said Eril, standing beside him. "They'll take anything we say as proof of Raerquel's guilt. They don't give a comet's fart what happens to us. Next time, they'll just wipe us. Until now, I just . . . I didn't see how easy that would be."

"That's what I thought, too," Kithri said, "or I wouldn't have tried that stupid stunt." She wondered what had happened to Raerquel, whether it was confined separately or still being interrogated by the Council . . . or already tried and executed?

*Why should I care what happens to the damned slug? It was Raerquel's peace schemes that got us in this fix!*

"Kithri, we were *all* jetted up for a fight," Eril said. "It could have been any one of us to make the first move."

"But it wasn't, was it?" she snapped. "The rest of you had the sense to stay put." She took a step toward him, jabbing one thumb against her chest. "*I* was the one who almost got us killed!"

"They were just using us to get at Raerquel," Lennart said. "And they didn't kill us offhand, the way they threatened to. Don't be so hard on yourself. Maybe what you did saved us, after all."

"If we could get them to just *listen* to us," said Brianna. "Let us *demonstrate* that we're civilized."

"They'd never give us the chance, just like Eril said," Kithri said. "You heard the Council. They think we're disgusting lower life-forms—*unevolved,* they said. If Raerquel's convicted, what do you think's going to happen to us? Goddamned slugs."

"Not slugs, *gastropoids,*" said Brianna. "Just because

evolution took a different path on their world, allowing molluscans to progress to sapience, while vertebrates remained largely instinctive—"

"Just *stop* it, would you?" Lennart said. "This is no time for a lecture."

"I disagree with you," Brianna shot back. "This is *exactly* the time for rational analysis. All you people think about is rushing from one avoidable predicament to the next. Use your brains for once, instead of your primitive hormones! We need to *understand* what's going on here!"

"If that Council is typical of the powers-that-be here, we're in one hell of a jam," said Eril. "I've heard that sort of posturing before, from the mouths of generals. 'Deterring escalation'—that's just a polite way of saying 'Bomb the blazes out of the other guy before he does it to you.' And we're the ones who'll be caught in the middle."

Kithri shivered despite the sunlight dappling through the overhead canopy. *Caught in the middle*—just as Stayman had been. Just as Albion had been.

"Raerquel's been our advocate so far," Brianna continued, undaunted. "But who knows how much longer that will be the case? It's no different from the others, it's only using us for its own purposes. While we may admire its pacifist goals, we still have our own survival to consider. Furthermore, as a scientist, I must avoid even the appearance of involvement in local politics. We know so little of this culture, how can we accurately evaluate what's going on? By accepting Raerquel's unsubstantiated statements? By imposing our own anthropocentric standards? In my professional opinion, our first objective must be to establish our legitimacy with the Council, with the rights and protections of citizenship. Then we can—"

"Let Raerquel just go hang?" Kithri looked up, stung.

Lennart shook his head. "Pinning our hopes on Council is a dumb idea. They wouldn't give us the time of day if we stood on our heads and asked pretty-please."

"We have only Raerquel's word on that, just as the supposition that war is imminent," Brianna countered. "It could have exaggerated the situation for its own purposes and manipulated us into acting as its advocates. May I remind you that it stands charged with *mental contamination*."

"You're as bad as the Council!" Lennart snapped.

Brianna whirled round, her face flushed, and for the first time Kithri saw her as less than beautiful. "So what do *you* suggest we do, throw our lot in with the Master of the Hopeless Cause?"

"At least it's trying to do something," Lennart replied. He got to his feet, looking as if he'd like to punch her. "Maybe it is hopeless, maybe we're all destined to be blown to smithereens, if we aren't chopped into little pieces first. Like they say, war is a whole lot harder to stop than to start. But I'll tell you one thing, lady, and that's if we don't give it our best try, we'll never find out otherwise."

Brianna drew herself up, still inches shorter than him. Her lips tightened into a thin line and her brows drew together. She looked like she was about to spit in his face. Kithri's shoulders tensed in anticipation, but Eril stepped smoothly between them.

"All right, you two," he commanded. "The best

thing either of you could say right now is nothing. Got that?"

"I—" Brianna began, her chin still at an ominous angle.

*"Nothing."* Eril repeated.

Lennart nodded and headed for the farthest corner, covering the distance in a stride and a half. He took a wide stance, facing the wall, and raised his hands to chest height. Slowly he began circling his hands, as if on an invisible table, his eyes half-closed, breathing deep and even. Brianna, watching him, wrung her hands and looked as if she were going to speak again, but managed not to.

Kithri shook her shoulders, trying to loosen them, but it was no good. Her heart pounded as if she'd been on the brink of a fight herself, her veins flooded with adrenaline and muscles battle-ready. She threw herself into the nearest empty corner to think.

Brianna had really gotten her hackles up, more thoroughly than Kithri would have imagined, and that disturbed her. Skies, she didn't even like the other woman, why should she care *what* she said?

Kithri's thoughts stumbled on. She'd always felt war was morally objectionable, but was she really any different from Brianna, who didn't care who got dumped on as long as *she* didn't? Since Kithri had been, through no fault of her own, at the bottom of the Federation social pile, she was also the first to be exploited, the first forgotten. By sheer fortune she was not also the first bombed, although that was only because of the Fed's need to protect its precious jaydium supply.

If she could have stayed, or done something, and Albion had been spared. . . .

*But I couldn't! I had no choice, I was only a child! If Father hadn't taken us away, we'd be cinders now, too.*

*If Father hadn't left. . . .*

Why had he left Albion, and gone to Stayman—bleak, heavily guarded, and out of the war zone? He was a scientist, intelligent and well-educated—he must have seen the war coming. What he'd done about it was run for the safest corner he could find, taking his only child. Kithri trembled inside, thinking, *Did he really want to fight, but was forced to run because of me?* She searched her memory for words like, *Maybe some day you'll understand* . . . but could find nothing clear, only his voice as he taught her to survive on Stayman. Only the pain and loneliness afterward. But had he really had a choice? Could he have stayed on Albion and worked for peace? Would anything he did have made a difference?

*Would anything I do now make a difference?*

Kithri ran her hands over her face, feeling her cheeks hot and dry, as if they burned with a sudden fever. Her mouth dried up like the Cerrano dust.

Without thinking what she was doing, she got to her feet. Her knees felt like powder and her stomach knotted into a lump. She took a step toward the center of the platform. Eril, leaning against the far corner, met her eyes, and she remembered how she'd locked on to his face in the pirates' courtyard. She looked away, for a moment terrified that her resolve would shatter and she'd go running to him.

Brianna was sitting along the opposite wall, playing with something in her lap. She'd teased loose a few strands of her gold-wire hair and was knotting them in an intricate pattern. She didn't look up at Kithri's approach. Lennart did, mildly interested, without Eril's sharp focus.

"I think—" Kithri's voice wavered. "—I think we should do what we can to help Raerquel. *Whatever we can.* Even if it means throwing in our lot with a bunch of losers."

Brianna tossed her head, puffing her hair into a golden froth. "That won't do us any good. Raerquel's a powerless dissident, an eccentric."

"We're going to die anyway, all of us. You think your little studies of alien architecture are going to save this planet?"

Brianna offered no reply. Kithri looked at the woman and two men who had, in a few days, gone from strangers to people she'd die for. She had no strength to argue with them. She barely had enough for herself. All her instincts, all her experience urged her to keep silent, to stay out of it. There might be nothing she could do, or she might die anyway. She thought again of her father, wrestling alone with his own choices, his own unknown future. How much more difficult it must have been for him with a child, perhaps already knowing he was dying. All these years she'd blamed him for being a coward because he'd run away.

"You do whatever you want," she said, closing the door on everything that had gone before in her life. "Me, I'm going to go out fighting for something besides my own skin."

## Chapter 26

Dawn came and the crystalline walls glowed with a faint iridescent sheen. Eril couldn't remember falling asleep, just lying there, staring at the expanse of featureless luminescent gray. Wishing he could see the stars. Feeling the emptiness inside him. The not-caring that made his promises empty syllables and turned his life into one long bid for escape. He was human, he told himself, not hollow. He cared—about the Fed, about Raerquel and the future of its world. Yet something had gone out of him even before he jetted down to Port Ludlow in search of the brushie *duo*pilot who was his only hope. Maybe in the bars and alleys of New Paris, one crazy scrape after another. Maybe as far back as Albion.

*Albion.*

Eril winced at the memory. Compared to Kithri, he'd lost nothing there.

He sat up, his hip and shoulder bones aching. When he reached his arms above his head and stretched, his spine popped. Next to him, close enough so she could easily have touched him in her sleep, Kithri lay curled on one side. In the far corner, Brianna had tucked up in a fetal ball, her back to the others. Lennart sat and stared blankly ahead, his legs folded in a complicated and uncomfortable-looking arrangement. His hands lay open, palms up, on his knees.

Eril clambered to his feet and continued his stretching. Even making allowances for the unforgiving sleeping surface, he felt stiff. He didn't like the thought of getting old. But at the rate they were going, they would none of them live that long.

*None of us,* he repeated to himself. *Not just me, none of us.*

A door opened in the wall and one of their unknown captors sat outside, ready to escort them singly to a newly sculpted sanitary facility in an adjacent portion of the holding platform. When they'd all made the requisite trip and an attempt at morning greetings to one another, the door opened again and Raerquel slithered in.

"Come, my human friends," it said with its usual graceful gestures. "We must return to the laboratory to prepare my defense."

"I thought we were just laboratory specimens, impounded ones at that," Eril said. "And now they're just going to let us go? What's happened, have they dropped the charges?"

"Make no mistake, the charges are very serious and in no fashion dismissed," Raerquel replied. "It is for this purpose that I am allowed to utilize all my resources. You are the crux of my argument of alien personness."

"Wait a second!" Eril held up both hands. "You've been charged with mental contamination for just associating with us. And now you say you're going to use us as part of your defense?"

"Of course." The alien paused. "How else would its validity be evaluated?"

"What a fascinating cultural—" Brianna began before Eril cut her off.

"Run first and talk later—before the Council changes its collective mind," he said, and shoved Brianna out the doorway after Kithri.

The whole trip back, Eril expected something to go wrong. In the city, he waited for silvery bodies to surround them, spewing forth liquid chains. Over the ocean, he watched for signs of pursuit. Maybe letting them go was all a ruse, so they could be killed "accidentally" while being recaptured.

Despite the empty expanse of sky, the gentle sunlight and breezes, Eril couldn't stop worrying. If something went wrong, he didn't know if he could pilot the platform. And if he, with his experience and training couldn't do it, he didn't trust any of the others to, not even Kithri. The only good escape route was one he found for himself . . . wasn't it?

Raerquel, on the other hand, had been expansive, almost ebullient, from the moment they moved out of range of the mass-communication panels. As they flew westward, it pointed out the various divisions of the city—the shallow living areas, the vertical food-growing corridors and deep-water nurseries, divided into areas for each clan.

Gastropoid fertilization, Raerquel told them, took place in the deepest trenches of the ocean, since the ciliated trochophore larvae required the high pressures of the depths. Comparatively few survived the larval stage. Some fell prey to genetic or developmental defects, others were eaten by predators or couldn't compete for the limited supplies of food and oxygen. All lived and suffered in the same anonymous preconsciousness. Only when the metamorphosis was complete and they made their way to the shallows were their nervous systems capable of self-awareness, let alone thought.

Eril, listening to Raerquel's crisply scientific description of the process, contrasted the whole arrangement to his own family. Raerquel would have dozens of siblings instead of a single bossy sister. A large part of its family loyalty would come from what was loosely called "survivor solidarity." Eril had seen this bonding in battle, the intense comradeship which pulled him and his crew through more than one hopeless situation during the war. But eventually they'd be reassigned to different missions, die or retire or get promoted. Eril never let himself get too dependent on the others, not when they might be blown to bits or off to Hyades when he really needed them. Your best ally in a jam was always yourself.

Not so with these gastropoids. Their earliest consciousness would have been of their unity as they burst upward into the light. Having survived the same brutal beginnings, it was no wonder they regarded everyone else as potentially hostile. As rational beings, they could extend that concept of "us" to the other generations of their clan, and with trepidation to other clans which had shared their birthplace. But to other creatures, no matter how phylogenically related, which didn't even come from the same water. . . .

In his musings, Eril had missed a beat of the conversation. Raerquel had left the subject of reproduction for a description of its peace faction. Eril had heard self-styled "peacemakers" before, but usually what they wanted was really a tactical advantage—"Don't bash us before we get so far ahead that we can bash you harder" or some version of, "Peace only on our terms."

But Raerquel didn't care what it gave up—its scientific career, the status of its clan, its adult alliances—everything but the truth, the basic unity of the gastropoid race. It spoke of compassion being the true test of self worth, that any injury done to another sensible creature was an irreparable loss to the offender.

*If the Fed leaders had such single-mindedness and dedication,* Eril wondered, *would we have ended up in splinters, held together by luck and hope?*

"All that sounds great," Lennart said when there was a pause in the oration. "But we humans had the same ideals, and look what happened to us."

"Your time remained peaceful," replied Raerquel.

"Yeah, but *theirs* didn't." He nodded at Eril. "They forgot everything we'd learned about peace."

Raerquel, with one of its characteristically fluid tentacle gestures, said, "Every day in which the bombs are not loosed is another day in which we can learn to avoid that catastrophe. Are you asserting that just because a thing has never been done that it is impossible? I cannot believe that of beings like yourselves, who have journeyed through the interdimensional nothingness of our possible future. Are we such hopelessly backward creatures that we cannot be learning from your example to dare something new? Are not your years of peace an accomplishment worthy of emulation?"

"You're right," Kithri said passionately. "We want to help, to do whatever we can to stop this war."

"Are you all crazy?" Brianna asked. Her voice was thin and reedy, strained to the edge. She held onto the low railing with white-knuckled hands. "Or is this some new melodrama-entertainment I've stumbled into? There's nothing we *can* do except get ourselves killed first."

"Is that what you believe in your Dominion?" Lennart said. "Then you're even more primitive than we were."

"What would our dying accomplish?" she retorted. "Even if we could act effectively, we'd be interfering with a culture we don't even understand yet. Callous as it sounds, we *must* allow the gastropoids to solve their own problems. It's the only ethical position available to us."

By this time they'd left the city proper and were now flying over the pleasantly warm ocean. The blue-gray water slipped along beneath the speeding platform. Eril took his eyes from the first shadowy lines of the coast and turned back to Raerquel.

During the first days of their captivity, Raerquel and its team had refused to answer even the simplest questions. They'd been almost paranoid about avoiding 'cultural contamination'—or even its outward appearance. Yet now the gastropoid was talking freely, almost eagerly. It had gone out of its way to show them the nurseries, surely the most sensitive and vulnerable areas of the city. The description of the gastropoids' life there explained much about their psychology, their inbred xenophobia. But why was Raerquel telling them all this now? What was behind this change of heart? Had it decided that since the humans were expendable, it could perform any sort of bizarre sociological experiment on them?

"There is no discrepancy," Raerquel replied tranquilly. "Whether or not you have true, independently-developed intelligence or are merely mimicking what you have seen is no longer the point in question. Now, with these charges of mental contamination as the basis for treason, the greater the commonality of your behavior and gastropoid values, the stronger our case."

"That must be a world record about-face," Lennart said wryly.

"What good will that do?" Eril asked Raerquel. "The Council isn't going to judge *your* guilt or innocence by how indoctrinated *we* are."

"Some of your Council members wouldn't believe us if we quoted cosmic constants at them," Lennart added.

"For my experiment to succeed, any insight into the principles of gastropoid civilization which I can be demonstrating in you will be of immense value. I am now attempting to answer all your previous questions."

"Why?" Eril said.

"Council-of-Ocean is expecting my defense to be a complete denial of the treason charges. That way, even if they acquit me, they can use my words to discredit the cause of peace. They can say, 'See, even Raerquel Hath'djan denies opposing our firm handling of offspring planets!' Even if I am convicted, this must not happen."

"What are you going to do?" Kithri asked.

"Agree with the charges."

"What! And let them execute you?"

"I am not intending to sacrifice myself needlessly," the gastropoid replied. "I am placing my faith in the inherent desire of the Council members for peace and understanding. I will say to them, 'Yes, Raerquel is agitating for peace, but with understanding comes fellowship, and then peace cannot be treason.' "

"That's just so many words," Lennart said dispiritedly. "If they didn't believe you then, why would they now?"

"Maybe there's a way to convince them *without* words," said Kithri.

Eril felt suddenly cold. He didn't like the tone of her voice or the set of her chin.

"What do you mean, *without words*?" Lennart asked.

"In my 'jet there's a device—the encephalosynchron," she said slowly, looking steadily at Raerquel. "We use it in *duo*flight to link the pilots' minds to shipbrain. That's a computing device like an artificial mind. It—"

"Hold it!" Eril interrupted. "We're talking about a third-class scrubjet here, not a psionics lab."

"But maybe we could adapt it for gastropoid brains, hook two of them up together. There's no way they could posture around then. They'd share each other's thoughts—they'd *know* how alike they are. Don't you see? This might change *everything* for them!"

"You have a device which is permitting speaking like this—mind to mind?" Raerquel asked.

Kithri said "Yes!" and Eril said "No!" at the same time.

"Of course!" Brianna exclaimed. "Computer-mediated telepathy!"

"My human-friends," said Raerquel, curling and uncurling its upper tentacles rapidly, "if this could be possible—to tie the minds of our Planetary and offspring leaders in this way—we could be resolving our differences without prejudice or misunderstanding. All would be agreeing on the necessity for peace. We would swim through one water, be illuminated by one light. War—war would become unthinkable. This can be done, this linking of minds?"

"I don't know," Kithri said. "It's just an idea. We'd have to modify the apparatus, reroute the morphoplex lines, maybe reprogram some of shipbrain. But we have to try."

Eril realized she might actually be serious. "The *duo*apparatus wasn't meant for telepathy," he said uneasily. "And that's assuming you can modify it for whatever kind of brains Raerquel's people have. They're not even in the same phylum as us—there's not a comet's chance in hell you'll find enough similarity to know where to start!"

They had now come to the first of the low hills separating the shoreline from the inland city. The platform rose in gentle waves over the lumps of land and Eril's body swayed with it. Sunlight gleamed on the dent in Kithri's nose.

"*I* know that!" she said. "*You* know that! But don't deprive these people of hope just because *they* don't know that!"

"Even if it were possible to modify the equipment, we'd have to test it on a human-to-gastropoid link first," Eril said, trying to sound calm and rational. "Who's going to be the experimental volunteer, *you*?"

"Damn right! Who else is qualified to test it? It's my apparatus, my brain."

"Your brain which gets fried! Kithri, I won't let you do it!"

"*You* won't!" she flamed at him. "What makes you think you have anything to say about how I risk my dustball brain?"

"It's completely unreasonable!" The proposal wasn't unreasonable, and he knew it. It was foolhardy and hazardous, but not unreasonable. What *was* unreasonable was how horrified he was at Kithri participating in it, how desperately he wanted not to lose her.

"So what is reasonable about *anything* that's happened to us?" she said. "Lennart popping out of thin space, the Cerrano Plain turning into a goddamned forest, Brianna's city—and now this! *This* is reasonable?"

"Will you stop it!" Brianna screamed. "Here we are on the brink of annihilation, and you two start a lovers' quarrel! Eril, the least you can do is help Kithri make the equipment work safely."

"I thought you were against our interfering in the gastropoids' affairs," Eril retorted. "Let them work out their own destiny, you said."

"I was! I still am. But improving their communications is *not* the same as dictating our own solutions to their problems. It might even enhance their own cultural processes. And besides, I didn't say I agreed. I don't know enough about it to have formed an opinion. I *said* that if you were determined to engage in the experiment at all, you ought to do it properly."

Lennart, still pale and quiet, added, "As has been said before under slightly different circumstances, we haven't got anything to lose, heyh?"

"It's a stupid, comet-crazy thing to try," Kithri said in a quiet, intense voice. "Nine chances out of ten it won't work at all. Or else it will, as you put it, fry my brain. Probably along with whichever leader is wired up to me, which will start the war for sure. But we've got to do *something,* and I don't see any other possibilities."

They were right, all of them, damn them. He understood, he just didn't like the feel of the whole thing.

Kithri shifted on the platform so she was facing him, almost brushing against him. Eril realized how rarely she ever touched anyone and when she did, it was deliberate and controlled. All except for that time after their first *duo* flight when something had broken loose inside her.

Behind her, the waves slipped by in hypnotic rhythm. Eril noticed them only peripherally. Her eyes were huge and dark, bruised-looking in the shadows of her lashes.

"In case it hadn't occurred to you," she said, "I can't rewire the damned thing by myself. You're the only other person who knows anything about the *duo* apparatus. I . . . *need* you. Or are you just pissed," she added savagely, "because you didn't think of it first?"

Shaken, Eril turned away, eyes blindly scanning the horizon. Her words stung as if she'd physically struck him. Thoughts rushed through his mind like poisoned memories.

*Whenever there's trouble, you never let anyone else make decisions for you. You live—or die—by your own mistakes. The only good escape route was one you found for yourself.*

No wonder he couldn't find a *duo* partner for Eades's Courier Corps. It was the pattern of his whole life, depending on himself and no one else, because every time he did. . . .

Sun and sky reeled around him. The gently lapping waves roared in his ears and the warm air turned to the chill of space.

He depended on himself because he'd had to. First his father, then Weiram . . . gone in an instant. They might all be gone tomorrow, blown to powder in the gastropoids' war. Now he couldn't promise Kithri a damned thing. And anything he did to dissuade or protect her would only expose all of them to greater risk. If she could make a difference, then by all the powers of luck and space, so could he. He had to let her try.

# Chapter 27

The Clan Hath engineer-scientists had moved the scrubjet to a huge, airy dome on the western outskirts of the city. As soon as they arrived, Raerquel turned the entire laboratory over to Eril and Kithri. They spent the better part of a day planning the modifications. At first, Brianna hung over Eril's shoulder, scribbling notes on the seaweed-gelatin sheets the gastropoids supplied. By the time they were ready to begin, she'd gone off on her own to explore the rest of the Clan Hath enclave. Once it became apparent Lennart would be of little use, he, too, disappeared. Eril was too busy to wonder what he was up to.

What Kithri suggested, the adaptation of the *duo*apparatus for gastropoid usage, proved to be far from trivial. The shipbrain and its sophisticated connections to the guidance systems were not designed for easy access. Rather the reverse; they'd been shielded from both the insidious Cerrano dust and the prying of incompetent, perhaps drunken, fingers. Spacebound installations were scarcely better protected.

In order to expose the connections between shipbrain and the headsets, as well as the sensors and flight control, they'd have to cut through *Brushwacker*'s ceramometallic hull. They both knew, without having to say it aloud, that without elaborate resealing, it would no longer be safe at *duo* speeds.

Eril squelched an irrational desire to maintain the flightworthiness of the tiny ship. *If the planet's blown to powder, where could a scrubjet take us that would be safe? Besides, we're not doing this to save our own skins.*

The jaydium cutter was cool and light in Eril's hands. He paused before slicing through the smooth patina of *Brushwacker*'s skin. He glanced at Kithri, standing behind the stubby wings and holding several of the sculpted *therine* tools. She'd always acted so possessive about the 'jet, as if it were everything she owned. Skies, it *was* everything she owned. Yet now she said nothing, only watched with her mouth so tight it looked white. Without a word, she slid beneath the ship and began to work through the rear panel.

Breaching the ship's seals without destroying the complex machinery inside turned out to be even more tedious and demanding than Eril had imagined. If he'd had any inclination to become a mechanic, it quickly vanished. Burned fingertips, creaking knuckles, aching neck muscles and red, watering eyes seemed to be an intrinsic part of the job. He groaned inwardly at the prospect of the hours of work before they could begin recalibrating the circuitry for the gastropoid nervous system.

Finally his eyes refused to focus on anything closer than his foot. His fingers on the jaydium cutter felt as if they'd been fused into permanent claws. He shoved himself out from under the scrubjet's nose and clambered to his feet. Kithri swore as she banged her elbow against the cut-away wall.

"We both need a break," he said, rubbing his fingers. To his surprise, they straightened, although with protest. He shook his shoulders, trying to loosen them.

Kithri rolled out from under the ship and sat up. She muttered, "You can if you want to. I'll just check—"

"You'll do no such thing," he said irritably. "We're so tired neither of us can see straight. Do you want to risk frying Raerquel's brain because you were too stubborn to rest when you needed it?"

Kithri's chin shot upward but after a moment, she shook her head. Eril decided that was about the best response he could hope for. She'd clung to her decision to modify the 'jet, resisting any distraction or delay. In her place, he'd want it over with as soon as possible, too. He left her sitting in the shadow of the scrubjet. There was no use asking if she'd walk with him.

He found Lennart squatting on the marblelike slab that served as their doorstep.

"How goes it, captain?"

"It'll take a few days yet, assuming everything keeps going this well. It's all got to be checked and triple checked."

"I was wrong about you," Lennart said slowly. "What I said before the hearing . . ."

"We were all swiping at each other. You were just—"

"Shut up and let me apologize! I can't hold you accountable for the crazy things your Federation did, any more than I can blame Kithri—or Raerquel.

Even Bri, with all her academic bullshit, she'd stand on her head to save these folks. Protesting all the while that her only interest was as a scientist. Maybe in my time, it was people like you that kept us from destroying it all."

"Hey, don't go making me into a hero," Eril said with an embarrassed laugh. "I'm just your everyday fly-boy. I followed orders, I didn't make policy."

"Maybe things would've been better if you had . . . Like they say, the time to stop a war is before it starts. Meanwhile, how about a stroll?"

"Such as, where?"

"We-ell . . ." Lennart drawled as he started down the wide avenue. "I was down at the spaceport earlier, having a look inside those glass ships . . ."

"They let you in, feeling the way they do about us *lowly mammals?*"

Lennart grinned. "That was the easy part. I convinced the technicians it was on Raerquel's orders. Clan Hath carries a whole lot of clout here in the city, even if it doesn't with the Council."

He paused, any illusion of humor draining from his face, and looked eastward, toward the glittering heart of the city. "My next question was how similar they were to our own. Everything else in their technology involves sculpting *therine.*"

"Which we can't do," Eril said unnecessarily. Raerquel's assistants complained about having to manufacture 'nonchangeable' *therine* tools for him and Kithri.

"So I tuned my new friend Araf'ex to the idea of creating a gizmo that would do the 'fixing' for us. After all, they seem to understand the chemistry well enough." Lennart shrugged. "So far no luck, but I keep hoping."

"A thing like that might open all sorts of doors," Eril said. He thought a moment. "How much of the ship has to be sculpted?"

"Nothing which has to do with power or navigation or life support." Lennart added, with deceptive quietness, "It's my guess we could learn to fly the thing."

Eril felt a sudden rush of adrenaline, as if he'd slammed into an invisible wall. To have a ship again, a ship which could take them all to the stars . . . and safety. He could . . .

Let the slugs blow themselves up? When he could do something to stop it?

*I'm starting to sound just like Kithri.*

Lennart hadn't meant skipping out while there was still hope, either. He'd only taken the initiative to do what he could, instead of sitting around like a useless lump. And he'd done more than Eril would have guessed, getting them into the spaceport, on friendly terms with an engineer, inside a ship. Even if the 'fixing' tool wasn't forthcoming, they could still see the ships, touch them. There might be all manner of possibilities.

The ship rose above the cream-colored pavement like a crystalline teardrop, tapering gracefully from a narrow nose to rounded body. Although the skin appeared to be clear and layers of structure could be easily visualized, the walls distorted so much light that the interior was completely obscured.

Lennart climbed the ramp like a man in a dream. Eril, watching him obliquely, felt uneasy with the way he kept glancing up at the hazy blue skies. When Lennart touched the ship's gleaming surfaces, it was with the intensity of a man approaching some revered object. Or the way a drowning man might cling to a lifeline.

Eril found himself studying Lennart and thinking, in a manner so calculating it disturbed him, *How can I use this passion as a strength instead of a weakness?*

They were met at the top of the ramp by Araf'ex Hath-si'in, a combination maintenance technician and engineer. Lennart greeted it warmly, like an old friend. They followed it inside.

Instead of the usual human arrangement of ladders and catwalks, the ship was built around a system of tunnels connecting the various compartments. Shallow ledges permitted the molluscan crew to leverage themselves along in any direction, even vertically.

The silvery bulk of the engineer filled the tunnel as it undulated upward. Slowly, feeling for each hand and toe grip, Eril climbed after it.

*If it slips, it'll sweep both of us along with it and squash our* pitouchees *flatter than a scalebug. Hell, it's probably wondering how we manage to get around with all those bones in our bodies.*

They reached the control room. The gastropoid chatted volubly with them as it modified the support structures to comfortably seat their human bodies. As he listened, Eril scanned the instrument panels. He saw nothing he could recognize or even guess the function of. Behind them lay a broad sweep of window overlooking the spaceport. Eril could make out only the larger features, so badly did the thick, spaceworthy glass distort the images. All he saw were masses of muted shades of gray and white beneath a swath of blue.

"Raw *therine,* such as used in buildings, is possessing relatively unspecialized optical and tensile properties," Araf'ex said. It sounded very much like Eril's chemistry instructor at the Academy. The man had a tendency to lapse into professorial oration in the middle of an ordinary conversation, but there were such gems to be gleaned from it—such as the contents of the next examination—that Eril had never minded. He did not mind now.

"Sculpted *therine,* on the other hand, is modified by the physiological signature of the individual secretor, resulting in reduced sensitivity to any other person, unless the object is 'fixed.' Fixture is thus a process of *removing* personal biochemical differences. Precision tools are usually 'fixed' to prevent individual variations."

"That's the process we call standardization." Eril hoped that what he'd understood was indeed what the gastropoid engineer intended. "You'd want to sculpt your own crash seats because they're more closely attuned to your own personal physiology. But tools which others use would need to be 'fixed' for less variability."

"That is a peculiarly mammalian interpretation, but essentially correct," said Araf'ex.

"This sculpting business is much more advanced than anything my civilization has," Eril said with a perfectly straight face. "I wonder if there's some way I could experience it firsthand. Could you make a device that would let me do it?"

The gastropoid's hide rippled in something like a shrug. "I have considered the possibility. It is an interesting technical challenge, but one I myself am inadequate to. It is simple enough to design an instrument to deliver biochemical catalyst agents to the *therine*. But the manipulation of the device itself by solely mechanical means—I cannot see how that can be done."

"But it's *theoretically* possible?"

Araf'ex answered, "If Scientist Raerquel authorizes further research, we can investigate."

Eril pointed to the collection of levers and switches spread across the broad pilot's panel. "What about these? They're the controls for the ship, aren't they?"

Araf'ex rippled to the side of his seat and caressed the nearest lever with a supple lower appendage. "All internal connections are 'fixed' to ensure reliability. These levers are for the control of forward propulsion, these are lateral stabilizers. Power for internal usage is generated from controlled-fusion engines and transferred as light energy along these channels. The technique permits direct monitoring of functions by this internal sensor panel."

Eril watched the gastropoid manipulate the lever switches below the bank of circular panels to the right of the main controls. There were few identifying features other than the location and shape of the levers and buttons, and no guidebook to refer to. He could only watch and memorize to the best of his ability, knowing that no one but a fool—or a glory-boy thrill addict—would try to pilot so alien a ship.

But if Raerquel's scheme failed, if war came and this was the only chance to get them out alive. . . .

"A small change in directional vectors here," Araf'ex

demonstrated the navigation system, "creates a large change in the projected final position here."

"Don't you use star charts or something?" Lennart asked. "Or a even basic altimeter?"

"Altitude is most accurately measured by changes in the light-transmitting qualities of different atmospheric densities," Araf'ex replied in its professorial mode. "This simulation shows our current planetside location," the flick of a delicate appendage, "now a progression through stratosphere . . . and finally, to space vacuum. From this point, sensors shift to a solar orientation, using the same scale for attenuation of a sun's ultraviolet radiation, coupled with the astronomical location displayed in simple wavelength coordinates."

*Simple, huh?* Eril had already realized from Raerquel's earlier comments that human vision was not sensitive to the spectral variations which were so vivid to the gastropoid optic disks. He wasn't sure it was even possible for a human to pilot the ship. Not using their instruments, anyway. But he still had his own eyes. "Do you have direct visual access to the outside?"

"Please to be observing behind you."

Eril turned to the window opposite the control banks. As before, the spacefield below was so badly distorted, both in shape and color tone, as to be virtually unrecognizable. He was able to identify sky and pavement and the distant green of the parkland only because he knew they were there. He could tell he was planetside instead of spacebound, but not a whole lot more.

"What good does it do to have an image that's so

badly warped? If the instrumentation failed, you'd never be able to fly this thing on visual."

"These images are not enhanced to mammalian eyes?" Araf'ex inquired.

*The damned window makes things clearer for them.* "Does it require special training to interpret the sensors?"

"Hardly! All postadolescent gastropoids possess adequate visual capability. The interpretation of extra-orbital position requires a screening grid, which is internal to the navigational controls. This ship is so elegantly simple, any *untranslatable* can fly it."

Eril restrained himself from retorting that certainly wasn't so in his own world. He said instead, "Does that mean *any* of you could pilot this ship?"

"With ease. Engineering, however, requires sophisticated training. Under normal conditions, civilians as well as military are having equal access to space. Now . . ." its voice trailed off, "all of Planet-of-Home is on war alert. Perhaps soon, the whole issue will become meaningless."

Araf'ex ran one gracefully tapering tendril along the ship's wall in unmistakable affection.

"Suppose some civilian wanted to pilot this ship. To NewHome, for instance, or Tomorrow," Eril said. "Aren't there diagrams of their locations, something you can look at?"

"You are meaning astrotopographic matrices. Naturally we have those." Araf'ex pressed a series of buttons and a star chart appeared on the screen, precise and clear. Lennart let out a soft whistle of appreciation.

Eril leaned forward to study the chart. He recognized Stayman as the viewpoint locus, then its nearest neighbors. New Paris and Pandora appeared at the extreme range of the diagram. Araf'ex pointed out the two colony planets, and Eril noted their locations among previously unexplored star groups.

*I could navigate to either of them, but what good would it do, hopping from one war zone to another?*

"It won't get you in trouble to have taken us aboard your ship—shown us all this?" Eril asked.

"What can it be mattering? *You* are not the enemy, you who are unable even to sculpt *therine,* you who have nothing at stake in current argument. Scientist Raerquel is desiring cooperation with humans, and I am merely complying."

"What if war does come? Don't you ever think of taking your loved ones into space and saving them, preserving what's decent about your civilization?"

Araf'ex swung its head around toward him, the four disks reflecting the pure light of the control chamber. They gleamed like highly polished silver with no trace of gold or copper overtones.

There was something so committed and so fatalistic, so utterly alien, in Araf'ex's silence, it made Eril shiver. If he had any hope of enlisting it to help them get off-planet, it was gone.

# Chapter 28

Kithri lay on her back beneath *Brushwacker*'s mangled nose, amazed that something was at last going right. After endless delays and mistakes, checking and rechecking, the basic modifications had been completed. She was now ready to fine-adjust the physiological parameters. Eril sat in the pilot's seat, monitoring the biohomeostasis functions. Behind him, Raerquel occupied all of the copilot's seat, as well as a goodly portion of the hold.

"Shipbrain says it's *mono*linking partially with Raerquel, so we're in the right orbital," Eril reported.

"So far, so good." Kithri used the optical stylus to guide a final connection before repositioning the protective panel. She clambered to her feet and stuck her upper body into the cabin, twisting to give Raerquel a clear view of her translator panel.

"How are you and shipbrain getting on?" she asked.

"I am not yet experiencing . . . linkage," the alien replied. "This ship's brain is different from other tools which are an extension of the self. Tools resemble water—they can be many things until instructed. Ship's brain also, only its limits are rigid. Like rock instead of water. It tastes dry."

*Dry?* Kithri wondered, withdrawing from the cabin. *Not the way I'd have put it. But at least Raerquel's getting* something *from shipbrain. We've done that much.*

Eril slipped off the headset and replaced it in its holder. "Everything's clear on this end. You ready for the next step, Kithri?"

"What, you mean right now?" she asked, startled.

He swung down from the pilot's seat. "I don't see any point in waiting. We're ready now, and besides, we'll have a whole day's worth of recalibration from just a few moments of synch. What's the matter," he asked, not entirely joking, "are you scared?"

"No." Her lips went stiff even as she said it.

He touched her shoulder, but she wouldn't meet his eyes. She had enough to deal with, just one task at a time, not letting herself think—*really* think—what she was doing, tearing out *'Wacker*'s insides.

She pulled free and climbed into the tiny cabin, brushing against Raerquel as she slid into the pilot's seat. The gastropoid's hide felt surprisingly smooth. It lay behind and around her, unmoving except for the gentle susurration of air through its neck slits. The seat under her was still warm from Eril's body heat.

"We don't need a full-out linkage at this point," he said. "Nothing fancy, understand? Just go in, get a solid contact and then get the hell out of there. Don't take any chances!"

*You don't have to tell me that.* Kithri slipped the auto-probes into place on her temples, feeling the gel contacts cool and familiar. She turned around in the seat. "You ready, Raerquel? This is your last chance to back out."

"There is still much work to do, and little time.

As friend-Eril has stated, what is the advantage of delay? Proceed now. Please."

She wet her lips. "I'll make the first part of the meld." She sank into synch with shipbrain's inhumanly steady rhythms. Her vision doubled as her mind began to make the usual adjustments. She blinked, searching for the visual focus that would tell her the first part of the meld was accomplished. It seemed to take much longer than usual. As she waited, her thoughts, like disobedient children, wandered to the last time she flew *duo* and how much had happened since that morning in Port Ludlow.

How angry she'd been at Hank's defection, which now seemed no more than a forgotten annoyance. How jealous of that raven-haired beauty he'd taken up with. How suspicious of Eril.

*Eril . . .*

"All right, Raerquel, here we go." Her voice sounded abrasive to her ears, as if it could scour away the demanding, sensual memory of that first *duo*flight across the Cerrano Plain. Belatedly, she realized that Raerquel couldn't see her translator panel. It didn't matter.

Slowly she shifted modes to bring the gastropoid into the *duo*meld.

*What if I have the same response to Raerquel as I did to Eril?* She stifled the thought. *It's not possible, Raerquel's too alien. I'll be lucky if I can understand anything I get from its mind. And besides, it would be automatic, a physiological reflex, nothing more. Just as . . . what happened with Father was.*

For the first long moments she thought the contact had failed, that there was nothing coming through the mechano-neuronal pathways. Then she sensed something, faint and far away from the usual human frequency. Leaving shipbrain's base pattern as an anchor, she began searching "upward" and "downward" along the frequency range.

"Upward" felt open and empty. Nothing to be gained there.

*It would help if I knew exactly what I was looking for. C'mon, Raerquel, where are you?*

She shifted her attention "downward." It was like slogging through molasses, thick and syrupy. The ambient mental energy resisted her with exactly the same amount of force she used against it. The harder she pushed, the harder it pushed back. In all her years of flying, both *duo* and *singlo,* she'd never experienced anything like it.

Frustrated, Kithri decided to follow Eril's advice and "get the hell out of there." To her surprise, she couldn't reverse her "downward" movement, couldn't even change her speed. She could go neither backward toward "normal", nor sideways, but only farther "down." Not only that, something was actively *drawing* her deeper and deeper, sucking greedily at her.

*What's happening? What kind of comet-crazy thing is this?*

Kithri struggled to think things through logically. There must be some rational explanation for what was happening. If she could only find it, she might be able to counteract it. People didn't get trapped in *duo.* It was designed to be foolproof. Yet something had gone wrong, terribly wrong.

What? Had the equipment modification failed? Or was the linkage between human and gastropoid impossible in the first place? Was the fault in her, or in the technology, or in Raerquel. . . ?

*Raerquel!*

Kithri reached out as far as she dared, but got no impression of the gastropoid's mind within the heavy, sucking darkness. But if Raerquel, like herself, were trapped here, then it was her responsibility to get both of them out. *She* was the one who had suggested this crazy experiment in the first place. *She* was the one who'd altered the apparatus. *She* was the experienced *duo* pilot.

No, she was only a novice, and now a man's bulky shoulders rose to blot out her view of the bleak terrain that stretched out beyond the scrubjet nose. She swayed in her seat, confused. She shouldn't be here, she *wasn't* here. Then the man turned around and leered at her with yellowed teeth.

*Dowdell!*

One dust-streaked hand reached for her, fingers splayed wide to grab her breast . . . and passed right through her. Like the space ghost, only this time *she* was the ghost, drifting. . . .

*It isn't real!* came a thin wail at the back of her mind, weaving through the whine of a badly-tuned jaydium cutter. She looked down at her hands and they were covered with blood and she knew her nose was broken.

*Not real! It's not real . . . I have to . . . abort . . . linkage. . . .*

Yet how wonderful it was to lie back against the flowers, looking up at the powder blue sky. How peaceful to swim in the clear warm water, the water reflecting and amplifying the living light. She could almost touch the softness of the petals, smell the ever-changing fragrances, feel the breezes.

The voice at the back of her mind kept on its annoying chant, weaker now but even more desperate.

*Abort command—give shipbrain the abort command! What is it, Kithri? Think!*

"It is . . . " Words formed in her mouth. The sky had gone all brown and she was rushing up into its murky heights. Her stomach growled, but whether with fear or hunger she couldn't tell. Her eyes ached from too little sleep.

"It is . . . escape . . . escape speed. No, that's not right."

The brown went suddenly black and still she flew along, dazedly watching the glassy reflections of a jaydium tunnel flicker past. Choking darkness filled her mouth and gills, the shallow waters murky, the fluid, changing light now blotted out. The shadow of a giant cacharon glided past, leaving the stench of terror in its wake.

Ship—there ought to be a ship around her, a ship she spoke to. But the words, what were the words? Why was it so important she remember?

*Escape? Escape speed?*

Still she rushed downward, steeper and steeper, more and more slippery so that she had no way to brake her descent. Between her knees something grew hot, glowing as with atmospheric reentry.

"Not speed, velocity . . . Escape something velocity . . . TERMINAL ESCAPE VELOCITY!"

The words were right. The abort command chosen by her father was unchanged since the day he programmed it into shipbrain. She'd never used it until now, never even whispered it, except in her dreams. But she knew it like the beating of her own heart.

Nothing happened.

She was still surrounded by dense, devouring blackness, and she had now lost all sense of movement and direction. Vaguely she remembered traveling "down," remembered fighting it with all her strength, but now the word no longer made sense. *Up, down,* what was the difference?

She felt herself slipping again along currents of mental energy, sliding, plummeting, no longer caring. Pressure squeezed her like a vise, the weight of hundreds of feet of water looming above her. Hunger seized her, hunger and blind terror. Her mind dissolved into primeval fragments, each scrabbling for survival.

And for one agonizing moment she no longer felt herself at all.

The tiny portion of Kithri's mind that clung to consciousness continued to struggle weakly. Around her shone a myriad pinprick lights, swimming in hypnotic arcs of color. She curled in on herself like a drying cinder, like an embryo.

*Like an embryo in a body!* Thought flared again. Somewhere—somehow—she *did* have a body. . . .

And that body was sprawled in a hauntingly familiar seat, legs thrust straight out and racked with spasm. Hands seized her shoulders, shaking her as her head lolled from a nerveless neck. Fingers peeled back her eyelids, probed for a pulse, stripped the autoprobes from her head.

"Damn it, Kithri," said Eril's voice. "I thought we'd lost you."

# Chapter 29

Kithri opened her eyes and gasped. Natural sensation flooded through her—the air whistling through her lungs, her heart pounding, the pressure of the floor under her thighs. Eril's fingers gripping her, digging into her shoulders. She lay in his arms just outside *'Wacker*'s open cockpit door. High above them arched a dome of sparkling crystal.

The sensation of incredible relief vanished instantly, replaced with the memory of who she was, where she was, what she'd tried to do.

"Raerquel . . ." her voice came out in a croak. *"Raerquel?"*

"It seems to be stunned, but you—"

"Never mind about me!" Kithri jerked free and hauled herself to her feet. "I'm fine, see? No aftereffects or anything."

Her knees suddenly turned to jelly and lost all semblance of structural integrity. Breathing heavily, she caught herself against *'Wacker*'s pitted side.

"You're about as *fine* as a space-sick rookie," said Eril. "What *happened* to you in there?"

"Forget what happened to me! What have we done to *Raerquel*?" Kithri reached into the cockpit and laid one hand on the gastropoid's silvery skin. There was no response.

She started trembling. It was the coolness more than anything else which reminded her of her father's hand, how she held it through the long night until the last bit of body warmth had seeped away.

"Eril, what if it's . . ." She couldn't bring herself to say the word *dead.* "It's different from us, how can we tell? Wouldn't the tentacles go slack or something?"

Eril grabbed her shoulders and told her to sit down until she could think straight. With a sense of grudging relief, she slid to the floor beside the scrubjet's landing gear, as limp as an exhausted child. Eril called the gastropoid's name, shouting it so loud she whimpered and covered her ears with trembling hands. He stopped only when Kithri reminded him it wouldn't do any good. He tried shaking it, at first gently, then slapping it and pulling on its sturdier lower tentacles, all without the slightest response.

"What are you doing?" Kithri asked when he climbed into the pilot's seat and slipped on the autoprobes. As his efforts had gotten more desperate, her own presence of mind returned, although she still felt uncertain, brittle.

"Trying to make contact with it myself," he said in a ragged-edged voice. "Or, failing that, getting shipbrain to give me some physiological readouts and praying I can make sense out of them."

Eril's face went blank for a split second and then settled into an expression of intense concentration. Kithri watched him with reluctant admiration. In all her years of flying with her father and then Hank, she'd never seen anyone slip into *duo* so quickly. He was good, very good. But good enough?

After what seemed centuries of waiting, fingers clutched around her knees, scarcely daring to breathe, she saw his eyelids flicker open.

"Damn!" He scowled as he pulled the headset off.

"What happened?"

"Not a ratshit thing, that's what! The whole system's gone neutral, as if it had never been activated. That moronic shipbrain of yours not only couldn't contact Raerquel, it didn't even know it had been in *duo*!"

"If there was a mistake, it was your morphoplex rerouting," Kithri snarled. "'*Wacker* would never—"

"Stuff it!" He jumped out of the cockpit. "The reroute was good. You checked it yourself."

Kithri bit her lip. It wouldn't help to argue whose fault it was. "So what's next?"

"Let's get Raerquel out of there. Lay it flat. Maybe we'll see something we can't from here. Or maybe just getting it out will help."

Kithri wrenched off the gastropoid's autoprobes. The sensor pads came free with tiny, sickening pops. Raerquel didn't respond. Its head and neck sections had completely retracted into its body so that neither the coppery eye disks nor the neck slits were visible.

Eril climbed back into the pilot's seat, facing backward, and managed to get a good enough traction on the far side of Raerquel's body so that he could push while Kithri pulled. It was a long, exhausting business, very much like trying to shift several hundred pounds of muscle-bound, boneless protoplasm.

Once they got enough of Raerquel's amorphous bulk out of the door, gravity took over and the extending curve of its body hit the glassy floor with a *plomp*! From that point it was relatively simple to ease the rest of the body out of the scrubjet. There was no visible change in the gastropoid's condition, nor could they see any sign of a wound or other damage. It lay on the floor, an inert lump. Kithri and Eril sat down beside it, sweating and breathing freely, wondering what their next move would be.

As if on cue, Brianna chose that moment to make an entrance. She burst into the laboratory dome, accompanied by one of Raerquel's assistants. Kithri thought it was Bhevon, but in her dazed state she couldn't be sure. She got to her feet, aware that Eril did the same.

Brianna rushed to the massive silvery lump that was Raerquel. "What's happened?" She glared at Kithri, her face contorted with emotion. "What have you done to it?"

Kithri's voice came in a stunned whisper. "I don't know."

"Leave her alone!" Eril grabbed Brianna's shoulder and spun her around. "She's been through enough!"

Without waiting for her response, he turned to the gastropoid behind her. "Bhevon—it is Bhevon, isn't it? We need your help. There's been a terrible accident. We don't know what's wrong with Raerquel. It seems to be unconscious, won't respond to anything we do, and I can't find its pulse. I don't even know if it has one."

Bhevon extended a quartet of antennalike appendages toward its clan-superior. The humans drew back to let it work. "We are possessing heartbeats like other large invertebrates," it commented without pausing in its scanning activities. "Bodies exceeding a certain minimum bulk are requiring the forceful pumping of nutrient and waste transport media. Human science is ignorant of this basic principle?"

"Is—is Raerquel still alive?" Kithri stammered.

"Indeed, my esteemed clan-superior is still living, having entered the protective state of estivation." It paused, its fragile-looking upper appendages writhing. "What can be causing such a drastic action? I demand an explanation! I am thinking that an unauthorized, unattended experiment has taken place here!"

"Just the first stage," Kithri said miserably. "Me and Raerquel hooked up to shipbrain. There shouldn't have been any problem. It wasn't a full linkage—it should have been perfectly safe."

"Irresponsible mammalians are risking the cerebral synapses of Scientist Raerquel in *untranslatable* scheme!" Bhevon boomed at her. If it were possible for the gastropoid's voice to carry any recognizable emotion, the ground would have trembled under its righteous indignation.

"Stop right there," Eril commanded. "If you're going to blame anyone, blame me. The procedure was my decision and my responsibility. Raerquel knew the risks, and it freely agreed to them. It chose to go ahead. But all this talk is beside the point. If Raerquel needs treatment, let's get it done and debate the issue later!"

"I should have been present for such-called *test,*" Bhevon said, its voice once more rising to a thunderous boom. "But you are correct that recriminations are accomplishing nothing. You will now be removing yourselves to sleeping chambers. I myself will summon healers to be reviving clan-superior Raerquel."

"Will—will it be all right, left alone like that?" Kithri said uncertainly. "Shouldn't one of us stay with it?"

"For what purpose? Obstruction of therapeutic procedures?"

"We only want to help."

"Mammalians are having *helped* sufficiently!" Bhevon cut her off with such force she flinched visibly. "We are now seeing the consequences of such so-called *help*!"

# Chapter 30

Eril stormed out of the laboratory with Kithri at his side and Brianna trailing behind. Kithri, her mouth set in an ominously tight line, kept pace with him as if she were his shadow. Every few steps, Brianna leapt into a trot to catch up to him.

"I can't believe you'd let Kithri proceed with her crazy idea!" she exclaimed. "I hope you realize she may well have jeopardized my entire research program— Will you slow down and listen to me?"

*Chattering on like a goddamned sand-hen,* Eril thought. He clamped his teeth together and kept on going, not trusting what was left of his nerves to risk answering Brianna. He'd never felt less sympathetic toward her—*pompous, insensitive, judgmental bitch!* It wasn't fair to vent his own feelings on her, but he was too upset to make allowances. He wished there were some merciful way he could shut her up before she said something unforgivable—or he did.

Kithri kept her eyes straight ahead and gave no visible sign she heard anything Brianna said. Eril remembered that taut carriage to her shoulders from just before she took *Brushwacker* and left them to be nabbed by the space pirates. Skies only knew what she'd do here, especially when Brianna said things like, "I know Kithri hasn't a shred of training in making evaluations like this, but I assumed *you* knew better. *You* at least seem to have some sort of education!"

They made their way past a plaza filled with free-standing, shoulder-high walls. Gastropoids wandered through the maze, either singly or in small groups, hooting softly to each other and sending ripples of brightness across the walls. What function the structures served, Eril could not guess, unless they were traditional designs, modeled after the tidal baffling systems of the aquatic city. This was his favorite part of the city, but he didn't stop to admire it now.

"Need I point out," Brianna rattled on in between gasps for breath, "there is a significant difference between helping these people develop better means of communication and engaging in irresponsible neuropsionic tinkering with our host scientist!"

Finally Eril snapped at Brianna to restrain herself from making public fools of them all. It was the mildest response he could think of.

"I'm only trying to make my opinion known. If you'd bothered to consult me, I might have advised you on a more prudent course of action. Aren't you interested in what an *expert* has to say?"

"Thank you," he replied, striding on, "I didn't know we'd made a mistake until you told me so."

The living quarters were quiet and empty, cool after the energetic pace Eril set. The broadcast unit which Raerquel had installed on one wall, its controls "fixed" for human operation, was silent and dark. Brianna's film notes and *therine* specimens lay scattered around the rim of the central dining table.

Brianna pushed her way into the common room, skirting the shallow pool. She whirled around in a dancer's graceful pirouette, and placed both fists on her hips.

Eril groaned inwardly. *Here it comes. She's been building up to it the whole way back.*

"I can see you simply don't understand the enormity of what you've done, either of you. Here I am, about to make a breakthrough in analyzing the gastropoidal architecture system and the role of hierarchically determined *therine* secretion patterns in clan dominance—oh, don't look at me as if that's so much nonsense! You understand my meaning. You know it's the first step in understanding this culture so that we could be sure we weren't introducing a fatal innovation—and you endanger everything we're working for with this criminally irresponsible escapade! You should have prepared suitable safeguards, in a scientifically acceptable fashion, not to mention waiting until we had a better idea of the implication of the impact of our technology upon the current situation! Why in *untranslatable* didn't you ask my advice first?"

Eril's first impulse was to laugh in Brianna's face. No one but his sister Avery could rant in such an operatic mode, and he thought Brianna would fare well in the comparison. But one look at Kithri's face convinced him that she, for one, was taking Brianna seriously.

"Calm down, Bri," he said as diplomatically as he could. "There's nothing to be gained by blaming one another. If there was a mistake, it was *my* mistake, not Kithri's."

"I don't blame her and I am quite calm already."

Brianna began gathering the sheets of seaweed-film into meticulous piles, as if to underscore her rationality. "After all, she's had no more education than a herd-beast. Not a shred of decent methodological training. It isn't her fault—"

Kithri had started toward her own cubicle, but now she froze and turned slowly back. Her face flooded with color and her old nose break stood out as a chalky brand. She strode to the table and swept the entire contents—all of Brianna's notes, styluses, and specimens—to the floor. Still without a word, she shoved one fist a hairsbreadth from Brianna's nose and made an emphatic gesture. Then she spun around and marched out the door.

Brianna looked at Eril, her eyes innocently wide. "What—what did she—"

"Never mind." Eril bent to pick up a pile of films. "You don't want to know what that meant."

"It's just as well the translator doesn't function for gestures," Brianna said as she knelt to gather up the rest of her materials. "Then we'd all have more to regret."

*There's nothing to do now but wait and hope that reviving Raerquel is as simple as Bhevon made it sound,* Eril thought as he dumped his armful of films on the nearest bench. "You'll be hours sorting all this out."

"That's not a problem. If it's one thing I've learned as a scientist, it's to label *everything* properly."

"I see that. You're very good at it." He paused. "Brianna, there are a few things we need to talk about."

"I agree. You've been so busy, we haven't had time to discuss our progress . . . or anything else." She smiled and took a few steps toward her cubicle. "Come on, see what I've done."

Somehow she'd found a curtain for privacy, now pulled back along a slender crystal rod. A comforter and overstuffed pillows covered her cot. The once-smooth walls had been replaced by an elaborate abstract frieze.

He stopped and stared. "Where did you get this stuff?"

"Not all of us have been cooped up in the laboratory for days at a time. I've been working this culture, and also learning how to extract a few favors in the process." She sat on the bed. "What are you waiting out there for? I thought you wanted to talk."

The bed surface yielded just the right amount under Eril's weight. The conversation was definitely going in the wrong direction. He searched his memory for the tactics which had worked with his sister, something outrageous enough to keep her off balance and never sure if he was really joking. But Brianna was not Avery and he had to work with her, depend on her. He cleared his throat.

"Look," he said, "you didn't sign up to be part of a team and neither did I. But we *are* one. We have to be. Maybe everything we're trying to do is hopeless. Maybe the *duo*linkage was impossible to begin with. Or maybe the war will start before we can get anywhere with it—space knows the situation hasn't gotten any better these last few days. But I'll tell you one thing for sure—Kithri's laying her life, not to mention her sanity, on the line for us. And you—you're treating her like ratshit."

While he spoke, Brianna sat very straight, hardly moving except for curling her fingers in the silky covering of a pillow and pulling it on her lap. The color drained from her cheeks, her lips, even her eyes.

"You're on *her* side—"

"There *are* no sides here," he said grimly. "And if Kithri had saved my skin with those pirates the way she did yours, I'd be a damned sight less judgmental about her."

In the shocked moment that followed, Brianna hung her head and began crying, at first soundlessly, then with throttled, almost hiccoughing sobs. Tears rolled down her face and splotched the pillow.

Eril watched her, still too angry to feel much sympathy for her. Whatever she was up to with her emotional outburst, he wasn't going to play into it. Then he remembered that this was the woman who dug herself out of a rock slide with her bare hands, who dealt calmly and effectively with the three of them when they'd appeared so mysteriously. Who went running into the pirates' arms to save *his* skin.

"It's the stress," he said awkwardly. "It's affecting all of us."

"No, you're right, I have been judgmental toward Kithri," Brianna said, visibly struggling to control herself. "Judgmental and unfair. It's always been so easy for me, I've never had much sympathy for other people's shortcomings. I had everything I ever wanted—money, academic advancement, work I loved. I thought I deserved it, and if anyone else had difficulties, they must be his own fault. I must have been insufferable."

She hugged the pillow to her chest. "And then when things did go wrong—the slide, the pirates—and Kithri refusing to go along with anything I proposed. She made me so angry—I felt certain her impulsiveness would result in catastrophe. I never stopped to think the problem might be my own expectations. Attitudes, expressions of speech—they get ingrained, like reflexes, even when you don't mean them. When things happen so fast, you keep on behaving the way you always have. Without thinking. I guess I'm trying to apologize. I'm not very good at it."

"It's Kithri you should apologize to."

"I know, but I'm not sure I can. This way—no matter what happens—I'll have said it to somebody."

She sounded so bleak, so desolate that Eril had to look away. Finally, in a voice that he wished wasn't his, he said, "The rest of the day's worthless. I'm going to find Lennart and fill him in, maybe catch up with Kithri and recivilize her. Hopefully, we'll have news about Raerquel's condition soon."

Brianna watched him as he left her cubicle and then slowly drew her door curtain closed.

# Chapter 31

Eril jerked awake and scrambled to his feet, ready to suit up and sprint for the launching port. His needle jet would be tuned to go, Hank already sliding into the copilot's seat. Heart pounding, he paused and looked around, his eyes searching the dimness. He could see only the blank walls of his own narrow cubicle, not barracks teeming with awakening pilots. No alarms shrilled through his ears. All he could hear were the normal sounds made by three sleeping people. From Lennart's cubicle came gentle rhythmic snoring. Whatever had woken him must have been a dream, nothing more.

Eril lay back and tried to relax. Late in the war he'd snatched hours and minutes of sleep whenever he could. He'd learned to simply *not think* about the problems he couldn't do anything about. Raerquel's condition would wait until the morning—the matter was entirely out of his hands. What had happened with Brianna was a different matter. He went over the conversation in his mind, wondering if there was anything else he could have said or done. Since then, Brianna had made no overtures toward Kithri, although she was no longer openly hostile. Not that Kithri cared what Brianna thought of her.

*Kithri . . .*

The thought came to him how alike they were, as if they each had their own poisoned memories. He thought of Kithri watching her father die by inches and of all his own years of growing up, desperately hoping there had been some mistake and his father had been found, that any day he'd walk through the door . . . and the moment on his tenth birthday when he realized, finally and absolutely, that would never happen.

Well, there wasn't anything he could do about those things, either.

In the end, Eril resorted to working out textbook navigational problems in his head until he drifted off to sleep.

The next morning, no word had yet come of Raerquel's condition. Brianna spread her notes over a section of floor, sorting and indexing. She said there was no point in sitting around worrying when there was work to be done. Kithri began pacing from her cubicle to the common room, biting her fingernails. Eril decided the situation was ripe for another confrontation between the two of them. He'd better get some action organized fast.

"Bri, you know the city best," he said. "You and Lennart check Raerquel's laboratory, the Clan courtyards, anywhere and anyone who might be able to tell you what's going on. Kithri and I will go back to the lab and recheck the equipment. Maybe we can find something we overlooked yesterday. We'll meet you back here, if one of you doesn't find us first."

He was a little surprised when the others did as

he suggested without protest. Even Kithri went along with him.

"Do you think we'll find anything, I mean some mistake that caused—what happened yesterday?" she asked as they passed the mazework of free-standing walls.

Eril shook his head. "If we had any idea there was something wrong, we wouldn't have gone ahead. Maybe we were too tired. Brianna might be right that it was a stupid thing to try under those conditions. But it was *my* stupid idea," he added, "not yours."

"Suppose we'd done all the things she said and the war started because it took us too long? Whose fault would it be then? You can't be responsible for *everything.*" Kithri paused, her expression thoughtful. Her eyes blurred, as if seeing some other time, some other place. "You can't *know* how things are going to turn out."

They went around to the far side of the laboratory dome, where a mechanically operated, "fixed" door had been installed to allow them access. The entire wall had been removed, leaving the building completely open . . . and empty.

No scrubjet, no tools, and no trace they'd ever been there.

"No!" Kithri dashed into the middle of the room. She halted where *Brushwacker* had stood, her hands extended in a gesture of utter bewilderment. Her breathing came quick and light.

"They—they took it—"

Eril walked up and touched her shoulder. She dropped her arms and turned toward him.

"Yes, but why?" he said. "I can see them calling a

halt to the experiment, but not this. Where would they take it?"

"It doesn't make any sense!" Her voice sounded strained, as if a giant fist were clenched around her throat.

"Unless something more has happened to Raerquel and someone else is making the decisions, unless . . ." He paused, seeing her horrified expression. "Let's get back," he said firmly. "Maybe Bri and Lennart have discovered what's going on."

Eril and Kithri burst into the common room, faces flushed, to find Brianna and Lennart seated at the central table, facing a gastropoid. It turned toward them, showing yellow-tinted head disks. Eril identified it as Raerquel's assistant, Bhevon. Bhevon, he reminded himself, had been unfriendly, almost hostile toward them.

"What's the news? Is Raerquel all right?" Eril's skin felt hot under its light sheen of sweat, and his blood-pumped muscles demanded action. He gulped air and forced his thoughts to slow down.

"My clan-superior is suffering no prolonged malaise from your endeavor."

"Thank all the powers of luck and space." Eril slid on to an empty bench. Kithri did likewise, visibly holding her tongue. "We just came from the lab. The scrubjet—our surface craft—it's gone. What's going on? Have you given up on the experiment?"

"On the contrary, clan-superior Raerquel is determined to persevere. It still holds to the goal of enhanced understanding between one gastropoid mind and another."

The adrenaline pumping through Eril's body left

him feeling jittery and almost preternaturally alert. He didn't need to study the unhappy expression on Lennart's face to know something else was at issue.

Lennart met his eyes. "They're going to try again . . . without you."

"That's just plain stupid!" Kithri bit off a curse and turned to Bhevon. "I know *Brushwacker* better than anyone living. There's no one—human or not—who stands a better chance of making the linkage than I do. Besides, suppose you did manage a hook up with one of your Council members. Suppose it gets stuck in this estivation state like Raerquel did, how will that get you anywhere? *You'll* get charged with attempted murder, *we'll* get blasted, and the war will start anyway!"

"De-estivation presents no significant problem. You are even now demonstrating that the differences between your mammalian and our evolved gastropoid brains are too great to be so easily crossed."

Brianna spoke up unexpectedly, "I agree with Kithri. I think entrusting your minds to an alien—that is, human—technology is too dangerous to try on your own. You ought to either keep us on as consultants or else abandon the project entirely."

*That was a quick change of opinion,* Eril thought. Kithri stared at her in frank astonishment.

"As I said before, if you're going to do it at all," Brianna added, "you ought to do it right."

Bhevon appeared untouched by any of their arguments. "If we shrink from this experiment because of hypothetical dangers, what will the doubters and followers think—that the cause of peace is to be pursued only when it is easy? That persistence and dedication are virtues only for the war-sayers? No, peace is too important to abandon because of a few initial difficulties."

Kithri turned back to the gastropoid and said between clenched teeth, "While all this is going on, what have you done with my ship?"

"They've taken it to their mountain city," Lennart said grimly. "Bhevon was telling us when you came in. The situation's gotten worse and the planetary leaders have moved there for security."

"You can't do this! She's *my* ship!"

"And Raerquel is *my* clan-superior, who spawned my Flesh-Before-Naming!" Bhevon drew itself up to its fully erect height. "Raerquel has ordered its removal to facilitate the complete dismantlement which is necessary for full utilization. The ship's brain and its connections must be divorced from its housing and amplified by our own equipment."

Kithri leapt to her feet, looking as if she'd like to pick up the table and smash it across the gastropoid's head section, the way she'd dealt with that miner in Hank's barroom story.

"Take it easy!" Eril put his hand on her shoulder and pulled her back down. He felt her resist for an instant and then yield, as if her bravado were only tissue thin.

"Personal alliances and preferences cannot be allowed to interfere with the cause of peace," said Bhevon. "Council-of-Ocean warned us that your cooperation could not be counted on. They said we were foolish to rely on your inconstant mammalian emotions. Raerquel insisted on your full participation in the experimentation, even over my own objections. Clearly, you cannot be trusted. Therefore, to prevent any rash actions on your part, you are now confined to these chambers."

After Bhevon sealed the door behind itself, the echoes of its final words lingered on. Eril stared at the blank wall, rapidly discarding all of the dramatic and completely useless courses of action that sprang to mind.

"What did I tell you?" Brianna said, but without any real malice. "Raerquel was only our ally as long as it suited its own purposes."

"But that purpose was stopping the war," said Lennart. "Like Kithri said, we had to try."

"Meanwhile," Eril added, "we're trapped here. Even if Raerquel manages to pull off its peace plan, we'll be no better than where we started. And if it doesn't . . ."

*There's got to be something we can do.*

"If Raerquel blows it, then we're all fried," Lennart said. "A lot of good my space ships will be to us if we can't get to them, heyh?"

Kithri had folded her arms on the table and buried her face in them. Eril remembered how she'd snatched the force whip from his holster and fired on Lennart's space ghost when she thought he'd threatened her scrubjet. She'd been furious when Eril suggested using it to ferry Brianna out to the jaydium site. But it hadn't been the jaydium that sent her off on her own, it had been the 'jet. Now its components were probably scattered all over some gastropoid lab, all its secrets exposed, and whatever the 'jet had meant to Kithri, it would never be hers again. There was nothing he could say to her, even if he could have found the right words.

He went to her and hesitantly laid one hand on her shoulder. Her muscles were so hard he couldn't tell them from bone. At first she didn't respond. Then a shudder went through her. He felt her relax, as if her body remembered his touch from that night under the stars.

"I'll be all right." She raised her head a fraction. Her voice was a ghostly whisper. "I know it's stupid to think *'Wacker* is still mine, or that it matters. Raerquel wouldn't care what happened to some old scrubjet, not when what's at stake is a whole world. I know all that, it's just I need . . . a little time to get used to it."

Eril let his hand drop from her shoulder and wandered over to the section of wall where the door had been. There was no sign of it now, not even a hairline shadow. The door seemed to have fused with translucent wall material.

The wall felt hard and smooth under his fingers. With a curious calm, as if the chill of the *therine* had seeped into his marrow, he saw himself hammering on it with his bare fists, clawing at it, hurling himself screaming against it. At first, the wall in his vision remained untouched by his efforts, even as his knuckles cracked open and his blood smeared over the impassive surface. Then he saw his fist pass through the wall, saw the *therine* splintering into tiny, glittering shards. Shards that blazed against the darkness of space for an instant before dimming.

He blinked, and the image fled, as ephemeral and overpowering as the dream which had awakened him that morning. His right hand ached from how tightly he'd clenched it. His stomach knotted around something hard and hot.

*The damned door is here somewhere, and I'm going to find it—find it, and open it—*

He began tapping along the wall at chest height. "I am not—going to sit here—like a dust-rat—in a trap," he said aloud. "There's got to be a way out, something we didn't think of before. Something we know now that we didn't know then. There's no such thing as an escape-proof prison, even one which *doesn't* have a door."

Lennart, behind him, said, "I wouldn't be too sure about there not being a door, captain. Ever since we got here, we've been razzled by all the things the slugs can do that we can't. We may be giving them more credit than they deserve."

Eril glanced back at him. "I don't follow you."

"Lennart's right," said Brianna. "There's so much that's alien in this civilization, we have a natural tendency to project that sense of the bizarre into areas where it hasn't been established." She smiled briefly. "It's a perennial temptation in my field. We call it xeno-resurgence."

Eril turned back to the wall. Maybe finding a door would get them somewhere, maybe it wouldn't. But working on the problem was a whole lot better than sitting around doing nothing.

Was he *assuming* the door wasn't there just because he couldn't see it? He'd been over the entire wall, rapping at regular intervals. There had been no trace of hollowness that might signal a hidden door. So what was he missing? Either the door was there or it wasn't. What other alternative could there be?

"Brianna, you've been studying these buildings," he said. "You know how they're put together. Are these walls as solid as they look? Do the slugs sculpt a new door every time they use one? Or does it slide back into the wall? And if there was a sliding door behind the wall, how would I find it?"

"I haven't examined this one in the closed configuration well enough to be sure," Brianna answered. "But it won't do us any good to know where the door is if we can't open it."

"We'll deal with that later. Tell me more about *therine*."

"Crystalline materials weren't in my area of expertise. My instruments did most of the preliminary scans, and I sent samples and spectroscopy data back to the Institute for analysis. I'm a xenoarchaeologist, not a physical chemist."

"But Kithri's father was," Eril said. "Or close enough." She looked up at him, her face waxy pale and her gray eyes opaque. "You said he studied jaydium. You said he taught you."

For a moment, Eril thought Kithri would tell him to stuff it. Instead, she slowly got to her feet. "I don't know what I could tell you that Brianna couldn't."

She touched the wall with her fingertips, as if comparing it to the jaydium she knew so well. For a moment Eril saw her stroking a living thing, testing its sensitivity, imagining it responding to her caress.

Brianna watched her for a moment. "If there's even a thin layer of air surrounding the hidden door, it should conduct sound at a faster frequency, so we could hear the difference in pitch it if we tapped on it with something hard enough."

"It sounded the same when I rapped on it," Eril said.

Kithri shook her head. "You couldn't tell just by knocking. This is more like glass than wood. You'd have to use something much harder than your knuckles. Metal would be better, a belt buckle if we had one."

Brianna disappeared into her room and came back with one of the styluses she used for her notes. Like everything else the gastropoids had furnished for them, it was made of *therine*. Kithri took it and tapped one end on the wall.

*Ping!*

"That doesn't sound hollow to me," Brianna said.

"Me either," said Eril. "Kithri?"

"It could be a sort of partial seal, like a fracture line through a crystal," she said. "Solid enough to maintain the strength of the wall, yet easy to split apart."

"An intact crystal lattice would transmit sound faster than one with a break, but the difference won't be as great as solid versus gas," Brianna said.

Kithri nodded. "Then we'll need a separation between where we tap and where we listen. If we're too close, the sounds'll be too similar."

She handed the stylus to Eril. "You tap over there and I'll listen here," she said, pointing. She put her ear to the wall about three feet away. "Tap there, and then an inch at a time this way. We'll work across and pray that I can hear a break at some point."

As Eril began tapping with the stylus, he remembered how Kithri taught him to chip raw jaydium. *Stroke it,* she'd said, *the way it* wants *to be cut.*

*Ping! Ping!*

"Damn." Kithri straightened up. "It's too muddy. If I had a tube to listen through . . ."

"Something to amplify the higher frequencies?" Brianna said.

"Like a rolled-up film?" asked Eril.

"Not my notes!" Brianna groaned, but Lennart had already snatched one from the table and handed it to Kithri. Brianna sighed and said, "I suppose we ought to be getting *some* practical use from them."

It was an exasperating process, progressing by inches across the wall, back and forth and then over again. Half the time Eril was sure any results they got would be purely hallucinatory, but he didn't care. It took their minds away from their present problem and gave them the sense they were doing something.

They changed pairs, Lennart tapping and Brianna listening because the women were able to hear the higher frequencies better. After three or four passes, both of them agreed they could hear a change in pitch over the same area. Brianna's marking fluid wouldn't stick to the slick *therine* surface, but they cradled a drop of it in the angle between the wall and floor.

"Okay, we've found the damned thing," Kithri said, stretching her neck and rubbing the tight muscles. "What do we do now?"

"If the break is like a flaw in a crystal, perhaps we could cleave it there," Brianna said.

Kithri shook her head. "I don't think so, not with any tool we've got. It took a laser cutter to slice through jaydium."

"Too bad we don't have that force whip of yours," Lennart said. "It packs a pretty good wallop."

"The last time I saw it was back with the pirates," Eril said, shaking his head. "I don't know if it even made it here with us. The next time a gastropoid brings us a meal, we could jam the door open. Maybe with the stylus."

"Worth trying, heyh?" Lennart nodded. "And then what?"

Eril stared at the wall, thinking hard. Kithri and Brianna also watched him, as if waiting for his signal. *Then what?* he asked himself. *Do we make a run for it as soon as the slug's out of sight? Do we wait until we hear from Raerquel—or until the bombs start falling?*

He knew, without having to ask, that he would be the one to decide. He was, for better or worse, their captain.

# Chapter 32

For the next few days, Eril watched and waited for a chance to try wedging the door open. He kept the stylus with him, tucked in the folds of his cloth belt. The gastropoids who brought their meals were alert and careful, or maybe it was only his own rising anxiety that made them seem so. Each time one left, it would pause in the corridor outside before sealing the door, watching him with its expressionless head disks. He would turn away, hoping no hint of his impatience showed.

They passed the rest of the time exercising, eating, and watching various programs on the broadcast unit. It had been installed with specially 'fixed' speakers in addition to the standard light panels. The only program which held any interest for Eril was the news, but Brianna took copious notes on other telecasts. Lennart and Kithri took shifts helping her, although they were seriously limited by the lack of a common written language. Everything had to be dictated and transcribed again.

One night, after everyone else had gone to bed, Eril found Kithri staring at the screen, studying a war report. She sat cross-legged on the floor, a sheet of seaweed film and stylus on her lap. As Eril knelt beside her, she bent and scrawled another note.

"Good news or bad?"

"It's hard to tell," she said, putting down the stylus. "I guess good, since they're still talking." She ran her hands over her face, looking bleaker than he'd ever seen her. "You know what's the worst of this whole mess? If I knew some good had come out of what Raerquel's trying, it would make losing *'Wacker* a whole lot easier. I don't know why else I bother watching this stuff. It's just a bunch of propaganda. But I keep hoping I'll see something—some news about Raerquel, some breakthrough. . . ."

---

Eril woke with a start to find Kithri's hand on his shoulder and her voice whispering his name.

"Eril! Eril, wake up! There's something you've got to see."

He sat bolt upright. His thoughts and vision seemed preternaturally clear, as if some celestial micrographer had cranked up the focus. Kithri sat beside him on his cot, leaning towards him.

"What's happened?"

"A cruiser blew up a NewHome ship just outside the solar system boundaries. From the size of the explosion, the NewHome ship was pretty heavily armed."

Eril could feel her trembling slightly, although her voice sounded steady enough. He felt a flush of empathy for her. She'd never been trained for war, her home world had been blown to bits, and now she was facing yet another catastrophe. All her instincts now must be telling her to cut and run, the way she had before. But she was here, at his side, thinking as straight as any of them.

"Let's take a look," he said.

Lennart rolled out of bed, alert and grim, but Brianna grumbled until Eril made it clear to her this was no trivial annoyance. They gathered around the broadcast screen, where the light from the panels played across their faces like a bizarre, moving camouflage.

". . . polar-orbiting intelligence satellites," droned the announcer's deep, expressionless voice.

". . . *untranslatable* are now making confirmation of unprovoked invasion of peaceful system territories . . . valiantly defended by our heroic forces . . ."

"And I thought *you* were a pompous ass at the Council hearing," Kithri murmured to Eril.

"That makes two of us."

"This stuff sounds like it's been censored," Lennart commented. "But is the *real* situation better . . . or worse?"

"Statement issued by Planet-of-Home High Council Defense Coordinator is following. . . .

" 'We are not violating the sacred responsibility of Flesh-Before-Naming in this confrontation with the degenerate inhabitants of planet NewHome. Instead, we are fulfilling our obligation in meeting any escalation with an even more definitive countermeasure. Our first priority must be the continuation of the true race, which cannot be accomplished by either appeasement or rabid peace-mongering.' "

"Now that," said Lennart, "sounds bad in anyone's language."

" 'We will not shirk from our duty and we will not weaken in our resolve. We will strive without reservation, to the utmost of our powers, until this pernicious influence has been permanently neutralized from the face of the universe!' "

"*That,*" said Kithri, "sounds even worse."

The next day there was neither breakfast nor lunch. When dinner came, the gastropoid which brought it was one Eril didn't recognize. It did not attempt to speak to any of them as it dropped the leaf-wrapped bundles of food. Duvach or even Bhevon would have exchanged a few words or perhaps waited while they began to eat. This one slithered back to the wall as quickly as possible.

As the gastropoid passed the threshold, Eril drew the stylus from his cloth belt. Flattening himself against the wall beside the door, he watched the opening grow narrower. He caught a glimpse of the corridor outside and the gastropoid as it crawled away. Slowly he bent down, concealing the stylus in his hand.

The gastropoid kept going.

Quickly Eril slipped the stylus into the opening. For a moment, the *therine* door flowed around it. Then it stopped before sealing completely. There was still a slender gap, barely enough to accommodate his fingertips. He tugged gently at it. The door slid open stiffly. He let go and it rebounded to its former position. To his relief, the stylus continued to hold it ajar.

He let out his breath, hardly daring to speak. The others clustered around him, touching the opening, touching him. Lennart mouthed something, but the translator wouldn't pick it up.

Eril took a deep breath. "We're getting out of here. Now!"

Beyond the abandoned courtyard, they spotted a few gastropoids moving at their usual undulating gait, murmuring to one another. None of them took any notice of the humans. It was past dusk. The shadows made it easier to move unobtrusively, but they dared not talk, not even in a whisper, lest their translator panels become beacons of brightness. For a short distance they traveled along the side streets behind a pair of gastropoids and overheard their conversation.

"This city is an easy target from space," rumbled one of them. "The Council are *untranslatable* if they think . . ."

"The only safe place is in the mountains," replied its companion. "Has your transfer come through yet?" Then the two gastropoids turned a corner and their voices were lost.

Toward the periphery of the city there was less traffic and more dark in the open spaces between the buildings. Between the clumps of parkland trees, shadows gathered like clotted blood.

The spaceport itself blazed like the heart of a brilliant-cut gemstone. Artificial light reflected off the ships, control buildings and scaffolding, splintering into minute rainbows. The four humans paused, squinting, at the edge of the field.

Eril led them quickly across the periphery of the landing pads, skirting areas where there was a concentration of workers. Groups of gastropoids formed and then dispersed in a frenzy of activity. There was no immediate outcry and he began to breathe easier.

*They're all so frantic, they haven't had time to notice us. We must act like we have every right to be here.*

Suddenly a gastropoid appeared directly in front of them. Its head section swung back and forth, exposing all four of its yellow-toned eye discs.

"Humans be halting! Be explaining your presence!"

They obeyed, clustering together more by reflex than design. "We are the guests of the scientist Raerquel Hath'djan," Eril said. "And we have permission to travel within the city boundaries."

"The space field is forbidden to all nonessential personnel."

A small crowd gathered around them, as quickly and silently as if it had been waiting in ambush. Eril recoiled, remembering the web restraints from the Council meeting.

"We were going to visit a friend—" Eril broke off as he recognized a gastropoid near the edge of the group—Araf'ex, the engineer Lennart had befriended.

"Planet-of-Home is on war alert status," the guard said. "Fraternizing with subsapient vertebrates is inappropriate behavior for a crisis. Human specimens are to remain motionless to be avoiding restraint enforcement! Subassistant, check their status."

"Look," Eril said in his most conciliatory tones, "we aren't trying to cause any trouble, and we don't want to interfere with your war effort. We didn't realize there was anything wrong with our being here. Let's not make a big deal out of a simple misunderstanding."

"Brigade-leader," said one of the lesser gastropoids, "Central Station reports that no permission has been granted for humans to be on the space field. They remind us that any such license, if given, would be automatically revoked during the war alert."

"What is the name of this friend you claim to be visiting?" the commander gastropoid demanded.

"Now that we know we're not supposed to be out here," said Eril, "we'll find our way back to our quarters on our own. Thanks, but we don't need any help. Sorry for the disturbance, folks." He raised his hand to wave good-bye, then realized the light panel couldn't translate the gesture.

The ring of silvery bodies closed in, now four or five deep with very little space between them. Only Araf'ex held back, watching . . . waiting. Eril's eyes darted around the circle, searching for the weakest point. He hesitated, unwilling to commit himself to a useless charge.

*We'll never break through. Not unless we can sprout wings or jump like sand-fleas.*

"The name?"

The threat in the deep-toned alien voice was unmistakable. It sent Eril's imagination reeling into the past, when he stood not in an alien spaceport but in a ruined, jewel-hued courtyard. And the voice which echoed through his skull demanded not a name but a location.

"*Jaydium? Where is jaydium?*"

"The name!"

Brianna screamed suddenly and pushed her way toward the ship. She stumbled over the first silver body, clawing and scrambling back to her feet. Eril leapt after her as the gastropoids turned, tendrils uncurling with ominous slowness.

Jets of colorless liquid shot from their tentacles, lacing Brianna with a network of gleaming strands. Even before she was frozen into immobility, the net settled on the remaining three humans.

# Chapter 33

Silence woke him. Eril blinked and struggled to focus on the nearest wall. It was about three feet from his nose and he assumed he was seeing clearly, for it was just as blank and unbroken by window or door seam as the other three. And he was still hanging in the restraint web, alone in his tiny cell.

He tried to stretch and then wished he hadn't. Even the slightest movement sent ripples of pain through his joints. He took a deep breath to clear his mind. It was no good. The air was stuffy, almost dense.

He could only guess how much of the day had gone by while he'd hung there, for the indirect lighting gave no sign of the sun's passage. There was no evidence of his hosts or the food and water they'd previously provided. Or the execution squad he expected. Neither was there any news of his companions or the progress of Raerquel's experiment on the far side of the ocean.

But news of war, that had surely come. Wave after thunderous wave had shaken the prison block while he'd hung there, helpless.

On the periphery of the spaceport, the prison building would be well within the first strike target zone, but Eril guessed the rumbling was caused by the blast of ships taking off under emergency scramble conditions. If the field had been bombed directly, he would not, in all likelihood, still be here to speculate about it.

Now, as he struggled awake from his fitful dozing, he heard none of the previous bone-shaking racket, only sepulchral silence.

*They've blown themselves up, damn them. We were too late. Or maybe Raerquel tried, and they just wouldn't listen. Now there's no one left to come looking for us, even if it would only be for a short march to the euthanasia chamber.*

Eril jerked against the restraining web and only succeeded in digging the strands deeper into his pressure-inflamed flesh. He tried to distract himself with thoughts of the others, hanging in their own isolated cells.

Some leader he'd turned out to be, with all his dreams of alien alliances. Or how about that nick-of-time escape plan? If only Kithri had laughed in his face, as he'd so thoroughly deserved, when he first proposed running jaydium with her. If she had, she'd be safe in Port Ludlow now, sipping brew with the other miners. It was all his fault she was here with him, waiting for certain death. No matter that she'd come to trust him, to reach out to him, to look beyond the dust on her fingers. . . . He wished they'd had a chance to make love because he had no words for what he wanted to say to her.

And Lennart would still be floating in that interdimensional gap. Time would have no meaning for him. He'd never know what happened to his age of peace or face the pirates. Neither would Brianna, who'd go on dreaming of alien civilizations and never see one. . . .

He was getting maudlin, thinking like this! Wallowing in self-pity, paralyzing himself with guilt. To hell with it!

From behind the seamless door panel came scuffles, so faint that Eril held his breath, listening. Over the sudden pounding of his heart he heard them again. Hairline cracks appeared in the far wall. The door jerked open, stuttered and came to a stop less than a quarter open.

Outside air, laced with acrid dust, swirled into the tiny cell. Eril coughed, his eyes watering. "Who's there?"

"Eril-human, you are still alive?"

Eril glimpsed a flash of silver hide through the partial opening, then the curve of coppery eye disc scanning his translator panel. A slender tentacle slipped through the opening.

"Who's there? Come on, you damned slugs, you've tortured me enough—don't keep me hanging here, tell me what's going on!"

"It is I, Raerquel."

"Raerquel! What the hell are *you* doing here?"

The scrabbling noises escalated into a rhythmic thumping, a pale echo of the previous blasts. Raerquel answered slowly, its normally resonant voice a tinny whistle, as if its vocal slits had been damaged.

"I am here—" *thud!* "—to rescue—" *thud! thud!* "—my mammalian friends—" *thud! crash!* "That is, if I can be opening—" *thud!* "—this *untranslatable* door!" *thud-thud-thud!*

The gastropoid paused, as if drawing breath. "It appears to be stuck."

*No shit.* "What's going on out there?"

"Skirmishing at outer planets has been escalating." Raerquel sank into a mound outside the door. Its tentacles drooped like wilted blossoms. "Several armed ships from Tomorrow were not destroyed."

"They got through—"

"Yes, to Planet-of-Home. We do not know if this was the intention of offspring-leaders, or only an accidental opportunity. These missiles were unguided and fell at random targets—some in the deep plains to the far south, some on polar regions."

"Did they—did they *all* hit uninhabited areas?"

"No. Some fell directly on Ocean-of-Light, destroying the Council chambers. Planet-of-Home has retaliated, sending our entire armed fleet into space."

"And the noise I heard? The ships taking off?"

"Those which were still spaceworthy. When the strike command was given, the offspring planets sent missiles armed with clean-fusion devices which they had based secretly in our asteroid belt. These were aimed at our most vital defense areas."

*All those ships . . .* Eril felt sick at heart.

"Is there any way of getting me out of this thing? I'd rather not die hung up like this."

The shadow outside heaved itself upright. "This door is not responding to normal biochemical controls and I am not able to pass through the available passageway."

"But *I* could slip through there if I were free." He eyed the opening. "Could you reach through and dissolve this thing off me?"

"Certainly. Your restraint web is designed to control vertebrate specimens and should be responsive to my manipulation."

Several slender appendages snaked through the open door. They extended to their full length and stopped, waving uncertainly as the eye disks moved back and forth. A lump of flesh slid along the foremost tentacle, like a bolus of food slipping down an elastic tube. It flattened out as it reached the tip, a wave which had dissipated its force. Eril watched, half in horror and half in fascination, as another swelling traveled the length of the appendage toward him.

"What—are you actually *growing* that thing?"

"The process is akin to that of protoplasmic streaming in protozoans. You are familiar with the concept?"

"No, but it doesn't matter. You're almost there. Now if you can only get this stuff *off* me—"

Raerquel's appendage stopped elongating a hand's length from Eril's thigh. The waves of added flesh slowed, thickening the tentacle. Feathery branches sprouted from its farthest tip, each delicate strand curling and reaching until it touched the restraint web.

Eril felt a sudden increase in pressure as Raerquel's appendage-tips slipped beneath the *therine* webbing. With an effort he kept still. What was the gastropoid scientist doing? Was it going to *rip* the stuff off him?

The restraint web continued to tighten, further constricting his breathing and digging painfully into his skin. "Raer—"

"Please be patient, Eril-friend," the alien said in its deep, toneless voice. "Even as water is expanding slightly as it is freezing into ice, this *therine* is partaking of minor volumetric changes."

The web clenched down harder and little black spots rose before Eril's eyes. His vision grayed around the edges. "I'm—having—trouble—breathing."

Suddenly the pressure dropped away. His knees buckled under him and he fell to the floor.

"Eril-friend, are you harmed?"

Eril pushed himself up on his hands, his ribs heaving with deep gulps of air. "I need a moment to catch my breath."

"My friend, can you do that as we proceed? We have only a little time before the retaliation is arriving."

"Go? Where is there to *go*?" Eril clambered upright and slipped sideways through the door opening. "I just wanted to die on my own two feet."

"To the mountains, to continue our struggle for peace. Yes, bombs are already falling, therefore we must be utmostly exerting ourselves. There is no longer any time for other concerns."

The corridor walls, once glassy smooth, were crazed and splintered. Toward one end, a mound of silvery bodies lay in a pool of colorless body fluids. One of them looked hauntingly like Araf'ex, but its distinctive neck slits were partly covered by rolls of limp flesh and he couldn't be sure.

Eril ran his hands over the ridges of swollen flesh crisscrossing his arms. The web had saved his life by cushioning the worst of the blast concussions.

"We must be rescuing your comrades without delay!" said Raerquel, undulating in the opposite direction at top speed. "Only human prisoners were retained during the crisis. All of our own people under confinement were summoned into military service or released to survive as best they can. Here is a cell with a living being inside!"

Raerquel came to an abrupt halt and ran its lower appendages over the wall.

"How are you going to open that thing? I thought the prison doors wouldn't answer to your signal."

"Prison structures are manipulable like any other *therine,*" Raerquel explained, continuing its scanning motion. "From the exterior surface, since only the inside is 'fixed.' We encountered a problem—" the door slid smoothly aside, "—because your door was *mechanically* stuck. Ah, it is the societies-scientist!"

Brianna turned a pale, swollen-eyed face toward them. She looked like a bedraggled butterfly caught in a spider's web. Raerquel dissolved the restraints and she staggered into Eril's arms.

"Time to get out of here, Bri," he said, hoping that she'd respond to the firmness of his voice. "This place is about to eat dust."

She didn't speak, yet Eril could see the fire in her green eyes as she drew herself upright. He'd thought her a fragile butterfly, but she was more like an ancient rapier, slender tempered steel. She followed Raerquel out the door, unsteady for only the first steps.

They found Lennart in the next cell, looking a little dazed. Raerquel disappeared down the hallway, where it began hooting that it had found Kithri.

Kithri blinked and scrubbed her eyes with the back of one hand as the gastropoid dissolved her restraint web. The strands left flaming welts on her bare arms. Eril remembered how she'd looked outside that rundown tavern in Port Ludlow, too proud to admit she'd been crying. Suddenly he hoped, with all the hoping left in him, that by some impossible chance they still had a chance to stop the war.

"You came back for us," she said to Raerquel. Her voice was scratchy but wondering. "I thought your peace movement was more important than anything. I thought we were nothing but tools—something to throw away as soon as we were no use to you any more."

Raerquel brushed a feathery tentacle against her bruised face. "We may not have shared Flesh-Before-Naming, but we have shared other things . . . a field of flowers, sunlit waters . . . and so many things I cannot yet be understanding. The fear, the rushing darkness, the loneliness. How can you humans live, so separate, so alone?"

"If we don't get out of here now, said Brianna, "*how we live* will be an entirely moot point." She stood in the corridor with Lennart, beckoning them to hurry.

*Sometimes,* Eril thought, *we live by leaving before those we love can leave us.*

Kithri stumbled as she crossed the threshold. Eril caught her and wrapped an arm around her.

*Sometimes we spend the rest of our lives afraid it'll happen again. Sometimes we get a chance to change things.*

The elegant spaceport towers lay in ruins, and those ships which had not already taken off had been reduced to splinters. The cream-colored pavement, designed to withstand the exhaust of the massive freighters, was peppered with blast craters. A few gastropoids moved slowly about the wreckage, pausing at the larger piles of debris. Above it all, the sky which had once been as clear as Ocean-of-Light glowered a deep, murky red.

"Atmosphere-pollution weapon to blind our forces by distorting light patterns," Raerquel commented as it led them in an eastward circuit.

"Ah!" Lennart said, as if he'd been punched in the solar plexus.

At the edge of the parkland, they discovered an abandoned transport platform. Raerquel slithered on board, followed by the humans. The platform rose slowly, as if in some demented mechanical way it mourned its fallen comrades. Raerquel kept it low, following the contours of the ground.

The city was less of a shock after the spaceport, which had sustained the worst of the attacks. Here and there buildings still stood, some of them apparently intact. From the distance, they could see a ripple of gray-toned bodies moving between the ravaged lacework towers. They were all very quiet as they skirted the city and began to wind through the hills.

Finally Kithri stirred. She'd been sitting, gripping the edge of the platform with white-knuckled fingers. "Are we going to ride this thing all the way across the ocean?"

Eril read her thought. They'd have no protection at all against another round of bombing.

"For the next part of our journey," Raerquel said, "we will be going underground, not over the water."

"Underground?"

"Indeed. Swimming through waters of light may be exquisite pleasure but hardly an efficient means of transportation. Do you think because you mammalians can dart about on your stiltlike appendages that we gastropoids have no need to get places quickly?"

# Chapter 34

The little village by the seashore was gone, along with its fairyland pier. Shattered *therine* lay everywhere, most of it in glittery splinters. Motionless gray bodies were heaped around the beach, clustered around the last remaining structure. A circle of quiet surrounded them, but off in the distance, toward the north, came muted, unintelligible hooting.

"Is this what's left of your underground station?" Eril said.

Raerquel answered as they slowly circled the debris. "I had been hoping, without any degree of reasonableness, that this entrance would not be inundated with refugees."

"What do we do now?"

"There are several other entrances which we might reach."

"Won't the same thing have happened there, too?" Lennart asked. "Mobs of frightened people trying to get to a safe place before all hell falls on them?"

"Very likely," Raerquel said. It guided the transport around the *therine* ruins and over the gently lapping water. "However, there is another entrance below the Council meeting platform, not known to the public."

"Your own *private* bolt hole," Kithri said, her voice bitter. "So the Council can get to safety while they let the brushies be blown to bits?"

"It is for the work we have yet to do," Raerquel replied, "not our individual survival—"

Its comment was cut short by a searingly loud whine above their heads.

"Duck!" Eril shouted. But there was no place to duck to and no shelter to duck under. Without thinking, he pulled Kithri onto his lap and covered her with his body.

An instant of whiteness shot through him and then raw, blaring sound, and then no sound. Kithri's fingers drilled into the flesh of his thighs. He held his breath as the platform rocked wildly. Something hot and wet drenched his exposed arms and legs. Blood—or water heated by the blast?

Behind his closed eyes, Eril's head reverberated like an echo chamber, quivering with soundless vibration. The residue of the blast went on and on. A howl of pain burst from the hidden creases of his memory like a genie freed from a bottle and condensed into a sound, a name.

*WEIRAM!*

He saw himself sitting in his stinger, watching the scintillating particles which had once been a flagship and the man who commanded it.

The name broke into fragments, each syllable a sob. The sobs echoed and multiplied, rolling through his body and spilling out into the cabin of the stinger. Each fresh wave hammered him thinner and thinner until he blew away like the darkening dust.

Eril had never admitted how close Weiram came to being the father he'd needed, the father he'd lost when his own disappeared into the reaches of space. He couldn't admit it now. But he remembered the unexpected touch on his shoulder, the kindly eyes, the ready smile. The words of encouragement given just as he'd reached his limit. Remembered the man who'd weaseled past the defenses of a rebellious young cadet, taught him, cajoled him, disciplined him. Loved him. And in the end, saved his life.

*I should have died at Albion. Or New Paris, or any one of a dozen places, trying to hide from what I'd lost.*

*No. I should have lived. I should not have forgotten.*

Eril opened his eyes and blinked. His ears brought him nothing but a dense silence. He struggled upright.

Beside him, Brianna sat with her mouth open, her fingers tearing at her hair and ears. Eril knew she was screaming, but he heard nothing. Kithri had collapsed ashen-faced against the rails. Lennart's head was down between his knees with his hands clasped over the back of his neck. Raerquel had retreated into a featureless lump of silver flesh.

Eril grabbed Brianna by the shoulders and shouted for her to get hold of herself. He couldn't hear his own voice nor, judging from her reaction, could she. He forced her to meet his eyes, mouthing, *Are you all right?*, forgetting that the implanted translator couldn't interpret it.

Brianna's eyes came back into focus and she pointed to her ears. *Me, too,* he mimed and then turned back to the others. Lennart gripped the edge of the platform, retching. Kithri crawled to Raerquel's side and hesitantly lay one hand on the gastropoid's hide.

Grimly, Eril considered their course of action if the gastropoid was dead or couldn't be roused. Raerquel had rescued them because it still had hope, because it thought that together they could still make a difference. It had gotten enough from Kithri's mind to convince it the experiment could still work. He'd be damned if he was going to let that go to waste because of freak bad luck. They'd have to make it to the Mountains-of-Darkness on their own, even if it meant paddling the transport like a raft. Skies only knew what they'd find there—maybe Duvach, who'd always been friendly, or one of the saner Council members. Someone who could carry on the project. But first they had to get there.

Eril was wondering how he could communicate this to the others when he noticed the faint, distant throb.

"Can you hear that?" Lennart's mouth opened and his throat moved as if he were shouting. Eril could barely make out the words. A few minutes later, his hearing had returned enough to activate the implanted translator.

Suddenly Raerquel's head section extended upward, popping up like a child's box-toy. "Sufficient time is having passed for recovery of all?" it inquired, and began uncoiling its appendages.

"Raerquel!" Kithri cried. "We thought you were—"

"I placed myself into a state of protective estivation," it said, quickly regaining its usual pear shape and sending the platform forward at top speed. "I could not be risking damage to my sensory structures, so I timed the duration of my estivation to my best estimate of your recovery time."

"You *timed*?" Brianna said. "But estivation is an

*involuntary* suppression of all but the most basic autonomic functions!"

"No time to be discussing!" Raerquel said. "We must move quickly now. We must be underground before the primaries hit."

Where the Council platform had once towered like an elegant dream, there now sprawled an irregular pile of shattered *therine,* interspersed with chunks of oozing gastropoidal flesh. A lone gastropoid, its skin a flat, yellowish gray, scored with abrasions and burn marks, swam slowly toward them. It halted, wavering as it studied them, and then dove out of sight. Raerquel called after it but it did not respond.

"Can't blame the thing for running away from us," Lennart commented. "*We're* the aliens here."

Raerquel brought the platform to a halt and they climbed out. The remains of a broad, rectangular landing was bordered by the wreckage of delicately fluted columns. Although they were forced to pick their away around the splintered *therine,* they encountered no unsurmountable obstacles. At the far end of the landing lay an oval-shaped pool.

Raerquel dove into the powder-filmed water and reappeared a few minutes later. They waited, shivering in the warm air.

"The entrance is passable," Raerquel said. "Let us proceed with haste."

"Will it take us that long to get through?" Kithri asked in an unsteady voice.

"Raerquel had to go down and check on everything." Eril tried to sound reassuring. "*And* come back out again. With full lungs, you won't have any problem going straight through." Her stricken expression didn't waver. "What's the matter?"

She wet her lips and swallowed hard. "I can't swim."

Lennart looked at her in astonishment. "How can you *not swim*?"

"I never needed to learn! Maybe I knew how on Albion, but I can't remember! There's barely enough water in Port Ludlow to drink, let alone *swim in*—"

"It's all right, *I'll* get you through," Eril said.

Kithri glared at him. "Goddamn war-hero, you think you're so hot, rescuing a lady in distress! And what are you staring at, Lennart? I suppose you consider swimming a basic requirement for civilization?"

"Shut up!" Brianna grabbed her shoulders and shook her. "Get control of yourself! What's the matter with you?"

"Matter with *me*? I'm only scared half out of my skin."

"You think you're frightened now, you should have been the decoy for those pirates!" Brianna snapped. Kithri ducked her head and twisted, as if to pull away, but Brianna held her fast. "You listen to me! The one thing—the *only* thing that kept me going was thinking, 'Sooner or later that *untranslatable* bitch will find something that's too big for her to handle, and I'll be around to see it.' "

Kithri flushed and met Brianna's eyes. She stopped shaking. Her chin lifted. "Maybe you will, but it won't be now."

Brianna let her go with a tentative, almost apologetic gesture, and Eril understood why she'd taunted Kithri like that. It was, in small measure, the repayment of a debt.

"Brianna, you go first," he said. "Then I'll take Kithri down with me, and you last, Lennart."

Raerquel's sleek shape disappeared into the water. Brianna slipped beneath the surface in a graceful dive.

"I'll be right with you," Eril told Kithri. "You don't have to swim, you just have to let me carry you along. You may feel like you're running out of air, but you'll have enough. I promise."

"I don't have any choice, do I?"

He shook his head.

"Then it doesn't matter *how* scared I am, does it? Let's go."

She took a few quick, deep breaths, filling her lungs as he told her to, and jumped. Eril dove in after her. The water was surprisingly cold, but clear. Kithri was right in front of him, her hair floating around her face like a halo of curly seaweed. Beyond her, Raerquel floated like a metallic teardrop. Kithri grabbed his shoulder as he turned and swam deeper, following the gracefully undulating gastropoid. After a few moments, he could feel the force of her kicking.

Unexpectedly Eril came up *bump*! against an intact *therine* wall. He recoiled, hardly able to tell where the water ended and the glasslike wall began. Raerquel swam downward, blue shadows rippling its silvery skin. With Kithri still clutching his shoulder, Eril dove deeper.

Fire began to creep along his diaphragm. Kithri was still hanging on, her fingers digging into his muscles. What would he do if she panicked at the unfamiliar suffocating sensation? There wouldn't be much he could do . . . except to die with her.

The next moment they emerged from a short,

wide tunnel into a small chamber. A few feet up, a final convulsive kick, and their heads broke together into a pocket of air.

Eril hauled himself onto a wide ledge in the oval-domed room and pulled Kithri up after him. She lay across the ledge, gulping air. A moment later Lennart's head popped through the surface. Brianna and Raerquel had already pulled themselves up on the landing.

Eril grinned at Kithri. "That wasn't so bad, was it?"

"Speak for yourself," she panted, grinning back and pushing her dripping hair back from her eyes. "I can think of easier ways of dying than drowning."

# Chapter 35

The domed foyer led to a spacious chamber, equally deserted and lined with *therine*. The air was cold but surprisingly fresh. The colorless light reminded Eril of times during the war when he'd gone without sleep for days, running on stimulants and adrenaline. His mouth tasted stale and metallic.

They followed the rail westward as it disappeared down a narrowing tunnel. Their footsteps, muffled by the tube socks, made faint, rustling echoes. After a short distance, Raerquel paused to run its sturdy lower tentacles along the *therine*-coated walls.

"What are you looking for?" Eril asked.

"Transport vehicle," the gastropoid replied. "Even shielded from above, we are not going to *crawl* all the way to Mountains-of-Darkness."

An oval door, truncated at floor level, slid open under Raerquel's manipulations. A long, narrow platform glided out on to the rail. Unlike the flat transport they had used before, this one was walled on three sides and had a bullet-nosed front and a gently arching roof.

At Raerquel's urging, the humans climbed on board, crouching under the roof. The platform was too narrow for them to sit side by side, so they nestled in a row like spoons. It took a few minutes for everyone to get settled, first the two women, then Lennart behind them.

Eril started to climb in back, but Kithri pulled him down between her and Brianna. He lowered himself into place, his slightly bent legs on either side of hers. Her damp curls smelled of the sea. He realized he was cradling her between his knees as a copilot would. The dark, curving tunnel loomed in front of them.

Raerquel crawled aboard, flattening itself to fit in the compressed space. They began to slide along the underground rail, rapidly gaining momentum. Their movement was smooth and almost silent, except for the air streaming past. Any resemblance to Eril's first *duo*flight down a Manitou tunnel vanished at once. This was much more like slipping through the greased tubes in the Academy scramble course. The nose piece sheltered them from the worst of the wind, but from time to time the chill air tugged at Eril's damp hair.

After a short distance, a second rail appeared on the tunnel ceiling. It dipped down until the carrier was anchored at both top and bottom. Once they were underway in earnest, the diffuse lighting disappeared. Occasional isolated spots passed so quickly they seemed no more than flickers in the darkness.

"Eril?" Kithri turned and spoke over her shoulder, her voice a reedy whisper against the hiss of their passage. "Do you think we've still got a chance?"

"Raerquel must think so, or it wouldn't have come halfway across the continent for us." The gastropoid couldn't see their translator panels, but Eril kept his voice low.

"But couldn't it have . . . just to save us? To take us to a safer place. . . ." Eril heard the undertones of anguish in her voice. He didn't understand what it was, only that it had nothing to do with Raerquel.

"After the way it skipped out on us when we were no longer any use?" Lennart said from in back of them. "Not likely."

"Raerquel's just as dedicated to peace as it always was," Brianna said. "We just don't understand its motives very well. I was wrong . . . about a lot of things. I confused personal affiliation with goal-alliances. What matters now is that Raerquel succeed, even though the odds are dismal. What's the good of refraining from cultural interference when the result is no culture at all? How can I justify sitting back like some damned observer when there's even the remotest chance?"

She flinched as if a bomb had just exploded nearby. There was no sound except the hiss of the air streaming by. "I've been so sheltered, so—*spoiled* all my life. Golden girl, golden career, what could go wrong? Oh, I *studied* all the sociocultural ramifications of war, but I never . . ." She flinched again. "I thought the cave-in was the worst thing that could happen to me."

Eril turned his head to look at her. "Are you all right?"

"All right? Will any of us ever be *all right*?"

*I can't change what happened to her*, he thought, *can't give her back the person she was before those three days in the dark.* She was, he realized, damaged in a way that could never be healed, just as Kithri was.

Just as he was.

*Albion . . .*

"I survived, then and now," Brianna went on. "By all rights, I shouldn't have lived through either disaster, but I did. Just as we will now. Maybe there's a reason, maybe we were meant to succeed."

"Maybe," said Kithri, "we can make that happen, whether it was *meant to* or not."

*By all the powers of luck and space,* Eril thought, *I hope she's right.*

Eril's muscles ached from sitting still. He'd been half-hypnotized by the rocking movement of the transport and the monotonous *whoo-oosh* of their passage through the tunnel. He hadn't noticed when the lighted ceiling strips reappeared. The vehicle slowed, then came to a stop in a large rectangular room with generously wide exit ledges.

"City-of-Darkness," Raerquel said in as quiet a voice as Eril heard any gastropoid produce.

"We made it," Brianna said. Her voice was light, almost breathless, her eyes fever-bright.

The climb to the inhabited levels grated on Eril's nerves. The angles of the ramps were all wrong for human legs, but Raerquel undulated up them at a rapid pace. After a sustained climb, long enough for Eril's muscles to become cramped and burning, they emerged into a rounded intersection of *therine*-lined tunnels. The few gastropoids they met hurried about on their own business.

Suddenly one of them called out. "Raerquel! Clan-superior Raerquel!"

"What news, Duvach?" Raerquel called back. "You are unharmed? Any major damage to the city here?"

"We are safe for the moment. But after you left, Ru-elliven halted all work on the project. The other

Council members were forced to agree. Even if the mind linkage can work, it is now too late."

"And you, Duvach? Are *you* thinking it is too late for understanding instead of destroying?"

"You are my clan-superior and have taught me otherwise. It is never the time to be giving up hope."

As they talked, the two gastropoids slithered up the corridor at a brisk pace, leaving the humans to follow. Kithri stumbled and had to run a few steps to keep up. She stared at the tunnel walls with a peculiar, almost mesmerized expression on her face.

Eril caught her as she tripped again. "You'd better watch where you're going."

"Eril, these are *jaydium tunnels.*" Her face had gone chalky, her eyes dark and haunted. "And this stuff on the walls—this *therine—it* will become our jaydium."

"But there *isn't* any jaydium on this world," Brianna said in a puzzled voice.

"They're jaydium tunnels, all right," Kithri answered in a deadly calm voice. "How could I fly them as I did—and hate them as I did—and not know them now?"

A thought snaked through Eril's mind, *If we somehow manage to stop this war, how will that change things in our own world? If there's no jaydium, will there still be a Stayman, an Albion, a Fifth Fed? Will our world die if this one lives? And even if we knew that it did, would we have any choice in what we do now?*

They came quickly to a smaller, downscaled version of the railway depot. The vehicles here were the familiar land transport platforms without any siding or nose cones. Raerquel and Duvach boarded the nearest, followed by the four humans.

They started off slowly. Eril studied the branching passages and tried to imagine them as the Stayman tunnels after some cataclysm had wrenched them into corkscrews. He didn't want to think what would happen to all of them, should they be inside the tunnels when that happened. *If* it happened, he reminded himself.

They traveled deeper into the mountain though there was no discernible change in the lighting or freshness of the air. Eril wondered how many tons of rock hung above them or how much firepower it would take to penetrate this far. Being underground couldn't be easy for Brianna, that was sure. She was sitting behind him and Lennart had one arm around her shoulders. She stared ahead, her features set, as if she were mentally working navigational problems—or whatever tedious and demanding calculations she did in her field. Her fingers laced together, knuckles white like bare bones.

Raerquel brought the platform to a halt at the side of a narrow tributary tunnel. They all climbed off. "The laboratory is now only a short distance."

At first the sound was so low Eril felt it only as a vibration. Before his mind could grasp what was happening, it escalated, rumble upon intensifying rumble. Pieces of *therine* tumbled from the walls and smashed into powder. Behind him, Brianna screamed, but her voice was soon lost.

Eril's senses went painfully acute. Each shard of *therine,* each mote of dust, each quiver of the rock beneath his feet, each sound—even the harsh breathing of the others—all etched indelibly on his mind. For an awful moment, his body wouldn't move. *Therine* fragments, sharp as knives, came tumbling off the wall in jagged sheets. They crashed on the exact spot where he would have been if he hadn't paused. He jumped backward, sweating cold.

Every instinct urged Eril to get away, back down the tunnel. Brianna and Raerquel were nearest the platform. He gestured to them to go back, then reached for Kithri, who was standing right beside him.

Suddenly, a giant fist of air slammed into him. Curling and rolling, he came smack against something hard and cold. Fist-sized rocks, dust and pieces of *therine* showered over him. He laced his hands protectively over the base of his skull.

A rain of stones struck him with bruising force. One hit his spine directly. A bolt of searing pain lanced through him. For a moment he couldn't breathe, couldn't move, couldn't feel his legs. Fire filled his head. He choked, hardly feeling a *therine* sliver from the ceiling slash through his outer arm. Luck was with him and it was only a superficial cut.

More rock cracked, toppling, adding dust to the splintered *therine*. At his back, Eril felt the curve of another warm body.

*Let it be Kithri. Let her be all right.* Then a thought shivered through him. Maybe it would be better if she were killed right away, rather than have to dig her way out and slowly die here in the dark, maybe alone. He thought of the scars on Brianna's hands.

The noise decreased suddenly, then rose again with more falling rock. Eril pulled himself into a tighter ball, his eyes squeezed shut. Then, suddenly, there was silence.

Eril waited for ten heartbeats, then ten more. Finally he dared to open his eyes. His lashes were wet and sticky. He dabbed at them with the back of one hand, but only made his eyes water worse. He sat up, blinking and waiting for his tears to wash the debris from his eyes. The light was dim and uneven, a fraction of its former brightness.

"Kithri? Kithri! Lennart—Brianna?" With every syllable, the light panel on his chest leapt to brightness, casting eerie shadows. "Raerquel, are you all right?" It hurt to swallow, to force the muscles of his throat into the pattern of speech.

Someone touched his shoulder—Kithri, her skin ghosty with dust except for one blood-dark cheek. Dust caked her damp curls. He grabbed her and buried his face against her neck. Her muscles tightened as she held on to him.

"Oh, my god . . ." Behind them, Lennart had struggled to a sitting position. He gestured in the direction of the transport platform.

Rock and splintered *therine* completely blocked the tunnel and spilled out along the landing. Brianna's foot, still in its sock of gray fabric, shone weakly in the light. The slender ankle disappeared beneath tons of wreckage.

"Bri!" Kithri struggled to her feet.

Eril grabbed her elbow, twisting her around. "It's too late!"

Kithri jerked away from him, scrambled through the debris, and knelt beside the rockfall. She pulled a few of the smaller chunks of stone and *therine* and threw them aside. A piece of rock the size of her head came hurling down, narrowly missing her.

"There's nothing you could have done," said Eril.

She sat back and took a deep, sobbing breath. "It's not fair, to have come so far and to end like this."

"Raerquel! Clan-superior, speak!" That was Duvach. Dust and gashes made a harlequin pattern of its skin. Raerquel had been at the extreme edge of the rock slide, while Brianna, standing behind it, had suffered its full force. Frantically Duvach hauled debris off its fallen leader, using all its appendages, even the fragile upper tendrils.

*Brianna may be beyond our help, but Raerquel . . . maybe there's still a chance!*

Eril raced to Duvach's side and grabbed whatever he could, rock, *therine* shards, handfuls of pebbles. Kithri and Lennart worked beside him with equal fervor. Eril's back cramped, threatening spasm, but he hardly felt it. Fury, red and hot, surged through him, masking his body's pain. He tore into the rock fall as if it were a tangible enemy, something he could rip apart with his bare hands.

In a few minutes, they were able to clear away a space around Raerquel's body. Eril felt a renewed surge of hope. Raerquel's hide was cool and sleek under his hands. Its head had sunk mostly into its body, its appendages tightly coiled but still visible. Duvach kept calling its name.

"Not dead—it can't be dead, too!" Kithri whimpered. "Do you hear me, you stupid slug? You can't die, too!"

"Don't waste your breath," Lennart said wearily. "It can't hear you."

"Don't tell me what I can't do!" she rounded on him. "We depend on this damned thing, it gets us all the way across the ocean—and then it dies on us—"

She punched the unresponsive gray lump with both fists. Her voice was half a sob and half a scream of raw pain. *"You can't die and leave me here!"*

Eril put his arms around her. He felt her loss as if it were his own and knew it was not only Raerquel she was crying out to. It was everyone who'd ever left her with nothing but a desolate chip of rock—her father, Hank, space only knew who else. And in a strange way, she cried out for him, too, for the fatherless boy he had been, and the young pilot. . . .

She bent her head to his shoulder, weeping openly. Her body, usually so taut and muscular, felt all bones, as if she would shatter at the slightest blow.

"My friends," came a familiar deep voice. Eril's head shot up. Raerquel's head was barely discernible above the battered mass of its body. The light glinted weakly off its silvery hide.

Kithri raised her tear-streaked face. "You're alive."

"But wounded," Duvach said, running its delicate sensory tendrils over Raerquel's head section.

Raerquel curled one slender upper tentacle with its old, characteristic grace. "Listen to me, my human-friends. We have lost the struggle here, but you must not. You must return . . . to your own world. . . . You must replicate . . . *all* the conditions. . . ."

"Beloved clan-superior, do not be wasting your life energies with these mammalians," pleaded Duvach. It wrapped its muscular lower tentacles around Raerquel's body, the flesh of one pressing into the other. "I will go for help."

"The . . . estivation reflex . . . is too strong." Raerquel's voice was fainter now. Its neck slits fluttered in between each hesitant word. "Duvach . . ."

"I am here."

"Take the humans . . . to the laboratory . . . my clan—my clan-inferior. . . . Remember all I have taught you, the dream which is your true inheritance. . . ."

Raerquel's voice trailed off. Slowly its head disappeared entirely into the rounded silvery bulk of its body.

A wave of sudden insight shook Eril. *All this stuff about "clan-superior" and "clan-inferior" has nothing to do with social status! It means* parents *and* offspring! *Duvach and Bhevon are Raerquel's* children. . . .

"Dead?" Lennart whispered.

"Estivating," replied Duvach.

*Not for long,* Eril realized. *It was saying good-bye.*

"It is not for me to question the actions of Raerquel Hath'djan. I only hope this task, and the extra time it takes me before I can bring help, will not—will not—"

"Duvach," Eril said, laying one hand on the gastropoid's hide. "We would not be the cause of Raerquel's death. We owe it too much, and we—admire it. We respect what it was trying to do." His voice almost failed him. "Let's go now, as it wished. . . ."

For a long moment, Duvach sat immobile and Eril feared it was too lost in its own alien emotions to help them. Then it extended a feather tendril and brushed Kithri's cheek. A droplet glistened on the silvery strand.

"Water . . . salt water. The water of life."

Behind Duvach's heavy, inflectionless voice, Eril

sensed its wonderment. Kithri, beside him, gulped and blinked, more tears streaming down her face.

"My clan-superior Raerquel was right all along," Duvach murmured. "The light is in each of us, however strange our outer forms. Beneath all differentness, our waters flow as one."

# Chapter 36

Duvach left them at the entrance to the laboratory. Kithri followed the two men into the eerily shadowed room, blinking as her eyes adapted to the light. Chunks of jagged underlying rock punctuated the splintered walls and *therine* instruments lay jumbled everywhere. It reminded her of Brianna's laboratory after the pirates ransacked it. *Brushwacker* sat in an undamaged area by the far corner. Sealed incisions crossed its hull like ridges of scar tissue.

Kithri pushed Eril aside and darted for the scrubjet, leaping piles of debris. Heart pounding, she yanked the cockpit door open. The *duo*apparatus looked intact, the headsets stored in their holders as neatly as if she'd done it herself. Eril's force whip lay on a stack of folded clothing. She recognized her own overalls, Lennart's space suit and Brianna's jumpsuit. Four pairs of boots sat in a tidy row.

Eril and Lennart came up beside her, but Kithri couldn't move. She stared at the force whip. Less than a week ago, they'd speculated whether it could jar open the hidden door to their quarters. Brianna had protested using her precious recording films to help locate the crystal fractures, as if anyone would ever read them.

*Brianna . . .*

Kithri took a step backward, suddenly revolted by the scrubjet. It was nothing but a piece of metallo-ceramic alloy and circuitry, its surface pitted like a gnat-bitten fruit. Yet she had once abandoned three people to the space pirates in order to keep the damned thing for herself. And Brianna, whom she hadn't liked but had come to respect, Brianna had suffered the most for it. There was nothing she could do for Brianna now to make it right, nothing she would ever be able to say. . . .

Lennart picked up the force whip. His fingers curled around the handle and his thumb settled over the firing stud. "How does this thing work?"

"Never mind, you won't be using it," Eril said.

*Brroom! Boom!*

Shock waves rippled through the ruined laboratory. Kithri jumped reflexively, her heart rate soaring. Sheets of *therine* broke from the wall behind her with an incongruous tinkling sound.

"We've run out of time!" Eril held his hand out to Lennart. "Give me the whip, then both of you get inside."

Kithri hesitated, eyeing the 'jet.

"Captain." Lennart spoke gently, his voice a velvet counterpoint to the staccato rumbling of the mountain. "What you're planning won't work."

"The hell it won't! It's how we got here, isn't it? And . . ." Eril's voice wavered, "we can't leave you here. Raerquel said to replicate the *exact* conditions."

*Exact conditions?* Kithri repeated to herself. *The 'jet, the whip, the three of us. . . .*

"We got here together from Brianna's world," she

said to Lennart. "Why won't it work now to send us back together?"

Lennart shook his head. The illumination was better here and Kithri could see his eyes. The irises seemed only a thin film covering the emptiness of space.

"When you dumped me out of that interdimensional whatsis, you displaced a whole lot of spacetime energy," Lennart said. "The same energy it took to put me there in the first place. I don't know why it took me so long to see it. Wishful thinking, I guess . . . not wanting to lose you."

*First Brianna's gone, then Raerquel and now Lennart, too. There's got to be some other way! If I can just get the whip away from him—*

"So we zap to some new place," Eril said. "We'll still be *alive.*"

*And together . . .*

The room shivered and swayed, as if the whole mountain range had suddenly shaken itself. There was a moment's stillness and then everything slid sideways. Lennart slipped and fell. Kithri lost her balance, twisted and bounced off the side of the scrubjet. The base of one stubby wing caught her in the short ribs.

Rolling, Kithri spotted the handle of the force whip where Lennart had dropped it. She grabbed for it. The next moment she was sprawled on her back, Lennart's weight pinning her down and his breath hissing in her ears.

"Give it back to me!"

She kicked out, searching for enough leverage to squirm free. Her fingers touched the control studs.

A spray of light spurted from the whip's barrel, illuminating the ruined laboratory in stark brilliance.

Chips of *therine* crackled and exploded as the beam lashed across the chamber. Kithri glimpsed the deep crack that ran through the floor, and the twisted bedrock underneath. More thunder rattled the room, and powdered rock showered down through the ceiling crevices.

Whatever happened, she must not let Lennart get the whip again.

The intense, white light of the whip shot out again, arcing over the humans toward the nearby scrubjet. It touched the edge of one wing. Sparks erupted in all directions.

Kithri blinked, her vision swimming. Suddenly the whip handle was torn from her grasp. She fumbled for it, but she couldn't see a thing, just featureless afterimages.

"What the hell?" Eril muttered from somewhere behind her.

"Where are we?" Kithri asked. "Did we— Did it work? Are we back home?"

The room swayed nauseatingly for a moment before her sight cleared. She saw Lennart getting to his feet. Behind him, the ruined laboratory looked exactly as before. He staggered as the mountain rumbled again, but his hands were firmly wrapped around the barrel of the force whip.

"Don't move. Either of you." He stepped back, too far for a quick grab.

"You don't know how to use that," Eril said.

"Want to bet I can't give a pretty good imitation?"

"Listen to me!"

"The only way for you folks to get out of here is to put me back where I was before," Lennart said bleakly. "If you were right, we wouldn't still be here now.

"Look," he continued, half-pleading, "it isn't so bad. I wasn't waiting out there for someone to find me. It happened in an instant—one moment I was in the light storm and then *poof!* into your tunnel. The next thing I know, somebody else will zap me out again."

*But it won't be us.* Kithri shivered.

"That won't happen, and you know it," Eril said, getting to his feet. He moved slowly, his hands carefully away from his sides. "It was ratshit luck you went visible when you did and there was somebody crazy enough to use a force whip on you. You tell me the odds of that happening again. Nobody's going to rescue you a second time—you'll drift on and on until time itself winds down."

"Couldn't we try—again—" Kithri stammered.

"Stop it!" Lennart's voice was practically a sob. "Do you think I *want* this? Do you think I want to float around some godforsaken void, that I wouldn't jump for it if there were any other way? I'm only one man, I can't stop the goddamned war. I don't know how! But I do know how to save two people that I love!"

Kithri stood up and walked slowly toward him. The rumbling had died down, so the only sound was the rasp of Lennart's breathing. She went on, one slow step after another, until the barrel of the force whip brushed her chest.

Lennart transferred the whip to one hand and put the other around her. She leaned forward, her breasts flattening against him. His face felt dry under her fingertips, as if a process of mummification had already begun. She curved her shoulders forward, cupping her body around his.

Kithri felt him drinking her in, imprinting her in his flesh so that his body would remember what his mind could not. She trembled, for a moment afraid he'd take so much that she'd be left a brittle husk. She knew that some part of her would float forever in the void with him.

He lowered the force whip. She could grab it, wrest it from him. It would be so easy. Standing here, saying good-bye, that was the hard part.

Lennart's lips parted from hers and his breath stirred the tangle of her hair. His heartbeat rippled through her body. Her hands rested on his chest, warm beneath the silken alien fabric. She would also carry a piece of him back to Stayman. She could never go back to being the person she'd been before she met him.

A shadow moved beside her shoulder—Eril, holding Lennart's space suit, bulky but light, and helmet. "I thought . . ." His voice cracked a little. "I thought you might need these . . . wherever you're going."

Lennart grabbed Eril in a back-pounding hug, almost knocking the helmet from his hands. Kithri took the gear and stepped back, her eyes stinging.

*It's getting to be a habit, going soft like this.*

Together Kithri and Eril fastened the catches on Lennart's suit. It was an eerie replay of how they'd helped him out of it under the umbrella tree on Brianna's world.

*Brianna's World . . .*

Reluctantly, Kithri flipped the last catch on the helmet. The thick rounded glass distorted Lennart's face. Eril placed the force whip in one of Lennart's gloved hands. Lennart backed up, fumbling for the controls.

"Come on." Eril touched Kithri's shoulder. "You've already said good-bye."

Kithri ran her hands over the battered pseudo-suede of her pilot's seat and sat down. The padding no longer fit her body perfectly. She'd lost weight and muscle since she last flew the Manitou tunnels.

"*Len—*" She meant it as a whisper, but no sound came from her throat. As she began to turn toward him, the brilliance of the force whip tore away her vision.

When she could breathe again, the first thing Kithri noticed was Eril's hands on her shoulders. She couldn't tell if he was comforting her or holding on to her for his own sanity.

"Eril, I can't see anything."

"Me either." He lowered his hands. "It's just like the first time."

*Did we make it?* She didn't dare ask aloud.

She swung her legs out the cockpit door and felt for the ground. It was solid enough, but irregular. Cautiously, she sniffed the slightly dank air. A familiar acrid tang flooded her nostrils.

Jaydium. Not *therine,* jaydium.

"Damned slugs—blew themselves up—after all."

Without any warning, sobs welled up in her, hot and dry like a Cerrano coriolis. They tore at her throat and ripped through her body, pouring out of her, one wave of wordless anguish after another.

Kithri crumpled to the ground beside *'Wacker'*s landing pads. Eril slid out of the cockpit and crouched at her side. He put his arms around her, rocking both of them back and forth. Through the shock and pain, she felt him tremble and silently gulp for breath.

Eril held on to her fiercely, almost desperately, as if she were the one comforting him, as if she wept for both of them. It filled her with a strange and inexpressible solace, a sense that she was not alone as she'd been through the hours and days of grieving for her father. She would never be alone. Even if they were half a galaxy apart, they would still be a part of one other.

After a time they both grew quiet. Kithri scrubbed the tears out of her eyes with the back of one hand and blinked, willing her vision to clear. She thought they were in a dimly lit, enclosed place, but couldn't be sure.

Eril pulled away from her. A moment later, he shoved a hard cylinder in her hands.

"The force whip," she murmured. "It came with us."

Brianna and Raerquel were long dead, thousands of years maybe. Lennart was lost someplace time didn't even exist. Grief—for them, for everything else she'd lost—welled up in her again. She'd learn to live with it, she knew, but not to forget. With time, pain would fade. Pain, but not memory. Every time she flew a tunnel or chipped a piece of jaydium, she'd remember.

Kithri looked up, making out the shape of the scrubjet against the faint, rosy light of the partly chipped jaydium face. The tunnels pressed in on her like a prison, the mountain above her an unbearable weight. Her muscles ached, out of long habit, to run.

"Let's see if this old 'jet will get us out of here," she said, startled to hear how calm she sounded.

*Brushwacker* came to life under her hands, as if it had never been tinkered with. They started off slowly westward.

The Cerrano Plain looked just like the Cerrano Plain. The radio static sounded just like radio static. The voice crackling above the static sounded just like the Port Ludlow tower operator.

"Bloodyluck! You better scramble if you want to get a haul down to the Fed Freighter."

She coughed, then remembered her hold was empty.

"They might not take off on sched," the tower operator continued. "They're missing a passenger—"

"This is Colonel Eril Trionan of the Federation Star Service," Eril cut in. "Convey my respects to Captain Tracey and tell him I'll board soonest possible."

After they signed off, Eril asked Kithri to land the scrubjet. "Anywhere," he said. Puzzled, she bumped to a halt on the uneven ground, disengaged the engines and pushed the cockpit door open. She slid out, reveling in the dry, alkali breeze. The ground was level but uneven, here in the shadow of the jutting, snow-capped Manitous. To the west, the Cerrano Plain stretched flat as far as the horizon.

"Skies, I never thought I'd be glad to smell *that* again." She held out her arms to the wind, then turned back to him. "Why did you stop? Aren't you in a hurry—to get back to your ship?"

*Off this chip of dust, to some place where there are no*

*tunnels and the only jaydium is sealed into star drives so you'll never smell it again?*

"They'll wait for us." Eril grinned as he climbed out. "I'm *not* reporting back wearing the latest in slug nightgowns."

Kithri watched him pull the gray tunic over his head. One shoulder was dark with clotted blood and gray rock dust caked his face. The skin on his body gleamed like old ivory, except for his arms, where it was the color of honey. Like her, he'd lost weight since they last stood on Stayman's desert plain.

He bent over to pull on his pants and she saw the angry, abraded bruise on his back. His muscles tightened suddenly. He gasped and froze, then slowly straightened up. The spasm passed. When his gaze turned outward again, she saw herself reflected in the liquid dark of his eyes.

*I can never forget this moment, never take you out of me.*

A vision came to her, that they were standing at either end of an intricate web, joined by strands so sensitive that if either of them twitched, the other would quiver. This thread was Lennart, this one Brianna, this one a field of rancid flowers, this one the dying embers of a once idyllic planet.

*Take some part of me with you,* she pleaded silently as she stepped into his open arms. *Up there, to the stars.*

He folded her close. His hair smelled of a dozen things—sweat, seawater, jaydium dust, his own masculine scent.

She thought of the people and places she'd lost. *Brianna and Raerquel. Lennart. My father. Albion. A planet of light and water.*

A new thought came to her, a thought that brought both peace and exhilaration. *My father ran and Raerquel stayed to fight, yet I owe my life to both of them.*

Compassion flooded through her. *I never understood why you took me away from Albion,* she whispered to her father's ghost. *Or what it cost you to do it. I won't waste what you've given me.*

*And you, Eril, I have to let you go, too. I have to make my dreams come true, instead of just holding on while they're taken from me.*

Eril wrapped her in his arms and held her tight, almost too tight to breathe. Kithri began to kiss him tenderly, hungrily. She felt a stirring in him and sensed again the things he couldn't say aloud. They each carried their separate grief, like a private darkness, but what they gave each other in this moment turned it from a burden into a source of strength. The dust of Stayman lay beneath her feet, while above her swept the high clear skies and beyond them, the stars.

# Epilogue

The Fifth Federation Star Service personnel lounge on New Paris teemed with men and women waiting to be shuttled up to their cruisers or for boarding permission to smaller ground-based ships. Almost everyone was in uniform—the beiges and greens of officers and pilots, the blues of medics and science, a scattering of diplomatic whites. By the western window, a huge curved sweep of double-glass looking out over the spaceport itself, a man and a woman in the severe black of the Courier Corps watched a stinger undergo its final safety checks. Refitted for prolonged travel for a crew of two, the graceful craft was packed with specialized equipment and the most modern, powerful jaydium drives.

"It still amazes me how beautiful it is," the woman murmured. "And it's ours."

The man nodded and put one arm around her shoulder. They moved away from the window, talking quietly.

Kithri, sitting at a table in one of the darker corners of the lounge, watched them go. They'd get their clearances soon, and they'd be off to the stars, bound on some secret mission. Everywhere they'd go, people would notice the black uniforms with respect and not a little envy.

She set her juice drink on the table of heavily varnished Terillium oak and watched the pink bubbles spiral upward. Her claret-colored shirt was loosely cut, gathered at the sleeves and yoke. The fabric was soft and heavy, so different from the crisp, tailored uniforms of the Service. She wore it tucked into her pants and belted with a wide strap of real leather. Only the small round patch on the left collar, a scout ship crossing a stylized "E", indicated it was something other than ordinary civilian clothing. Explorers didn't wear uniforms.

Eril slid in the bench beside her. "Half an hour, they said." He lay one hand over hers, touching the white-gold ring he'd given her.

"Any last minute problems?"

He shook his head. "No, they approved the flight plan just as we submitted it. According to their charts, it's just another unexplored sector, so they're happy to find someone willing to take it on. Then we'll find out how good my memory of Araf'ex's star charts is."

*And what will we find out there? It won't be NewHome any longer. Either a ruin, or another jaydium source. . . . Or if it or Tomorrow survived and Raerquel's people are out there, waiting for us. . . .* The light-translator panels were safely hidden in their personal gear.

*Either way, it'll shake the Fed up good.*

"Raerquel lied to us to make us go with Duvach, you know," she said. "It wasn't going into any estivation state."

"One way or another, it would be long dead now," Eril said slowly.

Kithri looked out the big window and imagined the slow whirl of galaxies beyond the clouded sky.

Space seemed so vast and the dark between the stars so deep.

*A planet I might find, but a space ghost who isn't even there most of the time. . . .*

Eril's fingers tightened on hers. "Len's still out there," he said, as if reading her thoughts. "And we'll find him. Somehow."

*Somehow . . . out of all that glory up there, what do I want, really want?*

After a moment Eril cleared his throat. "Once we're out of here, we won't have to get one permission after another. As long as our reports sound good, they'll let us go wherever we want. If we do find jaydium, we can use it to change the face of Stayman, maybe the whole Fed."

"And if we don't find it?"

"What?" he said, raising his eyebrows. "You want to give up and become the Fed's errand boys like those two over there?"

"Not on your sweet *pitouchee.* Then we'll see how much difference we can *really* make."

"Is that what you want, really want?"

She met his eyes and smiled. It was not a true question, she knew. It was a promise that wherever they went, whatever they did, they would do it together.